Boys of Fall

The Complete Series

Mari Carr

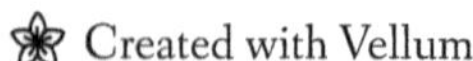 Created with Vellum

Free Agent

Pro-quarterback Tucker's romance with Lela was a force of nature – steamy, unstoppable, and tempestuous. Until a family tragedy made him run, leaving her behind.

When Tucker gets a call that his old coach needs help, he doesn't hesitate to return home. And when he sees Lela, he realizes the more things change, the more they stay the same.

Like she's still his, and right or wrong, he's reclaiming the woman he foolishly walked away from all those years ago.

Prologue

Tucker stared out the window of his bungalow in Turks and Caicos. The beauty of the sun setting over the crystal-blue water did nothing to ease the pressure pushing against his temple. He'd come here hoping to find some sort of peace and an answer to the question that had been plaguing him for months. But, for the first time in his adult life, the ocean was failing him.

He'd spent the last few weeks here falling into a mindless routine—one that offered neither comfort nor insight. He rose each morning after a restless night tossing and turning, and walked a couple of miles along the shore before returning for breakfast. After that, he sat on the porch, staring out at the horizon, his mind consumed with a million thoughts. If it was a good day, he could sit there until dinnertime, breaking the monotony with long jogs. On bad days, the headache returned and he would drag himself to his bedroom, pulling the room-darkening curtains and burrowing under the sheet for hours, waiting for the pain to subside.

Every few days, someone from the team called—his coach, the offensive coordinator, his agent or the trainer—to see how he was feeling. The phone calls always gutted him, sent him spiraling to a dark place. They needed a decision. Hell, he owed them one.

But everyone had a different opinion—and none of them had trouble expressing their feelings. His coach was in the this-too-shall-pass camp, suggesting he take the rest of the summer to recover so that he could come back strong when the season began. The trainer told him he was a fool to even consider stepping back onto the gridiron.

Meanwhile, his agent, Marty, was lining up commercials and interviews like there was no tomorrow, trying to pad Tucker's bank account—and his own—in case there really *wasn't* a tomorrow. The man had actually spent the better part of an hour with him yesterday on the phone, attempting to convince Tucker to consider a career in acting. He started listing all the great athletes who'd gone on to become successful in Hollywood. Tucker had laughed his ass off until he realized Marty was serious. Jesus. The man must have taken one too many hits to the head himself if he thought Tucker would entertain that idea for a split second.

Tucker rubbed his brow, praying the twinge of an ache wasn't the beginning of another migraine. He hadn't had one for more than a week and he was actually starting to hope he'd turned a corner. Of course, he'd had similar bouts of optimism before and they'd all been laid to rest by another round of agonizing, nausea-producing, head-splitting pain.

His cell phone rang. Tucker ignored it for one beat, then two. He ran through the list of people constantly calling him and acknowledged he didn't want to talk to any of them. He glanced at the screen, then frowned. It was a Texas number, but one he didn't have contact information on. Not that *that* was unusual. Tucker was sort of shit about filling in his contacts. His last girlfriend-slash-booty call had added herself to his phone when she'd realized that after two months of dating, he still hadn't attached her name to her number.

Curiosity won out as he reached for his cell.

"Hello?"

"Hi. Is that you, Tucker?"

Tucker recognized the voice immediately, his spirit lightening. "Yep. It's me."

"Hey man. I thought it was, but your voice sounded sort of off."

"How are you doing, Joel?"

Tucker's lips lifted as he spoke the man's name. It occurred to him he could count on one hand the number of times he'd smiled in the past six months. Hearing Joel's voice was a welcome respite from the depression he was drowning in.

"I'm doing fine. Just busy with work."

Typically Tucker tried very hard to avoid his past. He hadn't returned to his hometown of Maris since he'd made good on his escape twelve years earlier. However—that departure came with a cost. By cutting ties to his hometown, he'd left behind quite a few people he genuinely missed. The guys on his high school football team were pretty far up on that list. "Jesus, bro. It's good to hear your voice. What's it been? Two years? What the hell are you up to?"

Joel had been a decent center on the state championship team, but his friend hadn't stepped on the field since that last game they'd played senior year. For Joel, football had been a high school game, a way to make friends and be a member of something cool. His future—his entire life—hadn't depended on the sport like Tucker's had.

"Well, I'd like to say I'm calling to shoot the shit and catch up, but the truth is I have some bad news."

Lela.

Her face was the first to flash in Tucker's mind. He sat up straighter, his heart suddenly racing with a fear he hadn't felt since he was a young boy hiding in his closet to avoid his drunken father's fists.

"What is it?" Tucker forced himself to ask. If anything had happened to her—

"It's Coach Carr."

Tucker stood quickly, walking over to grip the railing of the porch.

Fuck. No. Not Coach.

"What about him?"

Joel blew out a long breath. "He had a heart attack three days ago. He's in rough shape."

From the strength in Joel's voice, it occurred to Tucker this wasn't the first time his friend had broken the news to someone. Joel had always been the responsible friend, the one who took it upon himself to keep their gang of guys up-to-date with what the others were doing. "Is he going to be okay?"

"Yeah. It was touch and go for a few days, but the doctors seem pretty hopeful now. Lorelie's been with him 'round the clock."

Tucker grinned as he recalled Coach Carr's willful, head-strong daughter. She'd been a couple years behind them in high school and more than a handful. Coach had charged the football team with keeping an eye on her, casting them all in the big-brother role as she was his only child. Tucker figured Coach had set up those parameters to ensure none of the lead-with-their-hormones teenage boys on his team looked at his pretty daughter with anything other than protective feelings. Plus Coach had made it perfectly clear there would be hell to pay if anyone on the team ventured toward her in a romantic way.

Not that any of the guys ever would have. And it wasn't fear of Coach's vengeance that kept them honest. It was Lorelie. None of the young bucks he called friends had been brave enough to take her on. So instead, they'd kept an eye on her at the parties down by Harper's Lake, thwarting her attempts to sneak away with older guys and keeping her from drinking too much. She hadn't appreciated their efforts.

"I'm damn sorry to hear that, Joel. Is there anything I can do?" Tucker would email his accountant as soon as he hung up to ensure that Coach's medical expenses were covered. It was the least he could do for the man who'd been like a father to him in high school.

"Naw. We got it covered. As you recall, Coach has a pretty substantial amount of property."

"I remember the ranch. Spent enough summers working there in high school."

Joel chuckled. "Yeah, conditioning through back-breaking work. It was Coach's standard training plan. I think I told you I've been working there full time along with another fella, Oakley."

"You did. Did we go to school with Oakley?" Tucker tried to recall that name, but came up empty. There were very few people from home he could remember after so many years away.

"Nope. He's from Austin. Moved to Maris a couple years back. Thing is, a lot of the chores were usually done by Coach. I've been telling him for years that the ranch is a five-, maybe six-guy operation, but you know how he is. His idea of a normal workload is always twenty times what the rest of us mere mortals can do."

Tucker recalled the sheer burly strength their football

coach possessed. The guy was a giant, a powerhouse. Tucker had no doubt Coach really was doing the work of five guys around that ranch and not even breaking a sweat.

"Lorelie's been trying to do as much as she can, but she's at the hospital most of the day. Me and Oakley have been pulling longer hours, but we're struggling to keep up. So I've been calling some of the guys to see if they'd be willing to come home for a couple weeks to lend a hand. I know that's not a possibility for you, with training camp gearing to start up in a few weeks. I'm not asking for that. I just...I knew you'd wanna know about Coach."

Tucker looked out at the ocean, trying to capture that sense of peace he'd felt the first time he'd stepped onto these islands years earlier. The white-sand beaches, the crystal water, the gentle breezes had eased his weariness, made him feel stronger. It wasn't working this time.

"I'll check out flights, Joel. With any luck, I'll be back in Maris tomorrow or the day after at the latest."

Tucker could tell from the silence on the other end of the line he'd surprised his friend. "Seriously?"

"I got some time. I'm on the injured reserve list right now anyway."

"Oh, damn, man. I didn't know. You okay?"

"Yeah," Tucker said, the lie bitter on his lips. "Just a concussion."

Just a concussion.

He wished that was true. In reality, he was on concussion number seven in six years, and this one wasn't going away. He'd taken a hell of a hit in the final game of the playoffs. The sack had benched him just after the third quarter started and he'd had to sit in the locker room watching his team's last chance at making the Super Bowl evaporate. Since then, he'd seen countless specialists as he suffered one migraine after another. In addition to the headaches, he kept experiencing bouts of dizziness that left him disorientated and nauseated. The general consensus was the migraines would eventually come less often and be less severe until they just stopped. The other thing all the doctors agreed on was the thing Tucker was struggling with.

Another hard hit to the head could cause serious brain damage. It could even kill him. His coach didn't agree, insisting the doctors were playing a game of cover-your-ass.

Tucker understood where his coach was coming from. Hopes were riding high that this would be the year their team made the Super Bowl. They'd come so close the last two, but injuries during the playoffs had knocked them out of contention both times. This year, all the sports analysts were pointing at Tucker, swearing *this* would be the season he took his team all the way.

While the coaches and the doctors disagreed on the prognosis, there was one thing they all understood as the truth. The choice of returning to the gridiron was Tucker's.

And so he'd spent months agonizing over the decision. Super Bowl or permanent brain damage. Both were very real possibilities.

"Coach will be beside himself to see you, Tucker. He never misses watching your games. Just about busts with pride every time you throw a touchdown pass."

Tucker grinned, then winced. The pain in his temple flashed hot, dark spots clouding his vision. He wasn't going to escape it tonight. The migraine was coming.

"I'll get there as soon as I can, Joel." He needed to wrap up the conversation.

Joel thanked him, and then said he had a couple more guys to contact. He told Tucker to call him when he got back to Maris.

They said their goodbyes and Tucker turned toward the

front door of his bungalow. He wanted to take his medicine and get into bed before flashing white lights behind his eyes blinded him.

As he entered the bedroom, the panic hit and he realized what he'd just committed to do.

He was going home. *Maris.*

He hadn't stepped foot in that town in a dozen years. At the time he'd left, he'd sworn there was nothing—no force on Earth—that would send him back there.

Time had a way of making a liar out of everyone.

As he crawled between the sheets, he tried to fight, tried to find something to concentrate on that would help him combat the fire blazing inside his head.

He imagined Coach, lying in a hospital bed, recovering from the heart attack that could have killed him. And Lorelie sitting beside him, holding his hand.

He envisioned the picture of the tombstone in the cemetery next to Maris Methodist Church, marking his mother's grave. He'd left town immediately after her funeral. His dad certainly hadn't had the money to give her a proper tombstone, so Tucker had sent money to Coach right after he signed with the NFL and that first pile of money hit his bank. He'd never seen it in person, but Joel had snapped a photo of it for him and emailed it.

He remembered the anguish, the devastation in Lela's eyes as he'd driven away, refusing to turn around to comfort her as she'd cried.

And he recalled the smell of the whiskey on his father's breath when Tucker turned the tables, throwing the punch instead of receiving it.

His last memories of Maris were that of his drunken father, lying in a pool of his own piss with blood trickling from his split lip, and Lela crying, begging him not to go.

Tucker closed his eyes.

Fuck it.

For the first time, the oblivion brought on by the migraine was actually a welcome relief.

Going home was a mistake.

Chapter One

Lela Whitacre stepped out into the sunshine and considered turning right back around to return to the hospital.

It was another scorcher in Texas. The late June sun beat down on them hard, offering day after day of humid, heavy, breath-stealing heat. As a result, Lela's summer break had consisted of moving from air-conditioning to long, refreshing swims in the lake before quickly returning to the AC.

She'd only broken the routine this week, stopping by the hospital daily to check on Coach Carr and to see if her friend, Lorelie, needed help with anything. It was hard to accept that the larger-than-life man she'd always looked up to and respected could be brought down so quickly. Coach had looked almost frail in the hospital bed, his face drawn, his eyes tired.

But even his failing heart couldn't dim his lively spirit. His face lit up when she walked into the room and for the first time in days, she felt genuinely optimistic that he would fight and defeat his health problems and be back on his feet in no time.

She was almost to her car when her cell rang. A quick

glance confirmed it was Carl. She briefly considered letting the call go to voicemail, but guilt won out. "Hello."

"Hey, pretty lady."

"Hi Carl. What's going on? Aren't you at work?"

"Yep. I'm not some lucky teacher lounging lazily by the lake for months." She knew he was teasing, but it was one of those jokes he'd repeated far too often. It was starting to wear thin.

"Did you need something?" she asked as she unlocked her car and climbed behind the wheel.

"I thought I'd see if you were available for lunch."

Lela considered briefly, trying to come up with an excuse not to go. Unfortunately, she wasn't quick enough.

"You're in town, right? I remembered you saying you were going to go visit Lorelie's dad in the hospital. Thought if you were nearly finished we could meet at Sparks Barbeque for a sandwich. It's Tuesday, which means the pork platter special."

Lela's stomach responded before the rest of her could come up with a reason to resist. "That sounds great. I'm leaving the hospital as we speak. Meet you there in ten minutes."

"I might be closer to twenty. If you get there first, you can just order me a sweet tea and the special. I'll get there as quick as I can. Okay?"

"Sure. I'll see you soon." Lela disconnected with a sigh, glad that Carl's call had come after she'd left Lorelie and her dad. Her friend had been encouraging her to break up with Carl for several weeks. It wasn't that Lorelie didn't like Carl. It was just that she didn't like him for her. Problem was Lela wasn't sure how—or even why—she would break things off. They didn't fight. He wasn't cruel. They had a good time when they went out.

Lorelie swore none of that was a good enough reason to stay with him. And lately Lela was starting to believe it.

Carl was probably one of the nicest men she'd ever met. He was polite, charming, intelligent...boring.

Lela chastised herself for the uncharitable thought. She'd been dating Carl for nearly a year. She would have gone on happily dating him forever, simply for the companionship, but he'd started dropping hints about them moving in together, marriage, kids. The idea of making a commitment to Carl freaked her out. He was fine to hang out with and her friends and family liked him well enough. And he wasn't the worst lover she'd ever had. She rolled her eyes. God. He wouldn't thank her for that faint praise.

He just didn't make her heart race. She wasn't counting the minutes until she saw him, and she was perfectly fine if a few days passed without her seeing or speaking to him at all. He'd gone to some bank convention two weeks earlier. He'd come back telling her how much he'd missed her, but the truth was... she hadn't felt the same. She hadn't really even noticed his absence.

To make matters worse, lately they'd fallen into the pattern of him sleeping over without having sex. He didn't seem to want her with any more passion than she wanted him.

She missed sex. She missed...

She shook her head, refusing to think the name, pushing it into her subconscious to that place where she didn't have to remember, to hurt.

She pulled into the parking lot next to Sparks Barbeque and found a spot near the door. Carl's car wasn't there. She killed the engine, sighing heavily. Then she leaned forward, resting her head against the steering wheel.

Tucker.

The name came anyway, unbidden. He'd been the ghost haunting her memories for well over a decade. He had—unbeknownst to him—impacted pretty much every relationship decision she'd made since the day he'd walked out of her life.

Tucker had broken her heart. It was as simple and as complicated as that. He'd really fucked her up. Stolen her virginity, her trust, her naïve view of the world. He'd ripped away every innocence she'd ever possessed.

And she still couldn't find it in herself to hate him. Because he'd been just as broken, just as destroyed.

Maybe even more so.

She closed her eyes and let herself drift back to that day—that one moment—she'd purposely tried to forget for twelve long years.

She'd gotten the phone call that would change her life from her friend, Bridget, whose mother was an ER nurse. Lela had struggled to digest the news as she drove to Tucker's house.

* * *

What the hell am I going to say to him?

As Lela stepped out of the car, she was surprised to find Tucker sitting on the front porch, his elbows resting on his knees, his head bowed. He was so still she wondered if he'd somehow turned to stone.

"Tucker?"

He didn't move at the sound of her voice, gave no indication he even knew she was there. She approached him slowly, a tiny part of her frightened, which was weird because Tucker was no threat to her. He'd never physically harm her.

But something in his stiff, rigid posture and the way he didn't acknowledge her presence told Lela he was going to hurt her.

When she stood directly in front of him, she said his name again.

He glanced up. Lela sucked in a quiet, painful gasp as she faced the shattered look in his eyes. She almost didn't recognize her funny, swaggering, self-confident boyfriend.

She knelt in front of him, grasping his hands in hers. She was taken aback by how cold they were. It was June in Texas and while the summer hadn't quite reached its full potential, it was definitely building steam. Even this early in the morning, she was starting to feel sticky and too warm in her shorts and t-shirt.

"I'm so sorry, Tuck. I came as soon as I heard."

He nodded wordlessly. And his silence left her tongue-tied, clueless about what to say next.

How did you comfort an eighteen-year-old boy who'd just lost his mother?

Finally, when the awkward silence drifted too long, she said the same thing she'd said before. "I'm just so damn sorry."

Lela preferred his silence to the derision that greeted her words. "It's not your apology to make, Lela. That honor belongs to someone else. And I don't hear him fucking saying it."

Lela bit her lip. Bridget had filled her in on as many details of the accident as she knew. Maris wasn't a particularly big town and there weren't too many people who were not perfectly aware of Mr. Riley's serious drinking problem. Apparently Nelson, the bartender at Cruisers, had called Tucker's mom around two a.m., suggesting she come pick up her husband, who was far too intoxicated to drive. Mrs. Riley had gotten out of bed and driven across town to retrieve him. The only thing Bridget knew about the actual accident was that somehow Mrs. Riley had wrapped the car around a telephone pole. She'd been killed instantly.

"How is your dad?" Lela asked.

"He's still in the hospital. The doctors wanted to keep him

overnight for observation. That's their nice way of saying he needed to dry out."

"Have you seen him?"

Tucker snorted, the grief she'd witnessed when she'd arrived slowly replaced with a fury the likes of which she'd never seen. "Yeah. I got the privilege of telling the drunk fucker he killed my mother."

There had never been any love lost between Tucker and his dad. Lela had started going out with Tucker their sophomore year and his relationship with his father during that entire time had been strained, to say the least. Lela had tried to talk to him about it a few times, but it was the one subject Tucker was resolutely silent on. He gave her the standard reply of "my dad's a drunk loser and not worth talking about," and then he'd change the subject.

"What are you going to do now?" Lela wasn't sure how Tucker would survive the loss of his mother. He'd adored the woman, was closer to her than anyone else in the world.

Tucker shrugged. "I guess I'm going to bury my mom." Lela winced at his harsh tone, but Tucker continued speaking before she could say anything. "Then I'm going to do the same thing I'd planned to do all along. Get the hell out of this shithole and never look back."

He bowed his head, his fists clenched in his lap.

Lela wasn't sure how to respond to his heated words. In her heart, she knew he meant them. Fear kept her silent for several moments, but Tucker didn't seem to notice. He was too lost in his anger, his grief.

Finally she cleared her throat and forced herself to ask the question. The one that was going to change everything for her. "Never?"

At that, Tucker's head rose, his gaze sharpened. For the first time since her arrival, Lela felt as if he was really seeing her. "Lela."

She recognized the tone. Could fill in the rest of the words. "Don't, Tucker." She raised her hand, hoping to ward off the inevitable. She'd seen this day coming. After all, Tucker had signed on the dotted line with Texas A&M way back in January. A full ride on a football scholarship. Tucker's feet hadn't touched the ground for weeks after that announcement. Of course, he was leaving town.

She'd known since they were fifteen about Tucker's desire to leave Maris and to play pro ball. His family couldn't afford to send him to college and his grades, while okay, sure as hell weren't going to get him into a great school. Football had been his only way out of town. He'd certainly said that enough times, but in the back of her mind, she'd always imagined him coming home on holidays and the occasional weekend to visit his mother...and her. Lela had always thought they'd keep the relationship going, despite the distance.

The thought that he never wanted to come back...

Well...never was a long time.

"You've had a shock today. We don't need to talk about any of this right now. Give yourself some time to process what's happened and—"

"Nothing's going to change later."

She struggled to get air to her lungs. Fear had weakened her breathing. "Tucker. Please."

She didn't explain her plea. It was clear from his expression he knew what she was asking. It was equally clear he wasn't going to stop.

"Lela. I can't do this anymore. I love you so much it hurts, but we're not going in the same direction."

"We can work it out."

He shook his head. 'We're eighteen years old. You know as

well as I do the odds are stacked against us. Besides, I'm not going off to college then coming back to settle down in Maris. I'm serious when I say I never want to come back here again. Ever."

She winced. As much as Tucker hated Maris, that was how much she loved it. It was home. The place she wanted to spend the rest of her life. She'd been accepted to Tarleton, preferring a smaller college campus, though she'd certainly considered following Tucker to Texas A&M. Ultimately, her parents convinced her she needed to choose a college based on what was best for her.

Suddenly she was regretting that decision.

"I can transfer after the fall semester. It'll only be a few months and then—"

"No. You'd hate a school that big. You're going to Tarleton. And you're going to stay there. It's the right place for you."

Tears filled her eyes before she could bat them away. Tucker had just lost his mother. The last thing he needed was her hysterics. But she honestly wasn't sure she'd survive if he broke up with her.

"Please don't do this."

He reached out, stroking her cheek, wiping away the tears. "We're the perfect couple, L.B., but that doesn't change the fact we were never going to go the distance."

A sob escaped when he called her by his pet name for her. He'd taken great pleasure in learning her middle name was Beatrice. From that point on, she'd ceased being Lela to him, becoming L.B.

He tugged on her hands, directing her to the spot next to him on the porch. He wrapped his arm around her shoulders, his voice quiet as he tried to explain. If she'd been able to speak, she would have told him he didn't need to bother. But Lela was struggling to accept the truth. Her heart refused to admit defeat even if her head could acknowledge that Tucker was right.

"You'd be miserable at A&M. And if I manage to catch the eye of the professional scouts, I'm signing and going. My future is football. And when I try to put you in that life with me, L.B., I can't make it work. You want to live in Maris and teach kindergartners. That's *your* dream. And it's perfect for you. You'd be unhappy living on the road, and even though you've never come out and said it, I know you hate football."

She laughed through her tears, sniffling. "Damn. I didn't realize you'd figured that out."

He smiled at her, his same beloved crooked grin. The sight of it sent a fresh round of tears to her eyes.

"God. I'm so sorry. I can't stand to see you cry. It's eating me up inside, Lela."

She turned to him, burying her face against his chest, not wanting to add to his pain, but unable to stem the flood. "I don't want to hurt you, Tucker. And I'm so sorry to fall apart like this." She wiped her eyes, willing herself to stop crying. After several deep breaths, she felt as though she'd composed herself enough to look at him again. "It's okay. I get it. I do. It just doesn't make it hurt less."

He tightened his arms around her. "I love you. So fucking much. I always will."

"I feel the same."

"I'm leaving for school next week."

She nodded. She'd had the date of his departure circled in red on her calendar for months. The damn thing had taunted her every time she looked at it, but she'd always consoled herself with the idea that he'd come home occasionally and she'd go visit him. Now that date marked a definite end. There wouldn't be anything after.

"So we have one more week."

He pulled back until he could see her face. "You're okay with that?"

"Jesus, Tuck. You don't really think I'm going to leave you alone now, do you? Your mom just died."

His composure cracked a bit as he bent his head and muttered the word "fuck."

It would take time for the reality of that loss to sink in. Lela wasn't going to leave him to face it alone.

"I guess I have to talk to someone about planning her funeral. And then there's her stuff to go through. I...I don't know how to do any of this."

If Tucker's father had been any sort of decent parent, he'd be here, consoling his son, taking care of the details instead of leaving it all to Tucker. Unfortunately, Tucker had no choice but to step up and take charge.

"We'll make a list," Lela said, standing and offering a hand to help Tucker rise as well. "And we're calling Coach. Right now. He'll help us sort it all out."

Tucker's worried expression cleared. "Yeah. Coach. You're right. He'll help."

* * *

Lela raised her head from the steering wheel and stared blindly at the diner. Coach had been at Tucker's house within twenty minutes of their phone call, and he'd guided Tucker and Lela through all the tasks associated with the death of a loved one. Tucker's dad—true to character—had crawled into a bottle about five seconds after he was released from the hospital, remaining completely shit-faced through it all.

She'd stuck by Tucker, holding his hand during the funeral, helping him pack up his mother's clothing for Goodwill. And she had been with him the morning he'd loaded his crappy, ancient Buick with all his belongings.

Lela wondered what she would give to go back to that one day—that one hour—and rewrite the ending. During that last week, she'd held it together, giving Tucker exactly what he needed, never once alluding to their breakup.

She'd arrived just as he'd closed the trunk to his car. Tucker had clearly been planning to leave without saying goodbye. She had fallen apart in pure dramatic teenage girl fashion. She'd pleaded with him to change his mind, insisted they could make it work, telling him he was wrong to assume they wouldn't last. She'd cried, screamed, cursed and even slammed her hands against his chest, but Tucker had held his ground.

Finally, he had opened the car door and climbed into the driver's seat—and that was when she'd *really* lost it, telling him he was a complete asshole, that she would never forgive him, that she would hate him until the day she died.

Tucker had accepted her venom, his jaw set, his posture stiff. All he'd said was "okay" and then he drove away, never looking back.

It had taken all of five minutes for the regret to appear. Lela had tried to call him several times a day for over a week. Tucker had never answered the phone. She'd emailed him apology after apology and had even written him several long letters, but he hadn't responded to any of them.

She'd spent the remainder of that summer shut up in her room, crying and swearing she'd never fall in love again. Then her freshman year in college began and time went to work, healing the broken pieces, dimming the pain, and even erasing some of the things she'd sworn she would never forget.

She had moved on. And, though her fondness for football hadn't grown, she'd never once, in twelve years, missed one of Tucker's televised games. Not one.

Lela climbed out of the car and wondered what had prompted that unwanted reminiscence. She supposed it was Coach's heart attack. Lorelie had mentioned that Joel was contacting some of the guys from Coach's old state championship team to see if they'd be willing to come back to Maris for a little while to pitch in at the ranch. Lela hadn't asked if Tucker had been called. It was too close to training camp starting up. There was probably no way he would come back to help anyway, but Lela still wondered if he'd been contacted, what he'd said, if he'd asked about her.

She blew out a frustrated sigh. She needed to get a grip. She was here to have a lunch date with her boyfriend, Carl. She was too damn old to keep mooning over a guy who'd probably forgotten she'd even existed. Tucker Riley was a football god, one of the most successful quarterbacks to ever play in the NFL. No doubt he had beautiful women throwing themselves at him nightly.

She had just reached the door of the diner when she felt a hand on her shoulder. She jumped as if bitten by a snake.

Carl reared back. "Damn. I'm sorry, Lela. I was calling your name."

She placed her hand on her racing heart and tried to play off her reaction. "I didn't hear you."

"Yeah. I see that. You were pretty deep in thought there. Everything okay?"

She nodded and gave him a breezy laugh that didn't sound a bit lighthearted to her, but seemed to fool Carl. "Oh yeah. Just trying to figure out what to make for dinner."

Carl accepted the lie easily, which didn't sit well with her. It was just another thing about this relationship that felt off. Everything between them was surface-y. He took whatever she said at face value and didn't seem compelled to dig much deeper than that.

Lela stiffened her spine, realizing what she had to do. Lorelie was right. It was time to break up with Carl.

He led her to a booth along the wall, claiming the side facing the front door and most of the restaurant while she took the other. Her view was of a few empty back tables and the kitchen. He always took the best seat. Her irritation flared as she studied the swinging door to the kitchen. At least she'd be the first to know when their food was coming. If they made it that far into the meal.

Now that she'd decided to end the relationship, she was anxious to get it over with. No reason to dawdle. She'd just say the words.

God. The next few minutes were bound to be uncomfortable.

Carl was an easygoing guy. She'd never seen him ruffled... ever. She used to think that was an admirable quality, but now she viewed it as a flaw. He wasn't passionate about anything— not his job, politics, sports or her. He just traveled through life, strolling along the path of least resistance. Just once, she wished he'd get pissed off, throw something, cry at the end of a sad movie or book. Do something to prove he possessed some sort of emotion.

Instead, he just smiled that same affable smile. She felt a bit like smacking him just to see if he'd still offer her that plastered-on grin.

Lela didn't bother to return his cheery look. She was tired of playing this game. Instead, she stared at him, scowling, daring him to ask her what was wrong.

He didn't.

Carl picked up his menu, once again oblivious to the fact she was troubled, and started musing aloud about his lunch choices, even though they both knew he was going to order the special.

"I'm absolutely starving," he said as he pondered breaking his usual routine by going with the cheeseburger or chicken salad.

Lela didn't bother to offer her opinion or pick up the menu. "I'm just going to have the special."

Carl nodded, acknowledging that was the best choice, and put the menu down.

Lela had just opened her mouth to speak when Macie came over to take their drink orders. Carl opted for his usual —sweet tea.

"I'll have a Coke," Lela said. Then she added, "And if a splash or two of Jim Beam happens to fall in the glass, I won't complain."

Macie laughed, declaring herself quite clumsy behind the bar, and left.

Carl gave her a curious glance. "Liquor? At lunch?"

"I'm on summer break. Why not?"

"Aren't you driving?"

She shrugged off his concern. "I'm only having one and I was thinking of spending the afternoon doing some window shopping along Main Street."

Lela gritted her teeth when she realized the opening she'd created when Carl responded with his usual, "Must be nice to have summers off to do whatever you want."

"Listen, Carl," she started, and then bit back a groan when Macie reappeared with their drinks.

"Y'all ready to order?" Macie asked.

"Two specials," Carl replied as he handed her the menus.

Lela picked up her glass and chugged half the drink. Carl lifted his eyebrow, but didn't make a remark. For the first time since they'd sat down, she thought perhaps he was starting to realize something was wrong.

However, rather than ask, he launched into a five-minute

recitation about some computer issue they had at the bank that morning. She only half listened as she tried to find the words—and the courage—to say what needed to be said.

When his story finally ended, she leaned her elbows on the table. "Carl. I was hoping we could talk about your suggestion that we move in together. I've been thinking about it a great deal and I..." Her words died away when she realized he wasn't listening. "Carl?"

He bent closer to her, his words an excited whisper. "Don't turn around too suddenly, Lela, but I swear to you, Tucker Riley just walked into the restaurant."

Lela's stomach lurched.

No. It couldn't be. Carl didn't have to worry about her turning around. If Tucker really was here, the last thing she wanted was for him to spot her. She was wearing cut-off jeans, a tatty old t-shirt that said *You Can't Scare Me. I Teach Kindergarten* and flip-flops. Her hair was pulled back in a messy ponytail and she hadn't bothered with makeup this morning.

Figures she'd run into her first love looking like this.

When she failed to react, Carl unnecessarily added, "Tucker Riley, the NFL quarterback."

"I know who he is." Carl had only lived in Maris a couple of years, but there was no way he wasn't aware that this was Tucker's hometown. Tucker Riley was touted as a hometown hero regularly.

Carl chuckled. "Yeah. I guess you do. I mean, I knew he was from here, but he's never come back, right?"

She shook her head slowly. "Not once in twelve years." Her words were spoken quietly, painfully.

Carl didn't recognize the emotion.

Lela heard several voices behind her calling out excited greetings as Maris' local superstar made his way into the restaurant. She prayed he would take a seat near the front, that he wouldn't claim a table close to them. Perhaps if she stalled long enough, she could hide in this booth until Tucker finished his meal and left.

That hope was dashed when Carl waved and called out to Joel, who walked up to their table.

"Carl, Lela." Joel shook Carl's hand. "Look who's back in town."

Joel took a step away as Tucker came into view. Lela sucked in a nervous, shallow breath, then had to make a conscious effort not to start shaking.

"Hey, L.B."

His voice was deep, sexy, and just a touch uncertain. She liked knowing he was as nervous about this unexpected reunion as she was.

"Tuck."

The nicknames, though unused in years, felt right. She hadn't been L.B. since he'd driven away from her. That girl had vanished along with his taillights.

He looked good. Damn him. His faded jeans hung low on his hips, his t-shirt—though not particularly tight—was straining against his massive muscles. His dark-blond hair was longer than he'd worn it in high school. She had no doubt it was cut professionally by someone who knew how to take a handsome man and make him stunning. A far cry from the buzz cut he used to give himself with an old pair of his father's clippers.

His face was older, more weathered, but it gave him the look of a dangerous, experienced man. Her sweet teenaged boyfriend had stolen her heart—and virginity—with his boyish good looks and charm. But this gorgeous, chiseled-in-stone, fucking hotter-than-hell man—God help her—was deadly to her libido.

Carl cleared his throat in an obvious fashion, reminding

Lela he was still there. Shit. She was all but drooling over Tucker in front of him.

"I'm sorry, Carl." She offered him a placid smile, trying to hide her sudden blush. "Carl, this is Tucker Riley. Tucker, this is Carl Wilkins."

Carl stood and shook Tucker's hand effusively. That's when Lela realized Carl hadn't even looked at her since Tucker's arrival in the restaurant. He seemed to be a bit awestruck as he fumbled for words to tell Tucker how much he'd enjoyed watching his team kick the crap out of the New York Giants last year.

Tucker was gracious, talking shop for a few minutes, but every time Lela got the nerve to look in his direction, she found his gaze on her. Carl might be oblivious to Lela's current state, but Tucker clearly wasn't. She could only imagine what he was thinking. He wasn't a fool. He knew what her flushed cheeks, shallow breathing and—Lela glanced down to check, then tried not to wince—hard nipples meant.

Finally, Carl ran out of gushing words and managed to regain some semblance of control.

Tucker took advantage of the opportunity, turning to her. "Looks like you got your dream job, L.B."

She frowned until he pointed to her t-shirt. "Oh. Yeah. I teach kindergarten." It was a stupid thing to say, but her brain synapses seemed to be short-circuiting. "You got your dream too. The NFL."

Carl decided to hop back into the conversation and Lela was grateful for the save. For about two seconds. "Lela and I never miss your games. Watch you every Sunday."

Tucker flashed her that crooked grin he used to give her in high school, the one that told her she was busted. "Really? I thought you didn't like football, L.B.?"

She narrowed her eyes, though she nearly laughed at his knowing smirk. "It's okay."

"Okay?" Carl asked with a laugh. "I thought you were going to go through the TV during that last game of the season." Carl turned to Tucker. "You remember, the one where you took a bad hit from that big-ass lineman, Rodney Jefferson, from the Chiefs? Knocked you out of the game."

From Tucker's expression, it was clear he recalled. For a moment, Lela saw that same pain in his eyes that she'd seen the morning she had found him on the front porch after his mother's death. However, he shuttered it away quickly, nodding. "I remember that."

Carl chuckled, oblivious to anything except the story he was telling. "Lela stood up and let out a stream of cuss words, and I swear to God, if she could have crawled through that television and beat the hell out of the guy, she would have."

Tucker smiled, clearly enjoying her embarrassment. "It's a shame you weren't there. I would have enjoyed seeing you take Jefferson down."

She didn't even bother to pretend she didn't care about the game. "It was a dirty hit."

Tucker lifted one shoulder, not commenting one way or the other.

"You staying in Maris long?" Carl asked.

Though Carl had asked the question, Tucker looked at Lela as he replied. "I'm not sure how long I'll be in town."

Something in Tucker's voice made her think part of his decision whether to take off immediately or stay awhile would be based on her reaction to his return.

Macie arrived with their food, so Joel and Tucker found a table nearby. Tucker made sure to claim the seat that faced her. Any hope she had of having a serious talk with Carl about their future—or lack thereof—was dashed.

She was too aware of Tucker's heated glances, the way he kept staring at her. She wished it made her uncomfortable because it was annoying, but the fact was, all his looks made her want to do was rip her clothes off and straddle him.

"L.B.?" Carl asked.

Lela forced herself to pay attention to her lunch date. "A nickname. Sort of a way to tease me about the fact my middle name is Beatrice."

Carl smiled. "I didn't realize you two were friends in school. You never mentioned it."

Lela tried to decide if there was suspicion in Carl's voice, but dismissed the thought. His tone was pure curiosity and maybe even a bit of jealousy. Not *over* her, but *of* her. Apparently Carl was envious of her past association with an NFL god. That idea would be funny if she were in a better mood.

"Maris High School isn't that big and we were in the same grade." As far as non-answers went, that one definitely fit the bill. Carl was bound to find out she and Tucker had been an item. She suspected the only reason he hadn't heard before now is because the locals who knew about her past relationship with Tucker never mentioned his name in front of her in order to spare her feelings. There wasn't anyone who'd lived in Maris all those years ago who didn't know Tucker had broken her heart quite thoroughly, completely.

Carl accepted her vague comment as enough and the conversation turned to mundane things.

Lela chanced a glance at Tucker. Sure enough, he was looking directly at her. Cocky bastard even winked. She turned away from him, blew out an exasperated breath and ate her lunch without tasting a single bite. She was vaguely aware of Carl talking, but she had no clue what he was saying. Finally, the meal ended.

She stood and threw Tucker what she hoped was a carefree, maybe-I'll-see-you-around wave, then left. Carl gave her a quick kiss on the cheek as they parted at the door. He returned to his car and work, while she decided to walk. She needed time to clear her head.

Within an hour, she'd decided to break up with her boyfriend and had been blindsided by the return of a man she thought she'd managed to get over.

Ha ha. Yeah right.

She was still in love with Tucker. Something told her she would be until the day she died.

That thought gave her no comfort.

Her life had just taken a hard left down a street she hadn't even known was there. Now she had to decide if she wanted to turn around to seek the familiar path or keep driving down this route to check out the changing scenery.

Chapter Two

Tucker stood on the porch of Coach's large ranch house. He'd started to knock on the door, but had felt compelled to turn around and study the view first. The large, sprawling landscape was a far cry from Turks and Caicos. Instead of the simplicity of white sand and sparkling blue water, Tucker found too many things for his gaze to land upon.

He soaked it all in. Fields of green and brown dotted with outbuildings and cattle, trees and scrub brush lining the horizon, as well as mile after mile of picket fencing surrounded him.

The only similarity between his hometown and the paradise island he'd just left was the sky. He'd spent weeks at the ocean watching fluffy white clouds riding the same endless sea of blue as he floated, letting the waves carry him along. He'd almost felt a kinship with the clouds, content to spend his days drifting without direction or purpose. A free agent. There was a freedom in letting go and letting nature take over.

He'd been seeking peace for the better part of six months.

When the beach had failed him, he'd latched on to home. He'd been back in Maris for three days and apart from that lunch with Joel and his unexpected face-to-face with Lela, he hadn't seen anyone else.

He had been brought down by the worst migraine he'd suffered since April. For two days, he'd barricaded himself in his hotel room, keeping the thick curtains closed, welcoming the darkness and whatever rest he could find. He'd sort of anticipated the pain would come. Flying did not agree with him anymore. He hadn't mentioned it to his doctors. Instead he'd credited the migraine to air pressure and accepted that if he wanted to travel these days, he'd have to suck up whatever came after.

Today—mercifully—he'd awoken and realized his head didn't hurt. After a quick shower and room service, Tucker had decided it was time to seek out Coach, who had been released from the hospital yesterday. Tucker was relieved to hold this reunion with Coach in his home. Joel had warned Tucker that the man had aged and the heart attack had definitely taken its toll on their strong-as-an-ox coach.

"Are you going to stand there all day or are you going to come over here and give me a damn hug?"

Tucker grinned at Lorelie's imperious tone. The more things changed, the more they stayed the same. He turned and just managed to get his arms up as she launched herself at him. He was blown away by the changes in her. Lorelie hadn't aged in his mind. Whenever he'd heard her name, he had seen that same gangly sixteen-year-old girl she'd been when he left.

But this Lorelie had grown up.

When she pulled away, Tucker gave her a quizzical look. "I'm sorry," he teased. "Do I know you?"

She punched him on the arm and he fought not to wince. Lorelie packed a wallop. Growing up around ranchers and football players without a mother to lead her along the path of all things feminine had insured Lorelie was a rough-and-tumble tomboy. It appeared that part hadn't changed, even if her looks had.

She'd gotten her father's height and, as a teenager, she'd sort of struggled with her long arms and legs. Somewhere along the line, she'd gotten used to her stature. She was much more at ease, graceful. Tucker suspected Coach found it harder to chase the men away these days. Lorelie was damn pretty.

She gave him a smirk. "Smartass. It's about time you got your ass over here. I was just on my way to the hotel to drag you out. Where have you been? Joel said you got back in town on Tuesday."

Tucker went with a lie. After so many months of pretending, it was getting far too easy to make up stories that wouldn't lead to more questions. "I must have picked up a flu bug on the airplane. Just spent a couple days in bed. Didn't want to see Coach until I was one hundred percent."

Lorelie bought the lie. "I'm sorry you were sick. And yeah, they wouldn't have let you see him in the hospital if you'd come in with the flu. He's sort of weak as a newborn kitten these days."

Though the words flowed steadily, Tucker could see the worry in Lorelie's eyes. Her mother had died in childbirth, leaving Lorelie alone with the loving man who had been a father *and* a mother to her. It was clear the fear of losing her dad hadn't left Lorelie since the night he'd keeled over shortly after dinner a week ago.

Joel had recounted the story of how Coach hadn't been feeling well that day, complaining of heartburn. Coach and Lorelie had eaten early as Lorelie had plans to meet some girl-friends for a movie. Coach had remained at the table while Lorelie cleared the dishes then grabbed her purse. She'd just given him a quick kiss on the cheek to say goodbye when Coach slumped over. Lorelie had tried to catch him, but despite her height, her dad had at least six inches and a hundred pounds on her. As a result, he'd gotten a nasty cut on his head from his tumble to the floor. Lorelie had called 911 and the doctors had insisted it was lucky she'd still been home. If the heart attack had come a few minutes later—after Lorelie had gone out for the evening—Coach would have died.

"How's the old man doing?" Tucker asked.

"Why don't you get in here and ask him yourself?" Coach's gruff reply came to them through an open window on the first floor.

Lorelie pointed to it. "He's in the living room. Been asking about you since Joel told us you came home."

Tucker started to enter the house, but Lorelie stopped him. "I'm going out to the barn to check on a few things. Give you two some time to catch up." Then she reached out and gave him another hug, whispering in his ear to shield her words from her eavesdropping father. "Thank you so much for coming back." Her voice broke as she spoke. Another hint of emotion. The poor woman was working overtime to put on a happy façade.

Tucker patted her cheek affectionately when she released him, then watched her descend the porch stairs.

"You still there, Tucker?" Coach called out.

Tucker let himself in the front door, grinning widely as he took in the same familiar foyer. He'd worked on Coach's ranch —along with several other guys on the team—for three summers. Coach claimed doing man's work would make them stronger on the field. Tucker had to admit that workout plan had definitely been as effective, if not more so, than simply lifting weights in a gym.

Tucker tried to keep his face impassive when he got his first glimpse of Coach, but he must have failed.

Coach grimaced, then pointed to the bandage on his forehead. "I know. I look like hell."

While Coach's hair had thinned and grayed over the past dozen years and his massive build appeared slighter in the aftermath of his heart attack and bypass surgery, his voice was as steady, deep and firm as ever.

Tucker approached the couch where the man was reclining. He'd put out his hand, intent on offering Coach a handshake, but was surprised when the old guy used that grip to pull Tucker down. Coach wrapped one arm around Tucker and gave him a strong squeeze and a hard slap on the back that immediately set Tucker's mind at ease. Coach might have been knocked down, but there was a lot of kick left in this old mule.

When they parted, Coach gestured to the chair across from the couch. Tucker claimed it.

"Damn good to see you, boy."

Tucker smiled. "Good to see you too." Apart from the occasional phone calls with Joel, the only other person Tucker had remained in touch with over the years had been Coach. Tucker had turned to the man for career advice time after time as he'd moved from college ball to the pros. Coach had never steered him wrong.

The only thing Tucker hadn't talked to him about was the decision he was grappling with now. He wasn't sure why he hadn't confided in Coach. Part of him figured he was too afraid to hear the man's response.

"So how long are you planning to stay in Maris?" As he spoke, Coach pushed himself up to a more comfortable position. The movement clearly caused him a bit of pain.

Tucker shrugged. "Not sure."

"Shouldn't you be heading to training camp soon?"

Tucker had known before he came here today he'd have to answer that question. He'd sort of evaded it with Joel on his first day in town, but folks were obviously curious about why he was here and not there.

"I'm on the injured reserve list."

Coach studied him. "Head?"

Tucker nodded, not bothering to lie. It was apparent he didn't have any broken bones or other visible injuries.

"That was a hard hit you took in that last game."

Tucker swallowed heavily. "Concussion."

Coach scrutinized his face too closely and Tucker resisted the urge to squirm uncomfortably. "Headaches?"

Again Tucker nodded.

"Still?" Coach asked. Tucker had said less than twenty words since entering the room, but it didn't matter. Coach was putting the pieces together pretty damn fast.

"Yeah."

Tucker held his breath, waiting to see what Coach would say next. Would he tell him to beat back the pain, fight through it? Or would he tell him to walk away?

"You're not sure if you're going back, are you?"

Tucker blew out a long sigh, then shook his head. "Another hit and the doctors say I'm in danger of permanent brain damage. I've had too many concussions. The thing is...I think we've got a real shot at the Super Bowl this year. A really good shot."

Coach folded his arms, his brows furrowed, while Tucker awaited his response.

Finally, Coach gave him a rueful grin. "Life's a bitch sometimes, isn't it?"

Tucker frowned. That was it? "That's your answer?"

Coach lifted one shoulder. "I didn't hear you ask me a question. Besides, this isn't my decision. It's yours."

"Yeah, but don't you have any advice?"

Coach tugged the blanket over his lap a bit higher. "I could offer you some. I've always got an opinion. You know that."

Tucker chuckled, despite the heavy pressure pushing against his chest. It was always this way with Coach. Even when he was at his wit's end and it felt like the world was falling apart, his coach always found a way to make him smile, to make it all seem a bit less dire.

"The thing is, Tucker, my advice is worthless to you. We all make the big decisions based on our previous experience. My experiences are different than yours. The things that would make *me* decide one way or the other aren't what are driving *you*. That's the beauty of being human. The freedom to choose our own paths."

"I don't know what to do," Tucker admitted.

Coach smiled. "I'm pretty sure you know exactly what you're going to do. You're just not ready to accept it yet. Give it time and stop thinking so damn hard. I can tell from the lines in your face and the dark circles under your eyes you've been letting this eat away at you for a long time. You need a distraction."

For a moment, Lela's face flashed in Tucker's mind. He hadn't stopped thinking about her since seeing her in the diner. She was absolutely beautiful. He'd seen her sitting in that booth and it felt like all the air in his body had flown out in a loud whoosh. It had taken him a few seconds to find enough breath to speak.

She'd be a perfect distraction if not for two things. For one, he'd broken her heart after graduation and been a grade-A prick for not returning her calls or emails. There was no way in hell he'd risk hurting her again. And secondly, the guy she'd been sitting with—according to Joel—was her boyfriend.

Lela was off-limits.

"A distraction, huh? What did you have in mind?" Tucker asked.

Coach's grin grew. "You look like you've let yourself go soft, my boy. What did I always tell you?"

Tucker didn't even have to think about the answer, though it was a lesson he had forgotten these past few months. "Sweat and hard work are the answer to every question."

Coach nodded, then his face sobered up. "I'm worried about Lorelie. She's been working herself ragged since my damn heart attack. Joel and Oakley are pulling long hours. Jack and Walt are back in town too. They've been helping out some. I'd give anything to be able to get off this couch and take some of the load away from her, but..."

Coach was a proud man, one who didn't like to be beholden to others. Tucker could only imagine how hard it was for him to accept his body simply wouldn't let him do what he wanted.

"I'm sort of between gigs right now," Tucker said, taking a page out of Coach's book, trying to lighten the mood. "And I'm in the market for some sweat and hard work. Maybe I could pitch in around here to help her out."

Coach gave him an appreciative smile. "I can't tell you how much it means to me that you boys came back." The older man's voice grew thick with emotion.

Tucker leaned closer, letting himself say things he should have said years earlier. Ever since learning of Coach's heart attack, Tucker realized he'd almost missed out on the chance to tell the man what a huge impact he'd made in his life. "I owe you so much, Coach. Everything. I can't imagine what my life would have been like if you hadn't handed me that football and taught me the game."

Coach tried to shrug off his comments, to say he hadn't done that much, but Tucker wouldn't let him get away with it.

"When my mom died," Tucker swallowed heavily. He hadn't talked about that night in a long time. "I don't think I would have survived if it hadn't been for you and Lela."

"Your mother was a fine woman, Tucker."

Tucker smiled, grateful for the compliment. He'd loved his mother and there wasn't a day that passed when he didn't think about her, miss her. Sometimes he thought she was the only person in his life who'd ever *really* understood him. Because she lived in that house too. "I just wanted you to know how much I appreciate your help. You got me out of this town. Away from..."

Tucker didn't bother to finish the sentence. They both knew how it ended.

He was surprised by Coach's harsh, almost angry reply. "I didn't teach you the game so you could use it as an escape. Courage means standing up, Tucker. Not running away."

Tucker felt the need to defend himself. "I stood up to him. Right after my mother's funeral—"

Coach's voice softened. "Throwing a punch doesn't count, Tuck."

Tucker ran a hand through his hair. He knew that. Knew the second his father hit the floor he'd done no more than stoop to the drunken man's level. He'd actually been ashamed of himself. Then that shame turned to a burning anger that hadn't left him. Not once in twelve years.

Coach sat up straighter, his expression one of concern. "Your father is still around, you know?"

"I know."

"You got a game plan?"

Tucker didn't. He'd flown to Maris without putting much thought into the repercussions. His only goal had been to see Coach, to make sure he was okay.

Then Tucker mentally chastised himself. Coach hadn't been the only person to bring him back.

Lela.

"Twelve years is a long time to sit on unfinished business."

Tucker nodded. It was clear Coach understood Tucker better than he did himself. It had been too damn long. If he accomplished nothing else while he was home, he knew he needed to put some sort of ending to the Lela and dear old Dad chapters.

"Yeah. It's too long." Problem was, Tucker couldn't see how the things he'd let fester for so long could end any differently. It was one of the reasons he'd stayed away. He'd never forgive his father. And Lela would never forgive *him*.

It appeared Coach could read his emotions as well as ever. He'd never failed to see when Tucker was losing his cool in a game or getting rattled. And he always found a way to help him rein in those feelings.

Coach began filling him in on how the ranch operated these days. Despite all the new technology, it seemed his coach was old school. He listed some of the tasks that needed to be done daily, many the same ones Tucker had performed during his summers on the ranch.

Tucker's former teammates had returned to Maris as well and would be pitching in to help. Tucker was looking forward to seeing them again. It would be great to reconnect with Walt, Jack, Caleb and Tyson. They'd been some of the best friends Tucker had ever had. They shared a past. A legacy.

State champions. Tucker couldn't remember any victory— not in college or the NFL—that was sweeter than walking off that high school football field with the state trophy in his hands. He'd always thought the only thing better would be winning the Super Bowl.

His heart lurched, a quick, sharp pain that pricked anytime

he thought about the Super Bowl. Some dreams were impossible to let go of.

Tucker pulled himself out of his thoughts when he realized the room had gone quiet. He grinned when he saw Coach dozing on the couch. The man had talked himself to sleep.

Tucker quietly rose and left the room, careful not to rouse the poor man. He needed his rest. The two of them would have plenty of time over the next couple of weeks to catch up.

He stepped back out into the Texas sunshine, and then froze.

Lela was standing beside his rental, admiring the sleek Camaro convertible, dark sunglasses hiding her pretty brown eyes.

She lifted them, the frames becoming a makeshift headband, when she saw him on the porch. "I wondered whose car this was."

He grinned, descending the stairs. He didn't stop until he was standing directly in front of her, too close for casual politeness. There was some perverse part of him that wanted to see if she still smelled as good as she used to, if she still used that coconut shampoo in her hair. He'd woken up more nights than he cared to admit, the memory of that scent haunting him.

Unfortunately, Lela took a big step back. That move gave him pause momentarily.

Then some devil lurking inside prodded him to challenge her, to decrease the distance between them again.

Lela started to counter that move with yet another step, but he caught her hands, held her in place. And then, God bless America, he caught a whiff of that sweet smell.

She tried to tug her hands from his, narrowing her eyes in warning. He ignored her unspoken admonition.

Tucker released one hand easily, but kept a firm grip on the other as he gestured to his car. "Wanna go for a ride? We can put the top down."

Tucker had played out this scene between them a million times in the past, always imagining what he'd say if he ever saw her again. He'd always begun with an apology and some lame explanation, but he couldn't find those words now. He owed them to her, but he would be damned if he'd fill this reunion with past mistakes. He'd missed her.

She glanced longingly at the car. Lela had always admired convertibles. If he were being honest with himself, he would admit it was what had prompted him to rent this particular car.

She shook her head, though he felt hopeful when her rejection wasn't immediate. She'd actually considered going with him. "No. I'm here to check on Coach."

Tucker looked back toward the house. It was still and quiet. "He's in the living room, but he's asleep."

"Oh." Lela fidgeted, clearly searching for some other reason to escape him. He refused to make it easy on her.

"So why don't we let the guy get some rest? We'll go for that ride and you can visit him afterwards."

"I'm afraid I...have...to..." She was searching for an excuse. And doing a terrible job at it.

He smirked. "You still suck at lying, L.B."

She shot him a dirty look. "Did you ever consider that I don't want to hang out with you and I'm looking for an acceptable reason, so that I don't hurt your feelings?"

He shook his head. "Nope. That thought never occurred to me. Because you're dying to go for a ride."

She rolled her eyes and started to walk away from him. "You cocky son of a b—"

Tucker had no idea what prompted his next move. Maybe it was because she was trying to get away. Or the adorable exasperation on her face. Or that damn smell that had his cock going hard in an instant.

Whatever it was, it had his hands on her upper arms, twisting her around to him, cutting off her words with hard, hungry lips.

Lela was motionless for several seconds. Tucker used her shock against her as he deepened the kiss. Her mouth had been open and he'd taken advantage of that fact, pressing his tongue against hers.

When she did move, Tucker tightened his grip and planted his feet to prepare, ready to halt her flight. But she didn't shove him away. Didn't turn her face away from his, didn't slap him for his forwardness.

Instead, she responded. Her lips softened and her tongue met his.

It was her turn to claim the advantage. She lifted her arms, wrapping them around his neck, her firm breasts pressed against his chest. Tucker released her arms, his hands dropping to her waist. He needed to touch her skin. He hadn't lived like a monk, hadn't resisted the perks associated with being a star quarterback. It wasn't unusual for beautiful women to invite him to their beds and he'd taken more than a few of them up on the offer.

He'd ventured into sex clubs and given in to dominant urges he'd never shown Lela when they'd been younger. He'd tied women up, down and sideways, but nothing, not one damn kinky, hot, sex-filled night, had turned him on more than this relatively simple kiss from Lela.

His hands drifted under her shirt. She shivered slightly when his fingers grazed her soft skin, despite the scorching heat.

Lela ran her hands through his hair before she closed her

fingers in the strands, tugging it harder, using her grip to increase the pressure of the kiss.

Tucker didn't try to escape, didn't acknowledge the prickling pain in his scalp. There was a new roughness, an impassioned hunger to Lela's response. It spoke to Tucker's own needs.

With his hands on her hips, he twisted them, lightly pushing her back against the side of the car, stepping closer. He pressed his cock against her, letting her feel how hard he was, how much he wanted her. She whimpered, but didn't seek to break the union of their mouths.

Tucker was vaguely aware of their surroundings. They were in the front yard of a fairly busy ranch. Anyone and everyone could be watching them, but Tucker couldn't find it in himself to give a shit.

Besides, Lela was too pragmatic. Common sense was going to raise its ugly head soon enough and she'd definitely shove him away. Until then he had to make sure to leave a lasting impression. Take care to ensure this encounter wasn't something she'd soon forget.

His hands still lingered beneath her shirt. Lifting them, he wasted no time cupping her full breasts. He squeezed the flesh firmly, loving the way Lela moved toward the touch, encouraging him to continue.

They'd been virgins the first time they'd come together. Tucker had been so much bigger than her and he'd been terrified of hurting her. That fear had never left his young man's heart, so their sexual history had been steeped in gentleness and slow, easy lovemaking.

This older version of Lela was stronger, self-confident, sexy. Tucker couldn't offer her softness if his life depended on it. Instead, he felt the intense need to conquer. To prove to her she wasn't the only one who'd changed. To take her in all the ways he'd dreamed of on those lonely nights when he gave in and let himself fantasize about her.

She'd been the face he'd seen every time he'd closed his eyes, wrapped his hand around his cock, and brought himself to climax. He'd envisioned her on her knees before him, her hands tied behind her back, sometimes blindfolded, sometimes not. She'd open her mouth upon his command and...

Tucker forced the sexy thoughts from his head before he really did do something neither of them was ready for.

Then, the devil inside pushed his way to the forefront again and Tucker pinched her nipples, letting the lacy material of her bra add to the pleasure-pain of the sensation.

Lela moaned, a throaty sound that demanded he give her more. He responded, then jerked slightly when she slipped her hands into the back pockets of his jeans, squeezing his ass cheeks roughly and using that grip to press his cock more firmly against her.

"You do realize my father is less than fifty yards away with a very clear view of all of this?"

Lela's hands disappeared instantly at the sound of Lorelie's voice. She ducked under his arm, desperate to put distance between them. Tucker found it more difficult to move. His dick was full to bursting and any sudden movements had the potential to maim him for life.

He rested his palms against the car door and took several long, deep breaths, trying to will away the painful erection. He was going to suffer the worst case of blue balls in history after this encounter.

It took several moments for him to realize that Lela wasn't fairing much better. She leaned against the hood, only a few feet away from him. Her cheeks were flaming, her chest rising and falling rapidly. He'd expected to see anger and accusation in her gaze. Instead he was met with the same confusion and shock he was experiencing.

Lela found her voice first. "I'm so sorry, Lorelie. I don't know what…"

Lorelie laughed. "Twelve years didn't do a damn thing to put out the fire that always blazed between you two. That was fucking hot. I'm probably going to have to go a few rounds with my vibrator later. Better than watching porn."

Tucker turned, shaking his head. Lorelie had never had a filter, always saying exactly what she thought and felt, no matter how inappropriate.

Lela covered her mouth, though her laughter escaped anyway. "God, Lorelie."

He was relieved to see she could find some humor in this situation, that she wasn't freaking out or giving him hell.

"Well, I guess I'll let you two sort out whatever the hell that was. I'm going inside for some lemonade." Lorelie looked at Lela. "Feel free to join me in a little while if you want to."

Tucker didn't have to be a woman to know Lorelie was dying to question her friend about what had just happened. Tucker wouldn't mind hearing Lela's thoughts on the subject either. Then he thought it was probably better if he didn't know.

Lorelie left them alone.

"Tucker." The resigned tone in her voice told him everything he needed to know in one word. She was going to brush it all off, pretend it didn't mean anything.

His temper flared. It damn well meant something to him. He raised his hand. "No. We're not discussing it."

Her brow creased. "What?"

"I'm not interested in analyzing what just happened or picking it apart."

"But—"

"No, Lela. I mean it. Neither one of us knows what that fucking was. It's too soon to try to reason it out or dismiss it."

She bit her lower lip, drawing his attention to how kiss-swollen they were. "Okay."

He hadn't expected her easy capitulation. It soothed him to know she was as staggered as he was.

"I'm sticking around for a couple of weeks." He wanted her to know this wasn't going to go away. Not easily anyway. Then before he could consider it, he added, "Maybe even longer than that."

She nodded. "Okay," she repeated.

He reached for the door handle, every instinct in his body demanding that he kiss her once more. But if he started again, he wouldn't be able to stop, no matter who was watching.

Lela took a few steps away from the car as he opened the door. He turned to look at her. "This isn't over, Lela."

She didn't wince, didn't deny it. Instead she held his gaze and said, "I know it's not."

He forced himself to get in the car and though it killed him to do it again, he drove away from her.

This time, however, he was definitely coming back.

Chapter Three

Lela stood at the edge of the small dance floor at Cruisers, staring at the gyrating bodies without seeing them. Lorelie had gone to the bar to grab them a couple of beers, insisting they needed some serious girl time. Against her better judgment, Lela had let herself be dragged along even though this was the last place she wanted to be.

She'd much preferred the state she'd been in a few hours ago, bra-less in sweat shorts and a t-shirt, curled up on her couch with a pint of Ben & Jerry's Cherry Garcia in hand.

The past week had been rough. She still wasn't sure what had possessed her to sort of sexually attack Tucker in the front yard of Coach's house. She'd tried to blame it on her distraught state. That same morning, she'd broken things off with Carl.

She had expected it to be an amiable, easy split. The relationship had been quite staid and uneventful, so she'd been unprepared for Carl's uncharacteristic show of emotion. He'd jumped from anger to pleading to utter devastation then right back to completely pissed off. She'd been floored by the sheer magnitude, the melodramatic way he'd responded. Where had that passion been when they were dating?

Regardless, she'd stuck to her guns, helped him gather the few things he had stashed at her house—a toothbrush, razor, change of clothes—asked for her key back, then watched him peal out of her driveway, spinning tires and kicking gravel against her garage door.

Then she'd gone to visit Coach and freaking lost her mind with Tucker. Since then, she'd been a complete basket case. She'd cleaned her house and her classroom like a woman possessed and when she'd run out of stuff to throw away, organize or alphabetize, she'd hit the grocery store, stocked up on wine and ice cream and hit the couch.

That was where Lorelie had found her this afternoon. The only thing that had offered her even the slightest bit of consolation was Lorelie's news that Tucker seemed to be just as off-kilter as she was. Apparently, he'd spent the last seven days working like a man possessed, repairing broken fencing, repainting the barn, and putting a nail in every creaking floorboard in Coach's house. Lorelie swore the place had never looked better.

"Earth to Lela."

She blinked, and then realized Lorelie was standing in front of her, holding out a beer. She hastily took it from her with a quick word of thanks.

"You're going to have to step it up," Lorelie said. "You're killing my buzz."

Lela laughed. "I warned you about that before we left the house. Told you you'd have more fun with Paige or Gia. You still made me come."

Lorelie shrugged. "I refuse to believe you were sitting in that house nursing a broken heart over Carl. Which means you were really only hiding."

"From?" Lela should have known better than to ask.

Lorelie didn't mince words. "From that hot stud of an NFL quarterback. And believe me, I don't blame you for thinking twice before taking on that freaking perfect specimen of a man. A man shouldn't be prettier than a woman, but damn, he looks fine. I'd be sincerely intimidated to take my clothes off in front of a guy who looks like he jumped right off the Photoshopped page of a men's magazine. I swear to God you can bounce quarters off that guy's ass. He was wearing these tight jeans today and I—"

Lela lifted her hand to cut her friend off. "Spare me the description. Please." She didn't need the visual. She'd spent too many hours over the past week recalling exactly how good that firm, muscular ass had felt in her hands.

Lorelie was right. Lela hadn't been nursing a broken heart. Instead, she'd thought of nothing but the feeling of Tucker's lips on hers.

How long had it been since she'd tasted that kind of desire?

She knew the answer. Never. Not even in her previous experience with Tucker had she felt that intense, breath-stealing, heart-throbbing, pussy-clenching need to rip off a man's clothes, toss him to the ground, straddle his hips and ride him until they broke bones. She wanted him with a hunger that bordered on painful and with a need that was nothing short of pure insanity.

She was a woman spiraling out of control with no desire to leave the chaos.

The problem was, Lela wasn't so sure Tucker was the right man for her any more than Carl had been. Their situation hadn't changed at all in twelve years.

They'd always set off sparks whenever they were within a fifty-yard radius of each other, but the reality was, he was in the NFL and she was a Maris girl through and through. This was her home. She loved her friends, her job, her little house by the lake and her life.

"Uh-oh," Lorelie muttered.

"What's wrong?" Lela looked toward the entrance to see what Lorelie had spotted, then she blew out a long breath. "Damn."

Carl was walking into the bar with a few of his coworkers.

It was times like this when she wished her beloved hometown were bigger.

"We're not leaving." Lorelie's voice was resolute.

"Lorelie," Lela said, hoping to convince her friend to see reason.

"There are a million people in here. We'll just give him a wide berth. I mean, you were going to run into him sooner or later. Might as well get this awkwardness over with."

Lorelie had a point. It didn't matter when they did this initial run-in. It was going to be uncomfortable. At least here, it was too loud and crowded to have much of a conversation. She could just wave, say hi, and then get swallowed up in the throng once more.

She took a sip of her beer. Two local farmers came over to ask them to dance. Lorelie jumped at the chance, tugging Lela onto the floor with her. It was an easy, fast-paced line dance and by the middle of the song, Lela was laughing, enjoying herself.

One dance turned into two and then into three. Lela's face was flushed from the heat, the nape of her neck growing damp with sweat from the workout. She was just about to excuse herself to step outside for some air when the music changed, the band playing a slow country song.

Perfect timing for an escape.

She pointed to the door over her shoulder as Lorelie nodded and partnered up with one of the farmers. The other guy accepted her departure, asking a cute little blonde near them to dance.

Lela turned, then found her nose pressed against a brick wall of a chest. A very familiar wall. She glanced up.

Tucker didn't ask her if she wanted to dance. Instead, he wrapped his arms around her and started swaying. She didn't take him to task or even try to leave.

One of these damn days, she was going to have to find some semblance of self-restraint.

He pressed his face against the top of her head. "You smell good."

She grinned, calling him on his lie. "I'm hot and sweaty."

"My favorite scent on a woman."

Just like that, her body went into overdrive. Her pussy fluttered, her nipples tightened and that same familiar ache she'd felt since he'd kissed her at the ranch reappeared. She'd never experienced such a simple—and terrifying—need. Basically she felt as though she needed to fuck this man or die.

"Tucker." She started to pull away. Lela needed to put some distance between them, hoping she could think rationally if he wasn't touching her.

He tugged her tighter to him, the pure, unassailable strength of his embrace turning her on even more.

"It's just a dance, L.B."

She lifted her face, capturing his gaze. "Liar," she whispered, the word disappearing in the noise of the music. He read her lips and gave her a crooked grin.

At that point, she simply let go. She rested her cheek against his chest and disappeared into the moment, enjoying the music, the dim lighting, the heat and his masculine scent.

Nothing else existed. They didn't have a past or a future. Just this place. This time.

She didn't realize the song had changed, another fast line dance starting up, until Tucker's grip loosened.

Lela accepted the hand he proffered and let him lead her to a corner table where Joel and Oakley were sitting.

"Look who I found." Tucker gestured for her to slide into the circular booth, then he followed her. She shot him a warning look when he plastered himself to her side, wrapping his arm around her shoulder. He ignored her when she tried to put some distance between them. Of course.

"Hey, Lela. Been meaning to call you about your lawn mower. It's just with all the stuff happening with Coach..."

Lela waved off Joel's comment. At the beginning of the summer, her fairly new mower had gone kaput. "Don't give it another thought, Joel. I know you've been busy. My grass isn't going anywhere," she said with a laugh.

"You need a handyman?" Tucker asked. "I took the same Small Engines class as Joel in high school, remember? I could come take a look at it."

She shook her head. The last thing she needed was Tucker anywhere near her house...or her bed. "That's okay. I know you're helping out at the ranch too. Coach needs you guys way more than I do."

Tucker looked as if he wanted to argue that point, but mercifully a waitress stopped by to take their order.

"What's your poison?" Tucker asked her.

Lela smiled at the waitress. "I'll have a Miller Lite, Denise."

Tucker crinkled his nose. "Miller Lite? Seriously?"

"Mind your own business," she teased.

"I'll just have a water," Tucker said before Oakley and Joel added their own drink orders.

"Water?" Lela asked after Denise left.

It took Tucker a second to respond. When he did, she knew

he wasn't telling her the truth. "Preseason conditioning. No alcohol."

"There you are. I thought you skipped out on me, Lela." Lorelie bumped Joel's hip, forcing him to scoot over and make room for her in the already crowded booth.

"I wouldn't leave without telling you."

Lorelie narrowed her eyes. "Of course you would. It's the only way you'd be able to escape, and since I had to drag you out tonight to begin with—"

"Drag you?" Tucker interjected.

Lela shrugged. "I wasn't in the mood."

"She dumped her boyfriend," Lorelie added.

Lela was tempted to kick her best friend under the table, but she was fairly certain she would hit the wrong leg. The booth was only made to sit four people comfortably and the men surrounding her weren't exactly small guys.

Tucker turned to her, his voice lower when he spoke. The loud music helped hide his question from the others at the table. "When did you break up with him?"

No doubt the cocky man thought she'd called things off with Carl after their kiss. She gave him a grin. "Two hours before the last time I saw you."

"Before, huh?"

She didn't bother to reply. In truth, she wasn't sure what to say. Did Tucker think her actions at the ranch were simply a knee-jerk rebound response? Or did he think she'd left Carl for him?

Neither was true.

Or...now that she considered it...both were actually true.

She should have stayed on the couch.

The band started playing *Day Drinking* and Lorelie yelled loudly. "Oh my God! I love this song." She grabbed Joel's hand to pull him out of the booth. "Come on. You and Oakley have to dance with me."

"Is this even a song you can dance to?" Joel asked as he stood up. His question was clearly rhetorical. Neither man bothered to refuse. They worked with Lorelie all day, every day at the ranch. They knew her well enough to know resistance was futile.

Lela tried to take advantage of the extra space and started to scoot over. Tucker's grip on her shoulder prevented that maneuver. "Tucker. You're going to have to stop manhandling me."

"Why?"

She gave him a dirty look. "Because it's annoying."

He laughed loudly. "No, it's not."

"Were you always this arrogant?"

He nodded. "Yeah." When he flashed her an of-course-I-was-how-could-you-forget-that look, she giggled. God, she hadn't giggled like that since high school.

Smugly, she said, "You're right. You were. No wonder I dumped you."

His grin faded. "Is that how you remember things going down?"

She'd meant her comment to be playful, but she'd missed the mark by about a mile. "I was just teasing."

She hoped he'd let that conversation die there. Lela wasn't ready to rehash those painful days with him. She was feeling too raw from his return.

He lifted his hand from her shoulder, picking up a strand of her hair and running his fingers through it. "Your hair is still soft." He leaned closer, breathing in her scent before whispering, "Coconut. Always loved that smell."

Lela's heart began to beat a little bit harder, the air in the room growing thick. It would be so easy to simply turn her face to his, cup his cheek in her hand, and kiss him.

But those memories of the past she'd managed to bury on the dance floor weren't staying down. They were sprouting up like ugly weeds. Letting herself get swept away in this, giving in to these sexual desires, would do nothing more than leave her with another bruise on her heart when he left again.

"Tucker. I don't think—"

"Well. Isn't this cozy?"

Lela looked up, surprised to see Carl swaying next to their table. He was clearly intoxicated—she'd never seen him drunk—and still very angry.

"Carl? Are you okay?" she asked.

Her ex-boyfriend practically snarled at her. "So let me see if I've got this straight. You dumped me the second this asshole snapped his fingers. Never pegged you for one of those shallow sluts who screw professional athletes, Lela."

Tucker rose, his face pure fury. If Carl hadn't been so drunk, he would have known to back down...quick. Tucker had at least six inches on the other man and he was probably twice as wide, made of pure muscle.

Instead, Carl clenched his fists.

The insane man had a suicide wish.

Lela followed Tucker out of the booth as quickly as possible, putting herself between the two men. "Carl. You've had too much to drink. You'd never say anything so cruel otherwise." She hoped her words would knock some sense into him and soothe Tucker's temper, calm him down. "The reasons I gave you for breaking things off were true. We both wanted different things from the relationship. It wasn't fair to keep you hanging on for marriage when that wasn't what I wanted.

Some of the anger in Carl's eyes faded. "I told you I didn't need marriage, Lela."

"I know, but that's not true. You want a family. Forever. Please, Carl, don't do this here." She could feel too many people looking at them, watching the unfolding drama, waiting to see if the NFL superstar would knock out the bank manager. From the corner of her eye, she could see a couple people holding up cell phones, no doubt hoping for some juicy video to share on YouTube.

Carl swallowed heavily. "It's only been a week, Lela. Was I that easy to get over?"

Lela's shoulders fell. It was official. She was the biggest bitch on the face of the Earth. He hadn't been hard to get over at all because her heart had never been engaged. It never was. She'd tried to gently explain that when she'd broken things off, but it didn't appear he'd heard her.

"Of course not. The thing is," she lowered her voice and leaned closer, "I wasn't completely honest with you about Tucker. He and I dated in high school."

"You dated Tucker Riley?" She saw a light bulb go on. "All those Sundays we sat and watched the games together, you weren't watching because you liked football, were you?"

"I was watching Tucker."

That answer was going to reveal more than she cared to Tucker, to Carl, to Lorelie—who'd left the dance floor, clearly ready to step in to defend Lela if necessary.

The wind went out of Carl's sails, his chest deflating. "I see." And she could see that he did. Lela's throat clogged up and she found it difficult to breathe. She took no joy in hurting Carl, but that was exactly what she'd done.

Carl walked away without another word and the phones disappeared, the gossipmongers clearly disappointed.

"I need to leave," Lela said to Lorelie, pointedly ignoring Tucker. She couldn't face him right now. She was fighting back tears and she refused to shed them in public.

Lorelie nodded. "Okay."

"I'll drive you," Tucker said.

Lela started to shake her head, but Tucker stopped the motion, his fingers on her jaw, forcing her to look at him. "I'm driving you."

"More manhandling?" She was trying for levity, trying to escape the heaviness of the moment, but the quivering in her voice betrayed her sadness.

He nodded, and then took her hand. They walked to his car without speaking. She felt numb as he opened the passenger door for her. Lela sat slowly, her head falling back against the headrest.

Tucker didn't speak as he started the car. For several quiet moments, they sat in the parking lot. Lela sensed Tucker was fighting back some emotions of his own. She had seen his face after Carl's cruel words. He'd been ready to go to war.

Finally, he turned to face her. "I don't know where you live."

She smiled. "Take a right. I have a little house on Harper's Lake. You remember how to get there?"

"Yep." He put the car into gear and drove in silence. It was the third time she'd seen him since his return to Maris. It felt like a million years had passed since the last time they'd ridden in a car together like this—him taking her home after a date— and yet it seemed so natural to be here again.

They continued to drive in silence. Lela was grateful for the quiet. It gave her time to try to gather her thoughts. As they got closer to her house, she started giving him directions. "Take a left here on Hollins Drive. I'm the third house on the right."

Tucker pulled into her driveway, and then turned the car off. Her mind whirled as she tried to do the right thing. If only her damn hormones weren't telling her how much fun the wrong thing could be.

He opened his car door. "I'll walk you to your front door."

"Tucker. You're not coming inside with me."

He chuckled softly. "Come on, L.B. Just to the front door. I promise."

She opened her own door and met him at the hood of the car. He grasped her hand, holding it as they walked down the little path that led to her porch. She loved the warmth of his hand, the strength in his grip. While she recognized so many similarities between this man and the boy she'd loved so long ago, there was no denying he was also essentially a stranger. There were parts of this older Tucker that were unknown to her and she longed to explore them, get to know the man he'd become.

Lela tucked that idea away as she searched for her house key in her purse. Once she found it, she thanked Tucker for the ride. She tried to make her tone dismissive, hoping Tucker would make this easy, give her a bye tonight. She wasn't thinking clearly and she wasn't feeling particularly strong. It wouldn't take much effort on his part to get inside.

"Did you break up with Carl because of me?"

She was surprised by his question. She shook her head. "No. Not at all."

He didn't press her for more. Instead, he accepted her response easily.

Despite that, she felt compelled to add more. "I realize the timing looks suspicious."

"Not really. I just wanted to be sure."

"I'm not the same girl I used to be, Tuck. I don't conjure fantasies; expect to create happy endings out of thin air believing that love and determination are enough. I'm glad to see you again and I'm sure there's a day of reckoning some-where in our future where we'll have to talk about the way things ended last time. But don't worry about that kiss at the ranch. I have zero expectations about that or us. It was just a kiss."

His expression darkened slightly. "No. It wasn't."

"Tucker—"

"You're right, Lela. We're going to talk. We're going to sit down and hash out all that crap that went down twelve years ago. I appreciate you being honest with me, so I'll give you the same. I think it's fucking sad that you don't believe love is enough to get you what you want. And I know I'm the person who stole that from you. I'm sorry."

She shook her head, tried to interject. "That's not what I meant. I—"

Tucker took her face in his hands and bent forward, pressing his forehead against hers. She could feel the heat of his breath as he spoke.

"You were the last person on Earth I ever wanted to hurt. And I did it anyway. You deserve to be happy."

She released a long sigh and closed her eyes briefly. "Life doesn't give us what we deserve, Tucker. It doesn't work that way. We get what we get, and then we figure out how to live with it. That's what I've done. And I'm happy. Honest."

She lifted her face when he suddenly released her. She'd thought the words would lighten what had become a heavy moment. Instead, something sad flashed in his eyes—and realization struck her. Tucker's trip home wasn't as simple as he made it out to be. She should have known the second she saw him in Sparks Barbeque. It was so obvious to her now.

But why was he here? Because of her? His father?

"Why are you home, Tucker?"

That same pregnant pause, the one that told her he was about to lie, followed. "I told you. To help Coach out."

She wanted to press him, but Tucker didn't give her a chance. Instead, he took the key from her hand and unlocked her door. Then, he offered her a chaste kiss that was no less beautiful for its simplicity. She felt it all the way to her toes.

"I'll see you soon, L.B." He walked away and was almost to his car before she found her voice again.

"Good night." She waved. He gave her a crooked grin and a wave and then he was in the car and gone once more.

Funny how his goodbyes never got any easier.

Chapter Four

Tucker walked into Cruisers for the second time a couple days later. After running into Lela on Friday night, he'd gone back to the hotel and kicked himself for being twenty kinds of fool. He found it very difficult to keep his hands off her anytime they were together, but the last thing Lela Whitacre needed in her life was another hit and run from him.

He'd returned to Coach's ranch the next morning and worked his ass off, hoping to gain some freaking control of his damn hormones while still seeking some answers to his problems. Instead, all he had to show for a weekend of hard work were stiff muscles and sunburn on his shoulders. So much for Coach's advice. He hadn't figured out a damn thing.

Joel waved him over. The bar was much less crowded tonight than it had been on Friday. No band played, so an ancient jukebox tucked against one wall provided the music. No one danced on the makeshift dance floor. Tonight, the bar's main activities were quiet conversations over pitchers of beer and a few guys shooting pool on a table that had seen better days. There appeared to be a stack of cocktail napkins under one foot to level the thing.

He forced a smile as he joined Joel, Oakley and several other old teammates at a large table. Joel had decided they needed a proper reunion, instead of the rushed attempts to catch up as they took shifts doing all the backbreaking work required to keep the ranch running effectively.

Tucker had searched for a reason not to come, not ready to field a lot of questions about the upcoming training camp and season. But in the end, he decided to put on his game face and make an appearance because when it came down to it, he really wanted this time with his old friends. He'd missed these guys a lot over the years.

He grabbed a seat between Jack and Walt. Like him, they'd come to town to help out Coach. Several of the other guys at the table—like Joel and Caleb—had never left Maris.

Tucker pointed to the beer in front of them. "What's on tap?"

Jack held up his glass. "It's Maris, Tuck. What do you think is on tap?"

They laughed as they said "Bud" in unison. Tucker had stopped drinking when he noticed alcohol seemed to trigger his headaches, but tonight he wasn't going to say no. He was nervous about this reunion.

Sadie came over with a new pitcher and an icy-cold glass for Tucker. Sadie was only a couple years older than them and had been the object of every boyhood crush for the men at the table. She'd been homecoming queen her senior year and as a hormone-driven gang of unruly teen boys, they'd lusted after her with a desire that bordered on zealous fervor for most of their high school years. "This one's on the house. It's damn good to see y'all in Maris again. This town has been hurting for hot guys ever since you all left."

Oakley clutched his heart, feigning injury at her joke as Joel said, "Hey, take it easy there. A few of us at this table have been here all along."

Sadie laughed. "Oh, I'm perfectly aware of that."

Oakley leaned back in his chair. "You really know how to hurt the ones you love, Sadie."

"Is that what this feeling is?" she teased. "I thought it was indigestion."

Sadie's family had been running Cruisers for decades. Before Tucker could push the thought away, he recalled it was Sadie's dad, Nelson, who'd called Tucker's mom to pick up his dad the night she was killed. He certainly didn't blame Nelson for making that phone call. He knew exactly whose shoulders carried the weight of his mother's death. So far, Tucker had been fortunate not to run into his old man. However, he suspected that luck would run out the longer he stayed in Maris.

Walt threw Sadie a charming smile along with a word of thanks for the free beer. Walt had made quite a smash on the country music scene after leaving Maris, though it had been a few years since he'd had a hit. Tucker always got a kick out of hearing one of Walt's songs on the radio, never failing to point out to whoever he was with that he'd played high school ball with the singer.

It had become a running joke with his current teammates. Whenever one of Walt's songs came on, Tucker reminded them that he knew Walt. The guys would always feign annoyance, then one of them would launch into an impersonation of Tucker, retelling how Maris High School won the state championship when Tucker has passed a lateral to Caleb who'd run it into the end zone for the touchdown that tied the game. It was Walt, the kicker, who'd come out on the field in the final seconds of the fourth quarter and scored the winning point.

Jack filled up everyone's glasses and they lifted them, offering cheers to Sadie. Sadie returned to the bar after a quick wink at Joel and Oakley. Tucker wondered briefly about the obvious flirtation going on between the three of them.

Before he could ask Joel about it, Walt leaned over to speak to him. "You ready for this season? Everybody and their brother seem to think this is the year you take your team all the way to the Super Bowl."

Tucker had prepared himself for this. He gave Walt the answer he'd rehearsed on the way over, talking about a few of the other players on the team and agreeing that he thought they had the potential to make it to the big game this year. He truly did believe that. It was one of the things making his decision so difficult.

Walt and Caleb started arguing about who the greatest running back in the NFL was. Tucker grinned, then let them continue to fight it out without him.

"What about you?" Tucker said to Jack, relieved that he'd managed to dodge any real questions about his appearance in Maris. "I understand you've only been back a few days and you're already ruffling some feathers around here."

Jack sighed and shrugged. "What else is new?"

Jack had run into some trouble during their senior year. Enough that it had gotten him kicked off the team, but from what Tucker had seen the past few days, Jack had really turned himself around, started doing some good stuff.

"What's this football camp thing about?" Tucker asked.

"You've heard about my camp in Omaha?"

"Everybody has. Coach is all about the one you're planning to start here," Joel said.

"It's awesome. But it's not football," Jack said. "It's actually a ranch. *My* ranch. I take at-risk kids and bring them to the ranch to give them a safe place where they can work to earn their keep, learn about being part of a team, and make something with their own two hands."

"No shit?" Oakley asked. "You've got punk city kids working as ranch hands?"

Jack quickly explained about the ranch and the program he'd put together.

Tucker was impressed by Jack's plans. "If you need anything, let me know," Tucker said. "I'd be happy to get involved. Come by and see the kids. Maybe donate money or something?"

Jack's eyebrows rose. "Seriously?"

"Sure. You're one of my teammates, man."

Jack was clearly surprised by the offer. "That would be great. I really appreciate that. The kids would love it. I was thinking of seeing if Coach would want to come over and help out some too. I could keep an eye on him so he didn't overdo it, but I know he misses coaching and, honestly, a lot of this is just *like* coaching. Seeing where the kids are going wrong, correcting them, giving them objectives and helping them dig deep to meet them."

When Caleb and Walt finally ran out of steam on their running back argument, Walt leaned closer. "What are you all talking about? That camp thing of Jack's?"

Jack shook his head. "How the hell does everyone know about this?"

Joel grinned. "It's Maris. News is rare so when it hits, it spreads like wildfire. I heard about it from Macie at Sparks Barbeque. I swear to God there is nothing that happens in this town that woman doesn't know about. She'd more informational than the daily newspaper."

Tucker chuckled. "I think inviting Coach is a great idea." Then he began comparing his current NFL coach to Coach Carr, and the conversation took off as the guys all reminisced about their favorite Coach stories. They polished off three more pitchers as they laughed, joked, and teased as if twelve years had never passed.

For the first time in ages, Tucker felt more like his old self than he had since that nasty tackle in January that had thrown his life into a tailspin.

He wondered why he'd avoided Maris for so long. In a world filled with groupies who sucked up to him, he found himself constantly questioning the motives of the people around him. He was used to women who were drawn to him because of his money and profession. The same was true of the men he'd met. Rich investors, CEOs, men with more money and power than sense. Men who thought it was cool to invite him to their parties, so they could brag about being friends with someone famous.

By comparison, these guys were genuinely happy to see him. They shared a past. With them, he was just plain old Tucker Riley, the guy they voted most athletic and who'd burned his initials into the practice field with a blowtorch he'd lifted from shop class on a dare. He'd paid for that prank dearly. Coach Carr had shaken his head and explained why it was damn stupid to put your own initials in graffiti. As his punishment, Tucker had to buy and plant the grass seed to cover the singed earth, watering it as well as mowing and chalking the lines on that particular field for the rest of the school year.

Suddenly Jack was up out of his chair, tossing money onto the table. "Hey guys, I gotta get going. Promised to work the early shift at the ranch and Lorelie will kick my ass if I'm not there before the sun rises."

They agreed Lorelie was running the ship as tightly as Coach would have, and they all said goodbye to Jack.

Joel returned from the bar with yet another pitcher as a few of the guys got up to play a game of pool. Joel claimed the seat Jack vacated.

"What's up with you and Lela? History repeating itself?"

Tucker shook his head. God. He hoped not. The ending to that history wasn't one he wanted to revisit, but he wasn't sure it could be avoided if he let things continue to heat up.

Unfortunately, it was only his head that understood. The rest of him was all for throwing caution to the wind and getting Lela back in bed. "Nothing's going on. I'm not in Maris to stay. She knows that. We're just catching up, getting reacquainted. Sort of like you and me and the guys are doing tonight."

It wasn't exactly the truth, but Tucker hadn't come clean with anyone but Coach about his reasons for returning home. He was getting pretty good at telling lies, though he hated doing it. Tucker wasn't sure why he hadn't told his friends about his injury or the decision he was facing. Maybe he was afraid they'd look at him with pity. Or perhaps he was simply tired of hearing everyone's two-cents' worth.

With the exception of Coach, every person he'd talked to about whether or not he should return had expressed strong feelings one way or the other. Tucker hadn't understood why all that unwanted advice had rubbed him the wrong way until Coach explained why he wouldn't tell him what to do. None of those people truly understood what Tucker was going through. They didn't know what made him tick any more than he knew what made *them* tick. So how could they say do this or do that with such assurance that it was the right thing?

Caleb leaned closer. "Hey, Tuck. Heads-up."

Tucker looked at his friend curiously, then caught sight of what Walt had seen. His father was walking over to their table. From the stagger in his step, Tucker could tell his dad was three sheets to the wind.

He'd known this day was coming. He'd tried to mentally

prepare himself for it. But now that it was here, he was overwhelmed by the desire to walk away. He had nothing to say to his dad. At least, nothing that wouldn't end in an argument or bloodshed.

Tucker sucked in a deep breath, grateful that most of the guys had wandered to the back of the room to watch the pool game and place bets on the outcome. The only men remaining at the table with him were Caleb and Joel.

All the guys on the team knew about his dad's problems with drinking. The asshole had been escorted out of no less than three games during their senior year for drunken belligerence, picking fights with anyone and everyone, before he was finally issued a No Trespass warrant and prohibited from stepping foot on school property. Tucker had started to breathe easier—and play better—with the knowledge his dad couldn't come to his games anymore.

The guys had always commiserated with him, been sympathetic without making Tucker feel pathetic. They'd looked to him as their leader—on and off the gridiron—and that didn't change just because his dad was a drunken shithead.

It was these guys who'd come to his mother's funeral and stood up for her—and Tucker—as pallbearers. He'd never forget the way they'd rallied around him the week of her death. He owed them all for that support.

Neither Joel nor Caleb stood to leave and if Tucker hadn't been so anxious about this unwanted reunion, he'd have grinned at the way they were flanking him in true we-got-your-back fashion.

"Tucker." His dad's voice was surprisingly clear, despite the glassy-eyed expression that revealed just how deep in the drink he was. "Heard you were back in town."

Tucker didn't move. "Looks like you heard right."

"You couldn't pick up a phone and call?"

Tucker frowned. "Why would you expect me to do that?"

The years hadn't been kind to his dad. Or, Tucker thought, the alcohol hadn't been. What hair remained on his dad's head was gray, thin, scruffy. He'd lost that large, imposing stature that had intimidated Tucker so much when he was younger. He seemed to have shrunk a few inches. His dad now had a large beer belly, saggy jowls, and dark circles under his eyes.

"Thought you might have outgrown some of your damned selfishness. That you might wanna see how your old man was doing."

The words would have tweaked Tucker's temper more if they hadn't been so slurred. His father was a complete asshole when he was wasted. Tucker was sure a meaner drunk had never walked the planet. He also knew his father enjoyed goading him, or whoever was in shouting distance when he was drunk, hoping to instigate a fight. Tucker wasn't willing to give his dad the satisfaction.

"You look like you're doing the same as always."

His father narrowed his eyes. "Still a smart-mouthed little prick, aren't you?"

Tucker considered standing up to prove to his father exactly how little he wasn't, but Dad would see that as an invitation to brawl. Tucker wasn't going there. Coach's words from a few days earlier still rang in his ear. Courage wasn't marked by who threw the hardest punch.

Tucker picked up his beer and took a sip, pleased by the steadiness of his hand. Years in the NFL had honed his nerves, taught him how to control his emotions under pressure. "Are we finished with this reunion?"

His father didn't acknowledge his question. Clearly he *wasn't* finished. "You know I almost lost the house."

Tucker shrugged. "So?"

Dad's eyes narrowed, radiating the same malice Tucker had

faced so many times when he was younger. "You saying you don't give a shit that the bank almost foreclosed on the home you grew up in? All that money you make in the NFL and you couldn't see fit to send me some after everything I've given you?"

That comment struck a nerve. Tucker laughed, though the sound wasn't one of pleasure. "I'm supposed to pay you for the black eyes? The bruises? The bloody lips? Because that's all I ever remember you giving me."

His father stumbled slightly and for a moment, Tucker thought he might fall over. He'd seen his dad drunk more than sober, but it was apparent so many years of abusing alcohol had taken its toll.

Once his father recovered, he lifted his hand and pointed a finger at Tucker. "You could'a sent me some money, could'a made sure your old man didn't get kicked out on his ass. But you always thought you were too fucking good for the family. A big shot, looking down on us."

Neither Caleb nor Joel had spoken during the entire scene, but Tucker felt the tension in the way they held themselves. They really were ready to defend him if Tucker needed it. Knowing his friends had his back helped. He wasn't sure he could have remained as calm as he was without their presence.

"Well, it sounds like you didn't lose it. Which means you either got a job or, more likely, you moved a girlfriend in and you're making her pay all the bills."

His father lurched forward, catching himself on the table. Sadie suddenly appeared next to them. "Mr. Riley. I told you, you can't come in here drunk and expect me to serve you. You need to get on home. Want me to call Wanda?"

A sharp pain pierced Tucker's chest, realizing Nelson had probably asked that same question all those years ago. And his father's reply had gotten his mother out of bed and across town, had led to her death.

"Call a taxi," Tucker said.

His father turned, scowling. "I don't have money for that."

Tucker reached into his wallet and pulled out a twenty. "This will get you home."

For a moment, his father looked at the cash as if it were a snake waiting to bite him. Then, slowly, he reached across the table and took it.

Sadie nodded approvingly. "I'll make that call."

His father didn't move away from the table.

The last time they'd spoken, his dad had admitted to slapping Tucker's mom as she drove him home from the bar that night. Then he'd had the nerve to say his mother had it coming. That she'd been nagging him. Tucker's vision had gone black and the next thing he knew, he'd thrown a powerful right that had knocked his dad out cold, leaving him bleeding on the kitchen floor.

Tucker had left him there, grabbed his duffel bag and car keys with the intention of getting out of Maris. He'd just closed the trunk when Lela had appeared. Tucker had forgotten about their plans to go out for one last lunch before he left. He'd handled the goodbye badly, but all he could think about was getting the fuck out of there before his dad came to. Tucker wasn't sure he'd have stopped with one punch if his father had come out of the house and the fight had continued. He could have murdered his dad that day and it had scared the shit out of him to realize he had the strength and the desire to do so.

Somehow his anger toward his father during those immediate weeks after his departure had made its way to Lela too. She hadn't done anything wrong, but Tucker had walked around for nearly a month after that scene outside his house, his vision covered in a haze of blinding, red-hot hatred—of everyone and everything.

His college coach had recognized the anger and known about his mother's death. He'd suggested Tucker talk to a counselor. It had taken several more months before he'd been able to drag himself away from the black rage that followed him. By then, too much time had passed and he hadn't known how to contact Lela, to explain, to apologize. Silence, though a coward's way out, had been much easier. The distance between them had helped as well.

His father muttered, "Don't know why the fuck you bothered to come back at all."

"I'm here to help Coach."

His dad all but snarled. "Oh, that's right. You run home to take care of the sainted Coach Carr, but God forbid you lift a phone to check on your father."

Tucker struggled to remain calm. "I thought I made it clear the last time we talked that you're no father to me."

"I see. Well, then I guess that makes us even. Because you've never been much of a son either."

His dad stumbled away from them. Tucker followed his movements, relieved when the old man left the bar.

Neither Joel nor Caleb spoke. Instead they let Tucker have some time to come to grips with what had just happened.

Sadie came over to the table. "I'm sorry, Tucker. I told him he couldn't come in and I thought he went away. He must have snuck in when I went back to the storeroom for some more napkins."

"It's okay." He needed to get out of here. Get away from all the shit that had just crashed down on his head. Tucker wanted to find some peace. "Sadie. Do you mind calling for another cab?" Tucker asked at last.

Sadie shook her head. "No, but the hotel is only a few blocks away. You could walk."

"I'm not going to the hotel. I'm going to Lela's."

Sadie smiled. "I'm on it."

As she walked away, Joel took a sip of his beer. "Just getting reacquainted, huh?"

Tucker grimaced. "Bite me, Joel."

His friend chuckled, and then slapped him on the back. "It's good to have you back in town, man."

Tucker said his goodbyes, then left the bar, relieved to see his father was already gone. He stood out in front of the building and tried to talk himself out of what he was about to do.

However, no amount of reason or common sense would convince him to alter his course. When the cab arrived, he climbed in the back and gave the driver Lela's address.

He was being selfish. He knew it. But it didn't matter. He needed something only Lela could provide. He'd been cold and alone and miserable for too fucking long.

He needed her. Wanted her.

This trip had been a mistake. He couldn't see any way it wouldn't end in heartbreak for both of them again. And yet he didn't tell the guy to turn the taxi around. Instead he closed his eyes and sent up a silent prayer.

Please be there, Lela.

Chapter Five

Lela was curled up on her couch in her pajamas by six. She'd seriously considered giving up on the day and heading straight to bed, but the last thing she wanted was to be wide awake at four a.m.

Why was it things that bothered you always felt a gazillion times worse in the middle of the night?

Seemed like all she could do lately was think about Tucker. About that set-the-house-on-fire kiss and the past and that little voice in the back of her head that said he was hiding something from her. And worst of all, that broken boy who'd left her didn't appear to be any more put together as a man. He was hurting about something. She wished he'd confide in her like he had when they were younger, but what right did she have to expect that? It had been twelve years, for God's sake. They were different people.

Except...they weren't.

Her feelings for Tucker hadn't changed one iota since the day he'd left Maris. She'd always tried to dismiss them, blaming her inability to get over him on those rose-colored glasses that tinged first love. But seeing Tucker again made her realize those feelings she'd dismissed as a teenage girl's crush had never been that at all.

She may have been young, but her love for Tucker had apparently been the real deal. And that realization had her reeling as she examined, then reexamined every romantic relationship she'd had since then. She had always found a reason to push away the men she was dating, be it chronic tardiness or no sense of humor or—as in Carl's case—a bad state of boringness. However, now she was starting to think the only reason she'd had for dumping the guys was the fact that they hadn't been Tucker.

Which made her way more pathetic than she wanted to admit.

Her phone beeped with an incoming message. She glanced at the screen.

"Want to come over for margaritas? Annie's with me. I'm inviting the other girls too."

The text from her friend Paige made Lela smile. Paige made great margaritas. Lela was tempted for two heartbeats, then realized she wasn't fit company for anyone.

"I'm in pjs," she texted back. "The bra is off." That was pretty much code that one of them was in for the night.

"So come without it. It's just us girls," Paige returned.

Lela laughed. Paige was the most conservative of their group. Not that it took much to be more conservative than Lorelie and Macie who were wild as the wind. Lela lumped herself in with the other girls, Lacy and Annie, who were more middle of the road—somewhere between crazy and conventional.

"Rain check." Then Lela considered Paige's sudden reason for alcohol. "Jack driving you crazy?"

"I'm so stupid," came Paige's reply.

Lela frowned. "How so?"

"I really like him."

Oh boy. Jack was a hell raiser. *So* not Paige's type. But Lela understood. Didn't all women go through a bad-boy phase? Paige's was just happening later in life. She'd get over it. Probably.

Then she considered her own inability to get over Tucker. Man...they were both screwed.

"It's the temptation for hot sex," Lela responded. Paige had shared that she and Jack had gone parking—that was exactly what she'd called it too—a few nights ago, and that he was an *amazing* kisser. "Keeps you stepping closer to the fire."

"Would burning up be a bad thing?"

"Not if Jack does it right," Lela replied.

Damn. This was exactly why Lela wasn't going for drinks. She was too screwed up to offer anyone advice tonight. Who knew what she'd suggest if she got tipsy on too much tequila?

"Yeah, I know. Hence the margaritas instead of more Jack." It was hard to read tone in texts, but Paige's reply was easy. Disappointment.

"I'll text you tomorrow," Lela promised.

She and Paige texted their goodbyes and Lela flipped on the TV. She found a Meg Ryan marathon, *You've Got Mail* and *Sleepless in Seattle*, on one of the movie channels and let herself escape into the romantic comedies. For five whole hours, she managed to put away thoughts of Tucker, grateful for the blissful nothingness provided by the lighthearted movies.

Lela had just turned off the lights and was about to head upstairs to her bedroom when she saw headlights turn into her driveway. A quick glance at the clock told her it was nearly eleven.

"Who on Earth?" she muttered, though a small part of her suspected who her visitor was. She walked to the front door and peeked out the window. Tucker was climbing out of a cab, paying the driver for the ride.

She unlocked the door and had it open before he hit the top step of her porch. She started to ask him what the heck he thought he was doing, visiting so late, but the question died on her lips when she saw his face.

She didn't say anything as he approached her. Tucker didn't stop moving. Instead, he placed his hands on her waist and propelled her backwards into her house. He kicked the front door closed with his foot a split second before his lips descended on hers.

Lela fell into the kiss. Not that she was given a choice. Tucker's grip was resolute, firm, unyielding. He didn't have to try that hard. She wasn't about to push him away.

She opened her mouth to his, their tongues meeting. One of his hands slipped beneath her shirt to touch the sensitive skin at her waist as his other cupped the back of her neck. After years of lackluster dates and lukewarm kisses, Lela wanted to kick her own ass for settling for anything less than this. This moment. This perfect kiss.

Several minutes later, Tucker pulled away—just an inch or so—and looked at her. She couldn't quite figure out the look in his eyes. The usual bright-blue orbs were suddenly dark with so many emotions, they took her breath away.

"I need you."

Three simple words, but the pure agony behind them was more than Lela could stand.

She took a step away from him. "Lock the door."

Tucker held her gaze for only a second, and then he turned, throwing the deadbolt on her front door. She held out her hand and led him upstairs to her bedroom.

Ever since his return, they'd promised to talk, to try to sort out the past. But now, Lela could see, at this moment, it didn't matter. It would still be there tomorrow. All that she cared about right now was what happened next.

She hadn't taken two steps into her bedroom, hadn't had time to reach for the light switch, before Tucker released her hand and took charge. He pushed her gently against a wall, his hands on the waistband of her sleep shorts. He followed them down, his face level with her pussy as the cotton of her pajama bottoms and panties hit the floor. His hot breath added even more heat to the fire raging. Her inner muscles clenched as her heart raced.

Tucker lifted one leg until her knee rested on his shoulder. She was completely open to him and he took full advantage. His tongue stroked her, starting at her opening and continuing forward until it landed on her clit. He pressed against the sensitive nub, a cry falling from her lips. Lightning raced along her spine as he continued to lick her. Then he upped the ante.

With his fingers, he held her pussy open and pushed his tongue inside her.

Her hands had been clenched into fists, pressed against the wall. When he began to thrust his tongue into her, she needed more purchase, something firmer to hold on to. Her head flew back as she gripped him, her fingers tangling in his hair. She was vaguely aware that she was tugging it too hard. Tucker grunted once, the sound producing the most delicious vibrations against her aching flesh, but he didn't shake off her grasp, didn't ask her to let go.

She wasn't sure she'd ever be able to release him. With just his tongue, he was driving her to the edge of sheer insanity, a white-hot blissful paradise where she would gladly buy property, build a house, and live forever.

Tucker used his thumbs to tease and pinch her clit as his tongue continued to glide in and out, in and out.

Beads of sweat gathered at her brow and Lela wondered if she'd suddenly come down with a fever. Her body was on fire, almost aching with the unquenchable need.

The lone leg supporting her weight began to tremble when Tucker ran one finger through the juices dripping from her pussy, then moved it farther back to press it into her ass.

She'd never been touched there. Never considered it something she wanted. Now...

Lela exploded, Tucker's tongue in her pussy, his thumb on her clit, his finger in her ass, pushing her into an idyllic, soul-shattering state of ecstasy. She cried loudly as her body shook violently. Tucker didn't grant her reprieve. He kept moving, stroking, touching until every last drop of pleasure fell.

When he finally moved away, he was there to catch her as she dropped to her knees next to him. He engulfed her in his strong arms and kissed her once more. She was overwrought and out of control. It didn't matter. She wanted more.

As her wits slowly began to return, she felt the overwhelming need to give something to Tucker. Anything. Everything.

She tugged her t-shirt over her head. She reveled in the hungry, appreciative look in his eyes. She'd never felt particularly beautiful, well aware that in a world full of gorgeous women, she was fairly securely ensconced in the just-average column. Her eyes were a dull brown that matched her equally boring brunette hair. She wasn't slim or overly endowed. She'd left the single-digit-sized clothing realm long ago.

None of that seemed to matter to Tucker. His gaze as it traveled along her body was nothing less than adoring. God, she'd missed this feeling of being special to someone. Tucker had always made her feel loved, as if she were vital to his happiness, to his life.

She'd let the terrible ending overshadow that memory. Now that he was here and looking at her as if she was the most beautiful woman he'd ever seen, all the reasons why she'd fallen in love with him years ago came back to her in a rush.

"Your turn." She pointed to his shirt. He didn't hesitate to comply. Lela couldn't resist running her hand along his incredible abs. It was as if he was built of steel. He sucked in a deep breath and held it when her hands drifted lower. She worked the button on his khaki shorts free, then tugged down the zipper.

His cock was straining against the material of his boxer briefs. Peeling back the elastic, she reached in, encapsulating the firm flesh and freeing it.

The air he'd held in his lungs came out in a loud whoosh when she added some pressure to her grip, then started to stroke him.

"God, Lela. When you touch me..." His words drifted away as his eyes closed. She increased her speed, and then dipped her free hand into his boxers to find his balls.

Tucker's hands found her upper arms even though he hadn't opened his eyes. He stroked along her arms to her neck, then he gave her tit for tat when his hands found her hair. His lids lifted and he captured her gaze, studied her face as he drew his hands through her long tresses, and then closed his fists around the strands. Her scalp pricked with the slightest tingle of pain as he pulled her hair tighter.

Her body responded instantly to the rough touch. This Tucker was so different from the boy she'd loved. There was something dangerously sexy lurking inside him, that made her want to throw caution to the wind, to relinquish total control to him. Which felt admittedly odd. She was typically the aggressor in bed.

"I want you too much to be gentle," he murmured.

She understood the sentiment. Shared it. She squeezed his balls in response, increasing the pressure until she saw the slightest trace of a wince.

Something in Tucker's expression eased. The emotions that had whirled behind his eyes when he'd first arrived seemed to fade a bit, his focus less on whatever had driven him to her bed, moving completely to her.

She wasn't sure what had sent him to her, but she was glad he'd come.

Tucker didn't release her hair, using it to direct her movements, to encourage her to rise. She found her feet the same time he did. Then he tugged her forward and kissed her again. It wasn't until that moment that she realized the restraint Tucker had been showing. Whatever had been holding him back had been freed.

She felt the same bonds falling away as well. She tightened her hold on his cock, moving her hand faster, harder. She couldn't tell from his grunts if she was hurting him or if he welcomed the rough touch. He didn't ask her to stop, so she doubled her efforts, gave him even more.

When she sensed he was close, she dropped back down to her knees, sucking his cock into her mouth.

"Ahh!" Tucker's hands pulled her hair harder as he used his grip to direct her mouth. She let him determine the pace, even as she struggled to keep up. His cock brushed the back of her throat. She gagged briefly until Tucker withdrew.

"I can't stop." He backed up that admission with another thrust, his dick going even deeper.

This time she opened her throat, ready for him. His hands shook, but he didn't release her hair. Instead, he continued to use them to drive her mouth on him harder, more rapidly. The pace was frantic, but neither of them sought to subdue it.

Lela drew his shorts down to his ankles, her mouth never leaving him as he lifted his feet and kicked them—and his shoes —off. She reached around him and grasped his tight ass, using her hands to take the tempo up another notch.

Tucker's hips pounded forward and back, Lela's mouth engulfing him over and over. She listened as his breathing grew harsher, his groans louder, as he gave up any attempt at remaining quiet or stoic. She could tell from his responses what he liked, so she put her newfound knowledge to use, stroking her tongue against the underside of the head of his cock, teasing him with her teeth at the tip, rolling his balls in the palm of her hand.

He was close to coming, so she decided to give him a taste of his own medicine. She released his balls and drew her fingers along the crack of his ass. Then she pushed inward, the tip of her finger finding the tight rim of his anus. She'd only managed to work the digit in to the second knuckle when he exploded. Come filled her mouth and she swallowed.

Tucker's hands slackened, leaving her hair to cup her face almost reverently. She didn't seek to move even as his cock softened in her mouth. Then Tucker pushed away.

Reaching down, he helped her to her feet and guided her to the bed. He pulled down the sheets and together they climbed between the cool cotton. Tucker wrapped his arm around her shoulders as she rested her head on his chest. They lay in silence for several minutes, neither of them seeking to break the magic or the solitude of the moment.

Lela was the first to move. She'd sensed Tucker getting ready to speak. She didn't want to fill tonight with talk. She had turned a corner and she was determined to keep the past in the past. Pushing up on her elbow, she raised herself enough that she could silence him with a kiss.

Tucker returned it willingly. Hours could have passed for all she knew as they simply lay there, getting reacquainted without words, only touch. She ran her fingers over his face, enjoying the prickly feel of his five o'clock shadow. His face had matured with the passage of time, a deep tan—indicative of how much time he spent outdoors—covered his face, enhanced the lines that had formed by his eyes and mouth. They had softened during the course of the evening, but they were still there, betraying that something was bothering him.

As she stroked his face, Tucker used the time to caress her shoulders and back. Though he'd said he couldn't give her gentle, there was no other word to describe the relaxing sensations his soft touch provoked.

Once Lela had finished exploring the new contours of his face, she dragged her fingertips along the line of his neck, then briefly played with the small patch of hair around each of his nipples. She couldn't resist the impulse to bend down to lick the tight nibs.

Tucker sighed as she did so. "I love your mouth on me."

After so much time in silence, his quiet confession caused her to jerk slightly.

He chuckled at her response. "Yep. I'm still here."

He meant his words as a joke, but they didn't feel funny to her. Instead, they filled a part of her that had been empty for too damn long. "I'm glad you are."

Her seriousness caught him unaware and his face sobered. "I don't know how I stayed away from you all these years."

Tears pricked the corners of her eyes, but she worked hard not to let them fall. Hearing that she hadn't been alone in missing him soothed parts of her that had never stopped aching. She'd chastised herself for being a fool, holding on to the memory of him for so long while she tried to convince herself that what she felt was nothing more than first love. Lela had actually wondered sometimes if she was somehow broken, stuck in the past, clinging to something that couldn't be.

She'd never truly committed to another man since Tucker. She could admit that to herself now. Breaking things off with Carl—and the few other men she'd dated over the past twelve years—hadn't been hard because she'd never given them her heart. That part of her had belonged to Tucker since she was fifteen years old and she'd never attempted to reclaim it.

"I didn't imagine this, did I? This thing between us?"

He shook his head. "No, L.B., you didn't imagine it. It's always been there. It always will be."

She smiled, her heart feeling a thousand pounds lighter. "I've missed you, Tuck."

He gave her that same crooked grin, then rolled toward her. She fell to her back as he came over her. "You remember our first time?"

She laughed. "Of course I do. You were a nervous wreck. I'm surprised we managed to do it at all."

He pressed his erect cock against her. "I didn't want to hurt you."

She lifted her hips, capturing his hard length in the slit between her legs. They both gasped. "You don't seem to be suffering from that same fear tonight."

He shrugged. "I guess I've just gotten better at hiding it." He kissed her shoulder, then buried his face in her neck. His voice was deeper when he began recalling that first night so long ago. "We were so young, L.B."

"Very young. Sixteen." They'd gone out for nearly a year before they gave in to the need to have sex. It hadn't been that hard to abstain as Lela's parents had been extremely overprotective, keeping a close eye on her. Since neither of them could drive at the beginning, they were never alone in private places. That all changed when Lela got her driver's license. Her parents had finally consented to the two of them going out on car dates. Even then, they'd continued to go to the movies or hang out at the bowling alley or roller rink with friends.

Tucker nipped her earlobe playfully. "The things we did in the backseat of that crappy old Buick of mine."

"We drove each other crazy for months, going a little bit further every time."

"Until New Year's Eve."

She smiled. He remembered that night as well as she did. Her parents had gone out to a party. Lela and Tucker had planned to go out with friends as well, but changed their minds at the last minute.

"We're lucky your folks didn't come home early and catch us. I'm pretty sure your dad would have kicked my ass, then expelled me from school."

Lela's father was the principal of Maris High School. She could only imagine how difficult it had been for Tucker, dating the principal's daughter, always trying to walk the straight and narrow in school. He'd had a bit of the devil in him in elementary and middle school, but he'd managed to control his mischievous nature when they started dating, always worrying about whether or not her parents liked him. It had been important to Tucker that they thought he was, as he used to say, "good enough for her". Sometimes she'd wondered if his perfect behavior was driven by his desire to prove he was nothing like his dad.

"But they didn't come home. And that night...it was perfect, Tucker." She'd lit a few candles in her bedroom, put on a pretty nightgown that was far from sexy. That fact didn't seem to matter to Tucker.

He lifted his head and kissed her slowly. "We took off our clothes, lay down on the bed and kissed for ages."

They still seemed to enjoy the taste of each other's lips. "You fumbled with the condom."

Tucker chuckled, and then surprised her by leaving the bed. She watched his progress across the room as he retrieved his wallet from the back pocket of his shorts and pulled out a condom. "These suckers aren't as easy to put on as you think."

As he spoke, he opened the wrapper and slipped the rubber over his cock with efficient skill.

"Looks like you've been practicing."

He crawled back onto the bed, covering her once more. She parted her legs in invitation. He placed the head of his cock at her opening. "I can still remember how good it felt to slide inside you. You were so hot and wet and tight." As he spoke, he pressed into her pussy.

Lela's chest constricted as the past and present melded, memories of her first time blending so perfectly with the here and now.

"Just like now," he whispered as he pushed in, not stopping until he reached the hilt, filling her completely. "I was so sure I was hurting you."

They both froze, then Lela shuddered. "So good," she gasped.

Tucker remained silent.

"You know, not all hurts are necessarily bad." She ran her nails across the top of his back, letting him feel the burn of the scratch.

His chest expanded then compressed several times. That damn restraint was back. She could feel it in his tense posture.

"I'm not that inexperienced girl anymore, Tucker. I know what I want, what I need from you."

He caught her gaze, forced her to hold it. "And what's that?"

"No holds barred." She wrapped her legs around his waist and tilted her hips, the motion driving him even deeper.

"Careful, L.B. That opens the door to options you may not be prepared for."

Her pussy clenched at the dark, almost threatening tone of his voice. If it was possible, Tucker's entire body went even harder. He wanted to move. She could feel it. It was taking a lot of strength and control for him to stay still.

She knew exactly what he was alluding to, what he was trying to warn her about. She didn't need his protection. She was a big girl. "Should we pick a safe word?"

His brows furrowed. "Lela."

The shock in his tone caused her to laugh. "You know, you don't have to leave Maris and move to the big city to learn a few things about bondage and submission."

"Have you—"

She shook her head quickly. "No. But I wouldn't mind exploring. With someone I trust."

"You're sure?"

The hunger on Tucker's face proved he wanted the same, yet even in that need, he sought to shelter her. Her heart almost ached, it was so filled with love for this man.

"So sure."

"Then it's yours."

All conversation ended as Tucker gave them both what they desired. He lifted his hips, then slammed home with a strength that drove the air from her lungs.

She'd spent a lifetime waiting for this kind of passion. It was time to reveal some of her own. She dug her nails into the muscles of his back, enjoying the wince and hiss that accompanied her brutal touch.

Tucker's gaze narrowed when she gave him a challenging smile. "Stop holding back," she taunted. With that, she lifted her head and bit one of his pecs.

He jerked, but his face showed no pain. Only pleasure and something more. "Behave, L.B. You're topping from the bottom."

She laughed. "I never said I'd be the bottom."

He captured her head, holding it firmly, as his gaze found her. "You're mine. Now hold on."

His hips thrust against hers, his cock burrowing deeper on each pass. The bed was rocking loudly and she wondered briefly if her bedsprings were up to the task.

That thought was wiped away in an instant when Tucker gripped one of her breasts in his large palm and roughly sucked on her nipple. Sparks of pain and rapture traveled along her spine, her pussy clenching.

Tucker growled—God, an actual growl—and repeated the same brutally wonderful suction on her other breast. Her back arched, then she pushed on his shoulder, catching him off-guard. He tumbled onto his back as she came over him, careful to keep his cock inside her.

He reached up to cup her breasts as she straddled his hips, driving the speed, the depth of their fucking. She was surprised he'd so easily relinquished the reins to her. Tucker had always had to be in control. Over the years, whenever she recalled their relationship, she'd played armchair psychiatrist, attributing his need to be in charge—on the football field and in the bedroom—to the fact he'd grown up in a house where he'd been powerless.

Even though she hadn't seen him since high school, she'd watched him on the professional field week after week and she'd recognized that same commanding presence. It hadn't faded.

The fact that he let her take over touched her, told her the trust between them flowed both ways.

"God," she said, her body freezing briefly when she'd taken him in at a slightly different angle. His cock rubbed against her G-spot and she trembled, the pleasure too much.

His eyes narrowed. Then his hand drifted to her waist. He lifted her body easily, driving her back down roughly, making certain to hit that exact same place. She planted her hands on his chest, trying to regain the upper hand, but she couldn't boost herself up again. Sheer pleasure stole her ability to move. She was so close to coming.

Tucker lifted her once more despite her attempts to remain still, to compose herself, calm down, buy herself more time. He found the spot again.

"Please." She leaned forward, her forehead resting against his chest as she struggled for breath. "Can't take any more. Just give me a second."

"No." Tucker raised her off him despite her protestations. She was no match for his sheer brute strength. She'd never met anyone so damn strong.

Within seconds, he had her facedown on the mattress as he knelt behind her. She startled when he swatted her ass. "Lift your hips. It's my turn."

She responded to his command without hesitation. He'd only just left her, but her body was rebelling against the unwanted emptiness.

Drawing her knees up, she started to raise her head as well. Tucker kept a firm hold on her shoulders, pressing her tighter to the mattress. "Just your ass. I'm going to show you exactly who you've invited to your bed."

She rested her head on the pillow, equal parts excited and terrified, Tucker's sexy threat ringing in her ears. Sex was so much more intense this way.

Before she had too long to consider that fact, Tucker placed another stinging smack against her ass, then his cock was back inside, pounding against her sensitive flesh. She came on the third thrust. She cried out loudly, but Tucker paid her no heed. On and on, he moved inside her. The second orgasm came right on the heels of the first. Or maybe this was still the first and she was setting the world's record for longest climax in history.

It didn't matter because Tucker wasn't anywhere near finished. If it weren't for his firm grip on her hips, holding her up, she would have collapsed on the bed. Instead, he continued his beautiful, hard, delicious thrusting. And she didn't have the ability or the will to call for a halt.

Slowly she began to recover enough from her orgasms to start to participate once more. She pushed her hips against Tucker's, her own motions increasing the stimulation.

When Tucker realized she had revived, he changed the game once more. Her pussy clenched around his cock as he withdrew, the action causing both of them to groan.

"Come here." Tucker had perched on the edge of the bed. Reaching for her hand, he drew her closer until she sat facing him on his lap, her knees resting on the mattress beside his ass.

They both sighed as she slowly slid onto his cock once more.

This time, Tucker set an easier pace, the two of them kissing, their bodies connecting in a wavelike rhythm that was no less potent than their previous fast and furious tempo.

Tucker left no part of her untouched as the brutality of their earlier fucking turned to the sweetest lovemaking she'd ever experienced. His hands caressed her back and sides, then gently pushed her tangled hair away from her face. He cupped her cheek, whispered the word "beautiful," then proved to her just how much he meant it.

Lela's hands rested on his shoulders as she reveled in his

touches, kind words, and gentle care. She'd been lonely for so long. Having him back was the answer to a prayer she'd never let herself pray. Her throat closed on unshed tears—of happiness, of relief, of fear.

Tucker tilted his head and she worried she'd given herself away when he frowned. "Don't be afraid." His words traveled to her on a whisper, but they did little to soothe her anxiety. She'd lost him before and the pain had been unbearable. She didn't want to go through that again.

He pressed his lips to hers. "Lela. I'll always love you."

At that, he lifted her, laid her on her back and rocked into her. Within seconds they hit the wall together, coming at the same time. Then Tucker placed his chest to her back as he spooned her. He kissed the nape of her neck and she listened as his breathing slowed, sleep taking him.

It was only then that Lela let reality slip back in. She'd let her hormones convince her that simply having him here was enough. And as long as Tucker was kissing her, holding her, she'd believed it.

What the hell was she supposed to do now? Nothing had changed between them. As far as she knew, Tucker didn't intend to remain in Maris any longer than it took for Coach to get back on his feet. And when he left her—again—she'd be left to pick up the pieces of her broken heart. Again.

She hadn't done such a great job of getting over him the first time, so she had no hope of doing so now.

Which meant she was destined to be in love with Tucker Riley for the rest of her life. A fact that pretty much ensured she was going to die a lonely, childless spinster.

Dammit. She hated this time of night. Everything always felt so dire and helpless. She tried to console herself, to tell herself she'd feel less freaked out in the morning.

Maybe.

Or maybe not.

God. What had she done?

Tucker rolled over, his hand flying to his forehead, a blinding pain jerking him awake. His stomach roiled. As he sat up, it took him a few seconds to recall where he was through the agonizing haze.

Shit.

Lela.

He didn't want her to see him like this. He hadn't told her about his headaches or all the reasons he'd returned to Maris.

He staggered from the bed and tried to quietly gather his clothing. Tucker stumbled slightly on the stairs, carrying everything with him to dress in the dark living room. Tugging out his cell phone, he saw it was only a little past three a.m. He called for the cab to return, praying the driver recalled the address. Tucker was having a hard time concentrating on anything besides not getting sick.

Once he was fully dressed and the cab was on the way, he glanced around the room, hoping to find some paper and a pen. He needed to leave Lela a note, some sort of explanation for his middle-of-the-night escape. Unfortunately, he found nothing.

Then another sharp pain pierced his temple. His stomach lurched once more. Tucker left the house quickly, doubling over in the front yard. How the hell was he going to make it back to the hotel without getting sick?

He wasn't sure how long he stood there, sucking in one deep breath after another, trying to will the pain away, fighting to contain it until he could get back to the privacy of his hotel room.

Mercifully, the cab arrived and Tucker climbed into the back, giving the driver the name of his hotel. During the entire ride, he concentrated solely on remaining upright, paying atten-tion only to his breathing. In through the nose. Out through the mouth. In. Out.

He made it back without being sick. And somehow he made it to the room. Tucker collapsed on the bed without taking off his clothing or his shoes, closing his eyes and praying for oblivion.

It was only when the pain subsided later the following night that he recalled he'd walked out on Lela without a word.

Chapter Six

Lela sat on the edge of the pier, her cell phone in hand. Lorelie had texted just as she'd been about to dive into the lake.

She'd spent the better part of the morning working in her garden, weeding, watering and picking the vegetables that were ripe. She loved summer's bounty, enjoying dinners made only of food she had grown herself. Tonight, if she could summon the energy, she would cook up some sautéed zucchini and squash, sliced tomatoes drizzled with balsamic oil and fresh corn on the cob. However, something told her that—just like last night—she wouldn't have an appetite.

"No word from Tuck?" Lorelie texted.

Lela sighed as she typed out the word, "No."

"Bastard" came back, and Lela grinned. She'd been blessed with some amazing girlfriends. Her mother liked to refer to Lorelie, Gia, Macie, Paige, and Lacy as Lela's gang, claiming when the whole group got together, things got wild...and loud. Lela had to admit there was some truth to that, but her friends could also be counted on to lift a margarita with her anytime something great happened, as well as share her indignant anger whenever someone pissed her off.

Yesterday had passed in a haze that started at six a.m., when she woke up and realized she was alone. Tucker's desertion had blindsided her, left her questioning everything that had happened.

It wasn't that Lela had expected any lasting commitments or promises from him. How could he offer those when his time in Maris was limited? Training camp started soon. She'd taken him to her bedroom knowing the affair would be brief. But she hadn't anticipated being treated like some casual one-night stand who wasn't special enough to spend the entire evening with. She had called him at least half a dozen times and left several voice mails.

She'd run the gamut of emotions yesterday, from confusion to annoyance followed by a brief bout of depression when he still hadn't returned her calls. Finally, around eight, Paige and Gia had shown up with a bottle of Jim Beam and they'd watched *Pitch Perfect* for the hundredth time. They'd gotten drunk and sung along—loudly and off-key—and taken Lela from hurt to pissed off.

It was a talent her group of friends possessed. Mob mentality. If someone hurt one of their own, the liquor flew and the pitchforks came out. It was actually kind of fun to get worked up, proclaiming the guy an asshole and swearing off men forever. She, Paige, and Gia had declared they were better off without two-legged creatures who possessed penises and her friends had spent a great deal of the night making her laugh.

With the help of the bourbon, Lela managed to sleep for a few foggy hours without wondering why the heck Tucker had left so suddenly and without an explanation.

"Yeah, I guess," Lela texted. "Probably not my brightest

idea. Starting up with him again. May be smarter to just move on."

Lorelie's reply was slow in coming. When it did, it simply said, "Mmmhmm," a sure sign her friend knew as well as she did Lela was nowhere close to getting over Tucker.

Lela rubbed her forehead, a slight hangover making her irritable. Fucker. He'd been back in town less than three weeks and he'd thrown her into a complete tizzy.

"I'm going to go swim." Lela wiped away the bead of sweat rolling down her cheek.

"Ok. I'm around if you need to talk later," Lorelie offered.

"Same goes for me." Coach's heart attack had been rough for Lorelie, and her friend was still reeling, even though she put on a brave face. It was going to take them some time—and probably several cases of wine—to come to grips with everything that had happened this past month.

They said goodbye and Lela set her phone on the pier. Rising, she held her nose and jumped in, anxious to wash away the sticky sweat from her morning's work. She'd always been the type to clean or garden or drive herself to exhaustion whenever something bothered her. Usually the busy work relieved the stress and made her feel better.

The gardening hadn't worked. So, Lela moved on to plan B. The lake.

Swimming around for a little while, she finally rolled over onto her back, floating weightlessly on the placid lake, her arms outstretched, the cool water a welcome relief on her overheated skin.

Lela's eyes were closed to block out the bright sunshine. While her face remained above the water, her ears were beneath it, the surrounding sounds muted. She loved floating on her back, disappearing into this peaceful world where she had no more significance than a feather as she let the water take her wherever it wanted. Her only job was to keep enough air in her lungs to remain afloat.

Some people found meditation soothing. For Lela, the water comforted her, all her worries drifting away on a breeze.

Unfortunately, no such reassurance came today. She was still pissed off. The longer she floated, the madder she got.

How dare he walk out on her like that? No note. No goodbye. She wasn't some faceless stranger he'd picked up at a bar for a quick screw. They had a history. At some point, they'd been friends. In love.

Maybe he'd lied about still feeling that way, but she hadn't lied to him. She'd meant it when she said she still cared. And for him to tromp all over her heart as if she weren't worthy of more respect enraged her.

Fuck it. She released a long breath, letting her lungs deflate, her feet drop. She dove under the water and started to swim back to shore. She was driving over to Tucker's hotel and she was going to tell that asshole where he could get off. She wasn't some weak-willed woman who was going to let him treat her like shit and get away with it.

She came up for air and to see how close she was to the shore. She was just about to go back down when she spotted him. Lela stopped swimming and began to tread water.

Tucker was sitting at the end of her pier, his bare feet dangling over the edge, barely skimming the surface of the lake. No more than twenty feet separated them, but she didn't seek to shorten it. It was apparent he'd been watching her for some time. And while his face appeared contrite, she wasn't going to pretend what he'd done was okay.

He'd hurt her. Again.

The old adage *Fool me once, shame on you. Fool me twice, shame on me* drifted through her mind.

He held her gaze, then when he realized she wasn't swimming closer, he called out, "Thought I'd come take a look at your lawn mower."

She narrowed her eyes and opened her mouth to tell him to go fuck himself.

Before she could speak, he added, "I'm sorry, L.B."

She considered accepting the apology, but discounted it in an instant. It wasn't enough. He owed her an explanation as well. "Why did you leave?"

He glanced around at the surrounding houses. There were a few kids swimming several piers down, but they were too far away to hear them.

If she were feeling more generous, she'd swim over to him. She wasn't feeling that nice.

"Lela. I shouldn't have left without saying goodbye, but—"

"You're right. You shouldn't have." There was no way Tucker could miss the anger in her tone.

"I was sick."

She frowned. She'd considered many reasons for his sudden departure, but she had to admit poor health hadn't entered her mind once. Probably because he'd been well enough to fuck her senseless for several blissful hours.

She felt the need to get a better look at his face, to see if he was telling the truth. Lela began to swim closer to him.

When she reached the pier, he remained silent as she climbed the ladder. Tucker handed her a towel. "Thanks."

She used it to dry off quickly, then she wrapped it around herself before sitting next to him. "Sick how? You seemed fine when we went to sleep."

He didn't reply right away. Once again she was struck by the notion that he was going to lie to her and it annoyed her.

Her temper flared and she rose. "Forget it, Tucker. Forget it all. We both knew going in nothing was going to come from this. Our futures aren't any different now than they were after graduation. We'd be smarter to let it go here. Now. Before we do or say things that can't be undone. It was really great to see you again."

Tucker stood, his face troubled, his eyes betraying a bit of anger. It struck Lela as odd. What the hell did he have to be mad about? She hadn't told lies about her feelings to get him into bed. She didn't run off in the middle of the night, then come back with some lame excuse. What had he expected? That she'd take his apology at face value, tear off her clothes and ring the bell for round two?

"Lela. I really am sorry. I—"

"I heard you the first time." She couldn't stand here any longer. Her heart was pounding, her chest tight. She was afraid of crying in front of him. She wouldn't do that.

"I get migraines. Bad ones."

She paused, uncertain how to respond, afraid to put her trust in him again. What if this was a lie too?

But what if it's the truth?

She didn't reply. Instead, she let the silence between them grow.

Finally, Tucker sought to fill it. "I took a hard hit in that last game."

Lela recalled the sack. It had been a brutal tackle from behind that had slammed Tucker's head into the turf with such vicious impact, Lela had feared he'd been killed. Especially when he didn't move for several minutes afterward.

"I know," she whispered. "I saw it."

"Knocked me out. I had a concussion." Every word Tucker spoke seemed to be dragged from him against his will.

Lela considered what he was saying, the consequences of that injury. "You've had headaches ever since?"

It had been months since that game. If he was still suffering from that tackle...

A light went on. "You're not going back to the team, are you?"

Tucker winced as if she'd struck him. Then he lifted his shoulders. "I haven't decided yet."

She tried to understand. That didn't seem like a decision that would be his to make. "Have you been cleared to play?"

He nodded.

She scowled. "Do your doctors know about these headaches?"

Tucker didn't reply. He was lying to the doctors. She could see it on his face.

"Tucker." She would make him answer her question.

At that moment, Tucker's phone rang. She hoped he would ignore it, but she should have known better. She'd backed him into a corner. The call would save him.

For the moment.

He pulled his cell from his back pocket, frowning when he read the number on the screen. "It's Lorelie."

Lela felt a shard of panic.

God. Coach.

Tucker answered. "Hello? Lorelie?"

Lela tried to read his face, wishing she could hear what Lorelie was saying. When he muttered the word, "Fuck," Lela's fear became full-blown.

"What? What is it? Coach?"

Tucker shook his head, but continued to listen as Lorelie spoke.

"Thanks for calling," he said after several moments. Tucker lowered the phone but didn't bother to put it away.

"Coach is okay?"

He nodded, though the action seemed sluggish, as if he was struggling to focus.

"Tucker. What happened?"

"It's my dad. He's in the hospital."

Lela wasn't sure how to respond. She knew he and his father were estranged. She didn't even know if Tucker had tried to contact the man since his return home. "Is he okay?"

Tucker shrugged. "He tried to kill himself."

"What?"

"Apparently he polished off a fifth of bourbon, then put a gun to his head. His hand slipped when he pulled the trigger. The bullet skimmed the side of his skull."

"Jesus."

"Neighbors heard the shot and called the cops. He'd passed out in a pool of his own blood. They have him bandaged up and in the hospital. A room on the psych floor."

"Oh, Tucker. I'm sorry. I—"

"I have to go." His response was wooden, abrupt.

"Are you going to the hospital?"

He shook his head. "Hell no. I'm not going anywhere near there. I just...I can't...fuck, Lela. I can't do this anymore."

"Do what?"

He ran a frustrated hand through his hair. "Any of it. I'm fucking it all up. Every goddamn thing I touch lately explodes in my hand."

Lela recalled Tucker's face the morning she found him after his mother's death. That same lost expression and utter desperation resided in his eyes. "Don't go."

He frowned, his voice growing louder as his anxiety increased. "Don't you see? I'm only going to hurt you again."

She lifted one shoulder. "Then that'll be on me. My fault. I don't want you to leave. Not like this."

"I'm numb, Lela. So damn numb."

She stepped closer, lifting her hand to his chest. She ran her fingers along his pecs, then up to his face. "Can you feel this?"

He released a long sigh, his eyes drifting shut. Tucker nodded slowly, tilted his face to keep her hand on his cheek. "Yeah."

"Let's disappear for a little while."

His eyes opened, his gaze finding hers. "I can't keep using you like this."

Tucker's comment sparked a realization. "Is that what the other night was?"

He didn't bother to lie or shield her from the truth. "I ran into my dad at Cruisers. We got into an argument."

"And then you came here?"

He nodded.

"Why?"

"Being with you is the only thing in my life that's not hard. I don't know how to explain it. We haven't spoken in twelve years, but when I'm with you, it feels like I never left."

She grinned. "You think this isn't hard?"

He frowned. "I think it's complicated and unsettled and we're moving way too fast. Hell, we're practically strangers now. But all that goes away when I'm with you. When you touch me."

All the anger and misery Lela had experienced since waking up alone evaporated instantly. Tucker had perfectly summed up exactly what she was feeling.

She stepped closer, raising her arms and placing them around his neck. Tucker didn't reciprocate. Lela reached for the phone he still held, taking it from him. She turned it off completely, then slid it into his back pocket.

Tucker stood motionless, even as she went up on her tiptoes to place a kiss on his jaw. He was fighting a battle with himself. He'd try to save her from herself if she let him.

She didn't intend to give him that chance.

. . .

Tucker took a deep breath, searching for the strength to walk away from her. His head was yelling at him, telling him he was too fucked-up to be good for anyone right now. Lela didn't deserve to be used like this.

Trouble was, he needed her. He'd been alone since leaving Maris all those years ago. He may have spent his days—and more than a few nights—surrounded by others, be it teammates, friends, or lovers. But that didn't change the fact he'd still been utterly and completely alone.

That loneliness vanished in Lela's presence. It had disappeared back when he was a scared, angry teenage boy fighting to escape an abusive father. And it had gone away the night before last when he'd walked into her bedroom, losing himself inside her body.

She kissed his jaw once more and he wondered if she could feel the tension there as he clenched it. He was stretched taut, a man on the edge. He'd tried to explain that, tried to warn her.

As always, Lela looked beyond the pain, dug through all the layers of shit that had him tied in knots and found the man he wanted to be. She saw something in him that he'd never seen in himself. Not once.

He reached for her hands, tugging them behind her back. Gripping them together with one hand, he tightened his hold.

Her face flushed, but she didn't try to escape. Glancing over her shoulder, he saw that the kids who had been swimming a few houses away had gone inside. They were alone. Lifting his free hand, he tugged the beach towel she'd wrapped around herself, dragging it away.

She wore the sexiest one-piece bathing suit he'd ever seen. If asked, he would have sworn bikinis were the hottest swimming attire on the market. Lela had blown that idea out of the water...literally.

He reached up to cup one of her breasts through the damp

material, squeezing the handful of flesh roughly. Part of him hoped she'd be too frightened of exactly what he wanted from her, while the other part prayed she'd respond to it.

He slipped a strap off her shoulder, baring one of her breasts. Lela started to look around, clearly concerned about who could see them.

"Look at me," he commanded. "Just me."

She licked her lips, the blush on her cheeks growing rosier. Her face revealed the most adorable mixture of embarrassment and arousal.

He grasped her bare breast, then pinched the turgid nipple. Lela gasped.

Tucker continued to play with the sensitive nub, using the grip he had on her hands behind her back to pull her closer. Her skin was cool, still slightly wet. It was a nice contrast to the heat his body was generating. Texas summers were brutal.

Her breasts brushed against his chest. There was something else he wanted her to feel. Pressing his hips forward, he made sure she felt the full length of his hard cock.

"Be very sure this is what you want, Lela, because once we start, it's going to get serious."

"I don't want you to stop." Her gaze found his and her voice was strong, sure. God, where had this powerhouse of a woman come from?

"Football," he murmured.

"What?"

"If things get too intense for you, I want you to say 'football'. That will be my cue to slow down or stop completely if that's what you want."

Her brow crinkled as she considered his comments. Lela had no experience with bondage, with submission. She'd admitted it to him. And God knew they'd never done anything much more scandalous than going down on each other back in school.

His tastes had evolved over the years. "And to be perfectly clear this time, I like to be in control."

She snickered. "Really? I had no idea."

He didn't laugh at her sarcasm, though he wanted to. Instead, he schooled his features, letting her see exactly how serious he was.

Her smile faded a bit. "Are you going to explain? Give me a hint about what's coming?"

Tucker shook his head. "No. I'm going to show you." He released her bare breast, but kept her wrists confined. Using his free hand, he tangled his fingers in her hair and pulled her face to his.

They'd always enjoyed kissing. That clearly hadn't changed with the passage of time. However, he wasn't giving her the same sweet explorations they'd always engaged in. This time, he wanted more from her. With firm lips, he forced hers apart, his tongue diving in. He tasted the slight tang of coffee and something sweet. Lela's tongue brushed his as she pressed closer. She wasn't shying away, wasn't intimidated by his hungry lips.

His teeth entered the game, nipping her lower lip, and she tried to jerk back. He held firm, keeping her still as he licked the sting away.

He tightened his fingers in her hair, recalling the way she'd pulled his hair at Coach's ranch, the prickle in his scalp. It was clear she was feeling the same now and it was turning her on.

"Get back in the water."

She frowned, confused when he released her in an instant. He let her hands drop and his fingers left her hair. "What?"

"Water. Now."

She ran her tongue over her lower lip. At first he thought

she was nervous, but her gaze didn't betray a single trace of fear. Instead, it was as if she was evaluating the damage his kisses had wrought.

Her lips were slightly swollen from his rough kiss. If he had his way, he'd keep them puffy all day and into the night.

When she still didn't move, he narrowed his eyes impatiently.

She tilted her head and gave him a saucy wink. "Are you coming with me?"

She may enjoy a strong hand, but Lela would never be a true submissive. She was too independent, too determined to make a few demands of her own.

"What do you think?"

She grinned at his reply, then walked back to the ladder, slipping down into the water. Her shudder as her stomach cleared the surface warned him of the cool temperature.

As Lela moved lower on the ladder, Tucker reached for the hem of his t-shirt, pulling it over his head before toeing off his sandals. Then he stripped off his shorts until he stood in front of her in just his boxers. He wasn't going to remove those until he was in the water, on the off chance the kids came back out.

Lela kicked away from the ladder as he began his descent. Once he was in the water, he turned, surprised to see she'd paddled several feet away.

"Come here," he demanded.

She laughed, then splashed him. Shaking her head, she taunted him. "Catch me."

Tucker sprang into action without a word, catching her off-guard. Lela squealed as she turned, trying to swim away from him. He caught one of her ankles after less than ten strokes, using his grip to pull her back.

She tried to kick off his hold, the fight turning him on. Reaching out, he managed to get his hands around her waist.

Careful to dodge her kicking legs, he dragged her closer until their bodies were connected, his chest against her back.

Wrapping his arms around her, he roughly palmed both of her breasts. Somewhere along the line, she'd slipped her bathing suit back up. That action annoyed him. He didn't want her covered, didn't want her body hidden from him.

Slipping both straps off her shoulders, Tucker worked the wet material of her suit downward until she was naked in the water.

"Tucker."

"Hush." He lobbed the suit back toward the pier, the dripping material landing with a loud slap against the wood.

Lela twisted in his arms, her hands finding the elastic of his boxers. Together, they stripped him out of the cotton. However, when Lela tried to toss them to the pier, her throw fell a couple of feet short.

"Oops," she said with a giggle as they watched his boxers sink.

He wiped away her grin with another rough kiss, his hands sliding along every slick, gorgeous inch of her he could reach. Lela took her own journey, stroking his chest and then reaching around to grip his ass.

His cock brushed her stomach as their feet bounced along the bottom. They'd remained in the shallow part, close to the bank. Brushy shrubs hid them from the view of Lela's neighbors and the opposite side of the lake was all woods. The water came just above Lela's breast, but with his height, it was only mid-chest level. They were well hidden, secluded, alone.

Tucker couldn't remember the last time he'd felt so secure about his privacy. On the road with the team, there was a continual battalion of tabloid and newspaper photographers flashing cameras in his face. Even while he'd been on his own at the beach bungalow, there had been more than a few tourists who'd tried to sneak pictures when they thought he wasn't looking. Right now, it felt as if he and Lela were the last two people on the planet.

Bending his head, he licked the water that ran along Lela's neck. She shivered and he recalled how much she liked having her neck kissed. Closing his lips on a small section, he sucked.

She tried to squirm away when it was clear his actions would leave a mark, but he held her tighter. Finally she stopped trying to fight, her arms wrapping around his shoulders as she let her head drift farther back. "I'm too old for a hickey."

He smiled even as he continued to suck and nibble. Then he pushed away. "I want to see my mark on you. Here..." He lightly brushed the red circle on her neck with his fingertips. "And here," he added as he reached lower, both palms cupping her ass.

"I have no problem with you kissing my ass," she teased.

Tucker flashed a dangerous smile. "It's not my lips that will be leaving their mark." As he spoke, he lightly tapped her ass, making sure she understood his meaning. Lela's slight intake of breath told him she knew exactly what was coming. He'd merely introduced her to the concept of spanking the other night.

Today, he'd make sure she got the full effect.

"Lay on your back, Lela. Like you were before. And open your legs."

She responded without question or hesitation. He watched her fill her lungs with air, then slowly she began to drift. Her legs were only a few inches apart.

Tucker gripped her ankles. Her concentration broke and she started to sink slightly before she remembered to hold her breath. He dragged her legs apart, then stepped to her side to place his hands under her back when she struggled to remain afloat.

"Stay up, L.B."

"I'm trying," she muttered before sucking in another deep breath.

He ran his hand along her thigh, then stroked the light smattering of wet hair at the vee of her legs. Lela sighed and started to sink.

He used one arm beneath her back to support her. Her gaze, though squinted against the sunshine, remained focused on his face.

"Close your eyes."

She followed his command and her body began to relax. That bonelessness turned back to steel when his hand left her thigh and touched her pussy. He chuckled at her sudden tension.

"Don't trust me?"

She peered at him through one cracked eyelid. "I think you're mistaking my response. It's not a lack of trust. It's nervous anticipation and fear of the unknown."

"Fair enough. And just so you know, you've earned yourself a punishment when I get you back to your bedroom."

She scowled. "For what?"

He loved that she didn't question the fact he was going to punish her. So far she was taking his commands and dominance in stride. He wondered how far he could push her before she'd balk...or push back. "For opening your eyes."

She rolled said eyes at him before closing them once more. Her body had gone limp as they talked, so he put her back on her guard by pressing one finger inside her pussy. His sudden action—sans warning—had her body sinking rapidly. He lifted her once more until she could control the air in her lungs again.

"Easy, L.B. Relax." He enjoyed the way his soothing words were playing in direct contrast to his actions, keeping her guessing about what he would do next. He added another finger to the first, then a third. The water made it easy for him to slide the digits in and out.

Lela's ability to remain afloat had deserted her as her breathing became more labored. He used one hand to hold her up as he fucked her with the other. He increased his speed, his strength, loving the way she writhed, the water splashing.

When he pressed his thumb against her clit, Lela was a goner. She jerked, and then cried out, her body curling into a ball. She pressed her face against his chest as he held her steady, careful to keep her above the water.

As Lela came back to her senses, she stood, smiling at him. "I can't believe I let you do that to me out here in broad daylight."

"I intend to do a lot more to you before the day's over."

She reached beneath the surface, her hand stroking his cock with a firm grip that sent stars flashing behind his eyes. It was difficult to control himself with her. He was used to having a lot more stamina, but with Lela, it simply felt too good, too right, and he wound up coming like an inexperienced schoolboy, exploding far sooner than he wanted to.

He gripped her wrist. "We need to move this show inside."
She frowned. "Why?"
He gestured back to his shorts on the pier. "Because the condoms are there and we're here."
Tucker reached for her hand, intending to help her back to the ladder. He was surprised when she dug her feet in.
"I'm on the Pill."
He swallowed heavily. "Lela." He understood what she was offering and he wanted it more than he wanted his next breath. Even so...
When he didn't respond, she tilted her head, studying his face. "You would tell me if there was a reason why we should use one, right?"

He nodded.

"Is there a reason?"

Tucker shook his head. "I've never had sex without a condom. Ever." Not even with her. They may have been young the first time they were together, but they weren't stupid. They'd never failed to use protection. Since then, Tucker had indulged in more than a few casual affairs, but he'd never had a serious girlfriend. He'd never thought it was fair to start dating someone, knowing he'd be on the road and away from them nearly thirty weeks out of the year. Besides, he'd never met a woman he'd wanted to have a long-term relationship with.

Lela had always been the yardstick and so far, no one had measured up. Reconnecting with her now, even after all these years, had just solidified that belief. After this interlude, he wondered if he'd ever find a woman he wanted more.

And her offer of going without the condom...well...Jesus...

"Come here," she said, shaking off his grip on her wrist. She tugged him toward her until they stood chest to chest.

When she wrapped her arms around his neck and lifted her legs about his waist, the pure heat radiating from her pussy amazed Tucker. He gripped her ass, and then used one hand to guide himself home.

Home.

The word pounded in his brain. For the first time since he'd returned to Maris, he felt as if he'd truly come home.

Chapter Seven

Lela took her time sliding down on Tucker's cock. He was definitely larger than her previous lovers and while she knew skill was as important as girth, she was damn grateful this man had both.

Then another thought drifted through her mind. *Tucker has never taken a woman without a condom?*

He'd been her first in so many things. It felt wonderful to be his first in this. His hands tightened around her waist. He released a guttural moan that told her this felt as good to him as it did her.

"Fuck me, L.B.," he muttered. She couldn't decide if that was a command or an exclamation. Maybe a bit of both.

She reversed direction, moving away until the head of his cock almost slipped free. He didn't give her time to make the return trip on her own. Instead he took control, dragging her hips back roughly.

At that point, all attempts at subtlety evaporated. Their lovemaking took on a brutal, almost animalistic quality. Their bodies slapped together, water splashing on their chests, their faces. Neither of them sought to wipe the drops away. Nothing mattered except pleasure. Dragging it out as long as possible. Pushing the limit, feeling it spiral higher.

Lela was dizzy with the sensations pummeling her. It was too much and not enough at the same time.

Tucker's fingers gripped her ass, seeking a better hold, intent on moving harder, faster.

Her head fell back, her long hair floating along the surface of the lake. It offered no cooling relief. She was on fire, and nothing would quench the flames short of an orgasm.

Tucker drove himself to the hilt once more, then held her there despite her attempts to continue the motion. She opened her eyes just in time to see him reach for her clit.

God. One touch there and she was a goner. She reached for his wrist, stopping him.

His eyes narrowed. "Let go, L.B."

A shiver racked her frame at his deep command. She loved his dominance, longed for him to expand on that concept. Years spent guiding her own pleasure, taking charge of her own orgasms—or going without—had caused her to grow apathetic about sex. It had always been more bother than it was worth.

Not so with Tucker.

The teacher inside her had no trouble giving up the role of instructor. In this, she was his most willing student.

She released his wrist. "If you touch me there, it's over. I'm too close." She hoped her confession would encourage him to slow down, to give her time to recover a bit.

He grinned. "It's not going to be over for a long time, Lela. I intend to spend the next few hours inside this pretty pussy."

Hours?

She felt light-headed. Was that physically possible?

"Oh," she replied stupidly. She didn't have time to form a more intelligent response when he stroked his thumb along her clit and lightning struck. Her spine arched and she almost dunked herself. Mercifully, Tucker cupped the back of her head just before she submerged.

After that, all of his actions seemed hazy, coming to her through slow motion as her climax continued.

"God," she cried out when Tucker sought to prolong the beautiful agony with more thrusting. In and out, he drove, her body floating away once more. This time, instead of the water carrying her, it was Tucker.

Always Tucker.

Her pussy clenched tighter and her lover fell as well. Tucker's arms wrapped around her, holding her, as he bent lower to place his forehead against her breasts. Water lapped around them but somehow, miraculously they managed to keep their heads above the surface.

Heat flooded her pussy as Tucker came inside her. Though they'd had sex countless times—both in the past and in recent days—she'd never felt this close to him, never enjoyed such a strong bond. Perhaps it was the knowledge that she'd given him something no one else ever had, or the idea that he was *truly* inside her now.

Tucker recovered first, rising slowly. Her legs lowered into the water, her feet finding the uneven floor of the lake. She was grateful for the water's support. Without it, she wouldn't have been able to stand on her own. Her limbs felt like rubber, her strength zapped.

Tucker kissed her forehead, then her eyes, his lips drifting down to find hers.

She was touched when he whispered, "thank you" against her cheek.

Lela captured his gaze. "Tucker..." She started to demure, to tell him she was the one who should be saying thank you, but he waved her words away, silencing her with another kiss.

"You've always trusted me." His tone was tinted with amazement.

"Of course I have."

He looked truly perplexed by that. "I don't want to betray that trust."

Once again, she suffered that niggling sensation Tucker had secrets he wasn't sharing. "You won't."

His body suddenly looked tense and his expression darkened with hunger. "I'm about to test the limits."

Before she could ask him what he meant, her hand was in his and he was dragging her toward the pier. He tugged her in front of him, encouraging her to climb the ladder first. She gave him a knowing look over her shoulder when she realized he just wanted a better look at her bare ass.

He didn't bother to hide the appreciative gleam in his eyes. "God, you're hot."

She rolled her eyes. "I have a fat ass and you know it."

"I honestly can't think of one man who prefers a skinny ass over a big booty. I like having something to wrap my hands around."

She laughed. "I'm not a damn football."

He slapped her ass when she reached the top. He'd been right on her heels during the four-rung climb. They both reached for towels, drying off.

Lela looked around, grateful that most of her neighbors worked year-round. The only person home at this time of day was the woman with all the kids, several houses down, and Lela knew she struggled to get them outside most of the time, the lure of Xbox keeping them glued to the TV.

"You ready for more?" Tucker asked as he gathered their things and started walking toward her house.

"I thought you were kidding about that. Don't you guys need recovery time?"

He glanced over his shoulder and gave her an exasperated look. "I'm spanking your ass as soon as we get inside."

"What for?"

"You settled, L.B. Didn't you? Didn't bother to find guys who deserved you, who made you come over and over again."

A lump formed in her throat. She'd never considered herself particularly low on self-esteem, but hearing Tucker's assessment made her realize she had sort of given up.

She recalled a plaque that hung in her foyer with a quote from Thoreau. It said, "Live the life you've imagined." She hadn't done that. Hadn't let herself believe she could find true happiness, passion or love. Lela recalled her lame reasons for staying with Carl, her claims that companionship and lukewarm sex were enough. How could she have believed that?

Lela didn't bother to reply. Her expression told him exactly what he needed to know. They climbed the stairs to her back porch and entered the house via the kitchen. She started toward the bedroom, but Tucker stopped her, his gaze focused on the counter of the island.

They hadn't bothered to put their clothing back on. Instead they'd simply wrapped the towels around themselves. Tucker tugged hers off, studying her naked body with obvious appreciation.

"Come here."

She began to step into his arms, longing for the warmth of his embrace, as the air conditioning was too cool on her damp skin. However, he didn't seem to have cuddling on his mind. He guided her to the counter and pressed lightly on the nape of her neck.

"Put your hands on the counter and bend over."

She shivered—with cold and anticipation. He'd made several comments about punishing her. Was he planning to follow through with it?

Lela wasn't sure why the idea appealed to her so much, but given the sudden moisture gathering in her pussy, she couldn't deny she wanted it. Wanted Tucker to claim control, take her hard. Somehow his rough actions didn't hurt as much as arouse.

Once Lela was bent over, Tucker lifted his hand and brought it down on her bare ass. He'd given no warning and he sure as hell hadn't held back.

"Ouch." She started to rise, but his hand reappeared at her back, applying the pressure needed to keep her where he wanted her. He spanked her again—two quick, hot blows, one to each cheek.

She tried once more to stand, but Tucker wasn't going to let her go that easily. "What do you say to end this?"

Lela struggled to understand his question as her body began to betray her. Her initial reactions had been pain and escape, but she noticed the heat in her ass didn't seem to sting as badly right now. The burn wasn't a bad one. She pressed her legs together, shocked by the jolt of blinding need that struck.

"God," she gasped. She was hot, horny. From three strikes to her ass? Seriously?

She tilted, then wiggled her hips.

Tucker chuckled, but didn't take her up on the invitation. "Nice try, L.B., but you didn't answer my question."

He'd asked a question?

"Um..."

Tucker stroked her ass gently, sending another round of vibrations rumbling through her. "What word?"

Lela pressed her eyes shut tightly, trying to force her brain to work. It was clear he wouldn't give her what she wanted until she responded, but she couldn't for the life of her—

"Football!" she declared loudly. Then she realized perhaps he'd misunderstand. "That's what I say. But I'm *not* saying it now." She felt it important to stress that point.

"Good girl." His hand landed hard.

Lela gasped, changing her mind. It hurt again. Then Tucker wiped the soreness away with light caresses that had her up on her toes, her empty pussy clenching, seeking.

"Tucker. Please." She didn't have enough functioning brain cells to form more than those two words. It didn't matter. Tucker was the quarterback and he was making the calls.

He placed ten more slaps against her ass, varying the speed, the strength. Sometimes it was a tap, other times the impact caused her to cry out. None of the touches made her want to call a halt. They only increased her longing.

She was gasping by the time Tucker stopped. He tapped on the inside of her ankle, bidding her to spread her legs without words. He ran his fingers through the juices there.

Lela released a long sigh of relief.

"Not yet, L.B."

She scowled, shooting daggers at him over her shoulder. She needed him to fuck her. And she wasn't in the mood to wait.

Her expression only served to fuel Tucker's determination to drag out this torturous, amazing foreplay. He grasped her upper arm and forced her upright. She wobbled a bit, but Tucker was there to support her.

"I love the kitchen," he said. "Probably the best room in a house after the bedroom." She was amused—and annoyed—by his steady, nonchalant tone. She was three seconds from splintering into a million pieces and he was casually chatting about the merits of a damn kitchen.

"Yeah," she muttered. "Great room."

He chuckled. "So many options."

She frowned, but Tucker continued.

"For instance..." Rather than complete his statement, he guided her to a kitchen chair, encouraging her to sit.

Once she was situated, he took two too many steps away from her. Rubbing his chin, he seemed content to simply look at her. Problem was...she was *not* content.

"I don't like this game, Tucker. I need you to fuck me."

Tucker tsked. "Don't remember you using such foul language when we were younger."

She narrowed her eyes. "That was then. This is now. Come here."

He gave her a grin she instantly distrusted and it occurred to her she was probably being very foolish with her imperious demands. Something told her he had every intention of making her pay for them.

Tucker didn't reply, didn't scold her. Rather, he turned around and started exploring her kitchen, opening drawers and cabinets, grabbing a couple of things, though she couldn't see what.

When he returned, she spotted her *I'd be a vegetarian if bacon grew on trees* apron and a clean dishrag in his hands.

"Still a fan of bacon, I see."

She shrugged. "Nobody's invented anything better yet."

"That's true."

He bent down and she lifted her face, expecting him to kiss her. She was disappointed when he clasped her hands instead and tugged them behind her back. That disappointment was short-lived when he used the apron strings to tie them together.

Ooh...bondage.

She started to tell him exactly how much she liked where he was going with things, but he cut off her words when he pushed the dishrag into her mouth.

Lela tried to shake her head, to dislodge the material, but he'd put in just enough to render her tongue useless without gagging her.

Once it was in place, he moved away a few inches, his gaze studying hers.

"Wink at me."

She paused as she considered his odd request, then she winked.

"That has the same power as the word *football*. Understand?"

She nodded, fairly certain she wasn't going to need the gesture. She sure as hell hadn't needed the word yet.

Tucker moved away from her. She hated the distance, but had no way to express her displeasure. She figured that was the purpose of the gag. He was going to keep playing with her and he'd stolen her ability to read him the riot act for it.

Clever bastard.

She hated him in that moment. And loved him. And wanted him.

He'd been back in her life for exactly nineteen days and Tucker had already finished the job he'd started in high school. She was officially ruined for all other men forever.

"Open your legs, L.B., and hook your ankles around the legs of the chair."

She obeyed, trying not to wince as the blast of cool air hit the inferno burning between her thighs.

"Scoot your ass forward to the edge of the seat."

Once again, she moved as he directed. She closed her eyes and concentrated on the air rushing through her nostrils. She was a powder keg set to blow and the damn man hadn't even touched her yet. Her ass stung slightly from the spanking he'd given her, but that only added more fuel to the fire.

"Look at me."

She opened her eyes.

Tucker reached out and ran one finger along her slit. One

ineffective finger. He lifted it to his lips and sucked off the moisture he'd collected.

Oh dayum. That was totally hot.

Almost sexy enough to make her forget how *not enough* his touch had been. Almost.

If she'd been able to speak, she would have slung a wide array of curse words and demands his way. He was going too fucking slowly.

She tried to convey that with an annoyed look, but Tucker either didn't recognize it or ignored it. Probably the latter, which just served to piss her off more.

"You're wet," he said.

No shit, Einstein.

Tucker chuckled and she wondered if he could read minds.

She groaned when he turned away from her and circled the island. She wanted to scream for him to come back, frustrated by the gag. Lela was tempted to wink just so he'd remove it, but she was afraid he'd untie the apron as well. She didn't mind that bondage.

He looked at the vegetables she'd picked from her garden earlier that morning. "Still have a green thumb, I see." He didn't bother to look at her for a response.

She sucked in a deep breath when he picked up a cucumber—the largest one—and returned to her.

"This is impressive." She heard the amusement in his tone, knew he was enjoying this interlude way too much. He was a master at sexual teasing. Back in the day, they'd been too young to explore the benefits of foreplay. If they ever managed to find a quiet moment alone, they just went for it, fucking like there was no tomorrow.

Tucker had clearly figured out there was something to be said for drawing out the moment, building the anticipation. She wanted to hate it, but she couldn't. This was shaping up to be the single hottest sexual experience of her life and if Tucker's promise/threat of hours spent inside her was to be believed, they'd only scratched the surface.

Lela's throat tightened when Tucker knelt between her outstretched legs, the cucumber still in his hands.

His eyes remained on her face and she sensed he was waiting for that wink. Lela's eyes began to dry out as she fought not to blink. She didn't want him to misread that involuntary action.

He pressed the cool vegetable against her clit. She bit down on the gag as visions of *9½ Weeks* flashed through her brain. Paige had lifted the movie from her mother's collection when they were freshmen in high school and they'd watched the scandalous film during a slumber party. Lela remembered how fascinating and arousing the kitchen scene had been. She hadn't exactly understood her body's reaction to it at the time, but she definitely got it now.

Lela wiggled closer to the edge of the chair in obvious invitation.

Tucker grinned. "If my ego weren't so solid, I think I'd be intimidated by this cucumber."

She giggled, the sound muffled.

Tucker's brow creased. "Dammit," he said, pulling the gag from her mouth. "I'll probably regret this, but I miss your voice."

She licked her lips, then lifted one eyebrow. "You realize that's my dinner you're fondling me with."

He laughed, the sound loud in a room that had been so quiet just seconds earlier. She loved how his whole face reflected his pleasure and it occurred to her she hadn't heard him laugh like that since he'd been home. He'd laughed all the time when they were in school, cracking her up with his off-color jokes and taking great delight in teasing her.

"I love your laugh," she admitted.

Her comment caught him off-guard. Then he shrugged. "Sounds rusty to me."

She tilted her head. "Lack of use?"

He nodded. "Yeah. I guess so. There hasn't been much to laugh about lately."

She opened her mouth to ask why, but Tucker always seemed to be two steps ahead of her. The question turned to a gasp when he pushed the cucumber inside her pussy an inch or so.

It felt weird, and Lela struggled to decide if she actually liked the sensation or if it was the naughtiness of the act that appealed to her.

Tucker rocked the cucumber inside her, slowly, only increasing the depth a little. "What toys do you have in your bedroom?"

"What makes you think I have any?"

He scowled. "Dammit, L.B. I better go upstairs and find at least a dildo or I'll be really pissed."

She laughed. "What? Why?"

"You like sex too freaking much. If you've been denying that to yourself all these years..."

"A dildo," she replied, cutting him off mid-rant. "And a vibrator."

"Butt plug?" he asked.

She snorted. "Dear God, no. I don't even know what that is, but it sounds ominous."

Tucker's interest was definitely piqued by that reply. "So you haven't explored anal play?"

She crinkled her nose. "No. And I'm perfectly fine keeping that island uncharted."

He didn't press the point. Instead, he murmured, "we'll

see," in such a way that told her the subject would be brought up again.

"Tucker," she warned.

He pulled the cucumber out of her and tossed it to the floor. Then he dropped the towel that had done little to conceal the hard-on he'd been sporting since they'd entered the house. It was pointing due north.

"Shit. I'm getting jealous of a damn vegetable." He reached behind her and untied her hands. Lela had enjoyed the restraints, but there was something to be said for freedom as well.

She reached for his cock, stroking it, loving the deep, guttural moans her touch produced. Tucker let her have her way for a full minute before tugging her hand away, standing and pulling her out of the chair.

"Finished with the kitchen?" she asked as he dragged her to the stairs. She wasn't resisting his attempts to get her to the bedroom, she just wasn't moving fast enough. He was suddenly in a big hurry.

"Fuck it," he said, pushing her to her knees on one of the steps. Then he was behind her, thrusting his cock to the hilt in one hard, hot shove.

Lela gasped, then she came. Just like that. "God. Oh my God."

Tucker didn't stop moving. "Holy fuck. You have no idea how good it feels when you come on my cock."

Lela began to add her own backward thrusts, increasing the pressure. Her vision went black a split second before white-hot lights flashed, another climax crashing.

Tucker shouted her name as he came, jet after hot jet of come filling her.

Minutes passed, but neither of them bothered to move. If Lela had an ounce of strength left in her, she would have laughed at the tableau they presented. She was bent over doggy-style, halfway up the staircase, Tucker's softening cock still tucked inside her as he knelt behind her.

Both of them were struggling to control their breathing. She'd been less winded after running the local 8K race on Memorial Day.

She was jerked from her sluggishness when Tucker's hand landed on her ass. It was a familiar, affectionate slap that betrayed his own exhaustion. "My knees are killing me, but I can't move."

She giggled at his confession. "Ditto." She wiggled a bit, disappointed when his cock fell out. She missed him instantly. "Shower or nap?"

He seemed to consider his options then said, "Both."

Tucker stood first, helping her rise. They moved upstairs slowly. "I had every intention of taking you in your bed. Couldn't make it."

She smiled. "No one's ever wanted me the way you do."

He wrapped his arm around her shoulders, placing a quick kiss on her forehead. "Every guy in this backwoods town is an idiot then."

Lela went up on tiptoe to kiss his jaw. She loved his height, his size. She wasn't a small woman—more average than anything—but she felt tiny with Tucker.

"Thank you," she whispered.

"For what?"

"For helping me remember some things I'd forgotten."

He didn't ask her to explain. Something in his face told her he understood what she meant.

That thought was confirmed when he said, "You're helping me remember too, L.B."

Chapter Eight

Tucker released a long sigh as he approached the house. Lela had shown up at the ranch a couple hours earlier. He'd been too far out in the field to do more than wave. They'd spent the last two days splitting their time between sex, sleep, food and work.

He hadn't had a migraine since his first night in Lela's bed, but the fear that the ticking time bomb in his head could go off at any minute never left him.

He hadn't said anything else to Lela about his injury and she hadn't asked. They seemed to share a sense that they were clicking up the tracks on an amazing roller coaster, but neither of them was ready for the plummet back to Earth. Instead, they filled the hours with kisses and cuddles in front of the TV, and so much sex his cock was actually sore from overuse.

She'd mentioned his father a few times, offering to call one of her nurse friends for an update on his recovery, but he'd turned her down. He didn't want a single second of his time with Lela to be dampened by his dad. He'd said good riddance to the man after his mother's death. Time hadn't changed his desire to keep his old man out of his life.

He climbed the stairs and stepped inside, following the female voices that told him she and Lorelie were in the kitchen. When he entered, he was surprised to find Coach with them as well.

"Tucker," Lela said, smiling brightly as he entered the room.

"Saw you pull up earlier."

She pointed to a pile of chocolate chip cookies on a plate on the table. "We're getting ready for the bake sale this weekend."

"They've put me in charge of packaging." Coach feigned annoyance as he lifted a baggie, though Tucker suspected the man was enjoying himself more than he let on.

"Six per bag, Dad." Lorelie lifted one of the Ziplocs. "This one only has five."

Coach grinned. "I got hungry."

"Speaking of..." Tucker walked to the table and snatched a cookie before Lorelie could smack his hand. "The whole house smells good. I can't believe you don't have every man on the ranch in here, mooching for sweets." Tucker popped the still-warm cookie in his mouth. "Oh damn. I'll buy the whole lot. Right now."

Lorelie waved her spatula at him. "I'm holding you to that, Mr. NFL. Bring that fat checkbook of yours to the fire hall on Saturday. In addition to the bake sale, we're holding a flea market, selling chicken dinners, and there will be games for the kids. It should be a fun day. Maris Fire Station needs a new tanker. Ours is on its last legs. Broke down on the way to a brush fire in April and poor Luc and Diego have been fighting to keep the thing going ever since."

Maris had exactly two firefighters and EMTs, mainly because the town wasn't big enough to need more than that. As such, Luc and Diego ran all the calls, and during the down-times, they filled swimming pools and taught fire safety classes to the elementary school kids.

Coach glanced at his watch, then stood. He was starting to move a bit faster, looking a bit more like his old self with each passing day. "I'm getting kind of tired, Lori. Think I'll take a little nap."

She smirked, then snorted once her father was out of earshot. "Tired, my ass. He's gotten hooked on *Days of our Lives*."

Lela laughed. "Really?"

"Yep. He turns the channel every time I walk in, but I've heard that theme music pretty consistently for the last week. And his naptime always seems to start promptly at noon."

Lela glanced toward the door Coach had just exited. "Wonder what's been happening lately."

Lorelie rolled her eyes. "Dear God. Not you too." She grabbed a box from the corner and began filling it with the baggies her father had packed with cookies. "So you're definitely coming on Saturday, Tucker?"

Tucker nodded enthusiastically. After years spent attending top-dollar, black tie affairs in swanky settings, he couldn't understand why a day spent at a fire station yard party was something he was suddenly looking forward to. But the truth of it was, he couldn't wait to go. Ty's Collective, the band his buddies Caleb and Tyson, had formed back in school would be playing after sundown and there would be dancing. It had been too damn long since he'd done the Texas two-step.

"Wouldn't miss it. So...are y'all just about done?" he asked, mentally wincing at the return of his southern accent. He'd worked hard to drive that telling twang out of his voice, but he'd noticed it coming back more and more as the days passed.

Lela nodded. "Yep. What's up?"

"I was wondering if you wanted to go for a drive with me."

Lela's face lit up. "Sure."

Lorelie walked to the sink with a dirty cookie sheet. "Is 'drive' code for 'fucking'?"

Lela laughed and said, "Hope so," at the same time Tucker said, "No."

"I'll be back in a little while to grab my car, Lorelie."

Lorelie waved her away. "Take your time. Have fun. I'll just be here, cleaning up the mess, horny and alone."

Tucker tossed Lela the keys when they hit the driveway.

Her eyes widened. "Seriously? I can drive it?" Lela was as car-mad as he was and too easy to please. She viewed driving the rental with the same glee as a kid waking up on Christmas morning.

"Yep. Just don't wreck it."

She opened the passenger door. "I would never hurt such a sweet car."

The top was down, so as Lela pulled the car out onto the main highway, Tucker tried to relax and enjoy the fresh air. Lela had cranked up the radio and was singing *Chicken Fried* full blast. He couldn't look away from her. She was so beautiful, full of life, fun. He could watch her all day and never get sick of the sight.

An old Dixie Chicks song played next and Lela turned up the volume even more. There would be no conversation until they reached their destination.

"Where to?" she asked at last, though she was seemingly content to just keep going until they reached the border.

"Beyer's Creek."

She gave him a sexy sideways glance that sent too much blood rushing to his cock. He should have picked somewhere else, somewhere public. Taking her to their old make-out place was going to distract him from his goal. And that couldn't happen. He needed to come clean to Lela, to explain his reasons for returning to Maris.

His future was still uncertain. And because he'd been unable to resist his feelings for her, he'd dragged her right into the well of what-the-hell-do-I-do-now with him.

He'd been trapped in limbo for months and guilt over putting Lela in the same boat had kept him up all night.

Lela pulled the car into the same parking nook they'd created years ago when they'd driven here after football games or summer picnics. Hormones had ruled the day and he recalled their rush to get away from everyone, to come together, under the foliage of the live oaks.

Shutting off the engine, she turned to face him. "Wanna take a walk?"

He nodded. "Yeah." They got out of the car and he took her hand as they traversed down the rocky path that led to the creek.

"I haven't been here since high school," she admitted.

Tucker was surprised. "Really? You always said it was your favorite place in Maris."

She shrugged, trying for casual, but failing. "It was our spot."

Tucker realized he wasn't the only one who'd been struggling to find a happy ending. "Why haven't you ever gotten married?"

She gave him a confused grin. "Where did that question come from?"

"I'm curious. I mean, back in school your master life plan was college, marriage, kids." He didn't bother to add that the dream had also included him.

"I haven't found the right guy yet."

It was a short, abrupt answer that said his question had bugged her. She punctuated her response by turning away from him and sitting on a large rock near the water. She tugged off her sandals. "So I'll ask you the same," she said once she was barefoot. "According to the tabloids, you're pretty high on the list of eligible bachelors. Where's your wedding ring?"

Tucker suddenly understood her aggravation. He didn't like the question any more than she did, but he'd come here for honesty, to open the dialogue and say what needed to be said. "I don't find it easy to trust the people around me. Once you achieve some level of fame and wealth, you start to question everyone's motives."

"Sounds lonely."

Lela always got it.

"The thing is, life has a way of fooling you, making you think you're content. Then, just when you believe you've got your shit together, it pulls the rug out and you realize you've been living in a fool's paradise and nothing is what you thought."

She tilted her head. "Very insightful. And completely cryptic. Care to explain?"

Leave it to her to call him out for bullshit. "You live alone long enough and you start to think it's normal, that it's what you want. I've spent years strutting around, gloating about being a confirmed bachelor, like it was some conscious decision I'd made."

"It wasn't?"

He shook his head. "No. Apparently, you're right. I'm lonely."

"Apparently?" she asked, amusement in her voice.

"I didn't realize it until I saw you again."

She bit her lower lip, but didn't reply.

"I sort of fell apart when my mom died, L.B. It took me a long time to come to grips with the fact she wasn't there. And the worst part was when I left Maris, I turned my back on all my friendships and pushed you away at the same time. So I did all the healing alone, on my own. I sort of forgot what it was like to have someone to talk to—who wasn't a shrink—who cared about me."

"I wish I'd known, Tuck."

He cupped her cheek fondly. "It wouldn't have mattered. I was in a dark place. I'm glad you weren't there. I don't think this...what's going on right now...would be happening if you had been."

"But you needed someone and I just let you drive away."

"No, L.B. As bad as things were then, they're worse today. I need you now."

She clasped his hand and pulled him to the rock. They sat on the large flat surface together. "I think the last time we sat on this rock was the day you told me you'd gotten a full ride to Texas A&M."

He smiled at the memory. "God. I don't know how you could stand being around me senior year. Between that and winning the state championship, I walked around like I was ten feet tall and bulletproof."

"Oh yeah. You were a cocky asshole, no two ways about it."

He laughed at her jest.

"But you were so happy. Ready to take on the world. And I felt lucky to be sitting beside you as you started your climb. Do you remember what we said?"

Tucker thought back to that day, recalling all the promises they'd made, all the dreams they'd conjured. "I was going to go pro—traveling with the team during season and living in Maris with you in the off months. You were going to get a job as a teacher and raise our kids. We were going to beat all the odds and live happily ever after."

"No. Not that part. Those words were said to give us some sense of control and security when we knew full well none of that would happen. There's nothing scarier than an uncertain future."

Tucker winced, trying to turn his head in hopes that Lela wouldn't see it. He wasn't quick enough.

"Tell me what's going on, Tuck. All of it."

He swallowed heavily. "I told you about the headaches."

She nodded.

"I've had quite a few concussions during my career. Enough that I'm skirting a line." He ran his hand through his hair, trying to find the words, some way to explain it to her without falling apart. His chest was tight, his lungs seizing.

"Just say it. Quick. Like ripping off a Band-Aid."

"I think this is the year my team has a real shot at the Super Bowl. That's been my dream ever since I was old enough to hold a ball. We've come so close the past few seasons, but something always happened to knock us out. This year...God, this year, we're going the distance. I can feel it in my gut."

"But," she prodded, when he paused too long.

"But if I go back and take another hard hit to the head, I'm facing permanent brain damage."

She reared back and though she tried to hide it, he heard her slight gasp. He waited for her response nervously.

"So you have to choose? Have the doctors cleared you to play?"

He nodded. "It's my choice."

"What are you going to do?"

He frowned. "I don't know. I was hiding out at my beach house in Turks and Caicos, trying to figure it out when Joel called about Coach. Before I could think about what I was doing, I was on a plane here. The last place I ever thought I'd step foot again."

Tucker turned away when he saw pain creep into her eyes. She loved Maris and he hurt her every time he claimed to hate the place, to want to escape. He didn't face her when he confessed, "I should never have stayed away so long."

"I don't blame you."

Her words surprised him. He glanced over to see her looking down at her lap, nervously twisting a thin silver ring on her pinky. "You don't?"

"The Maris you grew up in wasn't the same as mine. My childhood was pretty much idyllic. Yours was…"

He filled in the blank for her. "Less than ideal."

"I know how much you loved your mother."

He swallowed heavily, trying to dislodge the lump forming there. "I miss her every single day. Football saved me, L.B. I built my life with that game as the foundation. Without it…"

Lela lifted her head, forced Tucker to hold her gaze. "Without it, you rebuild." Her words were strong. Sure. "Football is only a small part of you, Tucker. You're so much more than just that game."

His mother used to say the same. She told him he had a talent and he should hone it, let it take him wherever he wanted to go. But she also reminded him that there was more to life than football.

Love.

There was love. And friendship. And home.

"Do you remember what we said the last time we sat here?" Lela repeated her earlier question.

"We swore that no matter where life took us, we'd always love each other, always care."

She smiled. "I didn't break that promise."

He leaned forward, pressed his forehead against hers, needing to be close to her. "Neither did I, L.B."

They kissed; a quick, chaste touch of the lips.

Tucker sighed. "I don't know what the hell to do."

She pulled away from him, studying his face. "I can't tell

you what to choose, Tucker. Only you know what will make you happy."

"I love that game. So damn much. I've never given much thought to what happens after."

"Really? No plans beyond football?"

He shrugged. "I'm making a lot of money. I hired a smart financial advisor who's made some really good investments for me. I don't have to work another day in my life if I don't want to."

She shook her head. "You see? This is what's wrong with the world. I'm teaching five-year-olds how to read and write and think for themselves and I'm struggling to pay my bills every month. Meanwhile..."

She stopped, looking somewhat chagrinned.

"Go ahead. Finish what you were going to say."

"No, I—"

He finished her rant for her. "Meanwhile, I make millions just throwing a football."

Lela crinkled her nose. "I'm sorry. I have a bad habit of opening my mouth and inserting my foot."

Tucker wrapped his arm around her shoulders. "I could never do what you do. And I do think teachers are grossly underpaid, while athletes are seriously overpaid. Not that I'm complaining about that disparity, mind you. I'm on the good side of the equation."

She elbowed him in the stomach as he laughed.

Then her face sobered. "Are you sorry you came back?"

He shook his head. "No. Not at all. Maris has forced me to open my eyes and look at some things I was trying not to see."

"Like?"

"Like...I should have called you back. Answered those letters. Sent you an email. I've thought about you a million times since I left. Regretted the way it ended. The way I hurt you."

She frowned. "The way you hurt me? Tucker, *I* was the raving lunatic. I was the one who said all those hateful things. I can't tell you how sorry I am. How much I wish I could take it all back. You'd just lost your mother and I...God...I was so selfish, so wrapped up in my own emotions."

He took her face in his hands. "You didn't do anything wrong, Lela."

She snorted. "I did it *all* wrong."

He smiled. "So basically I've spent twelve years regretting my actions, while you've done the same?"

She nodded.

"What a waste of time."

She clasped his wrists, then turned her head to place a soft kiss to his palm. "Time to let it all go?"

"I just did."

Lela giggled. "Me too."

Tucker kissed her again, harder this time. His emotions were so close to the surface, he felt raw. Lela always knew how to soothe his pain, take it away.

She answered the kiss, opening her mouth, her tongue touching his. She ran her hands over his chest, stroking the muscles, stoking the fire.

Tucker pulled away briefly, tugging his t-shirt over his head. He needed her hands on his skin.

Lela wasted no time taking advantage of the chest he'd bared for her. Her lips latched onto one of his nipples as her hands slid around him, nails scoring a path down his back. She understood the pleasure to be found in little pains. He wondered how they'd failed to recognize these shared needs all those years ago.

He found the hem of her shirt and lifted it off. Then he went to work stripping away her bra and shorts as well.

Lela's hands fumbled with the button on his jeans, struggling to free him. He stood and took care of the business himself.

Tucker used their divested clothing to form a blanket of sorts on the soft grass near the bank of the creek. He eased her onto it, then came over her.

Lela's legs were parted, ready for him. He accepted the invitation, sliding into her wet warmth. She was tight, hot. His.

Passion ruled the day as finesse was tossed aside. Tucker's needs were simple. Fuck or die.

Lela had given him her heart, her trust, her body. Her past and her present.

He needed to prove to her he'd given her the same. Over and over, he pounded into her, Lela's hips tilting up to meet him, her pussy clenching each time he retreated, as if her body resented him trying to leave.

"Tucker. God. Harder."

Her words, her cries of pleasure, drove him on. There was nothing he wouldn't give her. Nothing.

The world around them disappeared, shrank down to simply her and him and the need to come.

When his climax struck, Lela was right there with him. They jerked together, Tucker pressing to the hilt and holding, filling her.

He twisted, falling to her side in the grass. His chest rose and fell rapidly and he felt as if he could lie here, just like this, and sleep for a week.

After several minutes, Lela rolled toward him, wrapping her arm around his waist and resting her head on his chest. He soaked up her warmth, the closeness. There was no need for words between them.

Tucker closed his eyes—just to rest them—then opened them much later, surprised to find Lela dressed and sitting on the bank, her feet in the water.

"How long was I asleep?"

She turned around at the sound of his voice and smiled. "About an hour."

"I'm sorry."

She waved his apology away. "You were clearly tired. You needed sleep."

He pushed himself up and reached for his shorts. Once he was dressed, he joined her on the bank, dipping his feet into the water. Then he noticed the pensive look on her face.

"You okay?"

"Yeah." Her reply came too quickly and he recognized it as a lie. Unfortunately he knew what was bothering her. It was the same thing that occupied his thoughts 24/7. He longed to pull her into his arms and promise her everything would be okay, but he couldn't say those words. Not yet.

"So we're good?" she asked at last. "The past is dead and buried?"

"No." The word came out unbidden, without thought. "Not all of it." As he spoke, he realized there was still one more conversation to have. It was time to lay all the past hurts to rest.

"What's left?"

"I need to go see my dad. Will you come with me?"

"Yes."

Chapter Nine

Tucker stood beside the hospital bed, watching his father as he slept. His dad had been placed in the psychiatric ward once they'd stitched up his wound. Lela stood near the doorway, trying to give Tucker privacy. He appreciated her willingness to come with him. This conversation was going to be tough.

He struggled to make this version of his dad match the one that had haunted his nightmares for so long. The bandaged man in the bed looked tired, weak, old. The dad he'd grown up with had been a bear of a man, a bully who'd used his size and booming voice to intimidate anyone who dared to cross him.

Tucker glanced at Lela. She gave him an encouraging smile.

Bending forward, he quietly said, "Dad."

His father's eyes opened slowly, blinking rapidly against the bright sun shining through the window.

"Tucker?"

"Yeah. It's me."

The old man looked confused for a moment before an all-too-familiar scowl appeared. "What are you doing here?"

Tucker fought to remain calm, though he was sorely tempted to simply walk out of the room. Suddenly, this visit was starting to feel like a big mistake. "I wanted to see how you were doing."

Dad scoffed. "Bet you're sorry my hand slipped."

The anger lacing the hate-filled comment sliced Tucker like a knife. "No. I'm not."

His response seemed to catch his dad off-guard. The old man recovered quickly. "Come to see if I'm crazy? If I've gone off the deep end? Did that asshole doctor call you to come have me committed? I'm not going to the fucking loony bin."

"The doctor didn't call me."

His father fell silent. Tucker could see how much even this short conversation was zapping the man's strength. His dad's eyes appeared heavy and he struggled to hold them open.

Dad had been in the hospital several days, and according to the doctor, they had him sedated to counteract the effects of his withdrawals from alcohol. His dad was facing some rough times.

"Where's Wanda?" Tucker asked. He'd been curious about the woman his father was currently living with.

"Left me. Said she was tired of all my drama. Stupid bitch."

Tucker's respect for Wanda rose. He would have called his father to task for his rude comment, but his words were becoming more slurred, his eyes closing more often. It was clear nothing was going to come from this visit. His dad was too out of it and there was too much bad blood between them. Tucker was certain they'd never be able to have a conversation that didn't consist of malice, blame, and distrust.

Maybe it was time to cut his losses.

"I can see you're tired. I'll let you sleep."

Tucker was halfway to the door when his father's voice stopped him. "I know you blame me for your mom's death, Tucker."

Tucker wasn't sure how to respond. His father suddenly seemed more alert and the hard edge to his face had softened. Tucker longed to rail at the man, to curse him and the injustice. His mom hadn't deserved to die.

Before he could say anything, his father spoke again. "I blame me too. It was my fault. I haven't slept a peaceful night since she died. I wish I'd been the one killed in that crash. That I could go back and change that night. I wish it more than you'll ever know."

The remorseful look on his father's face was foreign to him.

"You can't change it. None of it." Tucker could hear the impassiveness in his voice, surprised by how little emotion this conversation was provoking. He'd been prepared for anger. God knew there had been enough of that running through Tucker since the night of the accident, maybe even before then. He'd spent the better part of his childhood as a punching bag for his dear old dad.

Yet now, as he looked at the broken man in the bed, he couldn't summon any emotion stronger than pity. Maybe it was because the man lying in this bed wasn't his father. Not really.

That honor fell to Coach. He'd been the man who'd tried to teach Tucker the difference between right and wrong, who had encouraged him to get good grades, had helped him shape his future and been there when his mother died.

"None of it matters anymore, Dad."

His dad shrugged, his eyes slowly closing once more, his words little more than a mumble. "I still wanted you to know."

Tucker watched his father give in to sleep. Then he grasped Lela's hand and they left.

"You okay?" she asked.

He nodded. "Yeah. I am." As he said the words, he realized he meant them. "I used to worry about becoming like my father."

She stopped walking to look at him. "What? No way. You'll never be like him."

He grinned and gave her a quick kiss on the cheek. "It's not completely unheard of. Children of abusive parents following the pattern."

"You're a good man, Tucker."

He appreciated her defense of him. "He's going to drink himself into an early death and die alone, isn't he? There won't be anyone around who gives a shit."

Lela tried to counteract the truth of his words. "Maybe he can shake free of the alcohol. There's always a chance—"

"No. Don't. Don't do that."

"Do what?"

"Pretend he can change. That hope, that belief in a fairytale ending is what kept my mother hanging on. I think it's better to accept the reality. That man has been an addict for over thirty years. If he wanted to change, he would have done it by now."

"If I concede to that, will you accept what I said as true? You're not like him, Tuck. Not by a long shot."

He chuckled. "So it's a draw? We're both right?"

She nodded, her pleased grin causing his cock to twitch. Jesus. He was starting to accept he'd never get enough of her.

Satisfied with his concession, she started walking once more.

However, Tucker couldn't shake the feeling he'd only just broken free of his father's fate. He had been following in his dad's footsteps in other ways, holding people at arm's length since leaving Maris. His mother's death had broken something in him. Something he hadn't realized was missing until he'd returned to Maris and experienced it again.

He'd eschewed friendships—never bothering to form the close camaraderie with his current teammates that he'd shared with his high school buddies.

He'd convinced himself he didn't need a family, but talking to Coach again, feeling that same protective brotherly instinct emerge whenever he was around Lorelie, proved he *did* need it. Not only that. He longed for it.

Finally…love. He'd chalked it up as a weak emotion, unnecessary. He had fooled himself into thinking sex was a much neater, easier arrangement because it wasn't messy or painful or long-term. Sex didn't require a commitment, didn't force him to reveal parts of himself he was ashamed of.

Lela had shown him exactly how stupid that idea had been. After years of hiding his true nature, she'd allowed him to be the man he was, flaws and all, without judgment. She loved him. Unconditionally.

And suddenly, just like that, the obvious answer appeared.

"Want to go back to my place?" Lela asked as they reached the car.

He shook his head. "Nope. Call your girlfriends. Get a group together. I want to take my girl out. Show her off."

Lela laughed until she realized he was serious. "Really?"

"Tell them to meet us at Cruisers."

Lela leaned back in the booth and enjoyed the warmth provided by the wine and Tucker's scandalously close proximity.

She hadn't realized how unhappy he'd been until now, when he was completely, unabashedly joyful. His good humor was infectious, drawing people over to talk to him, to ask for autographs and photos. Even now, he was signing a cocktail napkin for the waitress's ten-year-old son.

She hadn't seen Tucker in "star" mode since his return home. While he'd been back in Maris for three weeks, it was obvious the hometown people had picked up on his aloof mood and kept their distance. It was one of the things Lela loved about this small town. Folks were good at reading each other and they respected limits.

Tonight, Tucker was open and laughing. He'd spent several minutes talking football with a bunch of guys by the bar. He'd promised Gladys Lacey a signed football for her grandson and politely turned down at least seven invitations to dance, claiming he was saving all his dances for his girl.

Lela liked to think she wasn't as immature as some giddy schoolgirl, but she felt herself flush every time he referred to her as "his". What would she give to hold on to that position permanently?

He'd thrown her for a loop earlier when he'd discussed the seriousness of his injuries. While he seemed fine, carefree and happy, she understood the turmoil he was suffering.

What would she say if he told her he was returning to the team? How could she watch him walk away knowing he might not return the same...or return at all?

She wished she could share the same cheerfulness he was feeling. She was trying to put on her game face, to hide her concerns. Lela wouldn't dim Tucker's happiness for anything in the world. Especially considering she'd seen him laugh more tonight than he had during his entire visit home.

While she'd been calling their friends to invite them out, Tucker had phoned his accountant and made sure all of his dad's hospital bills were covered. Tucker genuinely seemed to have turned some corner tonight and she was happy for him.

But she couldn't shake loose of the fear, the sense of helplessness. He hadn't been home long. Did she really have the right to make any demands of him? To plead with him not to risk his life for a game?

Tucker jerked her from her thoughts as he reached for her hand. "Dance with me."

A fast-paced song was starting. "To this?"

He nodded. "My Texas two-step is a little rusty."

She laughed. "Well we can't have that, can we?"

They hurried to the floor and joined the throng of dancers, Tucker holding her tightly, spinning her so fast her head spun as Sara Evans sang about the *Suds in the Bucket*. He was strong enough to lead her through the steps, leaving Lela to merely hang on for dear life.

"You're a liar," she said loudly, her words coming out breathlessly.

He gave her a quizzical look.

"You're not rusty at all."

Tucker laughed and she practically went airborne on the next twirl. Fortunately, Tucker didn't release her immediately as the song ended and a slow George Strait ballad started. Instead, he held her tight to his chest, letting her catch her breath, helping hold her up as her dizziness faded.

She lifted her face as the final strains of *I Cross My Heart* played. Lela decided right then and there, she and Tucker had "a song" when he leaned closer and kissed her. Time ceased to exist as they continued swaying on the dance floor, even as a faster song began.

She vaguely recognized the sound of laughter, of people glancing their way, but Tucker didn't seek to end the dance. Or the kiss. Or the roaming of his hands when they drifted down her back to cup her ass.

Once they parted, Tucker winked. "Good thing Principal Whitacre isn't here. He'd nail us for PDA."

She laughed. "Oh, I think you'd have more to worry about from my dad than just a little after-school detention if he was watching us right now."

Tucker sobered up. "Oh damn. Did I fuck things up with your folks when I left? I always thought they liked me back in high school."

"My parents like you just fine. In fact, my mom has been after me to invite you for Sunday dinner ever since she heard you were back in town."

Tucker chuckled. "Dinner with the folks, huh?" He flashed her a horrified look intended to make her laugh, which she did, even though she couldn't help but notice he'd managed to dodge the invitation.

Maybe he didn't intend to be in Maris many more Sundays.

"Hey, Tucker."

They both looked over to see Walt standing by the pool table, waving. "I need a partner for this next game."

Tucker gave her a quick kiss on the cheek, then walked over to play.

Lela returned to their table to join Lorelie, who was sitting alone. None of the other girls had been able to make it out on such short notice. Lela followed Lorelie's gaze and noticed Oakley, Joel, and Sadie in what looked like a heated dispute across the room. "What do you think that's about?"

Lorelie shrugged. "No idea."

"Think we should go over there?"

Lorelie shook her head. "Nope. As a wise old man once said, 'It's not my circus. They're not my monkeys.'"

"You realize Facebook isn't a wise old man."

Lorelie chuckled, though she looked more tired than entertained. "It should be. God knows everybody quotes it enough."

"You okay?"

Lorelie reached for her purse. "Yeah. I think I'm going to head home."

"What? Have you ever left a bar before last call?"

Searching for her keys, Lorelie said, "Between the drama taking place over there with the ranch hands, and you and Tucker making out like the plane's going down, I'm starting to feel like a sixth wheel."

Lela instantly felt guilty. She and Tucker had been acting like a couple of teenagers on their first date, groping at each other more than was appropriate. "I'm sorry."

Lorelie waved her off. "Do *not* apologize. I'm happy as shit for you. You're exactly where you're supposed to be. I'm just feeling grumpy and sorry for myself. Everybody in this town seems to be having great sex while I'm still making love to my vibrator every night. If I don't leave right now, I'm going to pick up the next available redneck who looks my way and the only things that will come from that are lackluster sex and a lot of self-loathing come morning. Been there, done that, burned the t-shirt."

"You okay to get home?" Lela was worried about her friend, but she knew Lorelie was right. She'd had to build her friend back up after one too many of those regretted nights.

"Yep. Only had water tonight." Lorelie leaned forward and gave her a quick kiss on the cheek. "Tucker's perfect for you. He always has been."

With that, her friend made a quick exit, not bothering to say goodbye to anyone else.

Lela's heart gave a little pang as she considered Lorelie's comment.

Perfect or not, there was still a very good chance this go-round with Tucker would end exactly like the last. Only this time, the goodbye might be forever.

Chapter Ten

Tucker parked his car in front of Coach's house two days later, a spring in his step as he got out of the car and met Lela at the passenger door. He gave her a quick kiss. He was going to relieve Walt and Jack, taking a shift on the ranch, while Lela and Lorelie packed up all the sweets they'd baked for the sale and drove them to the fire hall.

"I'll see you later this evening at the yard party," he murmured when their lips parted.

"Save me a dance," she teased.

"I'm saving them all."

"You can give the Texas two-steps to someone else," she joked. Then she gave him a saucy wink and started for the house. She stopped when the sounds of shouting came from the barn.

"Help me! Oh God! Help!" The fear in Lorelie's voice sent a chill through Tucker's blood. He took off at a sprint, Lela on his heels. They nearly collided with Joel and Oakley, who were rounding the corner, heading the same direction.

When they entered the dim building, Tucker felt a sense

of panic as he spotted Lorelie bent over Coach. He was sitting with his back against a stall, looking pasty and far too weak.

"What happened?" Tucker asked.

"Is it his heart?" Joel's question came on top of Tucker's.

Tucker glanced at his friend and saw he'd already pulled out his cell phone.

"If you dial 911 on that thing, Joel, it's the last thing you'll ever do on this ranch." The strength in Coach's voice made them all pause.

Lela knelt next to the older man. "Are you okay?"

Coach nodded. "I'm fine. Do you mind helping me convince my girl? She's freaking out."

Tucker's gaze traveled to Lorelie and he had to admit Coach had a point. Lorelie was white as a ghost, her hands visibly shaking.

"I'm freaking out because you scared the shit out of me."

Coach narrowed his eyes. "Language, young lady."

Oakley chuckled, but the sound was cut short when Lorelie threw him a venomous glare.

Tucker wasn't able to laugh either. He was in the same boat as Lorelie, freaking out. Big time. "What happened?" he repeated.

Coach didn't have much more color in his face than Lorelie, his complexion pale with a thin line of sweat at his brow. He also seemed to be slightly out of breath. "I got tired of playing invalid in the house."

Joel slapped his dirty hands against his jeans. "Goddammit, Coach. I told you this morning, we got things under control."

"Yeah. I know that's what you said, but no work on a ranch is ever wasted. I didn't feel like sitting in that damn kitchen, bagging up cookies anymore. Figured I'd muck out a stall or two."

Lorelie added, "When I couldn't find him in the house, I came out here. He collapsed just as I walked in."

Coach rolled his eyes. "'Collapsed' is hardly the word I'd use. I just got a little tired. Thought I'd sit down for a second."

His daughter didn't buy that version of the story. "You went down, Dad. Hard." She looked at Tucker. "That's when I yelled for help."

"Overreaction," her father muttered. Coach tried to rise, but it was obvious his strength was completely gone.

Tucker and Oakley quickly stepped forward, helping him to his feet. Tucker kept a strong grip on the older man's arm as they left the barn and headed for the house.

"Joel, call Dr. Griffith," Lorelie said as they crossed the yard.

Coach stopped walking and turned to Joel. "Do not make that call."

Joel started tapping out the number.

"Did you hear me?" Coach asked.

Joel nodded. "Yep. But I'm way more afraid of Lorelie, and since *you* raised her, you're just going to have to deal with it."

Coach shook his head, but clearly he didn't have it in him to fight. Once they got him back to the living room, Lela went to the kitchen for a glass of water.

Lorelie perched herself in front of her father, sitting on the edge of the coffee table. "You can't do that again, Dad." She seemed only somewhat calmer.

Now that he was back inside, some color had begun to return to Coach's cheeks. "Lori, honey. I'm not a man who can sit on his ass and let others do his work. You know that."

"Coach, we came home to Maris to help. We don't mind doing the work. As long as it takes." Tucker was only just starting to breathe easier himself. Coach was the closest thing he'd ever had to a father and after all the turmoil and pain of the last year, Tucker wasn't sure he could get through what came next without the man.

"Not a question of what *you* mind," Coach replied. "It's what *I* mind. I hate this. All of it. I'm tired of being useless. Helpless."

Tucker could relate to Coach's frustration. It had been unbearable to sit in the locker room during the last playoff game of the season, watching his team struggle, then fail to get the win.

"Coach—" Tucker started, but Lorelie cut him off before he could continue.

"I don't care. Suck it up."

Lela had returned from the kitchen with water and Jack and Walt in tow. From the concerned looks on their faces, it was clear Lela had filled them in. "Lorelie," Lela said, frowning at her friend.

Lorelie ignored the tone of reproof from Lela. "I mean it, Dad. I know this is hard for you. It's hard for me too. And I know you hate sitting around. I've tried to come up with things for you to do around here to keep you from going stir-crazy."

Coach's face softened a bit. "I know that, sweetheart, it's just—"

"No." Lorelie wouldn't back down. "It's *just* nothing. You don't get it. I don't want to live in a world where you don't exist. You mean everything to me." Her voice broke.

Tucker felt his throat clog in the face of the absolute fear in Lorelie's eyes. Her words rang true for him too. Even through the years Tucker had been away, Coach had still remained an important part of his life.

"Lori." Coach cupped her cheek.

"I need you to swallow your damn pride, just this once. Do what the doctor says, rest, take time to recuperate. Do what you have to do to get better. I love you, Daddy. Please. Will you just do it for me?"

Tucker swallowed heavily as Coach reached out, Lorelie curling against him for a hug. "I'm sorry, baby. I'm so sorry. I'm going to be okay. I promise. I'll do whatever it takes."

Tears flowed down Lorelie's cheeks and it occurred to Tucker that he had never seen her cry.

After a few moments, Lorelie seemed to recall the rest of them were there. She quickly batted away her tears, the same tough façade Tucker had watched her wear like a coat of armor falling back into place. She turned away from them, attempting to compose herself.

Joel must have realized she was embarrassed, so he stepped closer to Coach. "When the doctor gets here, maybe we can ask him for a list of do's and don'ts. And I don't think it would hurt for you to get out of the house more, do some work in the barn."

Lorelie scowled, but Joel ignored her. "I just think mucking out stalls was a bad place to start. We've got some harnesses that need cleaning, stuff like that you can do sitting down. Nothing like the smell of manure to get a man back on the right track, right, Coach?"

Coach chuckled. "I do like the smell of horse shit."

Everyone laughed as Joel looked at Lorelie, trying to make amends. "I don't imagine Doc would have a problem with Coach doing stuff like that, do you?"

Lorelie shook her head. "No. That sounds good."

Coach gave Joel an appreciative smile.

"And as for the other stuff," Oakley added, "you gotta believe it when I say we got this."

"I'll never be able to thank you boys for all you've done for me. I'm not sure what I did to deserve such devotion, but—"

"Not sure?" Tucker interjected. "Damn, Coach. You were

there for us when even our own folks weren't. There's nothing we wouldn't do for you."

Coach blinked rapidly and Tucker realized his old coach was fighting back tears of his own. "Thank you, son."

Lorelie stood. Lela nodded her head toward the kitchen. "Want some help packing up the cookies for the sale?"

Lorelie wiped her eyes. "Sure. That'd be nice." She looked at Jack and Walt. "Y'all mind helping us load it in the car?"

The four of them left the room as Joel and Oakley excused themselves to head back to work.

Tucker walked closer to Coach. "You sure you're okay?"

Coach sighed. "Yeah. It's like I said. Helpless doesn't sit easy on my shoulders."

"I get it, Coach."

Coach studied his face. "I suppose you do."

Tucker gave him a sympathetic grin as he pointed to the couch and then said, "So you're staying put?"

Coach nodded, then glanced toward the door Lela just left. "Yep. And it looks like you are too. Finally ready to admit it, huh?"

Tucker narrowed his eyes. "Are you saying I knew when I came back to Maris, I was coming home to stay?"

"I think that's *why* you came home, Tucker. As much as you claim to hate this place, it's home. You've got family here who love you."

Family.

They may not be blood, but there was no denying Coach and Lorelie were his family. And he sure as hell wanted to make it legal as far as Lela's relationship status was concerned. "Yeah. I guess I do." He didn't bother to hide his big ass smile. He felt good.

"What's Lela think about all this?"

That dimmed his smile a bit. "Um..."

"Did you tell Lela yet?" Coach asked.

Tucker shook his head. "No. Not yet. Truth is…until you just said it, I wasn't a hundred percent sure I was staying."

Coach rolled his eyes. "Glad to know I'm not the only idiot in the room."

Tucker laughed. "You're right. I'm acting like a jackass. It's time I tell the woman I love that we're running a new play."

Coach chuckled. "You might want to say it in a way the woman will actually understand. She's never been much of a fan of the game. Just of you."

Tucker walked toward Coach and reached out. Coach took his hand to shake it, but it was Tucker's turn to lean down and give the man a hug. "Thanks, Coach."

"Get out of here, you lunatic. Go propose to the girl."

Propose.

Tucker was quitting the NFL. He was moving back to Maris.

Tucker walked to the kitchen to find Lela. "You got a minute?"

"Sure."

He took Lela's hand and dragged her to the porch. He suddenly felt nervous. He needed some air. Needed to set some things straight. Right now.

"What is it?"

He didn't bother to stop, but instead kept walking, propelling her toward the car. "I need to talk to you."

She nodded slowly. "Okay. Sure."

Tucker struggled to understand her sudden stiff tone, but he was still too shaken by what had just happened with Coach. He felt as if a ton of bricks had fallen on his head.

He climbed into the driver's seat and they rode in silence. Tucker had intended to take them to Beyer's Creek, but his attention was diverted when he spotted a sign.

"The Potter place is for sale?"

His question seemed to jerk Lela out of her own deep thoughts. "Yeah. The sign's been up there for months, Tuck."

He considered that. Typically he came to the ranch from the other direction. The only time he'd gone this way since his return was when Lela had driven him to the creek. He'd spent that entire drive enjoying the sight of her singing along to the radio, her hair blowing in the breeze.

He'd missed the sign.

"Where are they moving to?" he asked.

"Oh, gosh. You don't know. Mr. Potter died a couple years ago." She paused as if he'd need time to absorb that news, but the truth was Tucker could barely remember the man...or his wife.

When he didn't respond, she continued, "Mrs. Potter wants to move to Chicago to be closer to their daughter. Do you remember Emma? She was a few years younger than us."

"Vaguely." *Not at all.*

"Well, she got married and she's having a baby. Mrs. Potter is dying to be a hands-on grandma. And while their property is pretty small by Maris standards, it was too much for her to handle on her own."

Tucker stopped the car, pulling up beside the Potter fence.

"What are you doing?" Lela asked.

He didn't bother to answer. Instead he got out of the car and walked over to her door, opening it. She took the hand he proffered without question and let him lead her to the white picket fence.

She laughed when he climbed over it, but didn't put up a fuss when he gestured for her to follow him. "Are you trying to get us arrested for trespassing?"

He shook his head. "Nope."

"Good thing. Because Mrs. Potter is currently at the fire

hall with my mom making potato salad for the chicken dinners."

Tucker knew she was joking, but his heart was racing and his hands had suddenly gone clammy. Jesus. He was known for having the coolest head in the NFL, but right now, he was so nervous, he could almost taste the emotion.

"Lela—"

Lela raised her hand to cut him off. "No. You don't have to say it, Tuck. I already know."

His brow furrowed. "Know what, L.B.?"

"That training camp starts next week. I Googled it."

He frowned as the impact of what she was saying hit him. She thought he was leaving. "Listen, Lela—"

"I didn't go into this with my eyes closed, Tucker. They were just as open as my heart."

He smiled, touched by her honesty. Lela never hesitated to put it all out there, taking chances even if she did face heartbreak. She simply gave it all, withholding nothing.

"That's what I want to talk about."

She continued speaking as if he'd said nothing. "Twelve years ago, I asked for a long-distance relationship. You were right to say no. We were young and we had a lot of growing up to do. The thing is...my feelings for you haven't changed."

"Mine haven't either."

She reached out and clasped his hand. "If you need to go back..." Her words faded, but he didn't have to hear the rest. She thought he was leaving and telling him she understood. She wouldn't stand in his way.

For some reason, that idea rubbed him wrong—then Tucker saw tears in her eyes. "If I go back and take another hit, I risk serious brain damage, L.B. Maybe even death."

She sniffled. "God. Don't you think I know that?"

It was his turn to speak. He needed the answer to a question. "Do you want me to go back?"

She shook her head. "No. But that's not my call."

He cupped her cheeks. "I'm making it your call."

"What?"

"Tell me what to do."

"Hell no. No way. Tucker—"

"Just listen to me. I want you to forbid me to go back. The way Lorelie just put her foot down with Coach. I've spent my entire adult life alone without a single person to give a shit if I live or die."

"That's not true. I've always cared about you."

"I know that...now. Dammit, L.B. I don't want that fucking Super Bowl ring. I thought I did, but the fact is it's just a meaningless, inanimate object. It won't make me happy. Won't make me feel less alone. I want what Coach has. People who love him, who rally around him when he needs them."

"I'm not going to forbid you to go back, Tucker, because I don't have to. I can see you've already made that decision for yourself. And I'm glad. But I will say this. I would be utterly devastated and lost without you. I love you."

"I love you too." Tucker looked around, then pointed to Mrs. Potter's house. "What's that place like inside?"

"What?" She was clearly taken aback by his sudden about-face. He'd taken her from tears and proclamations of love to real estate in the blink of an eye.

He fought to keep his face impassive. "The Potter place. What's it look like inside?"

She shrugged, still struggling to switch gears. "I don't know."

"You've never been inside?"

"Yes, I have. I mean...it's nice, I guess."

"How many bedrooms?"

She laughed. "Seriously? You want to have a conversation about the Potter house? Right now?"

He nodded, unable to restrain his grin. Her exasperation was adorable.

"I have no idea," she said when it was clear he wouldn't relent. "Five, maybe six. Why?"

"I want to make sure we have enough room for our brood."

She narrowed her eyes. "Our brood?"

"Our kids. You know, eleven would give us enough to cover the football field."

She shook her head. "I'm not having eleven children. I've taught Kindergarten for eight years. We'll be lucky if I can come up with two names that haven't been ruined for me by all the demon seeds who've passed through my room in that time."

He laughed at her response, trying to decide if she was taking his comment in stride because she thought it was joke. "So is that a yes?"

She tilted her head. "Was that a sincere proposal?"

Tucker dropped down to one knee. "What can I say? I'm a quarterback. I like to get a read of the field before I throw the ball."

"And my response left you feeling confident? You realize I thought you were kidding," she said, gesturing to his pose.

He gave her a cocky grin. "Maybe so, but I'm going for broke. Throwing the Hail Mary. Marry me, Lela. Let's get hitched, buy this farm, make lots of babies, and grow old together."

Lela didn't bother to wipe away the tears suddenly streaming down her face. "That sounds completely wonderful."

Tucker stood and reached into his pocket. Lela's eyebrows rose when he pulled out a ring. He'd tucked it in there this morning. Just in case, he had thought. He'd been kidding himself right up until the moment Coach called him out for being a fool. "It was my mother's. I know it's not much. My folks were always poor and I'm not sure it will fit, but we can get it sized and add a whole bunch of diamonds to it. I'm pretty much richer than God."

Lela sniffled and giggled as he slid the ring onto her finger. It fit. "I don't need a bunch of diamonds, Tucker. It's perfect. I want to keep it just like this."

Tucker kissed her, certain he was the luckiest man on the planet.

"I should warn you," he started, realizing there was still one thing she hadn't seen since his return. "The headaches are bad. They put me in bed for days."

She narrowed her eyes. "I'm glad you've mentioned that. We're taking some of that pile of money you have and finding another specialist, the best there is. I want you to tell him all of your symptoms. No more hiding things from doctors."

He agreed. "Okay. So you want to buy this place? I sort of like the idea of having Coach and Lorelie as neighbors."

Lela studied his face. "You sure you're really okay with moving back to Maris?"

Tucker didn't even have to consider his reply. "Absolutely. Everyone I care about is here."

She smiled. "What about my house on the lake?"

"Keep it. We can spend weekends there."

Lela glanced at the Potter place. "I'd love to raise our family here with you."

Tucker picked her up and spun her as she laughed. He could see in her face that her joy rivaled his. When he put her down, he gave her a mischievous grin. "Are you sure Mrs. Potter is at the fire hall?"

She looked at him suspiciously. "Yes. Why?"

Tucker clasped her hand and pulled her toward a grove of pine trees away from the road, near the edge of the property.

"Because you and I are about to christen the first tiny piece of our new home. Then we're going to go tell our family and friends we're getting hitched. After that, we'll Texas two-step until we drop."

She laughed. "Sounds like you've got the game plan all figured out."

"Yep. So get ready, L.B.," Tucker teased. "Because I'm about to spike the ball."

Red Zone

Rancher Joel has a problem. He and his best friend, Oakley, are both hot for the same woman, sexy local bartender, Sadie. And while she's admitted an attraction to them as well, she refuses to choose between them, so...they're friend zoned.

Until a little too much champagne at a wedding reception leads to an unexpected sizzling encounter between the three of them, kicking off a no-strings affair.

However, things get complicated when it becomes clear there's nothing casual about their feelings. Add in a sensual, accidental touch between Joel and Oakley, and the threesome gives new meaning to the words "full contact."

To Mandee
*From Sunday school student to dear friend. Here's to secrets,
game nights and unexpected limo rides.*

Chapter One

Sadie Milligan was drunk. Well, okay. Maybe not *drunk* drunk, but she was definitely walking a thin line between tipsy and wasted.

Wait. Is that a thin line?

Damn weddings. They always depressed her. Not that she was unhappy for the couple who had just said their "I do's" a few hours earlier. She liked Sydney and Chas a lot and if anyone had a shot at happily ever after it was the two of them. After all, Sydney had waited for Chas as he served two terms with the military, stationed overseas in places no one wanted to fucking be. She knew Sydney was breathing a hell of a lot easier now that he was home to stay. If anyone had a shot at making it work, she figured Chas and Sydney topped the list.

Sadie did a mental eye roll. Yeah. Like she was capable of judging anyone's chances for success when it came to romance. Her batting record was a big fat zero. She'd struck out at the plate every single time. Enough times, in fact, that she'd decided to take herself out of that particular game. She wasn't destined for a forever kind of relationship. So she'd just settle for sex.

"That's a dangerous grin." Joel Rodriguez, the living and breathing embodiment of tall, dark and handsome, walked up and handed her another glass of champagne. It was his fault—as well as Oakley's—that she was three sheets to the wind. They'd been plying her with wine all night.

"I'm trying to pick out my hookup for the evening. Isn't that what wedding receptions are all about? Getting toasted and maudlin and desperately reaching out for some potential love match only to wake up naked the next morning in a strange bed, hungover and filled with regret."

Joel's brows creased. "Are you serious?"

At the same time, his best friend Oakley stumbled next to her and said, "Did I hear someone say 'hookup'?"

Sadie laughed as she tried for the gazillionth time to figure out how in the hell the two guys in front of her managed to remain friends. They were as different as tequila and water. Not that she'd mind a drink of either from time to time.

Oakley was just her brand of tequila, wild and uninhibited. She'd enjoy getting a buzz with him between the sheets. And, of course, after that, she could chug a gallon of Joel's refreshing, soothe-you-straight-to-the-soul water. Joel was the rock and Oakley the roll in their friendship. Somehow, it worked.

But Sadie wouldn't indulge in either. Both men had made their interest in her known, but she had no desire to come between them. They were closer than best friends, more like brothers. And she wasn't going to have the bad karma of messing up something like that riding on her head for all of eternity.

"Sorry, Oak. Neither one of you guys is even on my radar," she lied. She'd lived in Maris her entire life and, sadly, she was too familiar with the items on the sexual buffet tonight. She'd sampled more than a few already and decided they weren't worth the calories. In all honesty, Oakley and Joel were the only guys she'd consider going home with. Which was why she was sleeping alone.

Dammit.

Oakley pretended to be listening for something. "Really? Because I'm sure I heard the *beep beep beep* of a sonar getting louder when I walked over here. Wait." He raised his finger and tilted his head. "Yep. There it is again."

She raised her glass, her lips lifting as she launched into one of her typical teasing refusals. "There's not enough champagne in the world to make me want to sleep with either one of you guys."

Joel placed his hand over hers, guiding the glass to her lips. "Let's keep trying, just in case you're wrong."

She broke free of his grip, trying to ignore the tiny shiver of excitement that raced through her. Both men were always finding friendly, playful ways to touch her, be it Oakley ruffling her hair or Joel placing a protective hand at her back as they walked across the grass to find their seats at the wedding this afternoon. Worst of all was the way her body reacted every time they got too close. She found Joel's jet black hair and eyes as well as Oakley's bear-like, muscular physique irresistible. She was seriously attracted to both of them.

Fucking karma.

It was just her luck the only two guys she wanted to sleep with these days were the ones she'd sworn off.

The three of them watched the throng of wedding revelers going "just a little bit softer now" on the dance floor. They grinned when one of the more respectable, older ladies of Maris dropped a bit too low, then needed her husband to help her get back up.

"What is it about weddings that bring out the crazy in everybody?" Oakley asked.

Sadie jiggled her half-drunk glass of champagne. "I'm going to say it's the open bar."

Joel studied her glass. "How are you getting home?"

"Cab, I suppose. I caught a ride here with Lorelie and her dad, but they just cut out a little while ago. Coach was getting tired. What about you guys? I wouldn't say either of you is fit to drive." Joel and Oakley had matched her drink for drink.

Oakley shrugged. "We had the same plan as you. We were going to leave our truck here and ride back to the ranch with Coach and Lorelie, but they left too early. Guess we should have told them they were our designated drivers."

Sadie laughed. "The taxi route was always my backup. Lorelie warned me when we got here that she didn't see her dad going the distance. He couldn't sleep last night."

"Yeah," Joel said. "She told us this morning. He's chomping at the bit to get back to work and depressed that the doctor hasn't cleared him to do it yet. I suspected she'd get him out of here early. She worries about him getting too tired."

Sadie appreciated Lorelie's concerns. Like her, Sadie only had her dad left, and while they butted heads on a daily basis, Sadie didn't want to consider what life would be like without him.

Oakley finished his beer. "You mind sharing your cab with us? We can get the driver to drop you off at your apartment, then take us out to the ranch."

"We'll see," she said noncommittally. The idea of sharing the backseat of a taxi with the two muscular, sexy-as-fuck cowboys currently sporting their Sunday best would be too damn much for her champagne-induced horniness. Damn wine never failed to trigger some dirty, *dirty* needs in her. "I haven't discounted the possibility of a hookup yet."

Oakley laughed.

Joel didn't. In fact, his typically gentle smile faded as he leaned closer. "You don't want to go home with any of these yahoos. Shit. I wouldn't *let* you go home with them."

If she hadn't been so taken aback by his outright possessiveness, she would have raked him over the coals. Instead, she found herself incredibly turned on by his sudden dominant stance and dark tone. Her nipples budded and her pussy clenched.

Fucking champagne.

Oakley stopped laughing, clearly as shocked by Joel's comment as she was. The silence hovered for one beat too long as Sadie waited for the punch line. It didn't come.

"You wouldn't *let* me?" she asked when she finally found her voice.

He shook his head. "No, I wouldn't. I'm tired of pretending I'm okay with this, Sadie. Sick of watching you take guys to your bed who don't deserve you. Who won't treat you right."

"So, what's your solution, hotshot? I'm just supposed to be chaste for the rest of my life? Because I can tell you right now, I am not—"

"No," Joel cut her off. "You take me up on my offer to go out on a date."

"What about *my* offer?" Oakley asked. "Or do I fall into that yahoo category?" There was no heat behind Oakley's question. Yet.

Sadie's chest tightened. This was exactly what she'd been trying to avoid by rejecting their invitations.

"You're cool, Oak." Joel turned to look at her. "You have two decent guys standing right in front of you, Sadie. Why don't you stop messing around with losers and just pick one of us? You know we're both crazy about you."

If only it were that easy.

"I've told you a million times before. I'm not going to come between you two."

"What if we promise to accept your choice? No sore losers. I know I'd sure as hell rather see you with Oakley than any of the other guys around here."

Sadie didn't doubt for a minute Joel was sincere. But it didn't matter. He was forcing her hand. Forcing her to say something she'd so far managed to keep secret.

She wasn't rejecting them simply to protect their friendship. She was staying away because the truth was she *couldn't* choose. She was completely attracted to both of them. It would be like trying to decide between sour cream or bacon on her baked potato. Who the hell wanted one and not the other? She was a glutton—always ordering extra of both.

But there was no way in hell she'd tell the cocky bastards she was hot for them. With that knowledge, they'd probably double their efforts, her weak ass would succumb to one—or both—which would cause them to get into a fight and then she'd have that damn bad karma thing to deal with.

So, like a true coward, she dodged the issue entirely. "Actually, I don't think sex or dating or anything else is on the table for me tonight. This champagne is giving me a wicked headache. I might go ahead and get a cab. You guys can stick around and take your own chances with the crop of carbon-copy blonde beauties who've been batting their eyes at you all night."

Oakley laughed. "No thanks. We prefer our women with purple hair, tattoos, and pierced noses."

She rolled her eyes. She'd added the neon purple streak to her auburn hair as a lark because it matched the dress she was wearing to the wedding, but she kind of liked it. She was considering keeping it for a while. "Nice try. I'm still going home."

Joel nodded. "I'm done too. How about you, Oak?"

Oakley agreed he was getting tired, so Joel called for a cab. So much for her great escape. She may have managed to shut down the dating conversation, but she was still going to have to survive the ride to her place with Joel and Oakley's strong legs pressed against hers. Truth was, her morality was paper-thin and not up for that kind of test.

Neither man pressed her for an answer in terms of who she wanted to date. Thank God. So instead they continued to watch the dancers as they waited for the cab. The crowd had thinned a bit, as the older attendees had already taken their leave.

What was left was the hardcore, *came to the wedding to get wasted and dance until I drop* contingency. The playlist had drifted away from the old standards meant to get Grandma on the dance floor, to the younger bump-and-grind beats meant to get the rest of the group laid.

Laid. Damn. Sadie really wanted to get laid. It had been months. She'd never suffered this kind of dry spell. She was hitting critical mass and something had to give. She'd been hopeful about tonight...until Oakley and Joel had plopped themselves down next to her at the wedding. From that point on, they'd become her shadows. Fun shadows who brought her drinks, but shadows just the same.

None of the other guys at the reception had dared ask her to dance with Oakley and Joel next to her, looking intimidating.

And possessive.

That word kept drifting back to her. Tonight, they'd sort of claimed her. She wasn't sure what had changed, but they weren't playing that touch-and-go game with a healthy dose of proper distance they usually enjoyed. She'd expected to see them tonight, anticipated the teasing, and she'd even planned to dance with each of them a time or two. But other than that, she figured she'd be on her side of the room, scouting out the eligible bachelors, while they charmed the local hotties on the other side. After all, that's what they always did.

So why had they spent the entire evening attached to her hip, hovering around as if she was theirs? It felt as if they were calling her bluff, forcing her hand.

Or maybe it was just what Joel had said. They didn't like watching her hook up with losers. She didn't care for that herself, but what other options did she have? She was tied to Maris. Her dad owned one of the only bars in town, Cruisers. Sure, it was kind of a dive, but it was *her* dive. She was queen of the bar and when her dad was ready to retire from slinging drinks, it was going to be hers. All hers.

She loved the damn place, with its sticky dance floor, wobbly pool table, and old-fashioned cash register. Every inch of wall space was covered with sports memorabilia that her dad had collected over the years. Joel and his state champion teammates claimed a fairly large section of wall near the bar. She'd catch a glance of seventeen-year-old Joel's grin as he posed alongside his team with the huge state trophy sitting on the ground in front of them, and she had to force herself to remember that was him. While his face hadn't changed that much over the years, his body certainly had.

Years spent working on the ranch had honed his body into a Magic Mike paradise in a way football hadn't. She'd caught glimpses of him and Oakley shirtless whenever she hung out with Lorelie at the ranch. Since her sexual drought had taken hold, she'd actually gone to the ranch a lot more often, just in hopes of seeing their sweaty six-packs, so she would have something nice and juicy to fantasize about while her vibrator took care of the rest.

She jerked when Joel placed his hand on her lower back.

"Sorry, Sadie. Didn't mean to scare you. The cab's here."

Her face was on fire. Unfortunately, it wasn't embarrassment sending the heat. It was hardcore, *somebody fuck me already* desires.

She allowed Oakley to take her hand and lead her to the taxi as Joel pressed his palm against her lower back. She caught more than a few sideways glances from people as the three of them left together. God only knew what everyone was thinking.

Actually, Sadie had a pretty good notion what they thought. As she climbed into the cab—Joel and Oakley doing exactly as she'd expected as they trapped her in the middle— she wondered if the dirty-minded people didn't have a great idea.

Oakley kept hold of her hand, his fingers absentmindedly toying with her rings. Joel leaned closer, his arm draping around her along the backseat. Sadie gave the driver her address, though it was hard to speak with a dry mouth.

They hadn't been in the cab more than two minutes before the darkness of the night wrapped them up in a cocoon that wasn't lost on the guys.

Joel's fingers began to stroke the nape of her neck—dear God, that was one of her favorite erogenous zones—as Oakley's hand released hers in favor of her knee.

"I like your dress," Oakley murmured.

She'd wondered when she bought it if it was too short for a fall wedding, but had decided fuck it. She'd liked it because it showed off all the assets she felt like revealing perfectly. She hadn't cared about the old biddies giving her the hairy eyeball as much as she'd wanted to find a lover for the night.

Instead, she'd snared the wrong two guys.

Or the right two.

Oakley's hand drifted higher and, because she didn't have

an ounce of self-restraint, she parted her legs in silent invitation.

Neither man missed the movement. Joel turned toward her, his fingers gripping her neck more firmly as he leaned closer to kiss her cheek.

Her eyes drifted closed, savoring the heat from his breath as his lips lingered there, stroking the sensitive skin of her face.

Oakley didn't hesitate to explore deeper between her legs, his fingers lightly grazing her panties. They were wet, a dead giveaway to her desires, but it wasn't as if she was pushing them away or protesting. Instead, she slid her hips forward a bit more, making sure Oakley had even better access.

The smart cowboy never missed a beat. Oakley dipped his finger beneath her silky panties and found her clit almost instantly.

Sadie sucked in a loud gasp, then pressed her lips closed tightly. The cab driver's gaze found hers in the rearview mirror. There was no way she could play off the fact she was currently the cream filling in a cowboy Oreo, so she just winked at the guy.

What the hell did she care what he thought?

She didn't give two fucks about what *she* thought either. The champagne had done its job well.

Oakley applied some pressure to her clit and the world shrank down to just that tiny spot. Well, that one and the one Joel was currently sucking on her neck.

Sadie was in serious danger of spontaneously combusting when the cab pulled up to the curb outside her apartment.

Oh, hell no. She was about to tell the guy to circle the block a few times, but Joel spoke before she could make the suggestion.

"Thanks." He handed the guy a twenty, told him to keep the change and then he got out, reaching to help her. When she heard a second door close, she realized Oakley had gotten out too.

The cab drove away, leaving her on the curb, hot and bothered and still not alone.

"Did the plan change? I thought the taxi was taking you guys to the ranch."

Oakley chuckled. "Do you want us to call him back?"

She shook her head. "Fuck no."

Oakley gave her a sexy grin that made her pussy gush, but Joel's face revealed something way more dangerous.

She was tipsy. So were they. None of them would be here if they hadn't had so much to drink. Sober Sadie would have sent them packing.

Sober Sadie can suck it. She's no fun at all. Lame bitch.

"So, are you guys coming up?" Jesus. Where did that sexy, come-hither tone come from?

Joel nodded slowly, though she thought, like her, he was slowly starting to figure out this wasn't somewhere they should be. Oakley didn't give either of them time to let that realization take root. He clasped hands with her and led her up the stairs to the entrance of her apartment building.

When they reached the top, she glanced over her shoulder, relieved to see Joel was following them.

Relieved? Really?

When he reached out to take her key from her, unlocking the front door with big calloused hands that led her imagination down some hot paths, she knew that, yeah, she was relieved he was still here.

She lived in a three-story apartment building. Back in the day, the place had been a storage warehouse. About ten years ago, the owner sold the property to a big-city developer who converted it into three studio apartments. The place was damn trendy for small-town Maris, which was why she'd fallen head over heels for it. She'd scored the top floor eight years earlier when she started to fear she'd smother her father in his sleep if she didn't get out of her childhood home.

She loved her old man, but not as a damn roommate. First of all, he stifled her sex life. Bastard liked to show her dates his gun collection whenever they came to pick her up, and then he'd insist they bring her home at a reasonable hour. Like she was still a teenager in high school rather than a grown woman of twenty-five. No matter how hard she tried to break him of that habit, it was still there. Even now. In her dad's eyes, no one would ever be good enough for her. It was sweet, but annoying as crap.

Secondly, he was a freaking slob and she'd hit her limit when it came to picking up his shit.

"Nice place," Joel said when they entered her apartment. Neither he nor Oakley had ever been here before.

Because she'd never been stupid enough to get three sheets to the wind with them.

Because alcohol made her do crazy things.

Because her libido always switched into overdrive around them so she knew putting them anywhere near her and a bed would be the wrong thing to do.

"Yeah. I like it," she replied, distracted by the thought of her bed. Had she made it this morning? Did she have anything lying out in her bedroom that would be potentially embarrassing? Panties on the floor? Birth control pills? Vibrator?

Bringing both of them back to her place was ranking fairly high on her list of insane life choices. Right after getting her first boyfriend's initials tattooed on her ass. That tat had been turned into a butterfly after the breakup.

It also ranked after crashing her beloved first motorcycle into a tree because she'd taken a turn too fast. In addition to losing her sweet bike, she'd broken her leg in three places.

Those two decisions were worse than this one.

But not by much.

"Take a look around if you want," she said, inviting Oakley and Joel to roam around. She had eclectic tastes and it showed in her décor. She was sort of curious to know what they thought of it.

"Who took all the black-and-white photos?" Oakley asked, pointing to the pictures on the wall.

"Me. I went through a photography phase a few years back."

"They're good. *Really* good." Oakley's expression matched his words. He wasn't just bullshitting her, and she was flattered.

"Thanks."

Joel picked up a calavera. "Do I want to know?"

She grinned. "Sugar skulls. I collect them."

"You collect license plates too?" Oakley asked as he ventured farther along, getting closer to the kitchen.

"Not really. Those belonged to my mom. She was a bit of a hobo. She had a license plate from every state she'd ever been to."

Oakley's bright blue eyes widened as he took in the colorful plates, and she could imagine he was trying to figure out how many were there.

There were thirty-seven. She knew that because she'd counted them. About a million times. Sadie could only assume her mother had taken off in hopes of collecting the last thirteen. Hard to say that for sure, considering dear old Mom hadn't left a note or called to touch base. Not once. In twenty-seven years. She just vanished one day when Sadie was at school and her dad was working at the bar. Packed up a suitcase and left her husband and six-year-old daughter.

When Sadie was younger, she was convinced her mom

would come back once she'd found those final dozen or so plates. However, that belief faded as she got older.

Now, she hoped the bitch never showed her face in Maris again. Some people might say Sadie's attitude was unhealthy, but as far as she was concerned, she was in a better state of mind on her parental issues than she'd ever been. The license plates were her reminder that the only person she could really count on sticking around forever was herself.

"It's a great apartment, Sadie. Thanks for inviting us up."

She was surprised to see that Joel had moved closer to her. Sadie thought the heated moment in the taxi had passed, but she'd been dead wrong.

Joel reached for her with no hesitation, no uncertainty. He simply grasped her waist, tugged her close and kissed her.

Holy shit. She'd kissed enough frogs in her life to know she'd just found a prince.

He pressed her lips apart, his tongue dipping into her mouth. She tasted the tang of beer and a hint of sweetness—wedding cake?—on his breath. It was a heady combination.

She'd always wondered what it would be like to kiss Joel. And Oakley. So far her feeble fantasies didn't hold a candle to the reality.

She started slightly when Oakley stepped behind her, his hand brushing her hair to one side so he could press his lips to her neck. They kept overwhelming her with all these sexy/sweet touches.

How could their kisses blow her mind while making her feel almost cherished?

Joel released her. They sounded like swimmers breaking the surface in search of air.

"You kiss good." She was aiming for levity, but her voice was too breathy to sell it.

Joel didn't seem to mind. "So do you."

"My turn." Oakley twisted her toward him and within seconds, she was right back in paradise, with Prince Charming number two. And Oakley fit the part perfectly too, with his dirty blond hair, blue eyes and chiseled jaw. He was basically the poster child for the Disney heroes of her youth.

She'd done some wild things in her past, but she'd never made out with two guys at the same time. A girl could get addicted to this...fast.

Joel didn't care when Oakley cut in. Instead, he raised the bar as he pressed his chest to her back, his arms snaking around her so he could cup her breasts.

She gasped, the action breaking her union with Oakley. Oakley narrowed his eyes in confusion until he glanced down and saw what had prompted the sound. Then he grinned, gave her a wicked wink and started kissing her again. Joel squeezed her breasts, gently at first, but then he pressed tighter.

Her even-keel, no-nonsense-friend Joel had a dark side. She wouldn't have pegged him as such a dominant guy, but there was no mistaking he liked his lovin' with a rough edge.

That knowledge was dangerous because she liked the same thing. The way he was touching her, pinching her nipples —*holy fucking hotness*—was going to make it harder for her to put things back to right tomorrow. When she was sober.

"Take us to your bedroom."

Sadie broke off her kiss with Oakley to look over her shoulder at Joel as he made his demand. "Ask nicely."

Joel's lips tipped up at the edges. Then he lifted the hem of her dress to reveal her panties. Before she knew what he was planning, he slapped her ass. Hard. It hurt and turned her on all at the same time.

"Take us to your bedroom. Please."

Adding the final word certainly didn't make it sound like

less of a command, but Sadie didn't give a damn. She was into this side of Joel's personality.

"Jesus, bro," Oakley muttered. "You gotta scale back on that macho shit. It's starting to work on *me*."

Sadie giggled when she spotted Oakley's very apparent erection poking through his dress pants. Joel didn't seem quite as amused.

Oakley Fox was very open about his sexuality—his *bi*-sexuality. He didn't discriminate when it came to lovers. Boys or girls, he liked them all the same.

"Oakley." For the first time since they'd entered her apartment, Joel seemed to waver in his resolve.

Hell no.

She grasped his hand and dragged him to her bedroom before he could reconsider. She still had a lot of champagne flowing through her veins, heating up her girlie bits. She wasn't finished. Not by a long shot.

When they entered the room, Joel wasted no time taking things to a completely new level. He gripped the bottom of her dress and tugged it over her head in one fell swoop. The dress had a low back, so she'd gone braless. She wasn't packing enough on top for that to be a problem. She wasn't exactly-flat chested, but she was no stranger to padded bras either.

Neither man appeared to be disappointed.

"Shit, Sadie," Oakley murmured reverently. He stepped closer, compelled to run his finger along the edges of the water-color hummingbird tat that rested over her right breast. "That's incredible."

She lifted her shoulder, pleased. Not all the guys she went out with liked her tattoos. "I go to this guy in New Orleans. I figure if it's going to be there forever, I want it to be perfect. Carper is the best. He's done all my art." She turned to show them the hibiscus on her left shoulder. They'd already seen the

Celtic knot on her wrist, the fleur de lis on her ankle and the infinity symbol on her foot. Like her apartment, her tats were eclectic. If she saw something she liked, something that spoke to her, she got it.

Later, she'd give them a peek at the butterfly on her ass. Maybe she'd even confess to what it was covering up.

"I've always liked this," Joel lightly touched her belly button ring. Sometimes she wore crop tops just to show off a new ring or whenever she felt like annoying her dad. While he didn't mind the piercings or the tats, he hated when she wore clothes that were too revealing. Typical father response.

"Had enough of the tour?" she teased once they'd looked their fill.

Oakley laughed, his fingers stroking the side of her silk panties. "Sort of leaving out the best part, aren't you?"

She gave him a flirty grin. "You think you're up for the rest?"

He groaned and grabbed her hand, tugging her to the bed. He sat on the edge of the mattress, making it easy for her to straddle his thighs. She crawled on, facing him, kissing him and pressing her pussy against his hard cock, still trapped in his pants.

Oakley gripped her ass tightly, pulling her against him tighter. Neither of them seemed capable of getting enough.

She hadn't forgotten Joel was in the room, though she'd lost track of him. He remained somewhere behind her. She could feel his gaze on them, watching them. What the hell was he thinking of this?

She'd never considered herself a threesome girl, but she could definitely see the appeal. Like Oakley, she wasn't fussed with limits much. She'd done some hot-and-heavy making out and fondling with a girl back in high school and really enjoyed it. Sadie was a little too fond of being fucked with real dicks to go there permanently, but that wasn't to say she would turn down the experience again if it presented itself.

However, Joel was as straight as Oakley was wiggly. Sadie was sort of amazed he was here, taking part in this.

"God," Oakley groaned. "Gotta fuck you, Sade."

She reached for the button on his pants, but never made it to her destination. Joel suddenly made his presence known. He grasped both of her wrists and pulled them behind her back, holding them there, his large hands her shackles.

Her pussy clenched hungrily. Oh hell yeah. She may not have fantasized about a ménage, but bondage was another thing entirely. Unfortunately, she'd never dated anyone she trusted enough to tie her up.

Joel tightened his grip, causing her back to arch slightly, her breasts forced farther out. "What's your hurry?"

Using his hold on her hands, he pulled her off Oakley's lap. "Pull down the covers, Oak." Then—much to her dismay—Joel released her hands. Her annoyance was short-lived when he tugged off his tie, unbuttoned his shirt and stripped it off.

Oakley responded to Joel's demand, but Sadie could see what the dominant side of his friend was doing to him. Poor Oakley was as turned on as she was and fighting like the devil to hide it.

Once the bedspread was lowered, Oakley took off his own tie and shirt, climbed onto the mattress and scooted over to make room for her and Joel. Oakley was waiting for her as she and Joel lay down. He resumed their kiss, his hands caressing every part of her body he could reach, stroking her breasts, her waist, her hips.

Joel claimed the place behind her, his covered cock nudging against her ass. She pushed against it, seeking stimulation, hoping to encourage him to fuck her. Instead, he gripped her hips and rubbed his erection against her harder. She resented the feeling of his light cotton pants. She wanted flesh on flesh. Needed it.

Her head was swimming in a sea of alcohol and arousal. It was one hell of a buzz.

She flipped to her back when the heat of the kisses and the closeness of their two huge, muscular bodies became too much.

"God. Please." She reached down, intent on stripping both men out of their pants at the same time.

Both men.

Both.

Two.

The thought made her pause. Her hands were resting on two very hard, very ready cocks. She struggled to suck in a deep breath.

What the fuck was she doing?

"Um..."

Her arousal flickered out as if someone had dumped a bucket of cold water on her.

Joel must have sensed her hesitation and panic because he grasped her wrist, pulling it away from his dick.

"What are we doing?" he asked, his words mimicking her thoughts.

She shook her head slowly, common sense rearing its ugly head. "I don't know."

Oakley apparently hadn't caught up. "We're having sex. The hottest fucking sex ever."

She looked at him and bit her lower lip.

Oakley's expression fell as realization dawned hard. "Shit." He closed his eyes and sighed. "Sadie—"

"I'm sorry," she whispered. "I...this...it isn't..." She started to say *right*, but that was wrong. The problem was, this felt entirely too right. But sobriety was starting to clear a path and the voice of Sober Sadie was yelling for her to stop. "We wouldn't be here, doing this, if we weren't drunk. I know I said wedding hookups were all about sex and regrets, but I don't want to feel that way about you guys."

"You're right," Joel admitted. "We shouldn't be here."

Oakley didn't agree. "You're joking, right? I don't give a fuck how much we drank. There's no way you two can lay here and tell me this isn't fucking awesome."

Oakley was the only man in town capable of out-cursing her. Which was saying something, considering her gutter mouth.

"Oak," Joel started. Sadie recognized the tone as much as Oakley. Joel was about to issue one of his *you have to be responsible* speeches. She and Oakley had both been on the receiving end of them before, given their rather reckless approaches to life.

Oakley sat up, rising from the bed. "Save it. Tonight's not happening. I get it. I gotta take care of something." Sadie would have laughed when he pointed to his erection if she hadn't felt so guilty. "Where's your bathroom, Sadie?"

She pointed to a door on the left and Oakley stormed out. She released a long sigh. "Guess I screwed that up."

Joel gripped her shoulder, turning her toward him. "I share a room in the bunkhouse with that horny bastard. He's no stranger to his hand. Besides, we all got carried away. It's alright."

She studied his face, the dominant man had faded away and the friendly Joel she'd always known returned. "I have to admit your bedroom persona wasn't what I expected."

He rolled his eyes. "Sade." The word was laced with warning, so, of course, she ignored it.

"I mean in real life, you're just so..."

"I'm not going to like the word you fill in that blank with, am I?"

She grinned. "Passive."

He narrowed his eyes. "Seriously?"

Sadie laughed, glad that they could return to their usual teasing so quickly after such an intense almost-fuck-up. "I could always go with stoic, stodgy, serious, predictable or boring."

Before she knew it, Joel had pulled her toward him, tickling her as she giggled and tried to bat his hands away. She continued to wiggle, fighting to crawl off the opposite side of the bed, until he pulled her toward him, her back resting against his chest. He wrapped his arms around her in a friendly, relaxed manner, a far cry from their previous touches.

"I guess I should get up and call for a cab to take us back to the ranch."

She shook her head. "No. Sleep it off here. We're going to have to deal with the awkward morning after for this fiasco at some point. Might as well get it over with right away."

He tightened his grip, accepting her invitation without words. Then he finally said, "You're still not going to go out with me, are you? Or Oakley."

She twisted in his arms, wanting him to see her face as she tried to explain. "The thing is...I can't choose, Joel. I like you and Oakley. A lot. And as I think you saw tonight, I'm attracted to both of you. You say choose, but it's just not that simple."

He nodded slowly, though she could see her words didn't make him happy. Hell, they didn't make *her* happy.

She needed to lighten the heavy mood. "Let's face it, put together, you and Oakley make the perfect man."

Joel chuckled, the sound short-lived when Oakley walked back into the room.

Sadie glanced at him over her shoulder, wanting to put a smile on his face again as well. "Damn, Oak. That didn't take long. You know that doesn't really speak too highly of your stamina."

"Shut up and scoot over," Oakley said, no heat behind his words. He spooned her, snuggling close to her in a way that was far too comfortable. Sadie could sleep just like this every night of her life.

She sighed. "You mad?"

"Naw," Oakley said. "I could never be mad at you, Sade."

She snorted. "Yeah, right."

"Fine," he amended. "I could never *stay* mad at you."

She closed her eyes. Alcohol was a fickle friend. Now that the possibility of sex was off the table, it was taking the opposite route, making her very, very sleepy.

Her last thought as she drifted away was of Advil. She should have taken two. And had some water. Because there was no way she wasn't waking up without a headache.

Fucking champagne.

Fucking karma.

Chapter Two

Joel tossed a hay bale on the back of the tractor and tried to ignore Oakley's constant whistling. The damn man had been in an annoyingly good mood ever since they'd left Sadie's bed yesterday morning.

Sadie had claimed the morning after would be awkward, but she'd been wrong. Apart from the fact they'd all had wicked hangovers, there was no uncomfortable silence or stilted conversation. They had just gotten out of bed, dressed and shared some dry toast and weak tea while teasing each other the same way they always did.

That was one of the things Joel liked best about Sadie. She didn't play games or pretend to be anything other than exactly what she was. The woman was honest, with a great sense of humor and just the right amount of humility. She didn't take herself too seriously, but she wasn't afraid to tell you what she thought of you either. It was incredibly appealing.

However, unlike Oakley's sudden, irritatingly cheerful demeanor, their night together had left him in a foul mood. Mainly because he knew exactly how much he was losing out on now. He'd always liked Sadie, always been attracted to her, but he'd never realized just how cool she was. Hearing that she couldn't choose between him and Oakley was different from thinking she was uninterested and just trying to be a decent person. It made things harder, because now he knew she wanted him as much as he wanted her.

Oakley's whistling grew louder.

"Dammit, Oak. Will you stop making so much racket?"

Oakley paused mid-toss. "What the hell is wrong with you?"

That wasn't the right question at all. "Actually, I'm curious to know why you're so freaking happy?"

Oakley sighed. "You don't get it, do you, Joel? You haven't figured it out yet?"

Joel had spent the past eight years of his life working side by side with this man. And sometimes, it felt as if they were still strangers. Joel would never get used to Oakley's bizarre way of looking at the world. If Joel saw storm clouds, Oakley saw shade. If Joel saw an annoying deer eating all their vegetables in the garden, Oakley saw Bambi. And clearly, while Joel looked at Sadie and saw no possible future, Oakley found something different.

"Figured out what?"

"I heard what she said the other night. About liking both of us."

"You were eavesdropping?"

Oakley shook his head. "Not the entire time. Me and Woody had to have a little chat first. I was trying to talk him off the ledge."

Joel rolled his eyes. Oakley had named his cock Woody—the least inspired name on the planet—and actually talked about it like it was a real person. "Then I also assume you heard her say she couldn't choose. She's never going to date either one of us."

Oakley gave him a look that couldn't be described as anything less that pitying. It annoyed the crap out of Joel.

"Who said she has to choose?" Oakley asked.

Joel frowned, still confused. "You're going to ask her to take turns? And what happens if...when...we both fall for her? Because you know we're going to. We can't spend the rest of our lives going out with her every other day."

"You're so black and white, Joel. Think outside the box, man. We both date her. Together. At the same time. You were in that bed the other night. I dare you to tell me it wasn't fucking hot."

Joel wasn't about to admit that. Even if it was true. Mainly because his feelings about the whole situation were so jumbled and mixed up, he didn't know what to think.

That confusion was adding to his bad mood. He'd never made out with a girl in the presence of another person. Never considered sharing a woman with another guy sexually. However, that was all he'd thought about since the night of the wedding. He imagined it over and over, the idea keeping him in a constant state of semi-painful, half-hard dick mode.

It was becoming awkward and embarrassing. Every time someone came around, he felt the need to readjust his jeans to try to hide his erection.

"We were drunk."

"Bullshit!" Oakley said loudly. "You know as well as I do neither one of us was anywhere near as drunk as she seemed to think we were. Find another excuse."

Joel resented Oakley calling him out so boldly, even if the asshole was right. "I don't share."

"Wrong. You've just never shared in the past. You're

backing away from it because there's some fucked-up voice in your head telling you it's wrong. Did it feel wrong, Joel?"

"You gotta stop thinking with your cock, Oakley. That's not how the world works."

Oakley shrugged. "Maybe it should."

"So what's Woody's big plan? We just walk into Cruisers, tell Sadie she can have both of us, and we live the rest of our lives in some sex-filled threesome paradise?"

Oakley slapped Joel on the shoulder, his face filled with delight. "Exactly!"

Joel laughed despite himself. "You're insane."

"I'm creative."

Joel reached for another hay bale. "Even if I did agree to that—which I'm not—Sadie would turn us down flat."

"You're kidding, right? *You're* the stick in the mud, Joel. Not her. I think she'd go for it."

Joel wanted to argue that point, but he wasn't entirely sure Oakley was wrong. What had Sadie called him? Boring? Predictable? He had to admit, Sadie was more like Oakley than him. So what would she say if they presented her the option of a threesome?

Joel discounted the idea immediately. It didn't matter what she would say. He wasn't making that damn offer. He couldn't. Christ. He was raised in a devout Catholic home by a very strict but loving mother. He'd read enough of the Bible to know there wasn't anything in there condoning an orgy-like, ménage a trois relationship.

What would she say if he pursued the same unorthodox relationship? What would Coach say?

"Shit. I can see the wheels are turning. Which means you've probably already talked yourself out of this. So, you've left me no choice."

Joel didn't like the ominous tone of that. When Oakley took

matters into his own hands, things always took a twisted turn—sometimes fun, sometimes scary. "What do you mean?"

"I'm going to Cruisers tonight."

Clearly there was a hell of a lot more to it than just that. Joel took the bait. "What for?"

"To see my girl."

It was on the tip of Joel's tongue to correct Oakley, to say *our* girl. Because as much as he wanted to deny it, that was how he'd begun to think of Sadie. Regardless, he managed to refrain. Part of him was just contrary enough to tell Oakley to have fun while he stayed home. Sadly, that wasn't the stronger part.

"I wouldn't mind tossing back a couple cold ones." His nonchalance didn't fool his best friend for a second.

"Cool. Sounds like we've got a date." Oakley went back to throwing the hay bales on the trailer. Mercifully, the work distracted his friend enough that he couldn't see the impact his comment had on Joel.

It wasn't just the concept of a threesome that was holding Joel back. It was the way Oakley had looked at him the other night when Joel had taken off his shirt. They'd seen each other naked about a thousand times in the past. After all, they were roommates.

But Oakley had never looked at him with anything more than a passing glance; the typical once-up-and-down guys do to see how they compare.

The other night, Joel was certain he'd seen something more. Something that he *really* couldn't handle.

Desire.

* * *

It was close to ten o'clock before he and Oakley rolled into Cruisers. A couple of cows had gotten loose and it had taken them several hours to find the bastards, get them penned back up, figure out where they'd made their escape and repair the damn fence. Joel had insisted they call it a night and hit Cruisers later in the week, but Oakley wouldn't be swayed.

They walked in to find Sadie manning the bar as a couple of old guys sat nursing their beers, watching football highlights on the TV hanging behind the counter. A couple who appeared to be on a date was shooting pool. Other than that, the place was deserted.

Sadie looked tiredly toward the door as it opened, but her face quickly morphed to one of pleasure when she saw them enter. Joel liked that she was so happy to see them.

He and Oakley nodded hello to the other guys as they claimed stools at the opposite end of the bar. Sadie came over and leaned toward them. "What brings you guys in here so late on a Monday? I was just about to yell last call."

"Good," Oakley said. "Yell it and get these people out of here. We'll help you close up."

Sadie gave him a curious grin, but then she did as Oakley suggested. She poured them each a beer. Thirty minutes later, the place was empty save for the three of them. Oakley walked over to the old jukebox and threw in a few coins as Sadie finished washing the glasses.

She glanced up when the bar filled with the sound of "For You". Oakley was a hardcore John Denver fan and there wasn't anyone in town who didn't know it, as the man was infamous for belting out "Thank God I'm a Country Boy" whenever the spirit moved him. Which it did *way* too often.

Oakley lifted his hand. "Come dance with me, Sadie."

Sadie considered the invitation, and then she put down her dishcloth and met Oakley in the middle of the floor. Joel remained at the bar, though he turned to watch as Oakley took her in his arms, tugged her close and they swayed together.

He was reminded of the other night when Oakley and Sadie were kissing on the bed. Joel had stood apart from them, spellbound by how beautiful they were together. He hadn't felt like an outsider or like he didn't belong. Instead, it almost felt as if he were with them, a part of the kiss, the touch, the embrace.

It was odd. And enticing.

Oakley wanted to share her. It was a preposterous suggestion. Yet Joel had a sense that was the only way this thing shimmering between the three of them would ever work.

And as much as he denied it, he wanted to try it. Desperately. He'd spent a lifetime towing the line, doing predictable shit, playing it safe. What would be the harm in breaking character...just this once...and indulging a fantasy?

He rose as the song was about to draw to a close and walked over to them. As the last note faded, he reached out for Sadie. She didn't resist the pull, stepping into his arms as if it were the most natural thing and accepting his kiss.

Joel didn't seek to do anything more than kiss her. He was still trying to figure out if it was right to initiate this, to follow Oakley down this path. When Sadie lifted her arms and ran her fingers through his hair, he stopped worrying about it.

He'd wanted Sadie for years. Hell, his crush on her had started all the way back in high school. She was two years older than him and all the guys on the football team had been half in love with her.

Of course that was half a lifetime and another Sadie ago. She'd been so different in school, more like the women she made fun of nowadays. Sadie had been Homecoming Queen her senior year, a fact that made Oakley laugh his ass off every time someone mentioned it to her.

He pulled away and looked at her. She gave him a crooked, oops-we-did-it-again grin.

"We're going to have to work on our self-restraint," he said, half-joking.

"No, we're not." Oakley stepped closer. "You don't have to make a choice, Sadie."

Joel gritted his teeth at the way his friend dropped the bomb, but forced himself to keep quiet. Oakley was all-systems-go on this crazy scheme of his.

Joel was sort of hoping Sadie would reject it out of hand. At least that would save him the trouble of trying to sort out the feelings rumbling around inside him.

"What are you talking about?" Sadie glanced back at Joel questioningly. He lifted one shoulder. Oakley would explain it way better than he could. Knowing Oakley, he'd find a way to convince both of them.

"You'll date me *and* Joel. At the same time."

She laughed, but the sound died away quickly when neither he nor Oakley cracked a smile. "You're being serious? What do you mean? Like a threesome?"

Oakley nodded as if it was the most obvious answer on earth. "Yeah. You, me and Joel."

Sadie opened her mouth, rejection clearly her goal, but Oakley forged on before she could speak.

"Tell me you haven't thought about the other night, Sade. Tell me you haven't finished what we started about a million times in your head since then."

She bit her lower lip, the proof creeping out in the form of a blush. It was rare to see Sadie embarrassed. Joel enjoyed it more than he should.

Just how had she fantasized about that night ending?

Oakley moved closer and pressed his lips against Sadie's cheek as he whispered, "Tell me."

She grimaced, then—as always—held back nothing. "I've

played it out so many times I had to replace the batteries on my vibrator. Is that what you wanted to hear?"

Oakley chuckled. "That was what I thought I wanted. Now I'm sort of hoping for a more detailed description."

She batted Oakley away playfully. "You're the devil." Then she turned to Joel. "Are you seriously okay with what Oakley's suggesting?"

Joel wasn't sure of anything except the fact Sadie had called him boring. And passive. He had to admit that had stung. Enough that he felt the need to shake her impression of him.

"Yeah. I am."

Sadie's shocked expression was nothing compared to Oakley's. Sadie recovered first. And her answer was exactly what Joel had—and hadn't—wanted.

"Fine. We can give it a whirl if you guys are sure it doesn't bother you to share. This is actually sort of the answer to a prayer. I've been in a bit of a slump lately."

"Slump?" Joel asked.

"A sexual drought. That I'd be happy to see end with the two of you."

Neither he nor Oakley responded.

Sadie's brow creased. "Wait. That is what you meant, right? Sex? Because I'm not looking for a relationship or a commitment or anything like that. God. *Nothing* like that. I suck at it." And then, before either of them could respond, Sadie answered her own question with a light laugh. "I'm sorry. Of course that's what you meant. Because who dates two guys at the same time?"

No one does. Joel had been a jackass to follow Oakley's lead, doing exactly what he'd just yelled at his friend for today. He'd been thinking with his dick. Then, he realized Sadie had just confirmed what his gut had been telling him. Normal people didn't enter relationships in threes, just pairs.

"So should we put some parameters on it? A time limit?" she asked.

Joel shook his head. "No time limit. We ride the train to the end of the line."

She grinned at his analogy. "I had no idea you had such an impetuous nature, Joel. You've been hiding this guy. I like him."

He was careful to keep a smile in place, too afraid she'd be able to see beneath the surface and figure out he was freaking the fuck out.

"I don't..." Joel considered his mom. "I don't think we should advertise what we're doing."

Sadie's lips tipped up, her eyes widening. "No shit. I don't think your mom is ready for something quite so scandalous from her good little boy. And my dad would have a heart attack. After he murdered both of you, of course."

Joel tried to laugh, knew she meant her words as a joke. After all, she'd just offered him a sweet deal. He could have his cake and eat it too. He could sleep with Sadie and Oakley *and* keep it a secret from everyone else.

So why wasn't he happier about that than he was?

Then he realized why.

"Let's draw a line in the sand here, Sadie," Joel said, his mind hung up on one word. "We don't have to call it a relationship, but there is going to be some level of commitment."

She frowned until he explained. "No other guys but us."

"Oh." Her face brightened before she gave him a *duh* look. "I'm going to be sleeping with the two of you. Where the hell do you think I'd get the energy to look for more? I'm slightly promiscuous. Not a total slut."

Joel couldn't help but laugh. She was completely adorable. And like Oakley, uninhibited. Joel sometimes wondered if that was what drew him to them. He did tend to take his responsibilities too seriously. He never sang country songs loudly and off-key as he drove through town with the windows down like Oakley did. He didn't have tattoos or a motorcycle that he drove way too fast down the country lanes like Sadie did.

He didn't leave Maris after high school because he didn't want to leave his mother alone. Instead, he'd taken a job at Coach's ranch to help his mom get by. Even now, he paid her rent because he didn't want her to keep scrimping every month to get by. She'd worked three jobs when he was growing up to support them, to keep food on the table and clothes on his back. And while she'd never said college was out of the question, never asked him to stay in Maris, he had because he felt like he owed it to her.

Oakley wrapped his arm around her shoulder, dragging her close enough that he could kiss her on the forehead. "We don't mind you being a slut with us."

"Thanks for the permission." She lifted her face for a less platonic kiss than the one he'd just planted on her brow, and Oakley obliged.

Joel looked around the bar. They'd locked the door after the last customers left. The place didn't have any windows, more warehouse than classy pub.

Suddenly Joel recalled all the endings he had written to their interrupted evening. He stepped behind Sadie, lifting the hem of her shirt. She and Oakley broke apart as Joel pulled her favorite Sex Pistols tee over her head.

Oakley wasted no time reaching out to cup her breasts. She had a bra on tonight, one that pushed her breasts up and out.

God, everything was sexy on her. Or off her.

Joel turned her to face him, reaching for the button on her jeans.

"In a hurry?" She clearly meant her question as a joke, but there was no way she could hide the need for speed on her face.

Joel nodded. "Yeah. I didn't get to see you come the other night. I'm going to correct that oversight right now."

Sadie's hands met his, helping him drag her tight blue jeans down. The panties went with the denim, and he was treated to his first unobstructed view of her pussy. He wasted no time touching her. She was wet, hot, so ready for them.

"Go bend over that table, Sadie."

She kicked off her shoes and the jeans, and then walked over to the table closest to the dance floor. He and Oakley followed.

Joel shook his head when she glanced over her shoulder at him. "Don't worry about where we are. Bend over. Now."

Sadie let a groan escape. It was laced with hunger. So was Oakley's.

Joel tried to ignore it. Oakley had never pulled any punches with him. He'd moved into the bunkhouse and confessed to being bisexual the very first night they met. Joel had admitted to his straightness, and they'd lived in platonic best friendship ever since. What they were embarking on with Sadie felt like it was blurring the lines for Oakley.

He shoved that thought away, which wasn't a very hard task when his gaze landed on Sadie's beautiful, colorful ass.

Oakley beat him to the table, his fingers stroking the bright butterfly adorning Sadie's left cheek. She started slightly at this touch, and then grinned at Oakley. "Remind me to tell you the story about that tat sometime."

Oakley bent down and stroked his tongue along it, provoking a shiver from Sadie. "I'll do that."

Joel watched, trying to keep a grip on himself. He'd wanted Sadie for so many years. To have her here, ready and waiting for him...and for Oakley.

He sucked in a breath and dug deep for some control.

Joel stepped closer and lightly tapped the inside of her ankle. "Open your legs, darlin'." He noticed his southern accent seemed to grow thicker at moments like this.

Sadie moved into position without hesitation. She had such a powerful spirit that it amazed him when she offered herself to him—to them—like this. With absolute trust.

She'd chosen a small, circular, two-seater table to lean over. While her elbows rested on the flat surface, her upper chest and head cleared the other side. Oakley moved around to stand in front of her, his eyebrows lifting in appreciation at the view.

"God, you've got gorgeous tits, Sadie."

She laughed lightly. "Such a sweet talker, Oak."

His friend didn't seem to catch her joke. Instead, he added, "The way your bra pushes them up like that. I could bury my face between those and live there forever."

"I wouldn't mind." Her voice was husky, flirty, sexy.

Joel couldn't hold back. He stepped directly behind her and ran the front placket of his jeans across her ass, and then he knelt. He caught the sweet scent of her arousal, his mouth watering for a taste. He ran his tongue along her slit.

She gasped and jerked. "Ohmigod."

Joel lifted his gaze, catching Oakley's. His friend was standing stock-still, watching him. While the look was hot, Joel needed to put some space between them. This was pushing them too close together.

Oakley must have read the uncertainty in his face, because he glanced down and ran his hand through Sadie's dark-red hair. Sadie wasted no time reaching out. She unfastened Oakley's jeans and tugged out his cock.

Joel forced himself to look away, to focus on Sadie. On making her come. On making tonight so fucking good for her, she'd never want to let them go.

Them.

Him.

Fuck.

This train was going to hit a final station...somewhere down the line. It was inevitable.

Joel forced himself to return to the present.

Enjoy the moment.

He pressed his tongue into her opening, soaking up her groan of desire. Joel pushed in and out, trying to ignore it when Sadie's cries became muffled. He recognized the sounds. She was sucking Oakley's dick.

Joel closed his eyes, pressing her clit with his tongue. He felt her go up on her toes as even more arousal gushed from her. She was so wet. So ready to be fucked.

"God, Sadie." Oakley's deep, guttural cry was more than Joel could take.

Joel stood, though he kept his eyes averted. He focused on Sadie's gorgeous ass, the gentle rocking motion of her body on the table as she worked to bring Oakley to climax with her mouth. He unzipped his pants and reached into his back pocket for his wallet. He pulled out his cock and covered it with a condom. Through it all, he was careful not to look up, refusing to watch Sadie suck on Oakley. He was terrified of what—of how—that sight might make him feel.

Joel placed the head of his cock at her opening. All self-restraint abandoned him as he slowly slid inside and she let out a quiet cry of relief. He understood the feeling. She was hot and tight and perfect.

Then he couldn't resist it any longer. He wanted to see, *needed* to see, Sadie's mouth on Oakley.

"Jesus," he murmured, pressing in to the hilt, his cock growing thicker when Sadie released Oakley's cock with a pop.

She still held his friend in her hand as she turned to look at

Joel over her shoulder. All he could see was Sadie's pretty, flushed face and Oakley's hard dick. He couldn't move, couldn't take his eyes away from them.

He had no idea what Sadie saw in his face, but he prayed it wasn't the panic that was currently coursing through him.

There was no way he could do this again. No way.

Everything was getting mixed up in his head. He wanted Sadie. He would always want Sadie.

So why did it feel like he wanted Oakley too?

"Come here," Sadie whispered.

Joel wanted to say no. Leaning over her would bring him too fucking close. But it didn't matter. Sadie asked for something and he couldn't refuse.

He leaned over her body, his elbows resting next to hers as his chest covered her back. He had at least half a foot on her, so the position allowed him to turn his head, to place a soft kiss on her cheek.

She smiled. "Stay there."

Sadie was pretty good at issuing commands herself. Joel remained motionless, spellbound as she turned her face back to Oakley, her lips parting to take him inside once more.

Joel was mere inches away from them. He could see her saliva coating his dick as his friend pushed in and out. Her hand was wrapped around the base of Oakley's cock, stroking in rhythm with her lips, her tongue. Oakley's right hand rested on the back of Sadie's head as he used his grip there to slowly... Jesus...so slowly...fuck her pretty mouth.

Joel was still inside Sadie, and after several minutes, he realized he was moving in time with Oakley's cock in her mouth. It was a gentle thrust that mimicked their blowjob.

"So fucking hot," Oakley said, his movements picking up speed as he lost some of his careful precision. His friend was on the verge of coming.

Sadie felt it too. Joel saw her grip on Oakley's cock tighten.

Both he and Sadie were surprised when Oakley pulled out at the last minute.

"Lift her up, Joel." Oakley's hand pumped his own dick, keeping the orgasm there, but banked.

Joel didn't need any more instruction. He knew exactly what Oakley wanted. Joel rose from the table, careful to keep his cock tucked deep inside her. Then he reached for Sadie's shoulders and tugged her upwards, the action thrusting her breasts out.

Sadie's pussy clenched on Joel's cock. God, she loved this.

"Pull my hair," she demanded. Joel moved his hand to her long tresses and gripped tight, holding her up that way instead.

Oakley reached out and pulled one breast, and then the other, over the cups of her bra, taking care to pinch each nipple as he did so. His right hand still furiously pumped his cock.

And then Oakley jerked, a deep moan accompanying it as he erupted, jet after jet of come covering Sadie's chest.

Joel had stopped moving, too enthralled by what he was seeing. His hand was fisted in Sadie's hair, holding her up, though Oakley's climax had waned.

Oakley was the first to break the stillness. He pulled a nearby chair over and sank down onto it, his gaze glued to Sadie's breasts.

"Jesus, Sade," Oakley murmured.

Sadie shook her head slightly, reminding Joel to release her.

"I know," she whispered to Oakley.

She was breathing heavily, her face more red than pink as she glanced at Joel over her shoulder. They were both slick with sweat. "Joel."

He didn't need to hear more. He understood. Joel jerked his head toward Oakley. "Put your hands against that table to hold it steady, Oak." He placed a soft kiss on Sadie's shoulder. "This isn't going to be gentle, darlin'."

She gave him a hungry grin. "Good."

Joel stood straighter as he gripped her hips. He didn't bother to start slow. He couldn't. He felt the need to fuck her. Hard. He'd never been this aroused, never wanted anyone so much.

Oakley's hands rested against the opposite side of the table, pushing the wood to keep them from sliding the damn thing across the floor. Joel was a bit worried about the thing collapsing, but not even that fear could stop him now.

He plowed deeper, as Sadie met him thrust for thrust. She reared back and he shoved against her, both of them grunting, cursing, demanding more. Her sexual appetite was the perfect match. He'd never found a woman capable of handling his heavy-handed commands, his rough claiming. No one...until her.

The women he'd dated had expected a gentleman. So he'd been one. Sadie appeared to be just fine with the real Joel.

Then he closed his eyes when they landed on Oakley. What did that mean about his feelings toward Oakley? He shut that thought down. God help him if this was the real Joel because if it was...he was in trouble.

They moved even faster and Joel was vaguely aware of Oakley standing, leaning his hips against the table. Then Joel heard him. Heard Oakley speaking.

"Jesus. Yeah. Fuck yeah. You guys are so fucking hot. Harder. Go harder, Joel."

Joel responded to Oakley's voice, found himself turned on by it. Sadie's hands reached out for Oakley, her fingers digging into his hips as she sought purchase, stability.

"I can't...I'm..." Her words came out in gasps, her inner muscles clamped down on his cock so tightly, it almost hurt.

"Take him deep, Sade. Jesus. You're incredible."

She came with a scream and Joel was only one heartbeat behind her, his vision going gray as his balls squeezed, then exploded.

"Holy God," Joel yelled. His hands landed on the surface of the table, looking for something to hold him upright as he came so hard he saw stars behind his closed eyes.

For several minutes, Joel simply stood there, listening to the sound of his own breathing. Sadie didn't move. He wondered if she'd fallen asleep. He'd check, but he didn't have the strength to lift his eyelids.

Finally, a hundred years later, he forced himself to move.

The first thing he saw was Oakley. He expected to see his wild, uninhibited friend sitting there with a goofy, too pleased, *told you so* grin on his face. What Joel had *not* anticipated was the serious, almost dangerous expression painting Oakley's features.

Oakley was staring at him with an intensity that shook Joel to the core. He'd seen that look before on the faces of women he'd taken to bed.

Oakley wanted him. And his friend wasn't even trying to hide it.

Joel broke the connection first, scowling as he looked away.

Sadie lifted up on her elbows slowly as Joel withdrew. He offered a hand to help her stand.

Oakley moved as well, walking to the bar to grab a handful of napkins. He returned and carefully cleaned Sadie up.

Then Joel pulled her into his embrace.

"Are you okay?" he asked, suddenly afraid he'd hurt her.

"I...I think so."

Joel cupped her cheek and tilted her face up so he could look at her. Her eyes were clouded with the same confusion, the same overwhelming bewilderment he felt.

"I didn't realize it would be so..." She struggled for a word.

Oakley supplied it. "Intense. I've never done anything like that."

She looked at Oakley. "I just didn't know."

Oakley leaned forward in the chair, resting his forearms on his thighs. "And now we do. So what's next?"

His friend had directed the question at Sadie, but Joel knew it was his answer Oakley was waiting for. Oakley expected him to call a halt to it all, to say it was wrong, that it wouldn't work.

And that was exactly what Joel should say. They'd played with fire, thinking it would be a lark. They had all gotten burned.

Problem was, Joel wanted to burn some more. He wouldn't mind being consumed in it, turned to ash.

"We keep going," Joel said. If he weren't so exhausted, so wrung out, he would have laughed at Sadie and Oakley's matching looks of surprise.

Then Sadie nodded. "Oh hell yeah. I want more."

Oakley still didn't smile. "Are you sure?" This time he didn't pretend he was asking Sadie. His eyes were locked firmly on Joel's.

Joel gave him one, almost imperceptible nod. "Yeah. I'm sure."

Chapter Three

"Thanks for helping me plan all of this, Sadie, but I could have met you at the bar. You didn't have to drive all the way out here." Lorelie put down the pen she was using to take notes.

Sadie shrugged. "It's not like you live a hundred miles out of town. Besides I didn't mind. It was a good day to take my bike out for a spin."

"I swear I'd get my own motorcycle if I didn't think it would give my dad another heart attack."

"I could see you riding a hog," Sadie teased.

"I'm starting to get excited about this party. I mean it's been a ton of work, but I think it'll be worth it. My dad is going to love it."

Sadie agreed. Maris High School's current football team was undefeated, and everyone was already starting to talk about the state championship. The Titans hadn't brought home that trophy since Joel's class thirteen years earlier. The locals—Sadie's dad included—were foaming at the mouths for another win.

Sadie would never understand how seemingly normal grown men could lose their ever-lovin' minds over teenage boys tossing a football around. But the fact remained, Titan football was all anyone in town could talk about these days.

Since Coach's heart attack, a lot of the older guys, players on that last state-winning team, had come back to help Lorelie and her dad keep the ranch going while her dad recuperated. It spoke volumes about what Coach Carr meant to the guys, how they'd dropped everything to come back.

To commemorate the winning season and Coach's recovery, and with the old team in town, the school had decided to do something special this year for Homecoming. During halftime of the game, they planned to introduce the players from that first state championship team and then honor Coach for all his years of service to the school as football coach.

Lorelie had decided to throw a big-ass party after the game to celebrate, and as a way of thanking the guys for all they'd done by coming home to help them. Sadie had volunteered her expertise in setting up the open bar for the night. She and Lorelie hammered out the details on how many kegs to order, how many cases of wine, and whether or not to include liquor. Sadie was going to man the bar at the party, and Oakley and Joel had both promised to help her.

Sadie glanced out the window absentmindedly. "I'm looking forward to hearing Walt play. Always loved his music." Walt had enjoyed a successful music career in Nashville before coming back home to help Coach out. Sadie couldn't help but notice he was in no hurry to return to the big city, though she wasn't sure what was keeping him in Maris. He'd agreed to perform at the party.

Lorelie poured more iced tea in both of their glasses. "Yeah. Walt's got some friend who used to play guitar in his band coming as well. An *old times sake* kind of thing since it looks like Walt isn't planning to go back to Nashville for a while. So voila—now I have a band playing at my party."

Sadie took a sip of the sweet tea and sighed. Lorelie made the best tea in town. "Is the guitar-playing friend hot?"

"Lord, I hope so. I need some new eye candy. Not that having all the guys from school back hasn't improved the view in Maris lately."

Speaking of eye candy, Sadie glanced out the front window again, hoping to catch a glimpse of Oakley and Joel.

"Okay, what gives?" Lorelie asked.

Sadie twisted her head back to look at her friend. "What?"

"You've looked out that window no less than a hundred times in the last half hour. What the heck are you looking for?"

Sadie wasn't sure how to reply. She and the guys definitely weren't advertising their unorthodox relationship—for lack of a better description. In fact, they'd agreed to keep it on the down low.

She'd seen them three times since their first foray into the world of an explosive ménage, each meeting at the bar after closing and each encounter hotter than the one before. She was going to have to invite them to her apartment one of these days. It might be fun to actually have sex with them in a bed. That thought provoked a grin she couldn't hide.

Lorelie's eyes narrowed. "What the hell are you up to?"

"I'm not up to anything."

Lorelie rolled her eyes. "Sell it to someone else, sister. You have that recently laid air about you. So which one of the guys finally convinced you to do the horizontal mambo? My money is on Oakley."

Sadie laughed. Lorelie was four years younger than her, so they hadn't been friends in school. Hell, they hadn't even gone to school together. Lorelie had been in middle school when Sadie was a senior.

Sadie hadn't had any super close girlfriends in school. She wasn't a fan of drama or girlie shit, so she'd always hung out with the guys instead.

However, in the past year or so, she'd found herself in more and more social settings with Lorelie and her friends—Lela, Paige, Lacy, and Gia—and she had to admit she really liked them.

Though Lorelie was the one she had grown closest to. Probably because—like Sadie—Lorelie had been raised by a single father, spoke her mind, and didn't put up with a lot of bullshit.

"Why do you think it's Oakley?" she asked noncommittally.

Lorelie shrugged. "The guy is relentless. I've seen him flirt with you. And let's face it, there's just so long you can play hard to get before you start to wonder why the hell you're turning him down. He's not hard on the eyes and the man has a six-pack on top of a six-pack. So how was it?"

Sadie didn't reply. In truth, she didn't know what to say. She wasn't supposed to say anything.

Luckily, Lorelie didn't always need another person present to have a conversation. She continued speaking without giving Sadie a chance to answer. "Of course, if it was Oakley, it's probably over, right? I mean, that guy's never gone back for seconds that I've ever heard of."

Sadie hadn't considered that. Lorelie was right. While she'd heard some rumblings about Oakley's flings, he'd never seriously dated anyone, and she had never heard of him taking a one-night stand and turning it into a weekend. For a second, she felt a twisted sense of pride. She'd kept Oakley interested enough to come back. Quite a few times, if she counted the failed attempt after the wedding.

However, Lorelie misinterpreted her continued silence, her brows rising. "Joel? You fucked Joel?"

Damn. Sadie really was going to have to join this conversation or Lorelie was going to keep guessing. God help her if her friend landed on the right answer. Then she considered Lorelie's tone. "Why would that be so unheard of?"

Lorelie opened her mouth to answer, and then closed it again. Clearly Sadie had stumped her.

Sadie was really interested in hearing Lorelie's impressions of her entering a relationship with the guys and was tempted to tell her the truth. After all, Lorelie knew Oakley and Joel better than anyone, given the fact they'd worked on the ranch for years. The men treated Lorelie like a little sister, and although Lorelie claimed the protective-older-brother stuff drove her nuts, Sadie suspected the opposite was actually true.

"It's not that it's weird or anything. It's just, you and Joel are very different. I think you and Oakley have more in common. Joel is just so serious and..."

"Stuffy?" Sadie supplied helpfully.

Lorelie considered the answer and then nodded. "Not in an annoying way or anything. I mean it's not like he's judgmental or condescending or holier than thou. He's just..."

Sadie knew what Lorelie meant. She and Oakley were fly-by-the-seat-of-their-pants types. They tended to view everything with an off-color irreverence, making fun of stuff that wasn't really funny, and doing whatever they wanted just because it felt good. Joel wasn't like that—or at least he hadn't been until this week, when he'd agreed to something Sadie knew must rub against the grain for him.

Joel played by society's rules. He was hardworking, well respected. He was the man everyone wanted for a friend because he was just so damn nice. He'd give someone the shirt off his back if they needed it, even if it was the dead of winter, and he took his mother out for lunch every Sunday without fail. It was Joel who had gathered the troops after Coach's heart attack, calling his former teammates to let them know what was going on. Coach would never have requested help for himself, so Joel had seen to it, made sure his coach had gotten all the support he needed.

Oakley teased him sometimes, called Joel a people pleaser. Sadie admired that in Joel, even if she didn't totally understand it. Like Oakley, she preferred to live life by her own rules. She refused to make herself miserable just to make someone else feel better. That probably made her a bitch, but it was just the way she was.

"I guess Oakley and I *would* be a better fit," she admitted.

"Are you dating Joel?" Lorelie asked.

She'd given her friend the wrong impression. "Oh, no. I'm not dating either of them."

Lorelie's brow creased. "So you're just sleeping with Joel? You know, that doesn't sound much like him. Always had him pegged as a one-woman man, not the type to engage in sexual flings. Joel's very much a forever kind of guy."

Sadie had always thought the same thing. Which was why she'd been very careful to lay out exactly what she wanted from him and Oakley. She didn't want them to misunderstand or think that she could ever be their girlfriend. That was the beauty of their arrangement. It wasn't like she was in a serious relationship with both of them. By keeping it purely a sexual thing, she wasn't in danger of hurting them.

Because she sure as shit wasn't the commitment type. They could explore all the dynamics of their fun, mind-blowing threesome sex until they got tired of one another and then move on. And the best part was it had been Joel's idea to end it when it got old.

Not that it was anywhere near getting old. Sadie was starting to think they might actually have a few years' worth of sexual fantasies to indulge. Which was pretty exciting...and terrifying.

"It's just sex," Sadie said with conviction.

"And he's okay with that?"

Sadie grinned at the tone in Lorelie's voice. There was a definite warning laced with the question that left Sadie in no doubt Lorelie would kick her ass if she hurt Joel.

Sadie nodded. "Yep. He absolutely is."

She'd have to tell Joel that Lorelie knew they were sleeping together. She hadn't planned on revealing anything about them at all, but Sadie could see some benefit to Lorelie knowing at least half of the truth. This way she wouldn't question it, should Sadie stop by for a late-night visit to the bunkhouse.

"Well, then I'm sorry to break the bad news to you, but Joel headed into town with Oakley to run some errands. Don't expect them back until later this afternoon."

"Oh." Sadie was more disappointed than she cared to admit.

"Walt asked if I had any song requests. I figure you know what gets people dancing at the bar. Besides, my musical preferences run to pop, not country, and I can't really see Walt and his friend knocking out a few Beyoncé and Taylor Swift songs for me. Want to help me come up with a list?" Lorelie asked.

"Sure," Sadie said. They spent the next hour creating lists of songs, decoration ideas, and looking up recipes on Pinterest for the food table. The guys hadn't returned by the time Sadie pulled out of the driveway on her motorcycle. She watched for them the entire time she rode back into town, hoping to pass them on the road and entertaining herself with a fantasy of the three of them getting it on in the back of their pickup truck along the side of the highway.

Sadly, she made it all the way back to her apartment without an Oakley/Joel sighting.

She climbed the three flights of stairs to her place, her libido in overdrive. The men had turned something on inside of her and it was relentless. As she opened the door, she debated between a cold shower or a visit with her vibrator.

The vibrator that had gotten her through the past few months of a sexless existence suddenly didn't seem quite as inviting. It didn't hold a candle to all the amazing things Joel and Oakley could do to her body.

"Cold shower it is," she murmured. She was going to have to call the guys and make plans for a hookup. She hated cold showers.

* * *

"Mom at eleven o'clock," Oakley muttered under his breath as he and Joel got out of the pickup truck.

Joel looked over and saw his mother stepping out of the beauty parlor. She raised her hand and waved. Joel smiled and started to walk toward her, but pulled up short when he realized Oakley was still standing beside the truck.

"Aren't you coming over to say hello?"

Oakley grimaced. "Do I have to? Your mom does *not* like me, bro. Looks at me most of the time like I'm the son of Satan."

Joel chuckled. "Maybe it would help if you didn't cuss so much or adjust your dick in your pants all the time or chug beer like it was water or fuck anything that moves. Maris isn't that big, buddy, and you've got a bit of a reputation."

Oakley put his hands in the front pockets of his jeans. "I don't do any of that in front of your mom."

"Doesn't mean she doesn't hear about it. She's probably afraid you're a bad influence on me."

Oakley snorted. "Yeah, right. Because you were such a fucking saint when we met."

Joel didn't understand the wince that accompanied Oakley's comment until he heard his mother's voice right behind him.

"Oakley," Mom said as way of a greeting. Of course, she'd managed to lace it with an avalanche of disapproval. She'd clearly heard him say the F-word.

Joel gave him an *I told you so* look as he turned to give his mom a kiss on the cheek. "Hey, Mom. You look nice today."

She reached up to touch her bangs. "Just got my hair done. What are you boys doing in town?"

Apparently no matter how old Joel got, in his mother's eyes, he would always be a boy. "Just hitting the hardware store for some stuff we need to do repairs around the ranch. And then we're going to the grocery store. Lorelie caught us before we could make our getaway and gave us a list of food she needed."

Mom smiled. "That's nice of you. You still coming over on Sunday for lunch?"

He nodded. He'd only missed a half-dozen Sundays in the last decade, yet his mother always felt the need to double-check. "Of course."

Oakley fidgeted next to him, looking for a chance to escape. His mother was nothing like Oakley's folks, who were free spirits who laughed often and hadn't imposed many rules on his friend growing up. Oakley didn't know how to relate to Joel's strict, quiet mother and her devout religious beliefs. In fact, Mom seemed to be the only person with the ability to make Oakley nervous. So much so, he rarely spoke in her presence, always afraid he'd say the wrong thing.

Joel was probably an asshole for enjoying his friend's discomfiture so much. After all, his mother had never been rude to Oakley. She just hadn't been great at hiding her displeasure of his wild lifestyle and foul language. Oakley had expressed his amazement that Joel had grown up with any sense of humor at all. Joel tried to explain that just because his mother didn't smother him with hugs and kisses and care packages like Oakley's did, didn't mean she didn't love him. She just wasn't comfortable expressing emotion—*any* emotion.

"Good." Mom hitched her purse higher on her arm. "It's my week to clean up communion, so you might want to come a little later. Or you could come earlier and go to mass with me. I know Father Andrew would love to see you there."

His mother had been trying to get him to return to mass with her for several months. Joel had always gone with her to the Sunday morning services, but after Coach's heart attack, things had been too busy on the ranch. He'd used that as an excuse, but the fact was he'd only been attending mass to please his mother. He didn't find the same peace in the service that she did. Now that he'd made the break, he was finding it difficult to *unbreak* it. "I'm not sure I'll be able to make it this week, Mom. I'll just meet you at home for lunch."

Mom's expression was pinched. He'd pissed her off.

Oakley shifted uncomfortably. "Okay. So we probably should, um…"

Joel took the hint. "Right. We've got a lot of errands to run."

They were about to say their goodbyes when Sadie's father approached them.

"Hello, Ms. Rodriguez," Mr. Milligan said, tipping his baseball cap respectfully.

Mom's smile was friendly. "Good afternoon, Mr. Milligan. Lovely to see you."

Nelson Milligan was an enormous, hairy bear of a man. Joel and Oakley weren't small guys, both of them well over six feet tall. Mr. Milligan made them look like toy soldiers by comparison. The man was easily six-seven and pushing three-fifty—all of it sheer muscle. And all of that muscle was covered in tattoos of skulls, naked women, a huge dragon, and Sadie's name on one of his biceps. He looked like a cross between a Hell's Angel and a death-row inmate. The dude was fucking scary.

If Joel's mother intimidated Oakley, Sadie's dad scared the hell out of Joel. And Joel didn't spook easy.

So far they'd managed to avoid the guy since hooking up with Sadie. With any luck, they'd been successful in keeping their affair a secret, because Joel didn't want to know what would happen if Nelson Milligan found out about it. Sadie had mentioned murder and while she'd meant that as a joke, Joel was fairly certain that was a definite possibility.

Mr. Milligan smiled at his mom. Unfortunately, any bit of pleasantness on his face was gone when he turned to face Joel and Oakley. "Heard you two left Walt's wedding with my daughter."

Shit. Joel nodded. "We shared a cab." He didn't bother to add that the cab hadn't taken them to their own home.

Mr. Milligan's scowl deepened. "No shit. I own a bar, Joel. If there's anyone in town who knows the local cabbies better than me, I'd like to meet them."

Joel wasn't sure how to respond to that, so he didn't. He glanced over at Oakley, who gave him a slight *I don't know what the fuck to do* shrug.

"Man who drove you that night said he dropped the three of you off at Sadie's place. Said you looked pretty chummy."

"Chummy?" Joel's mom asked.

"Also heard you two have been showing up at Cruisers at closing time. Suppose you're going to tell me it's just a coincidence you picked the nights when I wasn't there."

That was no coincidence at all. Sadie had given them the nightly work schedule and told them exactly when to come.

"We're friends, Mr. Milligan." Joel didn't have a clue how to get out of this.

Mr. Milligan crossed his arms. "That all?"

Joel didn't want to lie. It didn't come easy to him, didn't sit right. Because in just a few short days, he knew he could never return to being merely friends with Sadie. He was crazy about her. At some point, he'd have to figure out what to do with those feelings because he'd backed himself into a corner— agreeing to a no-strings fling and including Oakley in the equation. He was fucked six ways to Sunday.

"Yep," Oakley answered, finally joining the conversation. Oakley teased Joel about his bad habit of being "honest to a fault". Meanwhile, Oakley was a master at stretching the truth. "We've asked her out about a thousand times each. She keeps turning us down. You got any advice for us, Mr. Milligan?"

Oakley's guileless grin didn't fool anyone.

"Yeah," Mr. Milligan said, suddenly appearing a foot taller. "Stay away from my daughter. She's too good for either one of you."

"What's going on with you and Sadie?" Mom asked Joel point-blank.

This conversation kept going from bad to worse.

Joel winced. "What Oakley said. We're friends."

"But you'd like it to be more?"

So much more.

Before he could reply, his mom turned to Mr. Milligan. "Sadie works in your bar, is that correct?"

Mr. Milligan nodded, clearly reconsidering his timing. He'd wanted to scare the shit out of him and Oakley, but he'd failed to take Joel's mom's presence into account.

"She's the girl with the tattoos and the earring right here?" His mother tapped her nose to demonstrate.

"Yeah. She is." Mr. Milligan's tone dared his mother to make a disparaging comment about either, but that clearly wasn't his mother's intent.

"I met her at a wedding last December. She was working the bar there. They had one of those Keurig coffee machines set up. I couldn't figure it out for the life of me. Sadie taught me how to use it and made me a cup. You have a lovely girl, Mr. Milligan."

Some of the aggression in Sadie's dad diminished at that. "She bartends part-time for special events, to make extra money."

"Are you and Oakley bothering this girl?" Mom asked him.

"No, Mom," Joel said, his temper sparking though he tried to remain cool. He was a grown-ass man, whether she wanted to believe it or not. "We aren't."

"Mmmhmm." It was a typical reply. Whenever she didn't believe him, she gave him that damn hum that let him know she'd be praying for his soul at mass. Joel tried to recall the last time his mother had paid him a compliment. It had been...years.

She turned back to Mr. Milligan. He cast a pretty big shadow over her, yet in this instance, his mother looked three times bigger than the giant standing next to her.

"You've raised a fine daughter."

"Thank you, Ms. Rodriguez." For a second, Joel thought Mr. Milligan actually blushed, but that could be remnants of the anger that sent him over here to threaten him and Oakley.

Oakley looked as bewildered as Joel by the exchange. "Uh, we gotta go...do some stuff," his friend said in what was probably the most awkward attempt at escape ever.

"I'll see you Sunday, Joel," his mother said. "Goodbye, Mr. Milligan. Oakley." The last name was added with the same unimpressed look she always reserved for Oakley.

Mr. Milligan tipped his hat once more, and then shot them a deadly look before heading off in the opposite direction.

Oakley slapped Joel on the back. "And that, my friend, is

why I moved as far away from my folks as I could. Doesn't matter how old you get. Parents are always going to stick their noses in your business."

"Nelson Milligan is going to murder us. Painfully," Joel said matter-of-factly.

"Oh yeah. That's a given." Then Oakley grinned widely. "But you know what? It'll totally be worth it."

That one line told Joel everything he needed to know. There wasn't going to be an easy resolution to what they'd begun. Oakley was as smitten with Sadie as Joel was.

This wasn't good.

* * *

Oakley had just finished unloading the truck when his cell phone rang. He grinned as Sadie's name popped up on the screen.

"Hey, gorgeous."

"Hi, Oak." The sound of her voice made him feel good all over. He'd been floating on this cloud of nonstop happiness since the wedding. Making a big enough jackass of himself that Coach had called him out for it this morning when he'd caught Oakley leaning on his pitchfork, his thoughts a million miles away and a goofy grin on his face. Coach had told him to get his head out of ass and pay attention to what he was doing.

Oakley figured that was easier said than done. He couldn't go two seconds without reliving some part of his time with Joel and Sadie. He was happier than he'd ever been in his life.

"What's up?"

"I was at the ranch earlier."

Oakley was instantly disappointed he'd missed her. "What for?"

"I'm helping Lorelie plan the after-party for Homecoming.

We worked out the alcohol list. I was hoping to run into you and Joel and Woody in the barn."

His cock rose at the sexy tone. "Damn, sweetheart. I wish you'd told us you were coming. We could have postponed our trip to town."

"My fault. I was hoping to surprise you. Believe me, I won't make that mistake again."

He chuckled. Woman had a sex drive that rivaled his. Which was scary considering he thought about sex approximately every three seconds.

"By the way, Lorelie knows I'm sleeping with Joel."

Oakley frowned. "Just Joel?"

"Yeah. It was a weird conversation. She could tell something was up by the way I kept looking outside for you guys. One thing led to another and she figured out there was some sex going down."

"Why would she think you were with Joel?"

"She guessed it was you at first, but I was trying to put her off the trail. She said something about how you never sleep with the same person twice, so if I was there looking, it must be for Joel. I realized I was being dumb to play it off completely. If she thinks I'm sleeping with one of you, she won't question it if my bike is parked outside your bunkhouse one night. Or several nights."

It was a good idea, but there was something about Lorelie thinking Sadie was just with Joel that rubbed him wrong. He knew he'd always given off a vibe of carefree Oakley, the guy who never settled down, but that wasn't for lack of desire. He'd always hoped to find someone and get married. Or at least someone to cohabitate with for the rest of his life. He was starting to resent that everyone thought he was a bad bet—Joel's mom, Sadie's dad, Lorelie. Maybe even Sadie and Joel.

The thought of those last two stung the most.

"That's probably a good idea," he said begrudgingly. "Ran into your pop today."

"Oh shit. What happened?"

Oakley climbed the three steps to the porch of the bunkhouse and sank down on one of the two rocking chairs there. The bunkhouse was small, built at the same time as the ranch house. It wasn't a huge spread, but it was big enough to keep them busy. It had been a shit ton of work when it had been him, Joel, and Coach. Since Coach's heart attack and recovery, the only thing keeping the ranch going was Joel's former teammates. If not for them, he and Joel would have been working twenty-four-seven.

"Let's just say no blood was shed. Yet."

Sadie groaned. "Dammit. Asshole cabbie came to pick up a drunk at Cruisers last night. Started running his mouth about dropping the three of us off at my place. I told my dad—and the driver—to mind their own business. I thought that had taken care of it. How bad was it?"

"It was a show. Especially when Joel's mom hopped in."

"She was there?"

Oakley understood her alarm. It had been a pretty uncomfortable scene. "Yup. Figure it's just our rotten luck that my folks are the only ones who don't live in Maris. They'd get a kick out of our relationship."

"We're not in a relationship." Sadie had made that point clear to them every single time they'd hooked up. She insisted it was just sex. That was all it could be.

Joel obviously agreed with that assessment. Neither of them thought a threesome could be more than a sexual fling. Oakley didn't agree. He believed he and Joel could quite easily share Sadie for the rest of their lives. The three of them fit together.

If that meant putting away a part of himself—the part that

was attracted to Joel too—then so be it. He was relatively sure he could do that. He was sure as hell willing to try if it meant keeping both of them in his life.

So he didn't push the relationship point. It was still early days. Wouldn't do him any good to spook them now. He was determined to show them exactly how good the three of them were together.

"Fine, Sade. But you're going to have to give me something to call this thing we're doing. Feels like more than just a fling, you know?"

"I'll give it some thought and get back to you," she teased. "And I'll talk to Dad again. Tell him to stay the hell away from y'all."

Oakley chuckled. "Yeah. I don't see that happening. He was pretty pissed."

"I guess that explains why he suddenly changed tonight's schedule. He's working until close with me. That's why I called."

"Fuck," Oakley muttered. They'd made plans to meet up at Cruisers. It had become a bit of a routine, locking the doors behind the last customer then meeting at "their table". Sometimes Sadie went down on him, other times she offered that paradise to Joel. Then they took turns fucking her.

It was completely hot, but Oakley was sort of anxious to break the pattern. He wanted to get Sadie in a bed, wanted to show her all the ways he and Joel could rock her world. "How late are you going to be?"

Sadie sighed. "No idea. Friday nights are usually hoppin'. Could be well after two. Which doesn't really work with those *up with the sun* hours you and Joel keep on the ranch."

She was right. During the week, Cruisers shut down around ten or eleven depending on the crowd. Even getting an early start, it was nearly three a.m. before he and Joel got back to the bunkhouse. Three hours' sleep was an ass-kicker, but they both agreed it was worth it. So much so they had been willing to pull an all-nighter tonight.

"Maybe we should just pack it in on this evening. Try to hook up another time."

Oakley knew Sadie's suggestion made sense. So many hours of lost sleep was catching up to him. But he didn't like the idea of not seeing her.

"I guess."

"I'm off Wednesday night. What if you guys come by my place? We can order pizza, drink body shots off each other, and get silly between the sheets."

Oakley laughed, even as her invitation had his cock twitching hungrily. "Damn. That sounds like my ideal night. Not crazy about having to wait so long though. Woody misses you."

She laughed. "Anticipation makes it better."

She was right, but he wasn't at a place where he was willing to put that theory to the test. If Oakley had his way, he'd be buried deep inside her every single night of the week. "Wednesday it is," he said at last. "I'll let Joel know."

"Cool. I'll call you later about a time. I gotta run. I'm late for work. See you Wednesday."

As they hung up, Oakley did some quick math in his head. Five days until he saw her. One hundred and twenty hours.

Jesus. He'd never make it.

Chapter Four

Sadie stood outside the bunkhouse and cursed herself for being a fool. And a nympho-fucking-maniac. She'd told Oakley that bullshit about anticipation making sex better just this afternoon. Instead, she'd gotten so hot and bothered and frustrated that she'd messed up at least a dozen drink orders and broken three glasses. She'd been so fucked-up her dad had told her to go home for fear she'd do some real damage. His exact words had been, "Get the fuck outta here before you burn the place down."

So she'd hopped on her bike, traveled two blocks toward her apartment, then turned around and headed here. She glanced at her cell phone. It was just after midnight. The lights in the ranch house and the bunkhouse were off. The entire spread was pitch black. Not that she was surprised. Days started early at a place like this. The polar opposite of her sleep-until-early-afternoon, then-stay-up-half-the-night lifestyle. She was the vampire in Oakley and Joel's early bird world.

She considered leaving them to their sleep for all of two seconds, and then she lifted her hand and knocked on the door.

Sadie only had a couple of minutes to second-guess her actions before the door opened. Joel stood before her in nothing but a pair of boxers. His hair was slightly mussed up and she suspected he'd actually been in bed for a while. Which made her feel really stupid for showing up unannounced.

"I, um—"

That was all she could say before Joel cut her off with a loud, "Thank God," and pulled her into his arms. His kisses could melt butter quicker than a microwave. She went soft in his embrace, letting his strength surround her, overwhelm her.

"Sadie?"

She heard Oakley say her name from somewhere behind Joel, his voice groggy from sleep. Joel either didn't hear Oakley or didn't care, because he didn't release her. His lips actually went hard and became more demanding, his hands gripping her head tightly when he thought she might back away. He didn't need to make that effort. She wasn't going anywhere.

When they finally came up for air, Sadie noticed Oakley leaning against the dining room table. His posture gave off an air of patience, but the rest of him betrayed his true feelings. His arms were crossed, his eyes hungry, his jaw clenched.

He radiated sex and need and desire.

"Hey," she said, realizing how silly it sounded in lieu of the kiss she and Joel had just shared.

Oakley's lips twitched. "Thought we were letting the anticipation build."

She lifted one shoulder. "That was bullshit. Have you ever known me to sit around idly and wait for something I wanted?"

Oakley didn't laugh as she'd expected. "Actually, yes. You kept me and Joel hanging on like lovesick puppies for years."

She couldn't tell if he was joking or if he was seriously upset that she'd put them off for so long. It didn't matter. He had a pretty good point. She *had* wanted them. But she'd denied it because she'd never in her dizziest daydreams, in her kinkiest fantasies, imagined anything like this. "You're right. I did. I'm sorry."

Joel reached out, grasping her upper arm and turning her to face him. "We don't need an apology, Sadie. We just need to make up for lost time."

She grinned, and then peeled off her leather jacket. Neither man stepped closer to help, but they certainly didn't look away as she pulled her t-shirt off, then her bra. She crossed the room to sit in a chair at the table where Oakley still leaned and lifted her foot. "Pull my boots off?"

Oakley wasted no time dropping down into the other chair and reaching for her foot. As he did so, Joel joined them, stepping behind her, his hands cupping her bare breasts.

Oakley licked his lips, his gaze glued to Joel's fingers as they pinched her nipples. They'd discovered her penchant for pain very early on. On top of that, Joel had her number when it came to dominance and submission. She wouldn't bend her will to any man outside of the bedroom, but there was something so sexy about the way Joel took over when they were fucking.

Once her boots were off, Oakley began to tackle the button on her jeans. He jerked his head at Joel, who moved his hands to his waist to help her rise from the chair. The men had spent years working side by side on the ranch. They didn't need words to make their desires known.

Oakley tugged her jeans down as Joel's hands returned to her breasts, his squeezes alternating between gentle and rough. He was a master at keeping her on her toes.

Neither man had bothered to dress when they answered the door, so it was a very simple matter of them dropping their boxers to join her in a naked state.

Sadie turned toward the table and started to bend over. At least one of them had taken her that way every night they'd come together at the bar, and she had to admit she loved the position.

Joel grabbed her upper arm, halting her. "Not tonight. Tonight we've got a bed. Let's use it."

She accepted Oakley's hand as he led her to the bedroom. There were two full-size beds in the room, each occupying an opposite wall. It wasn't what she'd expected to find in a bunkhouse, regardless of the fact they were the only two guys living there.

At her questioning glance, Oakley gave her a quick tour of the room. "When I first started working here, there were only twin beds. I got tired of squeezing my six-foot-two frame on that tiny piece of shit. Convinced Joel we could fit bigger beds in here," Oakley explained. Then he looked at Joel with a devilish grin. "Your bed or mine."

Joel rolled his eyes. "Mine. I have no idea when you washed your sheets last."

Sadie giggled, following Joel to the bed on the left. Both beds were unmade since she'd woken them, but where Oakley's sheets were just tossed on the mattress in a tangled mess, Joel's bed had been made with hospital corners, the cotton appearing almost pressed. The beds looked exactly as she would have imagined them.

Joel sat on the edge of his mattress and she wasted no time straddling his hips. They'd sat this way the last time they'd been together at closing time, her riding him as Oakley stood behind her, lifting her and pressing her down until she thought her body would implode under the intense, wonderful impact.

She shifted against him, his cock resting along her slit. She was soaking wet, her permanent condition whenever these guys were within a fifty-foot radius. She began to rock against him, moaning softly as the head of his cock stroked her clit.

Oakley gripped her ass cheeks, kneading them as she moved. Every now and then, she felt his erection against her back.

Joel kissed her throughout, his tongue plunging into her mouth the way she wanted his cock to do inside her. When she felt ready to explode, she lifted her hips, reaching for him, intent on guiding his dick in.

Joel's hand clamped down on her wrist tightly, halting her. She loved it when he used his undeniable strength to shackle her. He'd seen how much she enjoyed it when he held her hands behind her back, and he had promised her that one of these days he'd tie her up, he and Oakley tormenting her for hours before letting her come. The threat thrilled her as much as it frightened her. She had no doubt they would carry through on it.

"Turn around," he commanded.

As always, she responded without thought. She had no idea how he managed to do that when she had bucked pretty much every other authority in her life since the cradle.

She remained on his lap, his cock now resting against the slit in her ass. Her arousal crept higher.

"I'm going to fuck you this way while you suck on Oakley's dick."

It wasn't a request, though she only had to say no if she didn't want to. Not that they'd ever attempted anything she'd felt the slightest desire to refuse.

She started to rise up once more, dying to feel him inside her, but Joel gripped her hips and held her still.

"I need to borrow a condom, Oak. I'm out."

Oakley paused. "What do you mean you're out?"

"I was going to grab some on the way to Cruisers, but the plan changed and we didn't go into town."

"Fuck," Oakley muttered.

Sadie knew what he was going to say before he said it. She grimaced. "You're out too?"

Oakley nodded. "We've kinda been plowing through them this week. Shit. The last box I had lasted me a year. We bought that ten-pack three days ago and it's already gone."

Sadie started to laugh. It wasn't funny. Not by a long shot, but she loved the brutal honesty she shared with these guys. There was no game-playing, no second-guessing, or trying to pretend to be something they weren't. So many years as friends had left them with no choice but to speak the truth, because they knew each other too well to fall for bullshit.

Neither man seemed to share her humor. They actually looked like they were in pain. "Look, we probably should have had this conversation a week ago. I'm on the Pill and I'm clean."

Joel's arms tightened around her waist, his chin resting on her shoulder as he whispered, "I've never taken a woman without a condom."

"Me either," Oakley added. She and Joel looked at Oakley with raised eyebrows. He threw his hands up, palms toward them, as he quickly read their unasked question. "Or a guy. I've never fucked without a rubber, okay?"

"It's up to you, Sade. We don't have to have sex to come." Leave it to Joel to be the voice of reason at a time when she wanted nothing more than to be wild.

"I don't want to stop."

Both men studied her, neither moving for several moments. Then Joel lifted her up until the head of his cock rested at her opening. She cried out when he reversed the motion, pulling her down until she'd taken every lovely inch of him.

"God, Sadie." His voice contained an amazed sort of reverence that twisted her insides, made her heart beat a little bit faster.

Before she could reply, Joel was moving. Her feet fell to the floor between his and she put her years of doing lunges at the gym to good work. His hands remained on her hips, directing the speed, the depth. Even though she was providing the motion, she didn't forget who was driving the car.

Oakley stepped closer. Sadie was ready for him. Had been waiting. She lifted her face, reaching out to grasp his cock and pull him even nearer.

He pushed her hand away.

Joel, who slowed down so she could take his friend into her mouth, didn't miss the action. "Oak?"

"You've called the shots this whole week. Tonight, it's my turn."

Sadie shivered. Oakley had never given any indication that he possessed the same dominant streak that ran through Joel. The idea that both her lovers would want to command her had her inner muscles clenching tightly.

Joel groaned in response, his breath was ragged when he asked, "What do you want?"

Oakley didn't reply. Instead, he lifted Sadie's legs, placing her knees over Joel's. The position left her wide open, completely spread apart. Joel's cock was still buried inside her. Sadie leaned back against Joel's chest, her head resting on his shoulder. Joel kissed her ear, the side of her neck, and then he faced his friend again. "It's your show, Oakley."

Oakley grinned at Joel's offer. "Remember you said that."

Before Joel could take back his words, Oakley knelt between their outstretched legs, his breath hot and oh-so-fucking close to the place where her body and Joel's connected.

Oakley wasted no time doing exactly as he pleased—and as *she* pleased—when he ran his tongue along her clit.

"Holy shit," she cried out when he repeated the touch. Despite her limited mobility, Sadie found it impossible to remain still. She pressed her thighs against Joel's to lift herself, greedily seeking more stimulation.

Joel's hands gripped her waist tightly, adding his own strength to the thrust, lifting her once more. Oakley's tongue worked magic on her clit until she saw stars. She'd never come as quickly as she had with these two men this week. Sadie was used to having to work hard to find her own release with other lovers. With Oakley and Joel, the problem was the exact opposite. She couldn't keep herself from coming within minutes. Not that it mattered much. If the past week had taught her anything, it was that she was more than capable of having multiple orgasms.

Glancing down, she trembled at the sight of Oakley licking her clit, his hand wrapped around his own hard cock, stroking it. The image joined forces with the sensations of Joel's dick inside her and she fell over the edge, her hands digging into Oakley's scalp as she jerked roughly.

Neither man halted. There was no reprieve from the onslaught. In fact, as her orgasm started to fade, Joel picked up the pace, using his incredible power to bounce her more rapidly on his cock. Oakley replaced his tongue with his fingers on her clit.

She assumed he'd made the switch because it was too hard to keep his mouth on her, considering the almost brutal pace Joel was setting.

She was wrong.

Everything stopped when she felt it. Oakley's tongue had drifted lower, licking along her opening, around Joel's cock.

Joel froze, no longer moving her body according to his plea‑
sure, or hers.

For several captivating moments, she and Joel gasped for
air as Oakley explored their union with his tongue. Sadie's
head rolled backward as Oakley rubbed her clit with his finger,
using that super-sensitive nub against her. Part of her waited
for Joel to call a halt. Oakley was caressing Joel as much as he
was her.

Joel didn't move. Didn't make a sound. Sadie was afraid to
turn and look, terrified of breaking the spell.

Then Joel did make a noise—a deep-throated growl that
was equal parts hunger and pain. Sadie looked down. Oakley
had Joel's balls in his other hand. She marveled at his ability to
render both of them mindless. Oakley rubbed her clit and
squeezed Joel's balls while working his tongue around Joel's
cock and her opening with total ease.

Sadie's pussy clenched once more. "I can't, I need..." She
needed to come again.

Oakley lifted his face, smiled at her, then bent his head and
bit her clit. Sadie shattered. And her undoing was also Joel's.

He moved then, twisting quickly, tossing her facedown on
his bed. The quick movement sent Oakley backwards, landing
on his ass on the floor. That was all Sadie had seen before she
landed on her stomach on the soft comforter. Joel gripped one
of her ass cheeks in his grip as she listened to him pump his
cock quickly with the other.

"Look at me, Sadie."

She lifted up onto her elbows, watching him over her shoul‑
der. His dick was slick with her juices and he was jacking off
fast and furious. The second her gaze met his, it was over. He
grunted, jets of come landing on her back and her ass as he
continued to stroke, to push out every last drop.

He fell to his back next to her on the bed, but he didn't

close his eyes and he didn't look at her, his gaze focused solely on the ceiling.

Sadie started briefly when she felt Oakley's hand on her shoulder. He'd found a towel somewhere and was gently cleaning her off. The soft ministrations almost lured her to sleep. Until she felt Oakley's soft touch on her thigh and heard him call her name. Then she rolled over, opened her legs and lifted her arms, beckoned him to her. Oakley came over her without hesitation. He touched her pussy, found her wet, and guided his cock inside.

Something had been jarred loose, had changed the complexion of the game. Sadie had sensed the underlying sexual currents coursing between Oakley and Joel since the very first night. Now, it had all been laid bare and it was apparent Oakley felt the same fear as she. They fucked as if it was their last night on earth. Oakley pounded inside her deeply, roughly. She welcomed it, clawed his back, demanded more.

This couldn't be it. It couldn't be the end. She wouldn't allow it. Like Oakley, she felt reckless, wild, panic-stricken. She was losing control and she hated it.

She had no idea how long she and Oakley would have continued, would have torn into each other, but it was Joel who ended it.

He gripped Oakley's shoulder and held tightly. "Slow down, bro. You're going to hurt her."

Joel was right. But not in the way he meant. Oakley *would* hurt her. Not physically, but emotionally. She'd let them in. And now these men—both of them—had the ability to hurt her.

"I'm sorry, Sadie," Oakley said, trembling above her. He rested his forehead against hers. "God. I'm so sorry."

She shook her head. Refusing his words and her realization. If she didn't think about it, it wasn't there. She'd employed that philosophy for years and it had never steered her wrong. If she didn't want to feel something, she simply put it away and didn't feel it.

Instead, she concentrated on Joel's hand, the way it still gripped Oakley's shoulder. They were all caught in the silence.

Then Sadie understood. Joel felt the same fear she and Oakley did. None of them wanted this to end.

"I don't want to stop," she said at last, her voice sounding like a scream in the far-too-quiet room. For a moment, she feared they would misunderstand and think she was referring only to right now.

Oakley didn't move, but he did smile. It was a tentative one, but it gave her hope. "I don't want to either."

Joel's hand fell away, but he didn't leave the bed, didn't seek to move away from them. His eyes were dark but his face shuttered, unreadable. "Then we won't stop." His voice was expressionless. He might have agreed to continue, but Sadie knew there was a day of reckoning coming soon. For all of them.

Oakley dropped to his elbows and kissed her gently. Then he started to move. Unlike before, his thrusts were soft, slow. Wonderful.

Sadie had no idea she could find completion in something other than hardcore, knock-your-shoes-off fucking. Oakley and Joel kept proving all her previous misconceptions wrong.

Within minutes, she was there. Her orgasm helped along by Joel, who'd placed his hand between them, his finger gently stroking her clit. They knew she needed that extra touch and neither of them failed to offer it. In one short week, they seemed to know all her secrets.

Oakley came with her, her body's undulations milking his climax, and for the first time in her life, she learned what it felt like to have someone release inside her. It was warm and sticky, and she knew right then, she'd never allow either of them to wear a condom again.

Another barrier they'd broken down.

Sadie resolved that would be the last, even as she knew that was a lie.

Again, she shoved the wayward thought away and let herself drift off to sleep, nestled between Joel and Oakley.

Chapter Five

Joel stood next to Oakley outside the door to Sadie's apartment on Wednesday and cursed himself for being the world's biggest idiot. He shouldn't be here, but he couldn't stay away.

He and Oakley hadn't seen her since Friday night at the bunkhouse. Since the night he let his best friend lick his cock and squeeze his balls.

Neither he nor Oakley had mentioned the incident. He suspected Oakley wanted to talk about it, but he'd been too afraid of Joel's response. Oakley was right to be scared. Even now, Joel was torn between beating the fucking shit out of him or...God...pushing the man against a wall and demanding he suck his cock for real this time.

Now he was standing outside Sadie's house, having let way too much go unsaid. His gut was telling him to walk away right now. Turn around, get in the truck and fall into a bottle of bourbon until he was able to forget Sadie and Oakley even existed.

The rest of him—his heart, head, and dick—wasn't going anywhere.

Sadie opened the door looking completely adorable.

A fact Oakley expressed through a wolf whistle. "Damn, Sade. I love these miniskirts of yours."

His friend stepped inside the apartment, not stopping until he had Sadie in his arms. Joel had ceased wondering what exactly it was about watching Oakley kiss the girl Joel was in love with that turned him on so much. Some things, he figured, were simply meant to remain mysteries. Like whether or not ghosts were real, Atlantis had existed, and why the Texas Rangers couldn't win a freaking World Series.

When the kiss continued with no sign of letting up, Joel walked inside and closed the door behind him. The sound of it drove Sadie and Oakley apart.

"Hi," she said to Joel with a flirty grin.

"Remembered I was here, did you?"

She laughed at his joke and he realized why he was here. Because it was fun. It was easy. And because, despite all the shit rolling around in his head, he couldn't deny that it felt right to be here. Like he belonged.

Joel had spent most of his life feeling as if he was a peripheral player. While he'd been a member of the Titans' state championship, his position had been center. He'd basically snapped the ball to Tucker, then plowed into the first guy he saw. He'd done both jobs efficiently, but not in such a way that he got a lot of notice.

That seemed to be true of most things. Quite a few of his teammates had gone on to do amazing things with their lives—Tucker made it big in the NFL, Walt found success in Nashville, Jack molded kids' lives in the classroom, Tyson was a doctor, and Evan kept Maris safe as a cop. Meanwhile, he was still working on Coach's ranch, a position he'd started part-time while in high school. He'd gone nowhere and done nothing noteworthy.

"I didn't forget you."

Joel's cock rose rapidly in response to her sultry wink.

Oakley, who thought with his cock and then his stomach—in that order—walked toward her kitchen. "I smell food, but I don't see anything."

Sadie had offered to make them dinner. "We're not eating here."

Joel adjusted his pants and stifled a groan. He wasn't sure he could go out with Sadie and maintain any semblance of public decency. "We're not?"

She shook her head and pointed toward her bedroom. "Dinner—and dessert—are in there."

Joel grinned. She was the sexiest woman he'd ever met.

She started to walk toward her bedroom, but he grasped her hand and held her back.

"Not so fast," Joel said. Sadie was clearly used to being the aggressor in her sexual encounters. She was also as submissive as the day was long. He'd recognized that need in her their first night together. Knowing no one had ever given her the challenge she longed for was one of the reasons he'd spent most of the past week walking around with a hard-on. He had a list of bedroom demands that would keep them busy for the next decade or so. "Take off your clothes."

Sadie narrowed her eyes briefly. Just long enough that he thought she might balk. He secretly hoped she would. He was dying to show her how delicious punishment could be.

Then, as she had in the past week, she obeyed. It floored him to see such a powerful woman give herself over to him. Her skirt, blouse and bra fell away quickly. She hadn't been wearing panties, a fact that delighted Oakley.

"Damn, I wish I'd known that when I was kissing you," Oakley murmured.

Once she was naked, she looked at them, a spark of challenge in her gaze. "Your turn."

Oakley didn't hesitate. The man had two temperatures—freezing cold and boiling. He could be standing in line at the grocery store with nothing more on his mind than paying the clerk. Then a pretty woman—or hot guy—would walk by and the man would be raring to go. Joel had given him shit about it, but nowadays, he found himself in the same boat. One look from Sadie, the sound of her voice or even a whiff of her perfume, and he'd go from soft to steel in an instant.

Joel tried to keep his focus on Sadie as Oakley stripped off his shirt and pants. He'd seen his friend naked more times than he could count in the past eight years. After all, they shared a room and neither of them had any hang-ups about nudity. The difference was, seeing Oakley without clothing had never affected him before.

Even more disturbing was the idea of taking off his clothes in front of Oakley. His friend's bisexuality had always been there. Always. But Joel had never felt as if Oakley was attracted to him.

Was he now?

If not, then what the hell was all that licking and touching about? Was Oakley just trying to make sure Joel got off too? Or had it meant something to him?

Once Oakley was naked, he and Sadie turned to look at Joel. Sadie looked impatient, but Oakley's gaze was different. It felt like a dare.

Joel reached for his t-shirt and tugged it off. Then, before he could think of a reason not to, he kicked off his shoes and pants. Fuck it. He'd made his bed when he'd crawled into Sadie's with Oakley. There was no going back now.

They followed Sadie to her bedroom. Oakley laughed loudly when he saw her bed, and Joel grinned. She'd laid a red-and-white-checkered tablecloth on top of her comforter and lit candles on the nightstands. In the middle of her makeshift picnic was a bucket of KFC, a huge bowl of McDonald's French fries and a bottle of Don Julio.

"I forgot to mention," she said, crawling onto the bed. "I can't cook."

"Tequila?" Joel asked, reaching for the full bottle of Blanco.

Sadie shrugged. "Tequila makes everything taste good."

Oakley took the bottle from him, uncorked it and took a shot. "You got that right." He passed the bottle to Sadie, who followed his lead. Then she sent the tequila to Joel. He took a swig, enjoying the heat of the alcohol as it slid down his throat.

He and Oakley joined her on the bed, the three of them talking and laughing as if it was the most normal thing on earth to be eating fast food while naked in her bed.

Once they'd plowed through the bucket and put a big dent in the massive pile of fries she'd bought, Oakley "cleared the table", moving everything—except the tequila—to the floor.

"What should we do next?" Oakley asked, though the way he ran his fingers over Sadie's breasts made it obvious what *he* wanted to do.

Sadie, however, had other plans. She pushed his hand away. "Nope. No wham-bam tonight."

Joel scowled. "I'm fairly certain we've never done wham-bam."

She laughed. "You know what I mean. We get busy and then we get off. We're going to try that anticipation thing Oakley and I discussed."

Oakley scowled. "Thought we agreed we sucked at that."

"Which is why we need practice. I thought we could play a game."

Joel looked at their naked bodies. "I guess strip poker is out."

Sadie giggled, then took another quick shot of tequila. "I want to play Truth or Dare."

Oakley's brows lifted in approval. "I like the sound of that. Can we make it Kinky Truth or Dare?"

Sadie handed Oakley the bottle as she rolled her eyes. "You have a one-track mind."

Oakley took another drink. "Fine. Your game, you start."

"Okay." Sadie leaned against the headboard and looked at Oakley. It occurred to Joel she'd had time to consider her questions...and her dares. She was far too ready to play. "Oak. Truth or dare?"

"Truth."

"Tell me about your first time."

Oakley stretched out next to her, though the opposite direction, his head positioned at her feet. "Okay. With a guy or a girl?"

Sadie was undaunted. "Your *first* first. Was it with a girl?"

Oakley shook his head. "Nope. It was a guy. Friend of mine from school. We were sixteen. His name was Jacob." Oakley's gaze remained on Sadie's face and Joel got a sense Oakley didn't want to say more.

Joel was surprised to realize he didn't know this story. He and Oakley had shared so much of their lives with each other, it didn't occur to him until now that the one thing they didn't discuss was Oakley's affairs with guys. Had Oakley purposely avoided telling Joel about them? Had Joel somehow given him the impression those stories would make him uncomfortable?

"Details," Sadie prompted.

"Jake was an oops. A late-in-life baby for his folks. Which meant he had a lot of older siblings who were adults. Jake was housesitting for his older brother one weekend. His parents had said it was cool for him to stay at his brother's place to take care of the dog and stuff. I got invited to sleep over too. His brother left us a twelve-pack of beer in the fridge that Jake's parents didn't know about. Neither one of us really partied so it didn't take much for us to get tipsy. Next thing I know, Jake's kissing me."

Sadie tilted her head. "Did you know then? Did you know you were into guys?"

Oakley nodded slowly and for the first time since he started talking, his eyes drifted to Joel. "Yeah. I always knew I wasn't exactly like the other guys. My straight friends. They were all about girls, and while I could appreciate boobs as much as the other guys, I sort of got the same tingle whenever I caught a glimpse of a guy's ass in the locker room. Jake was completely out of the closet, one-hundred-percent gay. A lot of the guys stayed away from him because that freaked them out, made them nervous. It didn't bother me."

"What happened then?" Joel was strangely aroused by Oakley's story.

"Kissing turned to touching. Clothes came off. It wasn't Jake's first time. He put on a condom, filled my ass with lube and we fucked."

Typical Oakley description. Straight forward, graphic language, nothing extra or flowery.

"You liked it?" Sadie asked.

Oakley's grin grew. "I fucking loved it. Jake and I sort of kept going for a while, but he was a giver, not a taker, and not into girls at all. Six months later I was at a campground with my parents. We'd met and started hanging out with another family. They had a pretty daughter about my age. The two of us snuck out of the tents one night, started making out. One thing led to another and it was finally my turn to put the condom on."

"And you liked it?" Joel asked.

Oakley laughed. "I fucking loved it."

Sadie picked up a pillow and batted him in the head. "It occurs to me from your story, you clearly haven't grown up a bit since high school. An eternal man-child. Peter Pan."

"Growing up is for pussies. My turn." Oakley took Sadie's foot in his hand and sucked her big toe into his mouth as she gasped and squirmed. Oakley didn't release her. Instead, he said, "Sadie. Truth or dare?"

She narrowed her eyes. "God. Both choices are potentially dangerous."

Oakley gave her a wicked wink.

"Fine. Truth."

Oakley dropped her foot and sat up. "Good. I was hoping you'd pick that. There's something I've been wanting to know ever since I moved to Maris, but every time I bring it up, you change the subject."

It was clear from Sadie's groan she knew where this was going. Which sparked Joel's curiosity because he didn't have a clue.

"You don't strike me as the Homecoming-Queen type. Tell me how that happened."

Joel could understand Oakley's confusion. Hell, he knew her then, but he was still hard-pressed to remember the conservative, clean-cut blonde, run-of-the-mill girl she'd been then compared to the powerhouse, opinionated, take-no-prisoners, stand-out-in-a-crowd beauty she was now.

Sadie shrugged. "Why can't you let that go?"

"I'm curious too," Joel admitted.

She glared at him. "You were there, Joel. Didn't you vote for me?"

He nodded. "I was a sophomore."

"Oh yeah. Only the seniors voted." She looked at Oakley and confessed, "I guess I have changed a bit since high school."

"That might be the understatement of the century. You've changed completely."

"I was a typical teenager. High school was my rebellious stage."

Joel thought of the Sadie she was at seventeen vs. the Sadie she was now. The words didn't compute. "High school was your rebellious age?"

"I was six years old when my mom split. That meant my dad raised me. You've met the man. Have you ever noticed anything soft or girlie in him?"

"Jesus, no," Oakley muttered.

"That's because there isn't anything. He didn't have a clue how to relate to a little girl, so he basically just treated me like a boy. We went to baseball games together, he put me in little league. I did my homework at a table in Cruisers, surrounded by a bunch of drunks and foul language, and I watched more than a little inappropriate making out in the back room. None of that shit fazes you after a while."

Joel tried to imagine Sadie's childhood. Compared to his strict upbringing, it actually sounded ideal. Joel's days were more regimented. School, homework, chores, prayers, bedtime. He'd never heard his mother curse, never seen her drink, and she sure as hell had never gone out on a date. What she had done was work all day, every day, at two different stores while he was at school, then she took on tailoring jobs on the side, sewing at home until late at night to make sure they had enough money for the bills and food. It was a rather lifeless, humorless existence. Maybe that was why he was so attracted to Sadie and Oakley, with their colorful tales and larger-than-life personalities.

"So you decided to rebel?" Oakley asked.

"Yeah. Once I got boobs, the dad who used to let me do whatever I wanted went into meltdown mode. Turned into the overprotective bastard he is today." There wasn't a bit of malice lacing Sadie's tone. In fact, it was pretty obvious she adored her dad. "So I decided to push his buttons. Dyed my hair blonde, started wearing makeup and low-cut shirts. Went a little boy crazy, talking on the phone all night. My dad went ballistic. Didn't have a clue how to deal with a girlie-girl. It was okay for a while, but my outside didn't match my insides and that was pretty obvious to the other girls. I've never had a lot of friends who were girls. All that drama and squealing and giggling shit gets on my nerves."

Joel suddenly realized that was part of what made her so attractive. He'd thought it was her blunt honesty, but it was all that other stuff too.

"I guess the fact I was a late bloomer made me a bit more noticeable, more memorable when compared to the other three senior girls who were up for the title. It didn't help that—while they were all gorgeous—they were also snooty bitches who hadn't been particularly nice to many people in our class. According to the principal, I won by a landslide."

"When did you give up the whole rebellion thing?" Oakley asked.

"Just before graduation. Met a badass guy with a motorcycle and tats who smoked like a chimney and I thought I was in love. Turned out I was just in love with the tats and the bike. Even so, I stuck with the loser six months longer than I should have. At the end of the relationship, I had my own motorcycle, a really bad tattoo on my ass, and my father started sleeping better at night."

Oakley studied Sadie's naked body. "I love the butterfly tat."

She grinned. "So do I, but it's what's under the butterfly that sucked."

"Ah," Oakley said. "And so we get the story. What was it? His name? His face?"

Sadie narrowed her eyes. "Please. I would never be so stupid. It was just his initials."

Joel laughed until she turned her gaze to him. "Okay, Joel. Your turn. Truth or dare?"

In light of the revelations of the past few minutes, Joel decided to take the easy way out. "Dare."

"Awesome," Sadie said without a second of hesitation. "I dare you to kiss Oakley."

Joel froze, hoping he hadn't heard her correctly. "What?"

"Kiss Oakley. And nothing lame. Lips touching, mouths open, little tongue action would be cool. And maybe you can grip his hair like you do mine. Because that is totally hot."

"Sadie..." Joel didn't know what else to say. Didn't know how to get out of this situation. Shit, how to get out of this bed and this room.

Oakley didn't make a peep, his face completely impassive. What the hell did he think of her dare? Why didn't he step in and say no way?

Because he wanted it.

Oakley wanted his kiss. Joel knew that. Knew it deep down in his soul. God, he'd always known it.

Joel tried to fight down the panic gripping him. His next move had the potential to destroy so much more than this unorthodox affair they'd begun. He was terrified of losing his best friend.

The silence dragged on for too long. And while Oakley had one hell of a poker face, it started to slip, his eyes revealing a sadness Joel couldn't stand to see.

"One kiss," Joel whispered as he leaned across Sadie's body, gripped Oakley's face and pulled his lips to his.

Joel wasn't sure what he'd been expecting, but it wasn't the explosion of heat, passion, and desire that crashed over him like an avalanche.

Oakley had obviously considered what this would be like, and he was ready to take advantage of the opportunity. His best friend wasn't a passive lover. Joel had discovered that the other night. He may let Joel take the lead in most things, but when he really wanted something, Oakley took it.

Right now, Oakley wanted *him*. His hands reached out to grip Joel's upper arms tightly. He held him close, allowing no retreat. Not that Joel had plans to go anywhere.

There had been no slow start. They'd gone in with mouths open, devouring, claiming, taking everything and then demanding more.

Joel felt no need to be gentle with Oakley. Instead, he longed for a roughness he didn't dare show to Sadie. She was soft, sweet and, despite her penchant for pain, he held himself in check. He'd rather rip off his arm than hurt her.

The same didn't hold true for Oakley. Not that he didn't care about his friend—he loved him. But because Joel wanted to feel this. Really fucking *feel* it.

Oakley got it. He bit Joel's lower lip, the sting, followed by the bitter taste of blood, driving Joel out of his mind. He gripped Oakley's hair and pulled it, hard enough to provoke a pained groan. The sound was almost enough to make Joel stop. Until Oakley gave as good as he got—digging his fingers into Joel's scalp.

The pain morphed into a pleasure so intense, Joel feared he'd come right there. Oakley hadn't touched his cock, his hands weren't even near his dick, and yet, Joel was on the precipice of blowing. Hard.

The realization shook him.

He shoved Oakley away, then rose from the bed. His harsh breathing loud in the quiet room. What the fuck was he doing?

"That can't happen again." The words fell out before Joel could think about them.

"The hell it can't." Oakley looked just as wiped out, overwhelmed. Shattered.

Joel shook his head. Every molecule in his body was telling him to leave, but his feet were sunk in some imaginary quicksand. Something was holding him there. If he left right now, it would be the biggest mistake of his life.

But staying here was a mistake too.

"I'm sorry."

It was the first time Sadie had spoken since her dare. But Joel hadn't forgotten her presence. Not for a single second. And he knew Oakley hadn't either.

He'd felt her eyes on them as they'd kissed, her arousal wrapping around them, driving them higher.

Oakley reached over and ran a gentle hand through her hair. "What are you apologizing for?"

Sadie didn't look at Oakley. She never took her eyes off Joel. He couldn't stand the fear, the sadness in her eyes. This sure as hell wasn't her fault. Knowing Sadie, she'd thought this dare—this entire game—would help move along something that was inevitable. And it had.

"Not your fault, Sade," Joel said.

She gave him an expectant look. Clearly she hadn't given up hope that he'd accept what had happened.

He couldn't.

"I'm straight." It was probably the dumbest thing he'd ever said in his life, but for some reason, Joel felt as if he had to keep saying it. More for himself than for them.

Oakley snorted, shaking his head and closing his eyes. Joel

could almost hear the cursing dialogue running through his best friend's mind. Then, as always, Oakley found a place to put the anger. It was a skill Joel envied.

When his eyelids lifted, he captured Joel's gaze, giving him a smile and a shrug. "It's okay, man. We tried it. You didn't like it. No harm, no foul."

Oakley's words were a gift. He was letting Joel off the hook, pretending to buy into a big-ass lie.

Because they'd tried it and Joel had—to quote Oakley— fucking loved it.

If he'd been a better man, he would have admitted that. Given something back to his best friend. But in his mind, he pictured the faces of his mother, his teammates, Coach. How would they react if he came out? If he told them that not only was he in love with Sadie Milligan, he was head over heels for his best friend too?

He'd lived his entire life walking the straight and narrow, never rocking the boat. He couldn't see a way to stop doing that now.

So he greedily took the escape. He smiled and nodded, tried to play it cool. Truth was, he couldn't have spoken if his life depended on it. His throat was constricted, completely closed, the words trapped behind the steel door.

"Besides," Oakley said, "you can't fucking kiss worth a damn. Can't hold a candle to our sweet Sadie's kisses."

Oakley apparently sought to prove that point by kissing Sadie. She'd laughed lightly at his joke before Oakley's lips covered hers.

Oakley was trying to find a way to take the heavy, too-intense moment and turn it back into something they could all handle. It wouldn't work, but Joel loved his friend for trying.

Loved him.

When they broke apart, Oakley looked over his shoulder at

him. Joel hadn't moved an inch. He still wasn't sure which direction to go. That old song from The Clash drifted through his head. *Should I stay or should I go?*

"Coming back to bed?" Oakley asked.

For a moment, Joel had imagined their game was over. He was wrong. Oakley had just issued the final dare.

And just like last time, Joel found it impossible to resist.

Chapter Six

Sadie sat next to Oakley and pretended to watch the Homecoming football game. The Titans were currently pummeling their rivals and spirits were high. Even so, it would be no hardship for her to depart right after halftime. She was leaving early, heading to Coach's ranch to help Lorelie do all the last-minute stuff before her party. The rest of the guests would arrive about an hour or so later once the game was over.

It had been nine days since Sadie had instigated that ill-fated Truth or Dare game. Nine straight days of an unending fuck festival. Joel and Oakley had come back to her bed that night like two men possessed, and they'd found a way to be together every single night since then, five times at her apartment, twice in the bar, once at their bunkhouse and one time by a lake in the back bed of their pickup truck.

It was insanity. Beautiful, mind-blowing insanity.

And despite the unending litany of orgasms, Sadie knew they were living on borrowed time. The kiss Oakley and Joel had shared had jarred something loose and, though they were trying to ignore the fact that it was teetering precariously, they seemed to have accepted there was nothing that could stop it from crashing to the ground and shattering.

Worst of all, it was her fault. Neither man blamed her, but that didn't mean she hadn't opened Pandora's box. She had honestly thought Joel merely needed a little push in the right direction. She was certain she hadn't misread his feelings, but what she hadn't understood was how strongly he would fight against them.

Even though, she should have realized. She'd known Joel for years. Knew how strongly he stood by his convictions, how much he believed in doing the right thing, in keeping the people around him happy. He'd move heaven and earth for his mother if she needed him. And for Coach. For Oakley...and now, she suspected, for her. Once he cared about someone, there wasn't anything he wouldn't do to protect them. Even if that meant denying his own happiness or hiding some intrinsic part of himself that he thought others wouldn't understand or accept.

"Sadie?"

She glanced up at Oakley's voice.

"Man, that was a deep thought. I hope it was some dirty fantasy that involved me," he said with a sexy grin.

She hadn't mentioned her fears. How could she? She was the one who'd put the two of them in this untenable position to begin with. For years she'd refused their offers to date because she hadn't wanted to break up their friendship. Looks like she'd managed to drive a wedge between them anyway...and not in a way she had expected.

"Damn," Oakley frowned. "That's no fantasy. What's wrong, Sade?"

She shook off her uneasiness. "Nothing. Just bored. Football's not my thing."

"Don't let Joel hear you say that. High school football played a big role in some of the happiest days of his life."

"How long can you keep pretending?"

Oakley's brow creased. He knew what she was talking about. He glanced around the stands and she cursed herself for starting this now. Here. They'd chosen seats amongst Joel's old teammates and their loved ones.

She glanced down to the sideline and spotted the back of Joel's head. He was standing next to Tucker and Caleb, waiting to take the field at halftime to watch as their beloved Coach was honored for his contributions to Maris football. Lorelie stood near the guys, next to her dad, looking so proud she could pop.

That left her and Oakley in the stands with girlfriends, wives and friends, all those who had come to cheer on the Titans of today as well as the state champs from fifteen years ago.

"Sadie." Oakley stood up and offered his hand. "Come here."

She followed as he led them out of the stands to a private place near the gate. "It's not going to happen with me and Joel."

"But you want it to. And so does he. I can tell. When we're together, it's...like there's something missing."

Oakley frowned. "Wait. You don't enjoy what we do?"

She rolled her eyes. "Don't be stupid. You're right there beside me. You know I love it. But I'm not blind and I have a really hard time not pointing out something when it's wrong. What you and Joel are denying. To yourselves. To us. It's wrong."

"I don't have a choice, Sadie. If it were up to me, things would be different. But I can't force the guy to accept what I'm offering. He has to come to me."

She blew out an exasperated breath. "He can't do that. It's just not in him. We have to convince him, show him—"

"No." Oakley cut her off. "Absolutely not. We cracked the door with that kiss and we left it open. I'm not shoving him through. He's going to walk in on his own or he's not. There's nothing else you and I can do."

"Well...I think that sucks."

Oakley chuckled. "That's because you and me are doers. We want something, we just take it. Joel's a thinker. He has to analyze, weigh all the options and dangers. Shit like that takes time."

Sadie laughed. For someone who seemed to walk through life with a nonchalant, devil-may-care attitude, Oakley was probably one of the shrewdest people she'd ever met. He saw way more than he let on. And even better, he understood what made the people he cared about tick.

Meanwhile, she didn't have a clue. She'd always been the type to try to force puzzle pieces together that didn't fit. It was one reason she was so bad at relationships. She'd choose the world's worst guy, then work like a son of a bitch to hang on to something she'd had no business reaching for to begin with.

Even with Oakley and Joel, she'd found a way to make the possibility of something special impossible by choosing both guys instead of just one. The longer she was with them, the more she didn't have a doubt she could have made a happy ending with either of them. And, in typical fashion, she'd fucked it up by grasping at a short-term fantasy that likely wouldn't last through the rest of the year.

Whistles pierced the night, marking the end of the second quarter. The announcer came over the loudspeaker, inviting the crowd to turn their attention to the special halftime presentation.

Oakley wrapped his arm around her shoulder and turned her back to the stands. "Come on. Joel will be upset if we miss this."

Sadie returned to her place on the blanket she'd set down to share with Oakley and Joel. She'd caught more than a few sideways glances when she walked in with both of them. While Lorelie thought she was dating Joel—and clearly suspected Oakley was just a third wheel—there were plenty of other friends left wondering exactly which guy she was with.

Except for Caleb, a local businessman and a former teammate of Joel's. His stare felt a little too perceptive for Sadie's comfort. Caleb seemed to know it was both.

The announcer began to introduce the older players. She and Oakley screamed their fool heads off when Joel's name was announced and he walked across the field. She laughed as all the guys fist-bumped each other as they walked down the line. It was cool to see so many of the players back home and together in the same place.

Sadie remembered the boys who'd made up that team fondly, even though they'd been younger than her. Probably because quite a few of them had had crushes on her. She wondered how many of them had honed their flirting skills on her before landing their real high school sweethearts. Tucker and Walt had, for sure. And Jack—though he flirted with anything in a skirt.

The stadium was packed with current students and their parents, locals who lived and breathed high school football, and returning graduates, who had come home from wherever they'd moved to take that long walk down memory lane.

Sadie had never felt particularly nostalgic about high school. It was four years of her life that she'd basically just tried to survive. Not because she had been bullied. It was more like she'd been bored out of her mind.

She saw the Homecoming Court standing to one side, waiting for their time to shine under the stadium lights. Four girls nervously hoping they'd walk off with the crown. Sadie remembered standing in that exact same place. And she could recall her thoughts at that moment. She was hoping she wouldn't win because the whole thing felt like one big joke and she'd feel like an ass in a tiara.

"I know you told me the story, but I still can't quite picture you down there on that field in a crown," Oakley joked, leaning close.

"Neither can I. It was embarrassing as hell."

He laughed. "Yeah. That's sort of how I imagined you would have felt about it. Joel looks happy though. I wish I'd known him in high school."

She glanced at Oakley's face as he looked at his best friend. They were so close it was hard to remember they hadn't known each other forever. It seemed like they should have grown up together.

Sadie tried to think back to Joel in school, tried to remember some details she could offer Oakley. "He was a quiet kid. Not that he didn't have friends. He just wasn't showy or cocky. I remember being surprised when he made the Varsity football team because he didn't have that jock strut the rest of the guys had. He was a rule-follower, even then. And a good guy, which meant the girls steered clear. Most high school girls are only into the bad boys."

Oakley listened to her description in rapt attention. "Their loss, I guess."

She nodded. "Yeah. It was."

Once all the guys had been introduced, it was time for the main event. Coach Carr was called forward. Lorelie walked with him toward the superintendent of the school system and the Maris High School principal. The announcer read off Coach's accomplishments, the list long and full of all the things that made him the amazing man he was. And then they directed everyone's attention to the press box. A large white sheet was hanging above the concession stand, but at the principal's command, the covering fell away to reveal a new sign.

The Nicholas Carr Stadium had been named and dedicated to the talented coach who had given so much to the school, the community and to the players who loved him.

Sadie didn't consider herself a sentimental person, but she didn't hesitate to take the tissue Tucker's girlfriend, Lela, offered her at the unveiling.

Coach had been like a father to the boys who played for him, but he'd taken more than a few other wayward souls under his wing as well. She recalled sitting under these stands following the Homecoming game all those years ago and wishing that her mother had been there to see her crowned. She had truly believed that silly honor would've made her mother proud of her.

Coach Carr had found her there and he'd comforted her. His wife had died in childbirth with Lorelie. He understood how hard it was for a daughter to grow up without her mother, but he said that in his estimation, that missing part only made a woman stronger. Because she learned how to stand on her own two feet, to discover who she truly was—not through emulation, but through honest introspection. It was the first time Sadie had felt a kinship with Lorelie, a girl she'd barely known.

And then he'd said something Sadie had never forgotten. He told her that tears were fine as long as she knew what she was crying for.

Sadie had gone home that night and thought about what Coach had said. She thought she'd been crying for her mom, but when forced to face the truth, she realized she'd been feeling sorry for herself. They'd been wasted tears. She didn't need her mother's approval. She only needed her own.

Coach had set her on the path to discovering her own strength, her own sense of being. And she'd never forgotten it.

* * *

Joel walked into the barn with Caleb and Tyson. Sadie and Oakley had left the game shortly after halftime to help Lorelie get ready for the onslaught of people who were just now starting to arrive. The Titans had trounced the Pioneers 36-7, maintaining their undefeated status. The excitement level of the locals was reaching fever pitch as everyone proclaimed this team was going to do what none other had done since Joel's. Bring home the state trophy.

Sadie was already set up behind the bar, a few early arrivers standing in line, waiting for drinks. Oakley was just behind her, pumping the keg and making some off-color joke about two nuns and a cheerleader. Everyone was laughing. The evening had only just begun, but it promised to be a great night.

Joel stood back as he watched all the activity surrounding them. He and Oakley had spent the better part of three days getting the barn cleaned out and setting up a bar area, building a makeshift stage for Walt and his musician friend, as well as chiseling out a decent bit of space for dancing.

Lorelie and her girlfriends had spent all afternoon decorating and making the food. From the look on Coach's face, Joel suspected every bit of sweat and hard work was worth it. The guy was in his element, surrounded by so many people who loved him and who were delighted to see someone so worthy get the recognition he deserved.

"Hey."

Joel turned around to find Lorelie standing next to him.

"Aren't you joining the party?" she asked. "I thought you were helping Sadie behind the bar."

Lorelie had cornered him a few days ago to ask how things were going between him and Sadie. He'd given her a vague answer about everything being fine before making an excuse and getting away from her. He wanted to shout to the world that Sadie was his girlfriend. God knew that's what he wanted her to be. But he couldn't.

Everything was too screwed up. His feelings for Oakley were gumming up the works, and Sadie was still resistant to accept what was going on as anything more than a short-term fling. She was determined they'd ride the merry-go-round until they got dizzy and then they'd just get off. He didn't want off.

"I'm just soaking it all in for a minute."

Lorelie followed his glance at Coach, her own smile growing. "I'm so happy we're all here. Together again. And that Dad is getting better."

"I'm glad too. This party was a great idea."

High school had been one of the best times of his life. For a kid who'd always been a bit of a loner growing up, he'd hit his stride as a sophomore. Pretty much because of Coach. He'd been sitting on a bench outside school one day, waiting for his mom to pick him up. Tucker, who was in his math class, had stopped to ask him a question about an assignment while waiting for practice to start. Tucker had made starting quarterback for the Varsity squad as a freshman. It seemed to Joel his friend had been born throwing a ball.

Coach had stopped by to move Tucker along, and then he noticed Joel. Said he'd seen him sitting around after school every day. Joel hated riding the bus almost as much as he hated hanging out in an empty house alone for hours. So he'd elected to stay after school instead, doing his homework and watching all the other students come and go from extracurricular activities until his mom came to pick him up.

Coach invited him to practice and, since Joel's mom was still a couple hours away from getting off work, he'd figured why not. He joined the team that very day, never missed a practice after that and by junior year, he was the starting center at every game and working part-time on this ranch. Being a part of the team had given Joel some things he hadn't really had before high school—friends and a purpose.

Lorelie laughed as some of the guys arrived with their girlfriends in tow. Jack and Tucker came into the barn in style, Tucker with a ball in hand and yelling for Jack to "go long". Jack ran toward Coach as Tucker lobbed the ball at him. After Jack caught it, he handed it to Coach.

Joel knew what it was. All the guys had signed a football for Coach as a gift, a memento of the night.

"Wow." Lorelie's smile grew. "Look at Dad's face."

Joel couldn't look away. "Never seen the guy so happy."

Lorelie turned and hugged Joel. "Thank you."

"For what?" he asked.

"For calling the guys, asking them to come back. I think seeing all of them is what helped my dad get better. It reminded him of better times and made him feel young again. I know I never say it, but I'm glad you're here, Joel. It was just me and Dad for so long. With you and Oakley, it feels like we have a regular family."

Joel swallowed heavily and tightened the embrace. He understood what it meant to be light on family. Lorelie only had her dad. He'd only ever had his mom. Until she said it aloud, he'd never realized that they had begun to feel like a family. Joel thought he'd regretted not leaving Maris, but that wasn't true. He'd subconsciously stayed because he hadn't wanted to leave all the people he loved.

He placed a brotherly kiss on the top of Lorelie's head. "Love you, kiddo."

She laughed at the nickname he hadn't used in years. Mainly because she'd become a woman and threatened to emasculate him if he continued to call her that.

"Love you too."

The moment passed as they stepped apart and surveyed the room once more. Lela and Tucker had taken to the dance floor as music drifted from Lorelie's iPod. Walt was still getting set up, Tyson helping him move the amps into place. Jack and Caleb were playing a game of one-upping each other as they reminisced about the glory days.

He'd felt twinges of jealousy whenever he considered his friends and the places they'd traveled to, but the fact that they'd all returned to Maris spoke volumes to him. There really wasn't any place better than home.

The more Joel looked around at the people in his barn, the more he realized he couldn't leave here. He was happy.

His gaze landed on Oakley, who had taken Sadie's hand to spin her in time with the music behind the bar. She was laughing and trying to break free so she could pour a drink.

No. He couldn't leave.

"Damn. If all the girls around here are as pretty as you, I may never leave Texas again."

Joel and Lorelie turned around at the strange voice. Joel's hackles rose as a man he'd never seen gave Lorelie a charming smile to match his come-on. Joel started to tell the guy to back off, but as always, Lorelie was more than prepared to fight her own battles.

"Is that a pickup line?" To a stranger, Lorelie would sound sweet, flirty. But Joel recognized the tone. This guy was in danger. Joel stuck around for the show.

The guy stepped closer to her. "Did it work?"

"Not even a little bit."

He laughed. "Guess I'll have to figure out something else that might work with you then."

Lorelie narrowed her eyes. "Yeah. That's not gonna happen."

The man didn't look deterred. In fact, if Joel read his face correctly, it appeared he'd taken Lorelie's comment as a dare. "Never say never, beautiful."

Lorelie rolled her eyes. "You know, I made up the guest list for this party and I don't know you from Adam, which means you weren't invited."

The man pointed to a guitar case resting against the table next to him. "Actually, I was. I'm Glen Young, Walt's friend. I just got into town. Goddamn GPS on my phone took me all around Robin Hood's barn. Didn't think I'd ever get here."

Lorelie pointed toward the stage. "Walt's up there. I think he had given up on you. Said something to the effect that you were probably three sheets or *between* the sheets with some groupie."

Glen chuckled. "Walt always was a jealous bastard. So...if it's your party, you must be Lorelie. Walt failed to tell me how gorgeous you are."

"You realize all you did was reword the first pickup line that failed miserably. Your efforts are getting worse, not better," she teased.

Joel still stood close in case Lorelie needed him, but it was becoming more and more apparent she wasn't going to be calling in the troops.

Glen laughed loudly. "I'm going to sing you a song, Lori."

She shook her head, but she didn't look annoyed. "Don't bother. I'm not your type."

Glen gave her a curious look. "What's my type?"

"Blind, deaf, and stupid." With that, she gave Glen a wicked grin and walked away.

Glen's grin grew wider. "Damn."

Joel felt compelled to warn the guy off, in deference to Coach. "She's not a woman you want to mess with."

Glen only offered Joel a nonchalant shrug, his eyes still

locked on Lorelie's retreating form. "Maybe not, but I'm pretty sure I'm going to marry that girl."

Before Joel could say more, Glen headed to the stage, where Walt was just about to start playing. He watched the men high-five. Glen had his guitar out of the case and plugged into the amp in record time. Within minutes, he and Walt were jamming out and the dance floor filled up almost instantly.

"Hey, Joel," Sadie called out. "Thought you were helping us."

Joel walked over to the makeshift bar, joining Sadie and Oakley in the tight space. The lack of room meant they kept bumping into each other. He took advantage of the opportunity that afforded with Sadie, leaning closer, brushing her ass with his crotch whenever he could.

The sexy smile she gave him and the number of times she managed to run her breasts across his arm as she reached for something told him she was on to his game. And as always, Sadie found a way beat him at it. He had to adjust his pants several times as his cock refused to stay down. It was becoming painful.

The problem was Oakley. There was no way to avoid running into *him* as well. Each time they got too close, Joel backed away.

Twice he caught the hurt in Oakley's gaze as he dodged his casual touches. Joel hated pulling away from his best friend, but he couldn't figure out how to make his feelings go away.

It was that damn kiss. It haunted him. Replayed in his mind twenty-four-seven. He'd never kissed a guy. Never wanted to. Now he couldn't think of anything except kissing Oakley.

He reached out to grab another stack of red Solo cups, careful to avoid touching Oakley.

Oakley frowned, the expression drawing Joel's gaze to his lips.

God, he had it bad. Joel turned away and looked around the barn, studying the faces. Former teammates and friends surrounded him. Sadie's dad sat next to Coach with some other guys from town, the fellas who usually packed around the bar in Cruisers the night after a Titans game to dissect and discuss every play. His mother was even in attendance, standing in a corner, chatting with a couple of ladies from church.

What would they think if Joel reached over and kissed Oakley? Right here. Right now.

"Joel?" Sadie pulled him from his thoughts. "You okay?"

He nodded, even as he thought, nope. I am definitely *not* okay.

"Bunkhouse? After the party?" she asked. There was a twinge of doubt in her voice, something he'd never heard there before.

She knew.

How could she not?

But she and Oakley had gone along with him after that kiss. Joel had wanted to pretend it hadn't happened, had wanted to ignore it. And because Sadie and Oakley cared about him, they'd respected his wishes and pretended right along with him.

Joel couldn't understand how he could be this fucked-up inside. He was living a dream, sharing the girl he loved with his best friend. The sex was off the charts. He should be happy.

He wasn't.

He couldn't give Sadie and Oakley what they wanted. For the first time in his life, the king of people-pleasers didn't have it in himself to offer them the key to true happiness. It was clenched tightly in his white-knuckled fist. And it was staying there.

"Joel?" Sadie said when he failed to answer.

He was a coward. And a greedy one at that.

"Absolutely," he said in response to her question. "Come on. Dance with me. Oakley can hold down the fort back here for a little while."

Joel needed air, space, a chance to catch his breath. He couldn't let Sadie see him struggling. He feared she'd leave, walk away.

He couldn't let her do that. So they'd all just keep ignoring. Keep pretending.

Keep believing that this was working.

Even though it wasn't.

Chapter Seven

The sun beat down on them, the temperature pushing eighty-five, ninety. Sometimes Texas was a merciless bitch.

Oakley took off his hat and wiped away the sweat that was dripping down into his eyes. It was only midday and there were still too many hours between now and quitting time. Ordinarily, he didn't mind the long hours or the heat, but he was running on empty. Low on sleep, energy, and patience. It was a dangerous combination.

Especially since Joel seemed to share it. The two of them hadn't spoken three words to each other since they'd gotten up this morning, which left Oakley too much time to think, to fume.

He'd let Joel continue to push him away, to treat him as if he had some contagious disease because he'd genuinely believed his friend would come around. Joel wasn't stupid, and while he had more than a fair amount of stubborn, he usually did the right thing.

However, the dumbass had wrapped his head around his

feelings for Oakley and come to the wrong conclusion. Joel had convinced himself that being with Oakley would be wrong. Fucking idiot. Joel had been a part of that kiss. There was no way he didn't get it, didn't see exactly how right this was.

So, they continued to work in silence, trying to let the sun and exhaustion beat away all the heavy feelings. It wasn't working.

Oakley's temper sparked when Joel jerked his hand away as they both reached for a tool at the same time.

"Seriously, dude? I'm not going to jump you, Joel, so you can stop looking at me like I'm some pervert waiting to catch you in a dark alley."

"I'm not doing that."

"Bullshit. You think I don't see what you're doing? We lay in bed with Sadie and the second I get too close to you, you back away. What I have isn't catching, so you can take it easy. You're not going to turn into some raging queer if you get too close."

Joel scowled. "What the fuck are you talking about?"

"You don't want me. I get it. Okay? You don't have to keep ramming that fact down my throat. I'm choking on it already."

Joel's state of mind didn't appear to be any better than his, which pleased Oakley more than he could say. He'd tried to be understanding, tried to walk away, tried to pretend Joel's distance didn't slice through him like a knife, but he couldn't do it anymore. Couldn't swallow his feelings, pretend like they didn't exist.

"You don't know what you're talking about," Joel said.

Oakley laughed, the sound pure anger. "Fuck you, Joel."

Joel's eyes narrowed, the dark brown turning black. "Fuck *me*? Seriously? You fuck up everything. Everything! And you say 'fuck you' to me? No, Oakley. Fuck you!"

"What the hell did I fuck up?"

"We had a good thing with Sadie. Maybe it wasn't perfect and maybe it wasn't going to last forever, but for just a little while, we had her. With us. And it was fucking awesome! Then you...you..."

"Kissed you? Touched your balls? Licked your dick? Which part freaked you out the most?"

Joel exploded. A week of pent-up frustration just burst into flame.

And Oakley was ready.

Oakley only fell back two steps after Joel rushed toward him and shoved. He had enough time to plant his feet so that he didn't actually fall down, but barely. Joel wasn't holding anything back.

Never one to walk away from a fight, Oakley came back fast, his fist connecting with Joel's jaw.

Joel had anticipated the punch, dodging in time to lessen the intensity. He retaliated with a hard right that caught Oakley on the cheek. He was going to have a black eye from that. Unwilling to be the only one to wear a mark of this fight, he threw another punch, pleased to see blood welling at the corner of Joel's mouth.

After that, Oakley lost track of who landed what where. There was a flurry of dust, fists, curses, and pain—a lot of fucking pain. Joel was a scrappy fighter, and he was inflicting some serious damage. Not that Oakley wasn't holding up his own end pretty damn good.

The whole thing ended in an instant when they were hit by a blast of ice-cold water.

They fell apart and looked over to find Coach standing next to them with an empty bucket and an expression like thunder.

"What in blue blazes are the two of you doing?!" Coach roared.

Oakley bent over at the waist, holding himself up with his

hands on his knees, trying to recover from Joel's last punch, a hard one right to the gut.

Joel was wiping the blood dripping from his nose with his sleeve. "Nothing."

Oakley would have rolled his eyes if the left one didn't hurt like a mother. He could tell without a mirror it was swelling shut fast.

Yeah. Coach was definitely not going to let that non-answer fly.

"Try again, Joel," Coach said, through gritted teeth.

"It was a misunderstanding," Joel added.

Oakley snorted mirthlessly. "No, Joel. I'd say we understand each other just fine." He needed to get out of here, away from all this bullshit. It was starting to eat at him like a cancer. "Sorry about this, Coach. Things got a little out of hand. It won't happen again."

With that, Oakley limped back to the bunkhouse. He needed a shower. And then he needed a fucking drink.

"Come with me," Coach said, crooking his finger at Joel, and then pointing toward the main house.

Joel glanced back at Oakley, who'd made good on his escape. "Coach—"

"Get your ass in the house, Joel. And on the way there, get yourself ready to start speaking the truth about what just happened here. Because if you lie to me, I'll fire your ass so quick, it'll make your head spin."

Joel followed Coach into the house and plopped down on the couch heavily. He didn't have any more lies left inside him. He'd spent the past few weeks in a constant state of dishonesty. He needed help.

"Okay," Coach said. "Let's have it."

And Joel gave it to him. All of it. Sadie, Oakley, the fling, the kiss, the feelings, the shame, the fear. It all fell out of him in a giant heap.

And through it all, Coach was quiet. Joel had no idea what the man was thinking because he hadn't lifted his gaze from the floor. Joel couldn't make himself look into the eyes of the man who was like a father to him and risk seeing disappointment.

Once he'd run out of words, he held his pose, his hands still clasped together, his elbows resting on his knees and his head bent as if in prayer, eyes locked on the rug beneath his feet.

"What's the red zone?" Coach asked.

Joel was so taken aback by the question, he looked up. "What?"

"The red zone. Come on, boy. I taught you everything you know about football. Tell me what the red zone is."

"It's the last twenty yards before the end zone. It's when the playing gets rough, dirty even. Offense is fighting like the devil to score and the defense is kicking ass to keep them out."

"You're in the red zone, Joel."

Joel wasn't sure how to reply. It was a simple answer, and when Joel thought about it, he realized it did feel like that. He'd been under a cloud of almost blinding desperation for days.

The red zone.

Coach's words made sense of a situation that felt futile. Joel was on the verge of something big. Problem was he couldn't figure out if he was the offense or the defense. Something told him he was both.

"What do I do?" Joel asked.

"I can't answer that for you. You have to decide what you want. You in love with Sadie?"

Joel nodded. No hesitation. He was head over heels in love with her.

"You in love with Oakley?"

Joel nodded again. He was too tired to keep denying it.

"So why aren't you fighting to get into that end zone?"

"I can't have them both."

Coach frowned. "Who says?"

Joel threw up his hands. "The whole world!"

Coach's brows furrowed. "Bullshit."

"What the hell would my mom think? She's very religious, Coach. The ménage part is strange enough. If I tell her I'm in love with Oakley, that I want to have sex with him, she'll..."

"She'll what? Disown you? Hire a priest for an exorcism? Try to have you committed? What will she do?"

Joel shook his head. "I don't know. I just know I don't want to hurt her. I love my mom."

"And she loves you, Joel. Probably a hell of a lot more than you realize."

Joel still couldn't relax. His mother's approval was important to him. But so was Coach's. "What do you think of all of this?"

Coach grimaced. "You're still not getting it, boy, so I'll spell it out for you. You're responsible for one person's happiness in this world, and that's your own. Making yourself unhappy and denying a big part of yourself because you think it will please others has the opposite effect. I just had to break up a fight between two boys I consider sons because you can't get your head out of your ass. I don't enjoy watching you take a knee on the one-yard line. You know what would make me happy? Knowing *you* were happy, and I got a good feeling the same holds true for your mother. However you get to that place is okay with me. And even if it wasn't, I'd still expect you to go for it, to push through with everything that you have because I don't coach quitters."

Coach was right. If Joel went for what he wanted, he would have to deal with the disapproval of others. There were a hell of a lot of people in town who wouldn't approve of what he and Sadie and Oakley were doing. And there were some who would frown upon the kind of relationship he wanted to have with Oakley. Maris—like the rest of the world—had its share of homophobes.

But if he let fear of those people's opinions make this decision for him, it would be the biggest mistake of his life.

He'd find a way to explain it to his mom. And then he was going for it, making the play.

"I want to be with Sadie and Oakley. I want to spend the rest of my life with them."

Coach smiled. "Then it's time to stop playing it safe. Time to get out of the red zone and score."

Oakley sat at a table near the back door of Cruisers and glanced over at the bar. Sadie was talking to Jack, pouring him shots. From the way the guy was slumped over, he'd venture to guess Jack was having the same shitty night he was.

Sadie had walked over as soon as he sat down and asked him about the bruises on his face. He'd been a dumbass to come here, but he'd needed to get the hell out of the bunkhouse and off the ranch. He wasn't ready to face Joel. Or Coach. Plus he'd wanted to see Sadie and he needed a drink. Actually, a lot of drinks.

Sadie had gotten pissed when he mentioned having a disagreement with Joel. She'd muttered something about them being jackasses. When she had returned with his pitcher of beer, she'd merely set it down and turned her back on him without another word.

He was batting a thousand on pissing off everybody today.

Oakley sat alone in misery for a few minutes, and then

looked up when Jack dropped into the seat across from him. "Hey."

"Hey, Jack."

"Sadie said I had to move it over here. I'm bringing her down."

"That right?" Oakley looked past him to the bar. She really didn't look happy, but that probably didn't have a damn thing to do with Jack. "Well, I try not to argue with Sadie."

Jack chuckled. "Good policy. What's up with you?"

Oakley didn't even bother to lie. The beer was soaking in and doing its job, taking away some of the rough edges. "Heartbreak." Oakley lifted his glass in a silent toast to that bastard of an emotion.

"Is that what's wrong with your face too?"

Oakley grimaced. Pretty much everybody in the bar had snuck a peek at his black eye. He wondered if Joel looked this bad. "Yep. What's wrong with you?"

"Same."

They sat in companionable silence for nearly a minute, then Jack asked the question Oakley was hoping he wouldn't. "Someone I know?"

"Yep." Oakley didn't elaborate. He was pretty sure Joel didn't want the world to know what was going on between them. He took another drink of beer. His pitcher was running low. Given the dirty looks Sadie kept shooting at him, he wasn't sure she'd serve him another.

"What are you drinkin'?" Jack asked.

"PBR." Oakley pulled the beer closer. "Pitchers are on sale. I'm not sharing."

Jack grimaced. "PBR? You *are* having a shitty day."

"You have no idea."

Jack tipped his beer, draining the bottle before setting it down. "Bet I can top you."

Oakley was about to take him up on that when Sadie reappeared. Oakley sucked in a deep breath, the floral scent of her perfume calming him down as much as the beer. She always smelled so good. She set four shots of tequila on the table. Maybe she wasn't as mad at him as he thought.

"Looks like y'all might need these."

Oakley grinned up at her, resisting the urge to stand up and kiss her senseless. "Thanks, Sade, you're the best."

She narrowed her eyes.

Nope, he was wrong. She was still plenty pissed off.

"The *best*," Jack agreed, picking up one of the glasses.

She smirked at Jack, ignoring Oakley. "Yeah, I'm a regular humanitarian." She walked away before Oakley could stop her.

Jack clinked his glass against Oakley's and they both shot the liquor back.

"Okay, you want this next shot, you have to tell me why you deserve it," Jack said, pointing to the two remaining shots.

Oakley frowned. "I have to deserve it?"

"Yep. Two shots to the guy with the worst day."

"Fine." Oakley figured this would be a piece of cake. Because he'd just had the day from hell. "I hit one of my best friends today."

Jack arched a brow. "Okay, that's bad. *But*," he said, as Oakley reached for the tequila. "I'm in love with someone I shouldn't be. I'll never be good enough for her, but I can't let her go."

Oakley's eyes narrowed. "You really wanna do this?"

"Decide who most deserves to get shitfaced?" Jack asked. "Absolutely. Bring it. I'm the biggest asshole at this table."

"Don't be so sure." Oakley sat up a little straighter. It was a stupid contest to try to win, but Oakley needed a fucking win today. If it was for Asshole of the Year, then so be it.

Before Jack could drink the last shot, Oakley said, "I'm in love with someone who feels the same way but can't face his feelings for me." He paused, then emphasized, "*His* feelings" one more time, just to make sure Jack understood how fucked-up it all was.

Jack hesitated. "Dammit." He handed the shot glass over.

Oakley felt a strange sense of accomplishment as he swigged it down and then chased it with a gulp of beer.

"You know who you should be talkin' to?" Jack asked. "My best friend. Brian. Of course he's dead now. The bastard. He was in love with me. And I couldn't handle it."

Good God. Had Sadie known what was bothering Jack? Is that why she'd sent the guy over? "The sex thing, right?"

"You got it. Was never into dude on dude," Jack said. "Pussies are just too good. Why don't you want that?"

Oakley laughed. It was either that or cry. So he just laughed harder. It was on the tip of his tongue to tell Jack he shouldn't knock it until he tried it, but he remembered how much Joel had freaked out when Oakley touched him.

Instead, he focused on the one thing he and Jack had in common. "Pussies are *so good.*" Oakley clinked his beer glass against Jack's bottle. "I love pussy."

"But you like dicks too," Jack said.

Oakley nodded. It was pointless to deny it. It wasn't like everyone in Maris didn't know he was bi. "That I do."

"How come?" Jack asked, leaning in. "I'm being serious. What's the dude thing like? Not bad, huh?"

Oakley remembered the kiss he had shared with Joel. It had been intense. Brute strength wrapped in a need so powerful, it had made Oakley dizzy. "No, bro, not bad at all. You don't have to be nice about it. It's sweaty and rough and, well, it's a good way to get out some aggression and get your rocks off...all at the same time."

"Looks like you worked off some aggression today," Jack said, pointing to Oakley's eye again.

"Yeah, but I didn't get my rocks off."

"So you like being the fucker or the fuckee?" Jack asked.

Oakley snorted, grateful to be able to talk about this stuff with someone. "I'm pretty often the fuckee, actually." He fucked women, but when he was with a guy, he liked being on the receiving end. He could only assume it was because his first time had been that way.

Oakley wondered why he'd never hung out with Jack because from the gossip he'd heard about the guy, Jackson had been just as wild as Oakley when he'd been younger. Oakley had never been able to walk a completely straight-and-narrow line—smoking pot, stealing beer from the convenience store when he was under age, driving his car way too fast—and he'd heard similar stories about Jack.

"See, I was thinkin'," Jack said. "That if I was ever gonna do that... and I did *not* think about that until he brought it up...it would have been with Garrett."

Oakley leaned a bit closer, suddenly interested in Jack's perspective. Maybe it would help Oakley understand where Joel was coming from. "Yeah? How come?"

"'Cuz he was my brother from another mother, man," Jack said. "That doesn't sound right though. He was just, like, this great guy and if it would have made him happy, then maybe I coulda been into it, you know?"

Oakley considered that answer and decided he hated it. "You would have done that just to make him happy?"

Jack shrugged. "Well, you know, that's a lot of what really great sex is all about anyway. It's about making the other person happy. Giving them pleasure, right? That's what makes it so great. When it's someone you love, you just want to do everything you can to show them that."

Oakley started to get it. And it gave him hope. "Are you telling me that you think a straight guy could actually make love to another man?"

Jack nodded. "I think maybe so. If he loved the guy, you know? And maybe just that one guy. Maybe no one else in the whole world but that one guy and one girl. But yeah, I think maybe so." He leaned in and dropped his voice. "Because sometimes a good hard fucking is exactly what someone needs, and if you love them, you want to be *that* fucker, right?"

Oakley stared at Jack. He got it. He *really* got it. Maybe Joel would too.

Jesus. What a conversation. Oakley couldn't believe the absurdity of it. He was sitting in a bar, feeling sorry for himself and thinking he had the most fucked-up problems in the world. Then Jack sits down and shows him that his issues aren't that unique at all.

He couldn't help it. Oakley laughed. Hard. Because it was all so damn crazy. Jack joined in. They laughed until their sides hurt and everyone in the place was looking at them.

Oakley wiped a hand over his face. "Holy shit, man, I needed that."

Jack ran an unsteady hand through his hair. The guy was well on his way to shitfaced. Of course, he'd put down a lot more tequila than Oakley had.

"More tequila?" Jack asked.

Oakley groaned. "Man, stop, I can't take any more."

"Save that line for the bedroom," Jack said with a grin.

Oakley laughed. "You're a funny guy, I'll give you that."

"Glad you think so. So then here's my stellar advice for you."

"Can't wait to hear it."

Jack pointed at Oakley. "Don't fuck it up."

Oakley shook his head, laughing. "You kind of suck at this.

Though what you said about making the person you love happy was pretty damn smart."

"Jack."

Tyson Sparks stood next to their table. He had clearly come to pick up Jack. Sadie must've called the guy.

Then Oakley realized she'd made two phone calls.

"Uh, hey guys."

Joel walked over to the table. He looked like shit too. There was a bruise on his cheek and a cut above his left eyebrow. Oakley felt guilty about putting those marks there.

"What are you doin' here?" Oakley asked.

"Sadie called me."

Tyson managed to get Jack up from the table and out of the bar, while Joel continued to stand there.

Before Oakley could apologize, Joel jerked his head toward the back door. "Let's go."

Chapter Eight

Oakley stood, though it took some effort. He probably shouldn't have had those tequila shots. He was a little unsteady.

He followed Joel to the bar.

"Hey, Sadie. Can you take a break for a few minutes?"

Sadie bit her lip at Joel's request. This was it. Oakley knew what came next. Joel was going to get them alone and he was going to break it off. End it.

Just like that, all the alcohol he'd consumed evaporated as his heart lurched.

Sadie waved to a waitress, asking her to take over behind the bar. Then she lifted the hinged counter and followed them outside. The back alley behind Cruisers was deserted and only dimly lit. It was a cool October evening, the sky cloudy and the alley wet from the brief shower that had passed through earlier and killed the brutal heat of the morning. It was a dreary night. Perfect atmosphere for the hell that was about to descend.

"Listen—" Oakley started, hoping he could put off the inevitable.

"No. You listen. Or better yet, shut up."

Before Oakley could reply, Joel shoved him against the back wall of the building and stepped closer.

Then Joel kissed him. Hard.

Joel held back nothing as he forced Oakley's lips apart, his tongue stroking the inside of his mouth. Joel's hands were in his hair, gripping it tightly, using that hold to turn Oakley's head, so he could deepen the kiss.

Oakley's libido shot into orbit when Joel shoved a leg between his, pressing his knee firmly against Oakley's balls.

Oakley wasn't given the opportunity to do more than merely accept what was being given. Joel had taken over and there was no denying he wanted this, wanted Oakley.

After several head-spinning minutes, Joel moved away, his lips only an inch or so from Oakley's. Then he turned to look at Sadie.

"Come here," Joel commanded.

Sadie moved toward them, but Oakley could see the reticence, the confusion. She'd expected the same thing Oakley had. Had anticipated Joel ending it all.

Joel tugged her into their embrace, the three of them closing their ranks, connected. Joel kissed Sadie as deeply as he'd just kissed Oakley. As their lips danced, Oakley placed soft kisses on her cheek and then Joel's. When Sadie turned to Oakley, it was Joel's lips that skirted along her face and then to Oakley's neck.

"How long until closing time?" Oakley murmured when they broke apart for air.

Sadie grinned. "The second I get in there it's going to be last call. I can have that place cleared in forty minutes."

Joel groaned. "Make it thirty."

They started kissing again, none of them willing to leave the cocoon they'd created for themselves. Sadie ran her hands along their chests as Joel stroked her breasts above her shirt. Meanwhile, Oakley gripped Joel's ass cheek and squeezed.

"Too much more of this," Joel said through gritted teeth, "and I'm going to fuck you both out here. Right now."

"You say that like it's a threat," Sadie said with a light laugh.

"God." Joel pushed away. "Hurry up and close this fucking bar, Sadie."

She giggled as the three of them walked back inside. Joel and Oakley hovered near the back door, neither of them in a position to show themselves in public. Woody was hard enough to drive nails in concrete.

They leaned against opposite walls, hoping distance would help cool them off. It wasn't working for Oakley. He'd probably have to hide back here until everyone left and Sadie locked the doors.

He looked at Joel, but for once in his talkative life, words failed him. Or perhaps it was more like he was afraid he'd pop the balloon he'd just received. He didn't want to open his mouth and say something that would cause Joel to change his mind.

"It's okay, Oak. I'm not running from this anymore."

Leave it to his best friend to take one look at him and know what he was thinking. "You're all in?"

Joel nodded, but Oakley sensed the hesitation.

"I'm not going lie and say I'm not a little bit nervous about what comes next."

Sex. He was worried about the sex. Oakley recalled what Jack had said about a straight guy being willing to have sex with a man he loved. While there was definitely a strong attraction and a powerful pull, Joel had never considered sleeping with a guy before now. The rest wouldn't come naturally. There were still some barriers in place and it would take time to scale those walls. "It's okay, Joel. We can ease into that. There's no rush."

Joel looked back toward the bar, where Sadie was cleaning up like a mad woman. Oakley started to chuckle, but the serious look on Joel's face stopped him.

"I don't want to mess this up. Any of it."

Oakley understood. He'd felt the same way since the beginning. Joel had gone along for the ride, convinced from the start there were limits. Now that Joel had rejected any restrictions and admitted to his feelings, he could see exactly how much there was to lose.

"So we'll slow things down, watch our step. I got your back, bro. And you got mine. We can figure it out together."

"I don't think we have as much time as you think," Joel said, his gaze still glued to Sadie. "She's like a caged bird. I keep thinking we're going to leave that door open for one second and she's going to fly away."

"No." Oakley refused to believe that. He couldn't. Not when he was so close to getting everything he'd ever wanted. "We'll convince her to stay."

Joel gave him a crooked grin, but Oakley got the sense it was meant to comfort him, that Joel didn't really believe they'd succeed.

After a few minutes, they were decent enough to walk back into the bar and help Sadie clean up. It took closer to an hour, but finally, Sadie was able to lock the door and they were alone.

They wasted no time. Oakley grabbed Sadie and kissed her hard, Joel's words still troubling him.

After several minutes, she was the first to pull away. Oakley started to tug her back, but she shook her head and looked at Joel. Then, she walked over to the closest chair and sat down. She wanted to watch. *Them.*

Oakley had promised they would take things slowly—and

he meant that—but he'd waited too long for this moment. He gripped Joel's shirt by the front and pulled him close, kissing him.

Joel wasn't a passive lover, not with Sadie and—thank God —not with him. He cupped Oakley's face with his large, calloused palms and deepened the kiss.

Oakley released Joel's shirt, his hand drifting down. He stroked Joel's erection through the thick denim of his jeans. Joel sucked in a loud breath. Oakley wondered if his friend would shove his hand away when Joel released his face.

Then Oakley's eyes drifted closed as Joel covered his hand and pressed Oakley's fingers harder against his cock.

"Open my pants, Oak."

Like Sadie, Oakley was a goner whenever Joel issued his commands in that deep, sexy tone.

He unbuttoned Joel's jeans and slid the zipper down. They both went commando. Oakley was glad for that easy access now as Joel's cock sprang free.

Oakley wrapped his fist around Joel, stroking him. He'd seen his cock every night for weeks as they fell into bed with Sadie. He had longed to touch it, to hold it. To...

To hell with slow.

Oakley dropped to his knees. He could feel Sadie's gaze on them, watching their every move. It made the moment even more intense, hotter.

Joel didn't move away, didn't resist as Oakley opened his mouth and took the head of his cock inside.

He heard a quiet gasp from Sadie. Oakley hated that she was so far away. He released Joel and looked at her. "Come here."

She stood and walked over to them. "I thought..."

Joel pulled her close for a kiss. "This only works if it's all of us."

Oakley felt the same way. He loved Joel and he was truly attracted to him, but without Sadie, there would be no them. Not like this.

Oakley tightened his grip on the base of Joel's cock, prompting his friend to groan. Sadie glanced down and smiled. Then she dropped to her knees next to Oakley.

Oakley kissed her briefly, grinning when Sadie bent closer and ran her tongue along Joel's cock.

"Jesus," Joel muttered. "You two are trying to kill me."

For several minutes, he and Sadie took turns with Joel's cock—licking, sucking, even nipping at it—each trying to push their lover over the edge. Joel had a grip on each of them, one hand in Oakley's hair, the other in Sadie's. Each time one of them did something he liked, his fingers tightened. Oakley's scalp stung from the pressure, but the pain didn't make him want to stop. It made him want more.

Then Sadie moved back a little bit, handing the reins to Oakley. He lost no time grabbing them. He opened his mouth wider, taking Joel so deep, the head of his cock brushed the back of his throat. This wasn't Oakley's first rodeo. He'd mastered deep-throating in high school.

Joel groaned louder when Oakley swallowed the head. However, Oakley started to choke when Sadie's hand found *his* cock, squeezing it tightly through his jeans.

Oakley released Joel with a gasp. "God, Sade."

Joel must have caught a glimpse of their girl's game because he chuckled. "Now you can feel my pain."

So many hands and mouths. Oakley couldn't understand why anyone would choose to live with just one lover. He feared there was no way he could return to coupledom. Not when three was so fucking much better.

Sadie unzipped his jeans, her hand reaching beneath the denim to grip Oakley's cock. She lifted her head slightly, silently telling Oakley to start sucking again. He would never cease to be amazed by the power exchanges the three of them shared—each of them willing to submit to another's dominance.

He took Joel back into his mouth, working the hard flesh in earnest now. Sadie stroked Oakley's cock in time with the rhythm he created. He was in charge of her speed, her depth. His mouth was the remote control. It was the most incredible sensation of his life.

Oakley hoped Joel could hold off for just a moment more because he was so close. Jesus, Sadie's hand could be registered as a lethal weapon.

Through it all, Joel was anything but passive. He continued to pull their hair as he wove a litany of dirty, beautiful words around them. For a quiet guy, Joel had an arsenal of sexy shit to say, his deep-voiced, commanding tone only adding to Oakley's need to come. Soon.

"Deeper, Oak. God, man. So fucking good. Suck it harder." Oakley responded.

"Tighten your grip, Sadie. You make Oakley come before me and I'll throw you over a table and eat that sweet pussy of yours until you scream."

Sadie responded, clearly interested in the promised prize, and Oakley jerked, his rhythm thrown off as his balls filled. He wasn't going to make it much longer.

One more pull from Sadie's hand, one more pass of Joel's cock—deep in his throat—and Oakley erupted.

Joel grasped his head, holding him still as jets of come spurted from Oakley's dick, covering Joel's shoes and the bottoms of his jeans. Through it all, he still had Joel's cock in his mouth, the thick flesh muting his cries, his moans.

As the climax waned, Joel took over. Oakley had been a fool to think he'd ever had any control of this moment. It had been Joel and Sadie all along.

Joel used his grip to tug Oakley's mouth off his erection until just the head of his dick remained. Then he pulled him back roughly. Oakley let his friend fuck his mouth, opened his lips, and gave Joel everything he had left to give. He was being used. And he loved it.

Sadie remained on her knees beside them, watching. After only a moment, she lifted her gaze to Joel. "Come in his mouth," she whispered, her voice revealing exactly how much she was enjoying this show.

If Oakley was helpless to resist his lovers, it seemed Sadie had that same power over Joel. Within seconds, Joel came, his thrusts shorter, harder and punctuated by each drop of come that slid down Oakley's throat.

Joel pulled out of his mouth with a pop and Oakley's ass fell back on his feet, his strength drained.

At least it was.

Until Joel zipped up his pants, lifted Sadie from the floor and placed her on the table nearest them. He had her jeans and shoes off within seconds. Then he grabbed a chair and sat down for the feast.

Oakley found himself crawling closer, wanting a better view. He suddenly understood the soft mews Sadie had made while watching Oakley give Joel the blowjob. It was as if Oakley could feel what Sadie was experiencing when Joel stabbed her sweet opening with his tongue.

Though neither of them had touched her before this moment, Sadie was close. Oakley could see it, could hear it.

Sadie's pussy was covered in her juices and her back arched toward Joel's mouth, needing more.

"So sexy, Sadie," Oakley said, recalling the effect of Joel's dirty talk on both of them earlier. "You're so wet, baby. Dripping. I bet you want Joel to suck on that pretty little clit, don't you?"

Joel moved in response to Sadie's cry of desire, dragging his tongue out of her, his lips closing around the sensitive nub.

Sadie jerked roughly. "God. Yes!"

"Poor empty pussy. You need something inside. Something filling it," Oakley said, loving that he could direct Joel's actions.

Joel continued to suck on her clit as he pushed two fingers in to the hilt.

"That's it, Sadie." Oakley loved the way she lifted her hips in time with Joel's rough thrusting. Oakley had never taken a woman with such strength, reserving the more aggressive sex for his male lovers. Clearly he had underestimated exactly what women could take. What they enjoyed.

Sadie seemed to crave it hard. She beat her fist against the flat surface of the table as she made her own demands. Oakley had thought himself drained after her hand job, but when Sadie lifted her legs and wrapped her ankles around Joel's shoulders, driving her pussy harder into his friend's face, Oakley's cock began to stiffen again.

Joel had voiced his fear of death by sex. Oakley now understood his concern.

He rose from his place on the floor and came to the opposite end of the table from Joel, bending close to Sadie's face. She had clearly expected him to kiss her, but Oakley had other plans. He grasped her wrists and tugged her hands above her head, caging them there.

Sadie struggled to pull them free, but he merely tightened his grip. "You're ours," he whispered. Joel was afraid she'd fly. Oakley shared that same fear. Somehow they had to find a way to make her stay, to make her want this.

Joel stopped moving, lifted his head curiously. Sadie groaned, unhappy at the sudden lack of stimulation below her waist. She tried to pull his face back to her pussy with those sexy legs around his shoulders, but Joel was stronger.

"You're captured, Sadie. At our mercy. Ours," Joel said.

Oakley had known the night of the wedding what he wanted from this relationship.

Forever.

He got a sense that Joel had finally turned that corner tonight. There was one last person to convince, but it wouldn't be easy. Joel had compared her to a caged bird, the image conjuring up all the sexy ways they could shackle her. Maybe he'd see if he could borrow some handcuffs from his cop friend, Evan.

Sadie claimed she wasn't interested in a relationship, but Oakley got a feeling there was something else holding her back. So far she had managed to keep them at arm's length. Despite spending night after night inside her body, she hadn't let them anywhere near her heart.

Sadie's breathing had grown shallow, faster. Oakley wondered if it was her helplessness or their words driving the reaction. Was she turned on or terrified? He suspected it was both.

"You like bondage?" Oakley asked.

"I've never let anyone..." Her words faded. Bondage required trust. It appeared that feeling went hand in hand with love in Sadie's world. She wouldn't give either easily. If they could get her to trust them, perhaps the other would follow.

"Will you let us? Tie you up, blindfold you, gag you? Take you hard?"

Sadie licked her lips and swallowed heavily. Her gaze never faltered from Oakley's. The woman had courage, he'd give her that.

"Yes," she said at last.

Oakley smiled, her response giving him hope. She trusted them with her body. He wouldn't give up until she relinquished her love as well.

He looked at Joel. His friend's face was lined with desire. Like Oakley's, his cock had sprung back to life. Joel's erection was outlined clearly by his jeans.

Joel unhooked her legs and stood, unzipping his pants once more and running his cock along Sadie's slit.

God...it was never enough with these two. Never enough.

"Yes," Sadie hissed, her head spinning. She was used to Joel taking control, but this dominant side of Oakley was just as potent. It felt as if he'd looked inside her head and seen all of her deepest, darkest fantasies.

Oakley released her hands. "Don't move them or Joel will flip you over and spank that pretty little ass of yours."

If that was a threat, it was a weak one. She actually considered the option. Before she could test them, however, Oakley pulled off his t-shirt and ripped it in half. Joel continued to press his cock against her, the head of it caressing her from clit to anus, then back again. She tried tugging him closer with her legs once more, but the man was strong as steel. She couldn't budge him.

Then her attention was drawn to Oakley, who lifted her head to pull the soft cotton of his shirt over her eyes. She was instantly pitched into darkness.

She hadn't thought the loss of her sight would feel so intense or...scary.

She had agreed to Oakley's suggestion of bondage because she suspected she'd never get this opportunity again. She had spent her entire adult life longing for this type of experience, but she'd never, not once, found someone she'd trusted enough not to hurt her.

Sadie had no doubts about Oakley and Joel. Not one. They may get rough, but they'd never crossed the line into true pain.

They were able to read her expressions, to understand her cries, to give her exactly what she wanted without going too far.

She tensed up slightly before taking a deep breath, trying to relax, to play it cool.

Leave it to Oakley to watch out for her, to study her face. He knew the second she started to freak out a bit.

He leaned over, his breath hot on her cheek. "You only have to say stop, Sadie."

"Is that my safe word?" She meant the question as a joke, as her way of acting all tough and badass. Somewhere along the line, both Joel and Oakley had figured out she was anything but. It was dangerous. She needed that upper hand back.

"This isn't a game, Sade." Joel stopped moving. "You understand that, right?"

Sex is always a game.

She didn't express that dark thought aloud. How could she? Joel and Oakley had just shared a really special moment, acknowledging their feelings for one another. It had been beautiful, but it had also made her feel like a usurper. She didn't belong here with these guys. Despite everything they said, she knew—really knew—deep down in her gut, that they were looking for something serious. Something lasting and real.

For some insane reason and despite everything she'd said to the contrary, they thought they were going to find that with her.

She couldn't give into them.

Oakley pressed a soft kiss on her cheek. "We won't hurt you, Sadie."

She pursed her lips together, too afraid her thoughts would escape. Because despite Oakley's assertion, she knew they wouldn't have a chance to hurt her. She'd strike first.

Without her vision, Sadie felt lost. She was used to being able to read their expressions. It helped her understand what they were thinking and feeling. The blindfold was stealing that advantage from her. Neither man spoke for a moment, which left her adrift, confused.

She considered sitting up and calling a halt to the whole thing. She'd thought that was Joel's plan earlier, when he'd dragged her and Oakley to the alley. It struck her now that she'd actually felt a measure of relief as she had followed them outside. She'd believed Joel would do the hard part for her.

Sadie couldn't force herself to move. Neither of them held her, restrained her. Joel remained between her legs, Oakley standing just above her head. It would be a simple task to just get up and leave.

Yet she couldn't move. She may not be tied down, but she was captive. And the worst part was she had willingly allowed them to confine her.

"Please." Her voice was too quiet, too weak. What the hell was she begging for?

Joel ran his fingers through her slit once more and she moaned. Yes. This was what she wanted. What she needed. She couldn't escape on her own, so she'd let them take her away, help her hide from all the shit crowding in her head.

She was too much like her mother. Always feeling the need to disappear.

Somehow Oakley and Joel understood that.

Oakley reached for her hands once more, dragging them above her head and holding them against the smooth surface.

She waited for Joel to enter her, to thrust inside. He was right there and she was so ready for it. She should have known better.

One moment his fingers were on her clit, the next he had the front of her blouse in his hands. He ripped the material apart. She heard several buttons skitter along the floor.

She wasn't sure what was so freaking hot about a guy ripping her clothes off, but there was no denying her arousal went from hot to scorching. Even so, she sighed and feigned annoyance. "I loved this shirt."

Oakley chuckled. "I love it now too. Shows off some of my favorite parts of you."

She fought not to laugh. Oakley had a definite addiction to her boobs. The man was forever touching them, sucking on them or baring them the second they managed to get somewhere private.

"Put the rest of your t-shirt to use, Oakley. I need help."

Joel's voice was serious, sensual. Oakley released her and she heard another rip. Her freedom was short-lived when each man claimed a wrist. Joel bound her to one leg of the table, Oakley the other.

She tried to tug her arms free, but her lovers hadn't lied. This wasn't a game. Their knots stuck.

A slight unease crept in as her true helplessness soaked in. She couldn't see what they were doing and she couldn't move her hands. Her defenses were being stripped away.

"I..." she paused. She'd been about to call a halt to the whole thing, but something stopped her.

"Five more minutes, Sadie." Joel ran his hand along her chest and stomach. "Give us five more minutes. If you hate it, we'll stop."

Sadie could do that. She thought. "Okay."

She jerked slightly when she felt hands—Oakley's—reach beneath the cups of her bra to lift her breasts out. Then he shifted to her side and took one nipple in his mouth. He took a page out of Joel's book, applying more and more pressure until the pleasure morphed into the slightest bit of pain.

"Uh," she said, the sound coming out more breath than grunt.

At that point, everything started to move faster as both men touched, licked and bit her. Through it all and despite the blindfold, she knew exactly who did what. It was fascinating to her that in such a short time she'd become so attuned to them.

It was Oakley who'd drawn off one of her shoes and sucked her big toe into his mouth. The sensation made her giggle, which encouraged him to tickle the bottom of her foot.

It was Joel whose teeth latched onto her earlobe, applying pressure until she cried out. Joel liked her pleasure/pain noises. She was accustomed to his efforts at provoking them. And because she was *that girl*, she held off as long as she could in providing them. The end result was more pain, but also the reward because she really fucking liked it.

Her knees were pushed apart. Hot breath and a wicked tongue—Oakley's—hit at her opening. He drove his tongue inside her as her back arched in need. It wasn't enough.

"Please," she repeated again, wishing her hands were free to grab his hair, pull him over her and force him to fuck her properly. She knew exactly what she wanted. She needed it hard and deep. And now.

If either man—or both—knew of her distress, they didn't let that knowledge sway them. They simply continued to torment her with some of the hottest touches she'd ever experienced, pushing her to a hairsbreadth of climax before backing her away from it again.

Murder began to cross her mind when Oakley rose and Joel took his place between her legs, driving two thick fingers inside her. For a moment, she thought they were taking pity on her. After all, it wouldn't have taken more than two more of those rough thrusts to send her spiraling. The motherfuckers knew it. Once his fingers were buried deep, Joel held still, not moving, not giving her the satisfaction she craved.

"I will kill both of you the second you untie me."

Oakley chuckled, which sealed his fate. He was going to die first. As always, Joel remained silent. Without the benefit of sight, that left her to wonder what he was thinking or feeling. Knowing him, he was plotting ways to make her suffer even longer.

She was pleasantly surprised when she felt the head of his cock press against her pussy, seeking entrance. He slid in easily, given the fact they'd turned the water spigot on high as far as her arousal was concerned. Once again, he stopped when he was fully seated, not giving her the friction she needed so badly.

He bent over her body and she blinked rapidly as the blindfold was tugged away, the light too bright after so long in darkness. When she could focus her vision again, Joel was there. His lips mere inches from hers.

The look in his eyes took her breath away. He looked at her as if she truly mattered to him. As if he loved her.

Her heart lurched painfully and she tried to convince herself she was misreading it.

Not love. Lust. That was all this was.

Then Joel leaned closer, offering her the sweetest kiss she'd ever received. The tenderness lasted only a brief second before Joel stood upright and gripped her hips, plowing into her with all the force and speed she'd been begging for.

She came within seconds.

Joel pulled out and Oakley took his place. He found her sweet spot on the first thrust, pushing her to the hilt of yet another climax. Over and over, he stroked that magic place until she gasped, then cried out, then came.

She had mere seconds to recover before Joel returned, the hard, brutal, amazing thrusts dragging her out of her sated bliss and tossing her back into the red-hot flames of desire.

Sadie lost sense of time and place as Joel and Oakley took turns, marking her with their unique brands of fucking, playing her body like a finely tuned piano. She lost count of how many times she had come, certain it had to measure in the triple digits. Hell, maybe she'd hit a million. Who knew? At some point, her hands were untied, but she couldn't recall who had done it or when.

She'd been bound to the table, their all-too-willing captive. Joel flipped her to her stomach as he entered her again. She trembled with need and exhaustion. He bent over her, his lips caressing her shoulder.

"Last time," he whispered.

Sadie loved being taken from behind. The position allowed Joel to go deeper. Typically, she was an active participant, using her grip on the table to meet him blow for blow. This time, she was a rag doll, devoid of strength. All she could do was take, to accept what he gave.

It was a beautiful offering. Her orgasm struck hard and, finally, Joel was there with her. He pulled out at the last second, his come landing on her back in hot spurts.

Then Oakley filled the void. Only when his climax—and her gazillionth—came, he stayed inside her. There was something perversely fulfilling about allowing them to take her without condoms, to come inside her when she'd never given anyone else that privilege. Some nights, she'd hold off on showering for a little while after they left her bed, simply marveling at the sticky reminder of what they'd done together.

She closed her eyes, pressing her head against the slick wood of the table beneath her. Sadie couldn't look at them, couldn't face her lovers and see what she knew was there.

Love.

No.

She'd simply keep her eyes—and her heart—closed. She could do this.

She had to do this.

Chapter Nine

Joel leaned against a stall in the barn to take a breather. He'd woken up this morning with a smile on his face. A big one. Last night had blown his mind. And then some.

He hadn't anticipated how much he'd love the touch of another man on him. The memory of that experience alone would probably keep him hard for weeks, but when paired with the sight of Sadie, bound to the table, writhing in pleasure as their submissive captive, Joel found his knees going weak with need.

He ran a hand over his growing erection and tried to think of something less dangerous to his libido. There were too many hours to go between quitting time and climaxing.

They'd convinced Sadie to let them take her out on a real date tonight. Of course, they hadn't worded it that way. After they'd untied her, they'd taken turns cuddling with her, and then Oakley had said he wanted to buy her a big-ass steak dinner.

Sadie had laughed, but Oakley hadn't backed down. When she tried to reason with him about it being unwise for the three of them to be seen together too much in public, she'd tweaked Joel's stubborn streak. He'd thrown his support behind Oakley and after a few minutes of verbal—and physical—persuasion, she'd relented.

Joel glanced across the barn. Oakley was cutting boards with a table saw. He'd taken off his shirt, unwilling to see the clean cotton covered in sawdust. Joel took several moments to enjoy the sight of Oakley's muscular back as he ran each board over the saw. He had never found himself attracted to the male form before. Now he wondered how he'd been so blind.

Joel's head reeled over his friend's kisses, the blowjob, the unexpected pleasure he'd found in Oakley's touch. It was all so new, and while there were still parts of the intimacy they'd left unexplored, Joel couldn't deny he enjoyed being with Oakley every bit as much as he did Sadie.

So much for being straight.

He chuckled to himself, then crossed the barn, hoping to build on last's night's adventure. When he walked up beside Oakley, his friend turned off the saw, obviously thinking Joel needed to ask him something. The sudden silence after the loud roaring noise of the saw was instant.

"What's up?" Oakley asked.

Joel gave him a wicked grin and pointed at his crotch. "This."

Oakley's brow rose in approval, his grin growing wide.

Unable to resist touching him, Joel wrapped a strong hand around the back of Oakley's neck and pulled him toward him for a kiss.

Oakley didn't hesitate and didn't pretend he wasn't just as hungry for Joel. Their lips parted and the kiss went from lukewarm to sweltering in seconds. Things probably would have escalated very quickly from there if not for the female gasp coming from the barn door.

He and Oakley jerked apart and for a split second, Joel expected to see Lorelie.

Instead, he found himself gazing into the horrified eyes of his mother.

"Oh shit. Mom," Joel said, his stomach clenching tightly.

She slowly raised her hand, the trembling painful for Joel to watch. "You left your jacket at my house on Sunday." She placed the leather coat on a shelf near the door, and then turned and walked away without another word.

Joel started after her, Oakley's apology following him.

"God, Joel. I'm so sorry."

"No, Oak," he said over his shoulder. "Don't. Don't apologize."

He didn't say anything more as he raced across the front yard. His mother was nearly running to her car. Obviously the sound of the saw had prevented him from hearing her arrival. He caught her just as she reached for the door.

"Wait. Mom. Please. Just wait."

Mom looked at her car door, not turning to face him. "I think it would be best for both of us if I left right now."

"You can't leave like this. I can see you're upset. If you could just let me explain—"

Her head shook violently back and forth. "No. No no no no no no no no no."

Joel ran a hand through his hair, wishing there was something he could say to make this better for her. In the end, he couldn't offer her anything more than the truth. "Mom. We have to talk about this. You saw me kissing Oakley."

She whirled on him when he said Oakley's name. "It's that man's fault, isn't it? What has he done to you?" She stepped closer to look at his eyes as if he were delusional or sick. "Are you on drugs? Did he get you high?"

Joel sucked in a deep breath, determined to remain calm,

though her questions pissed him off. "No. He didn't. Jesus, Mom—"

"Don't take the Lord's name in vain!"

Joel closed his mouth and counted to ten in his head. Talking to his mom when she was upset was never easy. It was one of the reasons Joel had always attempted to toe the line, to keep the peace. It helped him preserve his sanity.

"*Why*, Joel? This isn't you. I didn't raise you to..."

"To what, Mom? Fall in love with a man?"

Her eyes widened. "You're not in love with him. You can't be! *The Bible*—"

"Stop." Joel raised his hand. "Stop right there. You're not throwing *The Bible* in my face as a way of justifying something *you* can't understand."

Mom's shoulders slumped. "You were a good man before he came here. You went to church, you prayed." She looked at his bruised face. "You didn't get into fights and you didn't get drunk."

That last wasn't true and she knew it, but she was grasping for anything she could, desperate to make Oakley the villain in all of this.

"You can't blame Oakley for any of that. I'm a grown man and I make my own choices."

"You've always been a *good* man, Joel. Respectful, polite, kind, hardworking."

"And suddenly—because I've kissed Oakley—I'm not that person anymore?"

His mother didn't reply to that, so he gave her the answer.

"I'm the same person I've always been."

She swallowed heavily, but didn't rebuff his assertion. "What about that Sadie girl?" she asked hopefully. "I thought you liked her."

Joel considered and instantly dismissed opening that can of

worms. He could only fight one battle at a time. And something told him he hadn't won that particular war with Sadie.

Something had spooked her last night. He'd tried to ignore it, to chalk it up to too much amazing sex, but there had been something almost...haunted—for lack of a better word—in her eyes. Until he got things settled with her, that element of this unorthodox, but incredible relationship was going to have to remain a secret. "I do like her. A lot. But that doesn't change how I feel about Oakley."

Mom took off her glasses and wearily wiped her eyes. She wasn't crying, but she looked like she might. It occurred to Joel that he'd never seen her cry. Not once. It was equally as sad to realize he'd never really heard her laugh, either.

"I don't know what you want me to say, Joel."

He wanted her to say she understood. That she accepted it. That she was proud of him and she loved him, but he knew that was too many emotions to ask for. "Then maybe I should be the one to do the talking. I'm with Oakley. I love him and I'm not going to hide that or pretend otherwise when we're in public."

She winced, but he continued anyway.

"And I love you, Mom. Nothing you say right now will ever change that. I know this feels wrong to you, but it doesn't to me. For the first time in my life, I feel like I'm being completely true about who I am and what I want."

"I've only ever wanted you to be happy, Joel."

"Well, then take a good look." He held his arms out. "Because this is it. I *am* happy." And if he could find a way to convince Sadie to remain a part of the equation, that happiness would turn ecstatic. He'd crawled into bed last night, put his head on the pillow and known—honestly and truly known—what he wanted his future to hold for the first time ever. And he intended to move heaven and earth to make it happen. The man who'd spent a lifetime trying to make other people happy was going to grab the lion's share of that emotion for himself.

His mother studied his face for several long, awkward moments. "I know you think I'm a hard, unforgiving woman."

Joel shook his head, but she waved away his denial, pointing toward the barn. "I know that's what he thinks too. And maybe I am, but I don't know how to be anything else. Your father died when you were two months old. I had no money, no job, no skills, no family to help."

Joel reached out and took her hand, relieved that she didn't pull it away. Instead, she tightened her grip, squeezing his. "I'm not good at saying how I feel. I don't understand what you're doing with that man. And I'm not sure I'll ever accept it."

Her words pierced him.

"But I love you, Joel. I'm very proud of the man you've become. I don't want to lose you. You're all I have."

He used their clasped hands to tug her close, wrapping her up in his embrace. "You're not going to lose me, Mom. And I know I've thrown you for a loop. All I'm asking is that you try to understand."

She nodded, her face still buried against his chest. Joel felt a bit of moisture seep through the cotton. She was crying. Strangely, he wasn't sorry about that. He'd spent too much of his life trying to make sure he never gave her a reason for tears. Truth was she'd always been sad, and he suspected she needed a good cry. She had probably held this one in for thirty-plus years.

He gently rocked her as she worked to pull herself together. Then she took a step away, the moment gone as his mother and her strict, stoic countenance was back in place.

"I'll try, Joel. I will."

He smiled. "Can I ask for one more thing?"

She nodded.

"Can you try to be nicer to Oakley? You scare the poor guy."

To his surprise—hell, to his outright amazement—his mother laughed. Loudly. Joel was so entranced by the sound he simply stood and watched her.

Once she'd regained control, she turned to open her car door. "I'm leaving."

"Is that a no?" Joel asked, relieved by the turn the conversation had taken. He'd had several weeks to fret over his budding feelings for Oakley and his mother's reaction. As so often happens, the reality of it was nowhere near as bad as his fears.

"That's a no," she said as she climbed in her car. "That boy needs a little fear to keep him honest."

As she closed the car door and started the engine, Joel began to laugh as well.

His mother was right.

Oakley did.

* * *

Sadie stepped out of the office and hitched her purse up on her arm. She'd left the bar last night with nothing more than her house keys, allowing Joel and Oakley to drive her home. It wasn't as if she could have driven her motorcycle home in a ripped shirt with no buttons. She might have a wild streak, but that didn't include flashing her tits to the whole town.

"Hot date, Sadie?" one of the patrons asked, clearly taking notice of her dressy outfit and makeup.

"Maybe. Maybe not," she said nonchalantly. "Why? You jealous, Teddy?" She hoped the question would turn the attention away from her as she wasn't about to feed the rumor mill. It worked. Teddy's drinking buddies started teasing him about his interest in Sadie as she kept walking. So far she'd managed to avoid her dad who was in the back alley, pulling in boxes from a delivery truck. She wanted that lucky break to continue.

Sadie had almost made it to the door when Jenna Mitchum walked in, her five-year-old in tow and an infant in her arms.

Sadie raised her hands to stop her. "Hey, Jenna. I'm not so sure this is a good place for—"

Before Sadie could say "kids," Jenna had thrust the baby into her arms.

"Please, Sadie. Can you watch them for just a second? I have a bone to pick with my husband. He was supposed to be home two hours ago."

Sadie glanced over her shoulder and caught sight of the back of Russell Mitchum, bent over the pool table, lining up a shot. Russ wasn't a bad guy overall. He just wasn't the most responsible dad...or particularly bright.

"Um..." Sadie had wanted to say no, but Jenna didn't give her the chance as she left the baby and her young son, Billy, in her care.

Sadie looked around, hoping to find someone else to pawn off this task on. She had zero experience with kids and, as such, they sort of terrified her.

"You got any ice cream?" Billy asked.

Sadie shook her head, and then she was distracted by the raised voices coming from the back of the bar. Billy noticed as well. Sadie didn't want the kid to see his parents fighting, so she grasped his hand and said, "Let's go outside. Sometimes the ice cream truck drives by here."

It was a lie, but the boy believed her just the same. They walked outside the door and claimed the bench set up there for the smokers. No one else was around.

Billy's feet swung madly as he glanced up and down the street hopefully for a treat that was never going to come. Sadie felt bad, but figured not getting ice cream would be less traumatic than listening to his parents screaming at each other.

The baby stirred in her arms and, for the first time, Sadie was forced to turn her attention to the tiny little thing. She did some quick math and figured the infant couldn't be more than two months old. "Boy or girl?" she asked Billy, unable to recall.

"That's my sister, Jane. You can tell she's a girl on account she doesn't have a dinky."

Sadie tried not to grin, though she decided right then, there were definitely worse things Oakley could call his penis than Woody.

"Oh."

Jane had been sleeping, but at that moment, her eyelids lifted and Sadie spotted the baby's bright blue eyes. They stared unfocused for a brief second before finding Sadie's face.

She expected the infant to cry. After all, Sadie was definitely not her mom. Instead, what she saw was no fear, just calm contentment. Jane seemed to realize she was in someone's arms and safe, so she closed her eyes once more and went back to sleep.

Sadie wished her emotions matched Jane's. Instead, they were going too far in the opposite direction. Her heart was racing, her throat closing, and she was starting to fear she would cry.

What the fuck was *that* about?

She was still reeling, shell-shocked, when Jenna opened the door, Russ in tow. "Oh, there you are. Thanks for watching the kids, Sadie." Jenna reclaimed the baby and her little son, moving both kids and her chastened husband to the car. Once she had them all loaded up, Jenna started the car and drove away, completely oblivious to the wake she'd left behind.

Sadie sat on the bench for several minutes, her thoughts whirling, her emotions in absolute turmoil.

Babies trusted.

Sadie had spent a lifetime avoiding kids because she'd always known she wasn't made to be a mother. Wasn't cut out for it. After all, she'd had the shittiest role model in the history of motherhood, and there was no doubt the fruit hadn't fallen far from the tree. Sadie possessed too many of her mother's wild, uninhibited characteristics.

Babies trusted.

Sadie couldn't shake that realization loose. How many times had Sadie looked at her mother with those same content eyes when she'd been little, so certain that her mom would always be there to take care of her? How could her mother have walked away from her so easily? Left her alone to fend for herself?

Sadie had trusted her. And her mother had shattered it in one selfish moment. Proven to her that the only way to survive, to live, was to trust no one.

All the reasons why she had avoided serious relationships crashed in on Sadie. She'd let things go too far, get too deep with Oakley and Joel. They looked at her with trust and they saw forever.

But what if she wasn't that girl? What if she began to feel trapped and ran? God, how could she promise some concept she didn't understand, offer a commitment that struck pure terror in her heart?

What if she turned out to be *exactly* like her mother?

Sadie was a few minutes late entering the restaurant. She'd opted to walk here, hoping the time outside in the cool fall air would help her regain her composure, gather her thoughts.

Find a way to break things off.

She fought against the butterflies in her stomach. They'd

been there all day, and the constant fluttering—maybe churning was a better word—had gotten worse after the incident with Jenna...and Jane. Her stomach ached and there was no way she was going to be able to eat.

Oakley had issued this invitation for a date last night after they'd reduced her to a pile of sexually replete goo in the bar. If she'd had two functioning brain cells left, she would have said a big hell no.

Instead, she'd been fucked almost mindless. The only part of her brain that could function was the panic region and it had told her to get the fuck out of there. So she'd said a hasty yes to his request when they'd gotten to her place, tugged her torn blouse closed, and left their truck in a hurry.

She had told them she would meet them here as the restaurant they'd chosen was only a few blocks from Cruisers. They had tried to fight her on that when they had called to confirm this morning, but she'd held firm. If they'd picked her up, it would have felt too much like a real date and she had been determined—at the time—to pretend this was just three friends sharing a meal out.

Now she knew it would be a lot less pleasant than that.

When they reached the table, Joel pulled out her chair for her. Sadie sat down and glanced around the fancy restaurant. There were a fair amount of diners—some familiar faces, others not. Joel pushed her seat in and Oakley reached for her hand across the table.

They were going to have to cease and desist on the touching. Her heart simply couldn't take it. Neither man was good at keeping his hands to himself when it came to their time together, which was why she should have moved the location of this date. Put them somewhere behind closed doors.

She pulled her hand away from Oakley and gave him a warning look, hoping it would encourage him to give up. As always, Oakley failed to feel chastised. Instead, she felt the tip of his boot touch her calf beneath the table, stroking it suggestively.

"This is a nice place," she said, grateful for the long white tablecloth that hung to the floor. It hid Oakley's foot as he got more adventurous. She kicked at his leg, then tried to move her own feet away from his. It didn't work. "Although it looks sort of pricey. We could have just gone to the Outback or something."

Joel reached for her hand, but unlike Oakley, he didn't relinquish it when she tried to pull away. He simply gripped it tighter and it was *he* who gave the warning look. His dominant streak was her fucking Kryptonite.

Joel winked at her. "It's our first time out together in public. Feel like that calls for something bigger than cheese fries and a pint of Fosters."

She wasn't sure how to respond to the "out together" comment, so she didn't. Instead, she picked up the menu, using it as an excuse to break free from Joel's grip. He released her hand and started looking at his own menu.

"I've never eaten here. What's good?" she asked.

Oakley shrugged. "We've never been here either. I asked Lorelie for the name of a romantic restaurant and she mentioned this place."

Romantic? Sadie's chest tightened. Did Lorelie ask who Oakley was taking out? Had he told her? Lorelie thought she was with Joel. If Oakley had said...

Sadie struggled to catch a deep breath. The air was getting thick and humid, the walls closing in on her.

"We felt like celebrating," Oakley said.

She frowned. "Celebrating?"

Oakley glanced at Joel and grinned. "Joel's mom caught us kissing in the barn and she didn't keel over. Or kill him.

Or me. We figured that was worth a big night out on the town."

Sadie experienced two emotions at once—horror at the thought of Joel's mother catching them in the act and relief that the event hadn't severed Joel's relationship with his mom. It also offered her a brief distraction from the fear that hadn't abated since she'd looked into Jane's eyes and known what she would have to do tonight.

"What did she say?" Sadie asked.

Joel didn't appear as overjoyed by the event, though he didn't look upset either. "She was surprised."

"She freaked out," Oakley said.

"We talked about it, and..." Joel shrugged. "I think she's going to be okay with it. Eventually."

Sadie smiled, though she wasn't particularly happy about his story. Not that she wasn't glad for Joel. He and Oakley would be facing some tough times ahead as the new nature of their relationship became public. She knew how much Joel cared about his mother, how much he worried about her. It would have devastated him to lose her approval, so she was glad for that.

However, once again, she felt like the outsider, the usurper. She needed to take a step away from them, so that they could move on with their lives, their futures. They had a shot at real happiness, but that couldn't begin until she set them free to find it.

Joel put his menu down. "Of course, I'm going to throw her for another loop when I tell her the rest of it."

"The rest of it?" Sadie asked.

"When I tell her about you," he said.

She scowled. "Why would you tell her about me?"

Joel's expression darkened. "Why wouldn't I?"

"You tell her about all the women you fuck?" She tried to

keep her voice calm, but there was no masking the fear creeping into it.

"No," Joel said. "But I would like to tell her about the woman I'm in love with."

"The woman *we're* in love with," Oakley added.

"I think we need to stop here." Sadie didn't like where this conversation was headed. Time to put them back on the right track.

Joel shook his head. "No. I think maybe it's time to talk about what comes next, Sadie."

"Nothing comes next." The words fell from her, but once they'd been spoken, she let them hover, hang in the air. She couldn't take them back, couldn't waver in her resolve.

Oakley's foot disappeared from her leg as he leaned back in his chair, his expression far too serious for her fun-loving friend. "What's wrong with taking this to the next level, Sade? Let's change the definition of this from fling to relationship. You gotta admit it feels right."

No. Nothing had ever felt less right to her.

Her temper piqued. She hated being afraid. Being weak. They were pushing her, putting on too much pressure. "I've never lied to you about what I wanted from this. Never pretended it was going to be more."

Oakley ran a frustrated hand through his hair. "It's not like we're asking you to marry us, Sadie."

"Well, that's a good thing. Since it's illegal. Little crime called polygamy. You might want to look it up."

Oakley didn't take offense at her cutting tone, which only served to annoy her more. She was purposely being a bitch, hoping it would drive them away, but neither man seemed willing to leave.

Joel frowned. "We just want you to be our girlfriend, Sadie."

She shook her head. "No."

Both men waited for her to elaborate, but she remained silent. Her head was whirling over all the reasons why she wouldn't, why she *couldn't* date them, but she struggled to find one that they would believe.

"Why not?" Oakley was ready to push the envelope.

"People wouldn't approve." Yep. That was the lamest one she could have thrown at them. They knew her far too well.

Joel scoffed, just as she'd expected. "You don't give a good goddamn what anyone thinks. Try again."

His arrogant tone sent her into orbit. "Listen. We have fun between the sheets and you have a nice cock, but that doesn't mean I want to wear your letter jacket and go steady. It just means you're a decent fuck."

Her words were deliberately cruel. Probably the meanest things she'd ever said, but they'd backed her against a wall. She'd never been the type to back away from a fight, so even as it ripped her heart to do so, she came out swinging.

If she had hurt him, Joel didn't let on. His face was impassive as he studied hers. She was terrified at what he might see, so she set her features in stone and held his gaze despite her desire to curl up in a ball and sob her heart out. It gave her no pleasure to say these things, but she needed to make a clean break.

"What about me, Sadie? Do you like *me*?" Oakley's softly worded question pierced her heart.

She didn't have it in her to keep going, to remain so cold. "Please don't make me say things that will hurt you."

Oakley lifted one shoulder, though his face made her feel as if she'd just kicked a puppy. "All we want you to say is the truth."

"That's all I've ever said to you."

Joel tilted his head. "Actually, now that I think about it, I'm pretty sure you've never said a single honest word to us. What are you so afraid of, Sadie?"

It was the worst thing he could have said to her. The Milligan family was notorious for its overweening sense of pride and determination to never be called a coward.

"Nothing," she said as she rose from the table. Her hands shook with rage and agony. "I'm not afraid of anything."

Joel didn't bother to stand. The son of a bitch was pushing her buttons. "Then why are you running away from us? From this?"

Sadie leaned closer, her voice dangerously low. "There is no us, Joel. And there never will be. I'm not yours. This train just hit the last station."

With that, she stormed from the restaurant. The steam from her red-hot anger got her back home in record time. And it was only after she closed the door behind her that her true emotions caught up to her.

She crumbled to the floor and cried like she'd never cried before.

Chapter Ten

Joel walked into Cruisers with Oakley at his side. It was a bold move, and probably not the smartest one. It had been five days, six hours and—he glanced at his watch—seventeen minutes since Sadie had ripped their hearts from their chests and stomped on them.

Since then, he and Oakley had done nothing but throw themselves into their work. Rising at the crack of dawn and doing the most backbreaking work on the ranch until sunset. Sheer physical exhaustion was the only thing saving them from feeling the emotional pain too keenly. They fell into bed each night and slept the sleep of the dead, too tired to suffer the agony of Sadie's desertion.

Today, Coach had stepped in. Told them they were taking a day off. He'd insisted despite their protests. So they'd endured an eternal day at home, both of them relieved when Tucker called and invited them out for a drink with him and Chas. Lorelie had hopped in the truck at the last minute, as the other men were bringing their significant others as well.

Joel had considered refusing the invitation at first, simply because he was certain Sadie wouldn't like seeing them here. Oakley, in typical fashion, had convinced him Cruisers had been their watering hole for years and Sadie would have to get used to seeing them, as none of them had plans to leave small-town Maris anytime soon. Or ever.

Joel hadn't been fooled by the bravado in his friend's words. Oakley hadn't given up hope yet. Hadn't accepted that Sadie wouldn't change her mind about this.

Oakley had believed they could console each other sexually. And it had helped...a bit. They'd crawled into bed together and kissed, touched, caressed. It had been more comfort than passion and both of them had missed Sadie. Maybe somewhere down the road that would change, but for now, neither of them could see beyond their broken hearts.

Unlike Oakley—the eternal optimist—it was the angry part of Joel that had brought him here. He wanted Sadie to see his pain, to understand what she'd done to them.

So here they were. For better or worse. Standing in Cruisers.

Sadie hadn't looked up upon their arrival. Probably because the place was hopping. It was Ladies' Night and there was a band playing. Joel hadn't known it would be so busy. If he had, he probably would have stayed home.

As it was, he was going to have to plaster a fake smile on his face and pretend he was having fun. Doing so would take more energy than he had.

He grabbed a seat at the table, surrounded by his former teammates and their girls. Everyone was laughing, talking and drinking. Twice, Lorelie had given him a questioning look and asked why he wasn't talking to Sadie. He'd shrugged it off, claiming she was too busy to chat.

Joel glanced at Oakley, who looked as miserable as he did.

"One drink," Joel muttered. "Then we're getting out of here."

Oakley shook his head. "Nope. Not going anywhere."

Joel hadn't expected Oakley to dig his heels in. His friend didn't have a stubborn bone in his body. Then he realized Oakley's gaze was glued to the bar.

Joel followed his line of vision and suddenly understood. There was a guy sitting alone, chatting with Sadie. Flirting, actually. When Sadie set a fresh drink in front of the man, he reached out to grasp her hand, pretending to look at her tattoo.

Sadie withdrew her hand, but the fact she wasn't responding to the asshole's come-ons didn't calm Joel down. He didn't consider himself a jealous man, but he realized that was because he'd never been in love. It appeared Oakley was suffering a pretty bad case of the emotion as well, his friend's hands balled into fists on the table.

Sadie must have sensed the heated looks honing in on her like laser beams because her gaze lifted and connected with his.

If he hadn't been so furious, he would have chuckled when her lips clearly moved and she said, "Fuck."

Her curse caught the attention of Mr. Can't Catch a Clue, who leaned closer, his face covered with fake concern.

Joel wasn't sure what Sadie said to the man, but she obviously hadn't mentioned him or Oakley. Instead, her scowl softened, her lips curling into a coquettish smile of her own. One that she gave to the man at the end of the bar. The man she hadn't given two damns about three seconds earlier.

Then she leaned over the counter, pointing to her tattoo. The man's interest in her ink vanished in the face of the ample eyeful of cleavage she was treating him to. Then she gave the guy a flirty look and flipped her hair. Joel knew exactly who her little show was for, but he wasn't sure what her goal was. If she'd wanted to solidify the fact she was no longer interested in them and was moving on, she failed. All she'd managed to do was trigger his temper and prove to him that she hadn't meant a damn thing she'd said in the restaurant.

Sadie was in love with them and fighting it. Hard.

"Oakley," Joel said, not bothering to look at his friend, refusing to take his gaze away from Sadie.

"Yeah?"

"I'm about to do everything wrong."

Oakley didn't laugh and he didn't ask questions. "I'll be right behind you."

Joel and Oakley rose from the table, ignoring their friends when they asked where they were going. They made a beeline for the bar.

Sadie's eyes narrowed when they stepped up to the counter, flanking the asshole.

"You want a drink?" she asked, her tone sheer belligerence. It was a dangerous stance to take, given Joel's current state of mind.

"You got a break coming up?" Joel asked.

That caught the attention of the man sitting between them. "Hey, back off, man."

Stupid prick must have thought there was some first-come-first-serve rule in effect.

"Excuse me?" Joel said.

The guy wasn't easily intimidated. "Sadie and I were having a little chat. I'm sort of hoping she'll take a twirl with me on the dance floor on her next break."

He gave Sadie a look that reeked of confidence. The man didn't have a clue she wasn't really interested.

"Yeah," Oakley said, drawing the man's attention to him. "That's not happening."

Sadie slammed down the metal shaker she was using to mix a drink with enough force that everyone in the surrounding area looked up. She pointed at both Joel and Oakley. "Come with me."

Every word dripped with fury. Joel welcomed it. They'd let her walk away from them in the restaurant without a fight. That wouldn't happen again.

She stepped out from behind the bar and led them down the small hallway that ended at the back alley. Joel remembered the last time they'd been together in that alley. How explosive it had been.

Sadie appeared to remember as well, because she took a sharp left just before the exit, leading them into a storeroom. Bottles of liquor, bags of peanuts, packs of napkins and trays of clean glasses covered the shelves. It wasn't a large space, but it suited Joel's purposes just fine.

Sadie clearly regretted her decision the second Oakley closed the door behind them, the three of them in very tight quarters. She recovered quickly.

"What the fuck do you think you're doing?" she asked, her voice dangerously quiet.

Joel crossed his arms. "That guy was a douche."

"No shit. I've been around the block a few times, Joel. I can hand out my own rejections just fine." Then she lifted her chin, her pretty face the picture of haughtiness as she added, "And I can accept whichever hookups I want."

Oakley shook his head, but it was Joel who answered her. "No. You can't."

If it were physically possible, Sadie would have rocketed into orbit at his cocky reply. Her face was flushed with fury and her hands were shaking with rage. "You fucking asshole! How dare you—"

Joel cut her off. Not with words, but with his lips. He'd told Oakley he was going to handle this situation wrong and he hadn't lied. But he also hadn't been able to stop himself. He saw Sadie flirting with another guy and lost it.

She pressed against his shoulders, trying to shove him away, but Joel tightened his grip and deepened the kiss. When she failed to dislodge him with force, she moved on to punching, her fists pounding against his chest. Joel took the blows, refusing to give up any ground. He might have backed away if not for the fact her lips weren't exactly agreeing with the actions of her fists. Her lips had softened and parted. And then, her tongue found his, touched it lightly before darting back into her mouth.

Oakley saved Joel from a continued beating by stepping behind Sadie and grasping her wrists, tugging them behind her back. Their bondage girl responded instantly. Her head rearing back as she gasped. Her chest rose and fell rapidly, drawing his attention to her very noticeable nipples poking through her t-shirt.

Joel's anger had faded, but it was still there. "You're killing us, Sadie."

Her face fell, and for the first time since she'd stormed out of the restaurant, he saw a trace of true regret in her eyes. "I'm not changing my mind."

"We're not watching you flirt with other guys."

"I'm not yours."

She'd said those same words when she walked away. Now, like then, she was wrong.

"You can say that as many times as you want. Still doesn't make it true," Joel said.

Oakley continued to hold her captive, though he remained silent, letting Joel fight this battle.

"Why can't you let this go?"

Joel shook his head. "We just can't. We told you we loved you, that we wanted to build a future with you. You said some shit about not feeling the same. Well, you know what? I don't buy it."

He looked at Oakley.

"Neither do I," Oakley said.

"There's something you're not telling us," Joel continued. "What it is, Sadie? Say it. And we'll fix it."

She snorted scornfully. "Believe me, this isn't something you can fix."

For the first time since they'd begun sleeping together, Joel sensed she was finally ready to confide in them. He silently prayed whatever was holding her back was something they could overcome.

"What do you mean?" Oakley asked.

"I don't want to get married."

Joel narrowed his eyes. It was a sentiment she'd voiced before. "Sadie—" he started.

She cut him off. "I'm not someone who can do forever. But it's more than that."

He and Oakley waited for the other shoe to drop.

"I don't want to have kids."

Neither he nor Oakley moved as they let that bit of information soak in. Until she'd said the words, Joel hadn't realized how much he did want a family. He wasn't exactly sure how it would work out logistically, but he knew he wanted a baby girl with Sadie's bright blue eyes and sweet smile. Now that the idea was out there, Joel felt that desire intensely.

Oakley was the first to ask the question left unanswered. "Why not?"

"I'm not mother material."

It was a vague response at best. Joel knew there was something else at work, something stronger. "Try again."

He should have known better than to take that arrogant tone with her. Coupled with the fact that he'd crossed his arms,

Sadie went off. Her emotions had been riding too close to the surface since they'd entered the closet. Joel had been stupid to push her, to set her off. But he was running on empty too. His heart ripped out, beating painfully in her clenched fist. One squeeze and she'd have him on his knees, begging her to come back.

"You asked for my reasons and I gave them to you. I'm not going to get married and I'm not going to wreck some poor, innocent baby's life the way my mother fucked up mine!" She was practically yelling at them.

And at last, they'd gotten to the truth.

"You're not your mother," Oakley said.

She turned on him, her face radiating pure fury. "You didn't know my mother."

Oakley was typically able to hold his shit together, but the tension was causing some cracks in his composure. "I didn't have to know her to know you would never leave your kid behind. Jesus, Sadie. You can't seriously believe what you're saying right now."

One look in her shattered, terrified eyes told Joel she believed every single word. And there was precious little he or Oakley could do to change her mind.

How did they fight against a lifetime of disappointment and mistrust? Something had broken when Sadie's mom skipped out of town all those years ago, and there was only one person capable of putting the pieces back together.

Sadly, that person wasn't him. And it wasn't Oakley.

"Sadie, if you'd just let us help you," he began, knowing there was nothing he could offer her that they hadn't already given. They'd given her love, trust, friendship, everything they had. It hadn't been enough.

"Please, Joel." His heart ached at the pain in her voice. It went against everything inside him to hurt her. Yet it was obvious that was what this conversation was doing. It was tearing them all apart. "Please don't ask me to come back, for any more than we've already had. I can't, I just can't give it to you."

Then he looked into her eyes and saw the tears and he knew.

Knew he had to walk away. Even though it would kill him to do it.

"Sadie," he whispered.

"Please," she repeated.

He nodded his reluctant acquiescence. Then he leaned toward her and kissed her gently.

Oakley didn't speak, but the utter devastation in his friend's eyes told him he understood it was over as well.

Oakley gave her his own sweet kiss and then they left the storeroom together.

Though he walked next to his best friend, Joel had never felt more alone.

Chapter Eleven

"**W**hat the hell is wrong with you?"

Sadie closed her eyes and prayed for strength. After tossing and turning, replaying everything she and the guys had said in the storeroom four evenings earlier, she had managed less than an hour's worth of sleep last night.

She'd seen Lorelie the second the woman had walked into Cruisers. And considering her friend had honed in on her like a homing missile, storming straight to the bar, it was obvious Sadie was in for a few unpleasant minutes.

She didn't need this shit. Sadie had only been back in Maris a few hours. She'd left the bar after her talk with the guys a few nights ago, climbed on her bike and taken off to San Antonio to recover, hoping the time away would help her get her shit together. All it had done was make her more miserable and lonely and horny—she really needed to get a handle on that last issue.

She'd still be away if her dad hadn't called her yesterday afternoon and told her to get her ass home before he fired her.

She hadn't given him a reason for skipping out of town without so much as a word of explanation, so she knew—in addition to this ass-chewing from Lorelie—she had that inquisition to endure later.

"Good to see you too, Lorelie."

"Don't pull that crap with me."

"I've been out of town. How did you know I was here?"

Lorelie pointed toward the front of the building. "Saw your bike parked in the lot. I've driven by here and your apartment every day for four days. Knew you wouldn't run forever. Where did you go?"

"San Antonio. Do Joel and Oakley know I'm back in town?"

Lorelie shrugged. "I doubt it. They haven't left the ranch since you split. They work from sunup to sundown, barely eat, hardly speak, and look like someone killed their best friend."

Sadie winced to hear how badly she'd hurt them.

"So you know why I'm here?" Lorelie asked.

Sadie had never backed down from a fight. And while she was tired as hell and her heart wasn't in this one, some small part of her was raring to go. "You shouldn't have put in so much effort. This is none of your business."

"Bullshit!" Lorelie said, her voice too loud. Sadie saw her dad's head pop up from the back of the room. The afternoon crowd was low, so he'd decided to take a break to play a quick game of pool with a customer.

Sadie leaned over the bar. "Can you keep your voice down? I'm not interested in giving the gossips anything to wag their tongues about today."

Lorelie glanced around, chagrined at having drawn so much attention to them. Even though she was angry, she obviously understood why Sadie wouldn't want the world to know what had gone down. "Joel and Oakley are like brothers to me. I love those two idiots. And you hurt them."

Sadie nodded. It wasn't like she could deny it. It was the truth. "How did you find out?"

"I was with them the other night. Here."

Sadie was typically very aware of who was in the bar when. It spoke to her distraught state of mind that she hadn't even seen Lorelie that night. Of course, it wasn't that surprising. Whenever Joel or Oakley were within a fifty-foot radius of her, her line of vision tended to go fuzzy around the edges, the only things in focus being them. "Oh."

"Yeah. Oh." Lorelie leaned her elbows on the counter. "They were pretty upset after talking to you, so we left early. Once I got them in the truck, I made them tell me what the hell was going on between all of you."

"Then you should know that I called things off."

"Which brings me back to my previous question. What the hell is wrong with you?"

Sadie closed her eyes, unable to shield the misery. She'd been living with a perpetual stomachache for days. "It can't work, Lorelie."

"You're wrong."

Sadie placed her palms on the lower counter behind the bar, using her hands to hold her upright. She was exhausted beyond belief and seriously considering curling up in a fetal position in some corner of the room for a few years. "It's done now. I've told them it's over and it is. We just need some time to move on and in a few weeks, we'll realize we dodged a bullet."

Lorelie shook her head. "I used to look up to you. Used to think you were so cool. I mean, you always seemed to have your shit together. You were self-confident. You knew who you were and you never let anyone's opinion keep you from doing what you thought was right or what you wanted to do. I guess that was all just a lie."

"Lorelie. You don't understand."

"Apparently I'm not the only one. Joel and Oakley don't get it either. So make us understand. Because you look every bit as miserable as them. Every bit as brokenhearted."

"Look, I get it. Okay!" This time it was Sadie's voice that was raised, but she didn't care. "I know I was wrong to get involved with them. Wrong to let it go on so long. I know that I hurt them. And I'm sorry about it. More than you know."

"So unhurt them."

Sadie grinned sadly. "Just like that?"

Lorelie gave her a small why-not shrug.

"I can't."

"They're in love with you. God, Sadie. I can't get one decent guy to fall for me. You've got two who would lay down their lives for you and you're throwing them away."

Lorelie's words cut through her like a knife, but someone had to be the voice of reason. Someone had to remain strong. While their hearts may be broken now, they'd have time to heal, to move on. Better to get this part over with quick rather than deal with the fallout later when it would be that much more devastating.

"I'm not a good bet, Lorelie."

"What's that mean?"

"I went into this..." She paused. She'd started to say "relationship". Then she realized that was exactly what it was. Not calling it by its name didn't make it something else. "I went into this relationship because I thought it was just going to be a physical thing. The three of us having some fun between the sheets."

"So what you got was something way better. Sex and love. Stop being an idiot, Sade."

"People don't live in threes." It was the same lame excuse she'd offered Joel. Lorelie rejected it just like he had, her eyes rolling back in her head.

"You're not the type of person who gives a shit what other people think, Sadie. That's Joel's hang-up and obviously he's gotten beyond it. He and Oakley took you to that restaurant, to that very public place, to declare their love because they happen to believe the three of you can make it work. He got beyond his fears. So it's your turn. Tell me why you're really saying no."

"I've never been in love. Not really."

"That doesn't sound like a reason to walk away. Love is staring you right in the face. What's stopping you from grabbing it with both hands?"

Sadie had never spoken her fear aloud, never told another living soul the terror she harbored deep down inside.

"What if I can't do it? What if I'm like her?" she whispered, her head bowed, her eyes closed.

Lorelie's voice betrayed her confusion. "Like who?"

"My mom."

"You're not a damn thing like your mother."

Sadie's eyes flew open, landing on her father's angry face. She'd been so upset, she hadn't even seen him walk over. "Dad."

"You really think that?" he asked.

She shrugged. She'd always believed it. Sadie had never found it easy to form close relationships and she had a wild streak inside her a mile wide.

Lorelie flushed as she stepped away from the bar. From her regretful expression, it was clear she knew she'd opened a can of worms. "I should probably go."

"Not yet." Sadie's dad blocked Lorelie's path. "Who's in love with Sadie?"

"What?" Lorelie hedged, glancing over her shoulder at Sadie, horrified. Her dad was a pretty intimidating fellow, but something in Lorelie's pursed lips told Sadie her friend wouldn't betray her. Even if she was scared spitless. Sadie decided then and there Lorelie was going to be her first real, genuine girlfriend.

Lorelie had come here because she loved Oakley and Joel. Her intentions had been good and Sadie was glad the men had such a fierce little protector. A sister of the heart to stand up for them.

Sadie couldn't make Lorelie stand before the firing squad for simply trying to help—so she stepped into the line of fire instead. "Oakley and Joel are in love with me, Dad."

Her father scowled. "Both of them?"

She nodded. "It's okay, Lorelie. Honest. I'll call you later."

Lorelie mouthed the word, "sorry," then took her leave without another word.

Her father jerked his head toward the back, indicating he wanted Sadie to move. Now.

"Roscoe," he called out loudly. "Take the bar."

He lifted the hinged counter and Sadie stepped out, following him to the small office in the back of the building.

Once the office door was closed, he turned to face her, his arms crossed. "Talk."

"I've been seeing Oakley and Joel."

"And they both knew you were dating the other guy at the same time?"

"I don't mean separately. I mean the three of us are together."

Her father scowled. "What? Like one of those ménage a trois things?"

She nodded, struggling not to giggle. It was the absolute worst thing she could do, but she always found humor in things that were not funny. Talking to her dad about a ménage a trois struck her as absurdly comical.

"I'm going to fucking kill those bastards."

Sadie stepped in front of the door, blocking his exit. "No. You're not."

"And why wouldn't I?"

Sadie licked her lips nervously. Then she said what she should have said to Oakley and Joel. "Because I'm in love with them too."

Her dad's arms fell to his sides, and then he raised his hands, almost beseechingly. "You can't be in love with two guys at the same time, Sade. That's not how the world works."

"I know," she said, hating the way her voice cracked. "Which is what I was saying before. I can't seem to conform, to do what's expected. I do what feels good, I have a strong disregard for authority, and I struggle with commitment. Sound like anyone familiar?"

Dad shrugged. "Yeah. Me."

She rolled her eyes. "No, Dad. *Her*. I'm like Mom."

"Jesus, Sadie. You're the polar opposite of your mother."

Sadie didn't agree, but wasn't sure how to plead her case without reopening a wound. She had been very young when her mother left. So young that her absence became a way of life before she was old enough to ask why she wasn't there. Why had her mom walked out on them?

Her dad sighed when the silence lasted too long. He pointed to a chair. "Sit down, Sadie." His tone proved exactly how uncomfortable he felt. The fact that he was still here, still trying to talk it out, made her love her dad more than ever.

He was a man of few words, most of them gruff or foul and never anything that touched on feelings.

She took the seat closest to the door should he decide to make good on his threat to do bodily harm to Joel and Oakley.

Dad crossed behind the desk and claimed the larger chair, placing his arms on the smooth surface. He clasped them together tightly, betraying his nervousness. It was odd to see her father like this.

"How much do you want to know?" he asked.

Considering he'd never said one word about her mother—short of the brief conversation they'd had when Sadie returned home from first grade and her dad had simply said, "Your mom had to leave town. It's just you and me from now on. Okay?"—she figured they were starting at zero.

Back then, Sadie had just said, "Okay," and held on to every single one of the million and twelve questions she had.

She couldn't do that anymore. "All of it."

He grimaced. "Some of it might be hard to hear."

After so many years of silence, she'd take anything. Not knowing was way more painful. She knew that for sure. "I don't care."

"Met your mom here at the bar. She was passing through Maris on her way to Arizona. One thing led to another and we sort of hooked up. She took off the next morning and I didn't really think about her again until she showed up three months later. Pregnant."

Sadie fought to keep her face impassive for fear her dad would stop talking. Once again, she felt the overwhelming desire to giggle. She was the product of a one-night stand. Figured.

When she didn't say anything, her dad forged on. "I told her I'd do the right thing by her, so we got married. I tried to make it work, Sadie. For you. And...for me. Saw you being born in that delivery room and I fell in love with your mom—right then and there. Never saw anything so incredible in my whole life."

Sadie smiled. "You always told me I came out screaming my head off and the racket gave you a headache."

Dad chuckled. "Yeah. That part was true too."

His face sobered up and Sadie recognized the look in his eyes. Knew instinctively what it was because she'd seen it in her own this morning. Pain.

"She didn't feel the same way about me. To be honest, she hung in there longer than I thought she would. But I'm pretty sure that was for you. Not me. Your mother was a free spirit and she was never meant to settle down and be anyone's mom...or wife."

"So she left."

Her dad nodded sadly. "Yeah."

His story had only proven her point. "Don't you see some similarities there, Dad?"

His expression grew thunderous, but a lifetime with this man had numbed her to his grumpiness. "No. I don't see one damn thing of your mother in you, besides her pretty eyes."

She had her mother's eyes? Sadie had a couple of pictures of her mom, but she hadn't looked at them in well over two decades.

"What I *do* see," her father continued, "is too fucking much of me."

"You make that sound like a bad thing?" She adored her dad and was proud that he actually thought they were alike. He was a badass who didn't take crap from anybody. He was his own man. She respected the hell out of that.

"In this instance, it is."

Sadie felt the need to make it clear to him how wrong he was. "You, of all people, should understand this. I'm a bad bet. I suck at commitment. I don't want to hurt Joel and Oakley."

Dad shook his head. "No. You got it backwards. You aren't

running because you're afraid you'll hurt them. You're running because you're afraid they'll hurt *you*."

She sat frozen, her body suddenly cold as ice, her mind numb.

Her father stood up and walked around to stand in front of her, leaning on the desk. "I tried to raise you to be independent, Sadie. I wanted you to be strong enough to handle all the shit life was gonna throw your way. Guess I taught you the best way to do all that was to never let anyone close. Good intentions. Bad lesson."

She grinned and stood up. Stepping closer, her dad was there, arms open to embrace her. "You raised me just fine. My problem is I'm a bum magnet."

"No, you're not. There were plenty of decent guys asking you out. You turned down the good ones because it kept you safe."

Sadie couldn't refute his words. She'd run through a long line of assholes, men who never had a snowball's chance in hell of hurting her because she would never love them.

Her plan had fallen apart when she'd embarked on the affair with Joel and Oakley. She'd strayed from losers and accepted the advances of two really great guys. Her safety net had been the threesome. And it had failed her. Because it worked.

Then she'd held Jane in her arms and though it killed her to admit it, she realized how much she loved holding that tiny little life in her arms. It had started some yearnings that terrified her. She didn't know the first thing about being a mom. The only thing she knew for sure was that she'd cut out her own heart rather than hurt a child the way her mother had hurt her.

"What do I do now?"

Her dad gripped her upper arms, holding her back so that he could see her face. "You really love those two men?"

She nodded.

He closed his eyes and blew out a long breath. There was no denying her father was not a fan of what her heart had chosen. However, he was her dad. And he was going to support her decision, going to defend her against anyone who dared to question it. He was going to have her back...just like he always did.

"Fine."

She stood up on tiptoe and kissed him on the cheek. "Don't worry so much. There's a pretty good chance I've already done irreparable damage to the relationship."

"No. If they really love you, it's gonna work out just fine." Then Dad cracked his knuckles. "But if it *is* over, it's still a win because I'll be free to pound their asses into the ground."

Sadie laughed. "I might keep that as my ace in the hole if they turn me down."

She meant her words as a joke, but her dad didn't laugh. "You can't tie someone to you who doesn't want to be there. If it doesn't work out, you stop picking up jackasses and go out with some nice guys. *One* at a time. I'll make you a list."

"Deal."

"And I should warn you, I'm taking my own advice outta this room."

"What do you mean?" she asked.

"I've had my eye on a woman here in town. I'm gonna ask her out."

Sadie's eyebrows flew up. "On a date? You never date."

"Well, I'm going to start."

"Who caught your eye?" Sadie had never heard her father express interest in any woman. Ever.

Dad chuckled. "Joel's mother."

"Ms. Rodriguez? You've gotta be kidding me."

Her father scowled. "What are you talking about? She's a beautiful woman. And very nice."

Sadie wasn't sure how to respond. When she did, her concerns came out in a jumble. "She's kind of...um...she goes to church every Sunday, Dad. We're atheists. And she's pretty straitlaced. None of that taking-the-Lord's-name-in-vain kind of stuff. Your favorite curse is Jesus Christ on a cracker. And... well, she doesn't drink, does she? You own a bar."

Dad shrugged as if none of that mattered. "Don't care. Still going to ask her to dinner."

Sadie sighed. Why was she fighting this? She was delighted her father was putting himself back out there. She sincerely hoped he found someone. Just...maybe not Joel's mom. "Do me a favor?"

Her dad nodded.

"Don't marry her. If things go well tonight, I could potentially be sleeping with my stepbrother. And that's just...ew."

Dad laughed loudly as he wrapped his arm around her shoulder and guided her to the door. "Take the rest of the day off. Go make things right with those guys. And once it's all worked out, tell them to stop by and see me sometime. I want to show them my gun collection."

Chapter Twelve

Sadie sat on the porch of the bunkhouse looking out across the ranch. It was late afternoon. She hadn't considered her timing after she'd walked out of the bar. She'd had a single-minded purpose and that was to come here.

And that was what she'd done after a quick pit stop at her apartment for a shower, some primping, a sexier shirt and the surprise she was hoping against hope she'd have the opportunity to use.

If she'd been thinking clearly, she would have realized the guys were working and called ahead. Or waited until quitting time. Which would have killed her.

Given the fact they hadn't seen or heard her approach, they must be well away from the main part of the ranch.

So, she would wait. Part of her thought this was a lucky break because it would give her time to think about what she should say.

She soon realized that was a very bad thing. She was much better off-the-cuff, unrehearsed. The longer she tried to figure out what words to use, the worse they got.

She replayed the night at the restaurant over and over, her own cruel words slicing through her. Within half an hour, she'd worked herself into a frenzy. She considered hopping on her bike and splitting, leaving Maris and never looking back. That would be the easy way out—her mother's way.

She didn't even bother to stand. She'd spent a lifetime hiding and the better part of two months denying what she wanted.

Gravel on the driveway caught her attention. She didn't move as she watched the pickup truck pull up to the bunkhouse and come to a stop. Sadie didn't even blink as Oakley and Joel climbed out of the vehicle, their gazes resting on her face.

Only once they'd approached the porch did she bother to rise.

Before either of them spoke, she raised her hand as a slew of ridiculous words flew from her lips.

"Don't read too much into this." Wow. Great start. Clearly the old Sadie wasn't going down without a fight.

"I mean, don't expect much." Oh yeah. That was much better.

Apparently it didn't matter. Oakley started grinning like a guy who'd just won the lottery, and Joel leaned against the railing of the porch, arms crossed, looking like the cockiest son of a bitch on the planet.

She scowled. "Don't look at me like that." Her words were growing softer. They lacked conviction.

"You're almost there," Joel prodded. "Try one more time."

His words were a dare. Fine. She'd show him.

"Don't leave me or I'll hunt you down and cut your cocks off."

Oakley laughed loudly at her very earnest and sincere threat. Sadie couldn't find the humor in this.

"I mean it," she said, her voice sounding pathetic even to her own ears.

Oakley sobered up as Joel walked over to her quickly. "Never, Sade. We're never going to leave you."

Oakley moved to stand next to Joel. "Never." He sealed that vow with a sweet, gentle kiss. Joel offered the same.

For several quiet moments, they merely held each other, their lips occasionally meeting for another quick, soft kiss.

Oakley was the first to break the silence. "Can I tell you I love you now?"

She shook her head. "No. I get to go first. I love you. And I'm sorry I was such a douchebag at the restaurant. I'm lugging around about two tons of baggage."

"Guess it's a good thing you fell for two strong cowboys. We can carry that shit away for you. No problem." Joel placed one hand on her hip. It was meant to reassure her, but it also fired up her libido. She wished he'd slipped his fingers under her shirt and found skin.

"I guess it is," she whispered, touched by his words and dizzy under his touch. He seemed to have read her mind, his hand drifting along her hip and around to cup her ass cheek. When he squeezed it tightly, she was done for.

"What's that?" Oakley asked as he pointed at the bag she'd dropped beside her chair as she waited.

"Plan B," she said, grinning as she recalled how she'd intended to beg for their forgiveness. They all seemed to be fairly evenly matched when it came to sexual appetites and lack of willpower. She had shamelessly planned to seduce them into accepting her apology.

Joel walked toward it but she stepped in front of him, trying to hold him back. His eyes narrowed suspiciously, then a wicked smile crept onto his handsome face. "I think I like the idea of plan B."

She shrugged nonchalantly. "Maybe so, but you've already forgiven me, so it's not necessary." Sadie had every intention in the world of enacting plan B, C, a few O's and the XXX one as well. But now that they'd turned the corner, it felt good to get back to the teasing, fun nature of their relationship.

"What's in the bag, Sadie?" Joel asked. Before she could reply, Oakley slid by her and grabbed it. His eyes widened with delight when he peeked inside.

"Jesus, Sade. I honestly didn't think I could love you any more, but I was wrong."

She laughed, slightly surprised when his words of affection didn't prompt the same familiar fear in her. Instead, they warmed her, made her feel good.

He handed the bag to Joel. Unlike Oakley, his expression didn't turn to humor. It morphed into hardcore lust. Instantly.

"Get in the house," he demanded. "Both of you."

Sadie followed Oakley, the three of them walking straight to the bedroom.

Their clothing fell away in one big heap as they raced to strip. It had only been four days since they'd seen each other, but to Sadie it felt more like years. She didn't want to live in a world where she couldn't touch these men, couldn't sleep nestled between them.

Once they were naked, Oakley pressed her down onto the bed and climbed over her. They lost *no* time making up for lost time. They were connected from head to toe, kissing, touching, exploring, teasing. She cupped his balls, playing with them as he pinched her nipple. Neither of them came up for air until the bag landed on the mattress next to them.

"Tell me about this plan B," Joel said, sitting on the edge of the bed. He hadn't attempted to break into her make-out session with Oakley. Instead, he'd seemed content with simply watching. She'd noticed his voyeuristic kink before. In fact, she shared it. There was nothing hotter than watching Joel and Oakley kiss.

It was so fucking incredible that she hoped for a longer show some time.

"I was wondering if the two of you had...um...you know..." She wasn't the type of woman to blush, but heat crept up her neck to her cheeks as she added, "done the deed?"

Sadie knew Oakley was anxious for that to happen, but he'd held back in deference to Joel, who had been a bit reticent.

Oakley chuckled, but Joel didn't. Instead he shook his head. "No. We haven't."

Given the look on his face, it was obvious Joel was more than ready to take it to the next level now.

Sadie wondered how he'd feel once she told him what she wanted to do. Then she decided some things were better felt than heard. She pressed on Oakley's shoulder and he fell to the side of her, allowing her to sit up.

"Kiss Oakley," she said. Joel narrowed his eyes. Unlike her and Oakley, he wasn't wired to take orders in the bedroom without question. It was difficult for him to give up the control. Even so, Sadie knew how she wanted this to play out, so she gave him a sweet smile that promised she'd repay the favor. "Please."

Joel reached for his friend, tugging him close. She was always enthralled by the sheer brute strength in her men. Though they'd taken her roughly, it was obvious they'd held back some of their power, unwilling to hurt her physically. With each other, those kid gloves came off.

As the kiss grew more heated, Joel twisted Oakley to his back, coming over him, their hard cocks knocking against each other. Sadie had never seen anything sexier in her life.

For a few minutes, she was content to watch their embrace, but then she couldn't resist joining in. She pulled the tube of lubrication she'd brought with her from the bag and uncapped it.

Joel jerked when her hand caressed his muscular ass cheek.

"Get on your knees," she urged him.

He shook his head. "No. It's not going to happen that way."

Oakley grinned. "If I weren't so fucking turned on right now, I'd fight you on that just to see your face."

"Trust me," Sadie said.

For a moment, she thought Joel would refuse. He was struggling with her attempts to take over. Finally he relented, going to his hands and knees, caging Oakley beneath him.

He grunted when Sadie squeezed a large dollop of lube into his ass. Joel held himself stiffly, a sure sign that he was ready to exit the bed the second she went too far.

She used just one finger to work the lubrication in and soon Joel began to relax. As one finger became two, he went down to his elbows and began kissing Oakley again, his quiet moans telling her exactly how much he liked what she was doing.

Fingers brushed against hers and she looked down to see Oakley toying with Joel's balls. She felt like laughing, so she did. Her giggles caused Oakley to break off the kiss with Joel and glance at her over their lover's shoulder.

"Something funny?" he asked with a grin.

She shook her head. "Not really. I'm just...happy."

Oakley laughed and she suspected Joel would have joined them as well if she hadn't chosen that moment to press her luck and add a third finger to the two already in his ass.

"Jesus, Sadie," Joel said.

She added a little bit more lube to her playground, and then decided to go for broke. She grabbed the remote-control butt plug she'd bought prior to *almost* losing the best thing in her life and pressed it inside Joel's ass.

His back stiffened once more, but he didn't resist or try to pull away as she introduced him to the toy. Sadie didn't stop until the plug was completely inside. Pulling it out would be a quick, simple matter if Joel decided he hated it. Not that *that* appeared to be a problem. Joel's hands had balled into fists by Oakley's head, his forehead pressed to Oakley's chest.

"Fucking amazing, isn't it?" Oakley asked.

Joel didn't reply immediately. When he did, his voice was gruff. "Yeah. It is."

"Switch places," Sadie urged, ready to put the next part of her plan into play. She had no idea if they could even do what she wanted, but damn if she didn't want to try.

This time, Joel didn't hesitate. Sadie suspected it was taking all his powers of control simply not to come at this point. That idea pleased her more than she could say.

Once Oakley had assumed the position on top, she grabbed the lube and repeated the same process on him. Unlike Joel, Oakley was obviously familiar with—and a big fan of—anal play. His hips pressed back against her fingers as she stroked him, slicking his channel with a generous amount of lubrication.

They all knew what she was preparing him for, and when Joel said, "Make sure you use enough." Sadie silently released a sigh of relief. Joel was ready. More than that. He clearly wanted it. Badly.

Once Oakley was ready, she removed her fingers and, after finding a towel on the floor—no doubt Oakley's, given it had just been tossed down—she wiped off the lube then returned to the bed.

Oakley and Joel had reversed positions once more, Joel kneeling behind Oakley, who was on all fours. When Oakley beckoned her over, indicating that he wanted her beneath him, she smiled.

"You guessed plan B."

Joel gave her a sexy, *hurry your ass up* look as Oakley nodded.

"If this hadn't been your plan," Joel said, "it was going to become it. There's no way we're doing this without you."

Sadie felt foolish for ever thinking she wasn't a part of this. "I just need one more thing."

Joel groaned when she grabbed the remote control for the plug. "I was hoping you'd forget about that. This isn't going to last long as it is. You turn that thing on…"

Sadie laughed. "We'll just have to keep practicing this way until we build up our stamina."

"Deal," Oakley said hastily. "Now get under me, Sade. I need to be inside you."

She crawled under Oakley, sighing when the head of his cock brushed against her clit. It would take precious little to set her off like a bottle rocket.

Oakley kissed her as she settled beneath him, his tongue stroking hers hungrily. "God, I missed you."

Feeling guilty for being too stupid to live and rejecting their affections, she kissed him back and offered him the same vow he and Joel gave her on the porch. The one that even now was resonating in her heart. "Never again. I'll never be so stupid again."

"You going to tell us what changed your mind?" he asked.

She nodded.

"Later." Joel's voice had taken on an almost pained tone that had her laughing again. She'd never been this downright giddy before. "She can tell us later."

Oakley didn't bother to disagree. Instead, he grasped his cock and guided it into Sadie. She gasped as he continued to push in, not stopping until he was completely lodged within her. Then, he paused.

She started to give him hell for stopping, for teasing her, but

Joel wasn't wasting any time. She heard the crinkle of the condom wrapper, then heard Oakley hiss.

Joel tried to go slow, tried to wrap his head around what was happening. There were too many good things, too many amazing sensations overwhelming him. Oakley pressed back against his cock as Joel pushed into him. He was doing it. Making love to Oakley. God. And Sadie.

He'd never once—in all his life—considered having sex with another man. However, he had been able to think of little else since that Truth or Dare game. Then, like now, it was Sadie who'd given him the push he'd needed to take this chance.

Joel tightened his grip on Oakley's hips. He hadn't been joking when he said this wouldn't take long. Having sex with a man was so different from being with a woman. Joel suddenly understood Oakley's desire for both sexes.

Oakley groaned once he was fully lodged. Joel couldn't resist making the journey again, so he withdrew instantly. As he moved out, Oakley moved into Sadie. Within a half-dozen thrusts, they had found a rhythm that had each of them gasping, clenching and begging for more.

Joel had anticipated an easier ride for their first time, but none of them ever seemed content to take the path of least resistance. Each thrust grew harder and the pace increased. Joel wondered how in the fuck Oakley was hanging in there and for a moment, he considered what it must feel like to be doubly penetrated.

Sadie reminded him.

He'd forgotten about the vibrating plug she'd placed in his ass. *She* hadn't. He jerked when the damn thing started moving and his balls filled. He had foolishly thought he would be able to outlast them.

Sadie seemed determined to win that race as the vibrations increased.

"Fuck me," Joel muttered when the plug hit top speed, beating a tango in his ass that had him rutting like a wild beast. He pounded harder in Oakley's ass, driving his lover deeper into Sadie.

Oakley was the first to plummet as he came loudly, cursing fluently. "Jesus mother-fucking Christ. Son of a goddamn bitch."

Sadie followed, her nails scratching deeply into Oakley's shoulders. His friend didn't appear to feel any pain from her scoring.

That was Joel's last cognizant thought before his climax struck. For one brief, astounding moment, the world went black. And then he tumbled, crash-landing into a heap of sweaty, trembling bodies gasping for breath.

"Holy shit."

He chuckled at Sadie's perfect summation of what had just happened. They slowly untangled body parts and, in the end, Joel found himself sandwiched between Oakley and Sadie. He reached for Sadie's hand to tug the remote control from her clenched fist. Joel turned it off as Sadie giggled and said, "Sorry."

"Someone is going to have to get this damn thing out of me," he said, which prompted laughter from both sides of him.

"You aren't fooling anybody, Joel. Why don't you just go ahead and admit you like having your ass filled?"

Joel turned to give Oakley a warning glance. "Don't start getting any ideas." Then, he grinned, deciding he was an idiot to deny the truth. "Yet."

Then he sat up and made his way to the bathroom to dispose of the condom. He was surprised to find Sadie and Oakley right on his heels.

Oakley pressed on his shoulders and Joel bent over at the sink so Sadie could tug her wicked toy free.

"Where the hell did you get that thing?"

She winked. "Ordered it online the night you stopped being a stubborn ass and kissed Oakley at Cruisers."

"Dammit, Sadie. There you go again. Just fell *even more* in love with you."

Sadie laughed at Oakley's proclamation. "I think that might be Woody talking. Are you sure you aren't mixing up love for lust, Oak?"

Oakley kissed her on the cheek. "Is there a word that combines the two? I have to admit I've never had trouble figuring out what feelings were attached to my heart and which ones were cock-driven. I can't separate the two with you. You've taken over everything, Sade. My heart, my head, my dick. So what's the word for that?"

Joel could see Oakley's words had touched her. "Maybe you could just combine the two words," Sadie said.

Oakley nodded as he considered that suggestion. "Lost. Damn. That sums it up pretty fucking good. I'm lost, Sadie. And I don't ever want to be found."

She took Oakley's hand, and then reached for Joel's. "I'm lost too."

Joel kissed her forehead. "Me too."

Oakley stepped away first. "Shower?"

Joel shook his head. "Got a better idea."

He grabbed three towels and led them both out the back door of the cabin. Night had fallen, but a full moon provided enough light for them to walk with ease. None of them bothered with clothing. It only took them a few minutes to carefully make their way along the path and down a slight incline to the creek that ran through several miles of the ranch property.

They'd had several afternoons of rain, so the water level

was high enough to reach Joel's mid-thigh. He'd noticed that fact this afternoon as they worked a couple of miles downstream and he'd considered stripping off and jumping in then, but Lorelie had called to say there was a motorcycle parked outside the bunkhouse. He and Oakley had dropped everything and hightailed it back home.

Joel stepped into the chilly water, then reached back to offer Sadie a hand. She shivered as she dipped one toe in.

"You sure you wouldn't prefer a hot shower?" she asked.

He shook his head. "Nope. Like the idea of skinny-dipping with you. What's the matter? Too cold for you?" His words were laced with a challenge, and it worked.

Sadie could never pass up a dare. She walked into the water and then, in true one-up-man style, sank down until she was sitting on the bottom.

Joel was convinced Oakley was a born polar bear, so he wasn't surprised when his friend splashed in next to them and joined Sadie, the water reaching both of them at shoulder level.

Joel took a deep breath, and then sank down too. The cold water was a shock to his system for only a minute and then it felt good, cooling off his muscles, soothing away some aches produced from four days of nonstop, backbreaking work followed by one hell of a gymnastics routine in the bedroom.

Oakley had wrapped his hand around the back of Sadie's neck, pulling her close for a kiss. Joel watched them, letting the peaceful night and the realization that Sadie was here sink in.

"You ready to tell us why you came back?" Joel asked when she and Oakley broke apart for some much-needed air.

She gave them a rueful grin. "As you know, I apparently have some unresolved mommy issues. I was trying to help you out, save you from yourselves."

Oakley tugged her closer with an arm around her shoulders. Joel knew she was joking, but it was clear Oakley was still worried she'd take off again.

"We told you," Oakley said. "We're not going anywhere."

"I know. It's just going to take me some time to believe that, to trust it. But it's nothing you guys have done. You're wonderful. Like I said, it's something I have to work on."

Joel appreciated her honesty. It was one of the things that had drawn him to Sadie in the first place. "We have a lot of stuff to figure out, Sadie. As long as we're committed to making it work, it will."

"Like how to make a threesome permanent?" she asked.

Joel grinned. He loved the hell out of that question. "Yeah. That and other things."

"Like where you stand on kids now," Oakley added. Until he spoke Joel didn't realize Sadie's insistence that she didn't want a baby had bothered his friend as much as it had him.

Sadie licked her lips, drawing Joel's attention to their plumpness, a slight swelling caused by their kisses. "The idea of becoming a mother still terrifies me, but I want a baby. Desperately."

Joel breathed out a long sigh. "Thank God."

She ran her hand down his upper arm as if she was unable to be so close and not touch him. Joel understood the feeling.

"I want this to stick. I've never felt this happy," she admitted.

Oakley found a smooth rock near the edge of the water. He scooted over to it, leaning back with his hands behind his head. Joel rolled his eyes at his friend's lord-of-the-manor pose. "It's smooth sailing from here on out. I got a good feeling about this."

Sadie raised one eyebrow. "Do you? Are you forgetting who my father is?"

Oakley frowned. "I say we wait a few dozen years before we tell Mr. Milligan about us."

Sadie shook her head. "Sorry to break it to you, but he already knows."

Though it was dark outside, Joel could swear he saw Oakley go pale in the moonlight.

"He knows about both of us? And you?" Oakley asked.

Joel recalled his mother's comment about keeping Oakley grounded. He suspected his mom would have some help in that area. Mr. Milligan was going to kick their asses.

"Yep. He wants the two of you to stop by some time so he can show you his gun collection."

Sadie laughed and the sound set Joel at ease. While he didn't pretend for one second her dad was okay with what they were doing, something in Sadie's face told him that—like his mom—her father was going to try to accept it.

Even so, Joel said, "I'm never going to your dad's house."

Sadie winced at that. "You may have to reconsider that if…" She paused, clearly searching for a word. "If future events work out in a way that may or may not be in our favor."

"What the hell does that mean?" Joel asked.

Sadie crinkled her nose. "It means my dad has the hots for your mom. He plans to ask her out."

Oakley's eyes widened in true terror. "Jesus Christ. We can't let that unholy union form. If they combine forces, I'm a dead man."

Joel didn't reply as he let Sadie's words soak in. Then he felt…happy. "I think that could actually work."

Sadie and Oakley gave him matching astonished glances.

"Seriously?" Sadie asked.

"Yeah." The more Joel thought about it, the more he hoped it did. "Yeah. I think they'd be really good for each other."

Oakley remained unconvinced. "I think the blood flow hasn't returned to your head yet. It's obviously still pooling around in your crotch."

Joel splashed Oakley, and the dirty bastard that lived in his cock actually responded to the word *crotch*. If the water weren't so cold, he suspected he'd already be fully erect.

"Like I said. Lots of shit to figure out. Let's put it all on the back burner for tonight. What do you say we go get hot and sweaty again?" Joel suggested.

"I thought you'd never ask," Sadie said as she rose from the water, the drops sparkling in the moonlight as they slid along her silky skin.

Oakley clasped hands with Sadie, the two of them heading back to the bunkhouse. Joel was slower to follow.

He'd done it. Somehow he'd come out of the red zone and scored the biggest win of his life.

"Joel?" Sadie called out from somewhere in the darkness. "You lost?"

He was. Completely. Head over heels lost.

Joel stepped out of the water and onto the path. "I'm coming."

Wild Card

Following her dad's heart attack, Lorelie put her own life on hold. However, as his health improves, she struggles to find her way back to life as normal. Her girlfriends insist the answer is simple. Get laid. Enter Glen Rodgers, the sexy country singer she met briefly at a party where he sang her a song.

When Glen returns to town several months later, intent on taking a break from his own screwed up life, he decides Lorelie is just the cure for his blues. Flirtation turns to seduction...the two lovers swept up in something neither of them is prepared for.

Unfortunately, reality rears its ugly head, leaving Glen no choice but to show his hand, forcing him to decide if he should fold and return to life on the road...or go for broke and play the wild card.

For my Family

Prologue

October

Lorelie Carr stepped out into the cool evening air and sucked in a deep breath. The temperature in the barn had risen steadily as more people took to the dance floor. The party wasn't even halfway over and she was already declaring it a success. Maris High School had done a special dedication at the Homecoming Game, naming the football stadium in honor of her dad. The fancy new sign for the Nicholas Carr Stadium had been revealed tonight.

Best. Thing. Ever.

Lorelie couldn't recall the last time she'd seen her father so relaxed and cheerful. It made her happy...even if she couldn't manage to accomplish the same feelings of contentment.

Drifting farther away from the party, she took the path that led to a small, meandering creek that ran through the ranch. The sky was crystal clear and the moon full, allowing her to find her way with ease. It was a beautiful night, and while she loved every minute of the party, she was fairly certain no one would notice her absence.

Unlike so many of her friends, she was here stag, one of the few people in attendance without a date or a significant other to dance with. That solitary state had never bothered her before, mostly because, up until a few months ago, all of her friends had been single as well. Slowly, that was changing—and Lorelie was struggling to keep up.

She was almost to the creek when she realized she wasn't the only one who'd escaped the music and the heat. Someone was sitting in her usual grassy spot on the bank near the water. The end of a cigarette glowed. Though she couldn't see the smoker through the shadows cast by the surrounding trees, there wasn't anyone at the party she didn't know, so she continued forward without hesitation.

"You shouldn't smoke. It's bad for you," she said.

"Yeah. I figured that out when I was twenty-six, which is when I quit."

She recognized the voice, and realized there *was* one person here that she didn't know all that well. This guy. Walt's former bandmate, Glen.

Lorelie stepped closer, finally able to see his face.

He hit her with the full force of a sexy-as-sin grin, and she actually stumbled slightly. She'd noticed how attractive he was the moment he'd walked into the barn. However, along with the handsomeness, she recognized the cockiness in his stance and the look in his eyes that told her this man was no stranger to charming women out of their clothes and into his bed.

"Come join me," he invited, patting the ground next to him.

She wasn't interested in playing the groupie for some here-today, gone-tomorrow musician, but she had really been looking forward to tugging off her cowboy boots and wading through the cool creek water. Her feet were killing her.

So she dropped down next to him as he took another drag.

"You quit, huh?" she countered.

"This doesn't count."

The smell suddenly hit her and she glanced at his fingers. "Pot? Seriously?"

He took another drag, and then held it out to her. "Wanna hit?"

"You realize that's illegal in Texas, right?"

"You a cop?"

She snickered. "Hardly."

"Give it a couple of years. Laws are changing. Besides, I bought this in Colorado."

"Which is where you were supposed to smoke it."

God, when did I become such a prude?

He shrugged, unconcerned. "You ever smoked pot before?"

"Yeah. A few times." She was no saint. In truth, she was tempted by his offer. She'd been stretched taut as a drum since her dad's heart attack and marijuana wasn't exactly rampant in Maris. A year ago, she would have taken a hit. Or three. Or...

Now?

She couldn't afford to let her guard down in case her dad overdid it tonight. For months, she'd put away the parts of her that felt as natural as her skin and pulling out this boring saint who spent every minute living in fear. She was worn out, and the idea of staying out here by this creek the rest of the night and getting stoned was more appealing than she wanted to admit.

Hell, she hadn't even had more than a beer tonight. What would she give for a shot of tequila?

She leaned back on the bank, looking up at the sky.

Glen looked down at her and held out the joint. "Last chance."

"In case you forgot, I'm currently hosting a party for my dad. Every single person in town, including our pastor and my fourth-grade teacher, is in that damn barn. You don't seriously expect me to walk back into the room stoned, do you?"

"One hit might do you good, Butterfly. I've been watching you tonight, flitting here and there without ever landing. Do you ever relax?"

"Of course I do." It was a lie.

She used to be a champ when it came to taking it easy, but since her dad's heart attack, she'd been living life in constant motion. For some reason she couldn't explain, part of her felt that if she stopped, *he* might stop. And she couldn't imagine one single day without Dad.

Glen stubbed out the joint on a rock and put what was left into a bag he tossed next to the cowboy hat resting on the ground. Then he laid back too, the two of them looking up at the night sky.

"So what do you do for fun around here, Lori?"

The only person who ever called her Lori—and got away with it—was her dad. "Lorelie," she corrected. "And I do the same thing most people do for entertainment in a small town."

He waited for her to elaborate and she wondered if he didn't really know.

"I hang out at Crusiers or Sparks Barbeque or by Harper's Lake. Occasionally, I go to weddings or yard parties at the fire hall or celebrations like tonight. I go to high school football games in the fall, baseball in the spring, rodeo year round. Then there are trail rides, camping. But more often than not, I just stay in and play games or watch movies with my dad or some friends, and consume a lot of wine and margaritas."

Glen's brows furrowed, completely unimpressed. "Sounds dull as dirt."

"I guess you think it's more fun to be in a different city every night, hanging out with a bunch of strangers, club hopping, getting drunk and stoned and…"

She didn't finish her statement. She had intended to say something about him getting laid by a bunch of groupies, but she realized that would be a rude thing to say to someone she didn't know very well. She wasn't sure why she assumed Glen was a playboy. The guy was a stranger. His wild lifestyle meant nothing to her.

"And?"

"You know," she added. "The usual."

"I assume you meant to add something about my sex life. After all, you hit the other biggies. Sex, drugs and rock and roll. Sort of all go hand in hand, don't they?"

"You play country music."

He chuckled. "Guitar-playing cowboys get laid too."

"Spare me the details."

"You got a boyfriend, Butterfly?"

Lorelie pretended she hated the nickname. In truth, no one had ever given her a pet name. It made her feel kind of warm and squishy inside.

Dammit.

"Nope. I'm footloose and fancy free."

"That seems like a waste. What's wrong with the guys around here?"

She shrugged. "Nothing. I'm just not that easy to get to."

"What do you mean?"

"I mean my dad is one of the most respected men in the community, and he used his position as head football coach to ensure that I had a legion of big-ass protectors surrounding me at all times."

Glen turned his head and studied her. "Please tell me you're not a virgin."

She huffed out an amused breath. She had never indulged in such an oddly personal conversation with a complete stranger before. And honestly, she didn't want it to end. Talking to Glen was refreshing, a challenge. Something different.

She'd spent her entire life in Maris, Texas. There was precious little she didn't know about every single man, woman, and child who resided there.

"No. I'm not a virgin. I've had plenty of lovers, thank you very much."

"Define 'plenty'."

She couldn't tell if Glen was teasing her or sincere. "None of your business."

"Tell me anyway," he urged.

The devil had her spilling all her secrets. Part of her was curious to see how he'd respond if she gave him the truth. "Four."

Glen's brows lifted. "Butterfly, when you get home tonight, look up 'plenty' in the dictionary. Then flip back to F and check out the definition of the word 'few'."

"Four was plenty for me," she said, wishing she'd managed to temper her tone a bit. As it was, she suspected she might've made it obvious she hadn't really enjoyed her encounters—few, plenty or otherwise.

"Is that right?"

She sat up. "That wasn't a dare."

Glen chuckled, not bothering to rise. "I didn't take it as one. Until you said it wasn't."

Lorelie considered pulling off her boots. Then she reconsidered. She needed to get back to the party.

"Shouldn't you be playing?"

Glen sat up slowly. "Walt wanted to dance with his new wife. Nobody seemed to mind the recorded music, so I figured I'd take a break."

"It was nice of you to come tonight to perform for my dad's party."

He gave her that damn lethal grin that had her insides fluttering uncontrollably. There were deep laugh lines around his eyes that betrayed his older age...and his love of laughter.

"Walt thinks the world of your dad. Quoted the guy at least a million times when we used to tour together. I always wanted to meet the famous Coach."

His words pleased Lorelie, though they didn't surprise her. She'd heard the same sentiment expressed countless times throughout her life. "My dad is the greatest man I've ever known. He raised me all alone and I've never—not one single day—felt as if I wasn't completely loved."

Glen reached out and took her hand, holding it. The touch felt friendly, comforting. "You strike me as the type who's damn easy to love, Lori."

She blushed and dismissed the praise. "Lorelie. And I'm an opinionated, stubborn pain in the ass."

He chuckled and squeezed her hand. "Just part of the charm. Gotta admit it though, I'm not so sure it's the football team keeping the guys away from you, so much as what you just said."

"What do you mean?"

"Coach sounds like a pretty hard act for a man to follow."

Lorelie had never considered that until Glen spoke the words. "I..." She wasn't sure how to respond to something she realized might be true.

Glen read her sudden distress. "Well, I didn't mean for that to upset you. Kind of intended it as a compliment for your dad, but I obviously missed the mark. So let's change the subject."

"Okay." She'd have plenty of time to fret over that tomorrow. And the day after. And...

"The reason I'm here is because I had a rare weekend off from playing with the band, so I thought I'd take advantage of the time to come see Walt."

Since Walt's retirement from music, Glen had moved on and was now lead guitarist for Trent Maxwell, the hottest thing to hit country music since Garth Brooks. According to Walt, Glen spent at least fifty weeks of the year on the road, so she couldn't imagine why he'd want to travel to Maris on his weekend off.

"If I was you, I think I would have spent my downtime at home, sleeping in, binge-watching Netflix and doing a whole lot of nothing."

Glen shrugged. "Guess I'm too used to moving to sit still for long. In fact, I think I just hit my limit on relaxation, so..." He put his hat back on, stood up, and then reached down to help her rise as well. "I think it's time we got back to the party."

She agreed. She'd been gone too long. The food platters would probably need refilling and she wanted to make sure her dad wasn't overdoing it.

They walked back to the barn in silence, but it didn't feel awkward. Typically, Lorelie was the type to fill all the quiet times with the sound of her own voice. She knew perfectly well she talked too much. Her friends teased her about it enough, but tonight she was happy to just listen to the breeze rustling the leaves on the trees and the crickets and the distant strains of music and laughter coming from the barn.

When they reached the entrance, Glen stopped and looked at her. "I'm going to sing you a song, Lori."

"Lorelie," she corrected, though now, like earlier, Glen pretended not to hear her. "And that would be really nice."

They returned to the party, both of them instantly enclosed

in the hubbub. Glen returned to the makeshift stage to play with Walt, while Lorelie toured the room, stopping to converse with the guests, making sure they all had enough to eat and drink.

Later, as the evening began to wind down, Glen stepped up to the mic and kept his promise to sing her a song as he traded places with Walt.

He strummed a few bars of a song. "This song is dedicated to tonight's hostess, Miss Lorelie Carr. Let's give her a hand, folks. She's thrown one hell of a party."

Everyone clapped and she felt herself blush. Not because of the crowd's attention, but because of his.

Glen's.

He looked directly at her as he began to sing. The entire night, he'd sung backup, so it was the first time she'd gotten to really hear his voice. It was deep and rich and so clear, it almost moved her to tears.

She smiled as she listened to the words of the song, "Butterfly Fly Away." She recognized it as an old Miley Cyrus one, but Glen changed the words from first to third person as he sang about her relationship with her dad.

As if on cue, her father crossed the room and took her hand. "Dance with me, Lori."

She swallowed the lump in her throat as her dad led her to the floor, the two of them moving in time to Glen's guitar.

"We haven't danced together like this since you were a little girl. Remember?"

She nodded. "I do."

"You'd put your feet on top of mine and we'd shuffle around the kitchen."

Tears formed in the corner of her eyes. "And you'd sing along to the radio at the same time."

Her dad placed his forehead against hers. "Didn't sound anywhere as good as this young buck, did I?"

"You sang just fine."

"Tonight was perfect, Lori."

She couldn't speak, her throat clogged with tears, so she just nodded.

"It's been a rough few months for us, baby girl. I know that. But we're turning a corner tonight. Okay?"

"Okay."

"No more sneaking into my room in the middle of the night. I'm not going anywhere. Not for a long time."

All the heavy feelings and fears of the past few months slowly started to fade away. For weeks following the heart attack, she'd watched her dad closely, too terrified to take her eyes off of him. She had been there the night her dad had grabbed his chest, hitting the floor unconscious, as she called 9-1-1 and screamed for Oakley and Joel, their ranch hands. The memory of that horrifying event wouldn't leave her.

It woke her up night after night, restless and frightened. She would toss and turn for hours, knowing she wouldn't be able to sleep again until she tiptoed down the hall to determine that he was still breathing.

Luckily her dad snored, so more often than not she didn't even have to walk all the way to his room. On the nights when nothing but silence met her ears, she would hold her breath, her heart racing with every step as she played out her worst fear.

Losing him.

"I didn't know you knew about that."

"It's an old farmhouse. Floorboards squeak something terrible."

"Wait. If you heard me coming, why were you usually snoring?"

Dad chuckled. "Thought I'd save you the trip."

"But sometimes you *weren't* snoring."

"Those were the times I was really sleeping."

They both laughed. Dad frequently saw the things she thought she'd hidden. And as always, he knew how to make everything better.

"I still gotta walk you down the aisle and spoil a couple dozen grandkids."

"A couple dozen? You better have at least eight illegitimate kids tucked away somewhere if that's your plan."

Her father chuckled. "I love you, Lori. And I'm proud of the woman you've become. You're so much like your mama."

Lorelie had never known her mother—not personally, anyway. Her mom died the day she was born. Her father had taken on the role of both parents, raising her with love and understanding, treating her as if she were his greatest gift. He often spoke of her mother, drawing pictures of the woman in Lorelie's mind until sometimes it felt as if she *had* known her.

She gave in and let the tears fall, her dance with Dad morphing into a swaying hug that neither of them was anxious to let end.

As the song faded, Dad pulled away with a grin, wiping her tears away with his thumbs. "The party's a hit. So stop flitting around worrying and go have fun with your friends."

Lorelie was reminded of Glen's description of her earlier. Her father walked backed to rejoin his cronies in the corner and she glanced toward the stage.

Glen tipped his hat to her and winked.

"Thank you," she mouthed as he and Walt switched places once more, picking up the pace with a rousing version of "Dixieland Delight" that had everyone out in the middle of the room, stomping, swinging and singing along. She was floored when Glen picked up a fiddle midway through the song and brought the house down.

As the music played, Lorelie was drawn into a huge circle of her friends, laughing and dancing with Paige, Macie, Gia, Tucker, Caleb and the whole gang.

The night couldn't have been more perfect. And as people began to leave, the party coming to an end, she knew her dad was right.

It was time to turn a corner.

Chapter One

TOBY

Where are you?

GLEN

Almost to Texas

TOBY

Texas? Thought you went back to Nashville

GLEN

I did. To pack a bag

TOBY

Didn't mean for you to leave town

GLEN

Needed a break

TOBY

Probably a good idea. Take some time. Get
your head screwed on straight. I'll be in touch

Three months later

"Well, this is one hell of a surprise."

Walt reached out to shake Glen's hand as he stood up from his barstool at Cruisers.

Walt wasn't the only one surprised by Glen's impromptu return to Maris. Glen was pretty shocked himself. It certainly wasn't a trip he'd intended to make, but after the nightmare that was the past three days, this was the only place he could think to take refuge, lick his wounds, and figure out where the hell he'd gone so wrong with his life.

"Yeah. Tell me about it."

Walt gave him a funny look. "So...?"

Glen grimaced. "I was just sitting on my couch the other night, thinking to myself 'you know what would be great? An impromptu trip to Texas in late January.' Who wouldn't want to be in Texas in winter?"

His sarcastic tone clued his friend into the fact this visit wasn't purely a social one.

"Shit," Walt said as he claimed the stool next to Glen's. "What happened?"

"Trent Maxwell happened."

Walt nodded. They had discussed Glen's current job before, so Walt was perfectly aware of his issues with the arrogant lead singer. Glen had spent the past two years touring with Nashville's biggest rising star. While most musicians would give their left nut for such a great gig, Glen was miserable.

Trent was—hands down—the biggest son of a bitch on the planet. Cocky, with more ego than musical ability, he strutted around like God's gift to the world. He was insufferable, annoying... Jesus, the list could go on and on.

"What did the asshole do?"

"Talentless little prick," Glen muttered.

Walt groaned again as a light went on. "Let me reword my question. What did *you* do?"

Glen blew out a frustrated breath as he picked at the label on his bottle of beer. "I beat the shit out of him."

"Fuck." Walt raised his hand to the bartender. "Hey, Sadie. Can we have a couple of whiskeys over here?"

Sadie walked over with two glasses and filled them. "Good to see you again. Glen, right?"

Glen nodded. He'd met the cute bartender at Coach's party a few months earlier. She'd made sure his cup of beer was never empty, always checking on him, while thanking him for providing the music. He'd been touched by her kindness.

Actually, most of the folks he'd met at the party back in October had been really nice. Accustomed to city life, Glen had been instantly struck by the fact that everyone in Maris seemed to not only know everyone else, they appeared to like each other.

Part of him thought that was cool. And another part of him figured that kind of *Cheers*-like, everybody-knows-your-name lifestyle would drive him insane. There was a lot to be said for anonymity. He didn't want to have to deal with anyone else's shit. Which was good, since he was currently rolling around in enough of his own.

When Sadie started to put the bottle away, Walt waved a hand. "No. You might as well leave that right here."

She gave Walt a quizzical look, but didn't question him about why they were planning on putting a dent in a bottle of whiskey at one p.m. on a Wednesday afternoon. In Glen's opinion, that meant she was a damn good bartender. The fewer questions the better right now. He sure as hell didn't want it getting out that he was the reason Trent Maxwell had cancelled his last two concerts. Hard to sing with two loose teeth, a split lip, and a black eye. Their manager had told the media Trent had laryngitis, and then hid him away from the public.

Sadie put the bottle of Jack Daniels in front of them on the bar. "Have at it."

Walt lifted the glass and downed it in one long drink. "Okay. So give me the details. Thought your fighting days were well behind you."

"Before three nights ago, I hadn't gotten into a fistfight since that night you and I took on those three drunk rednecks in that bar in Santa Fe."

Walt chuckled. "Jesus. That was a hell of a night. Thought Marty was going to let us rot in that Podunk jail cell."

Glen grinned at the memory of their band manager's ire when he'd come to bail out his band. "Figure he probably would have, if we hadn't had that sold-out show to play in Tucson."

"You get fired?" Walt asked, turning the conversation back to what had brought Glen to Maris.

"Not yet."

Wade seemed surprised by that. "Any news stations pick it up?"

Glen shook his head. "Nope. It appears the record label did a good job covering it up. Either no one knows about it or they paid a pretty penny to hush it up."

"That's lucky."

Glen nodded, waiting for the inevitable question.

Why?

"Not sure it has to do with luck so much as they're trying to save face. This gig used to be a hell of a lot easier. I'm getting too old for this shit, man."

"You're only thirty-eight."

"And I've been on the road since I was sixteen. Twenty-two

years. I'm worn out. Things have changed a lot. Nothing about touring with Trent is like *our* time together on the road."

Walt refilled his glass and tapped it against Glen's still untouched one. "Is this where we relive our glory days while bitching and moaning about the younger generation?"

Glen laughed. "*You're* the younger generation to me, dammit. I've got nearly a decade on you."

"That's true, old man."

Glen rolled his eyes at the nickname.

Walt and the other guys in the band had always called Glen that. It used to piss him off. Now it was starting to feel way too accurate.

Walt's eyebrows rose when Glen didn't get riled about the name the way he used to. "Wow. You *are* in a funk. You're only eight years older than me, Glen."

"Feels like a lot more. Like I'm aging in dog years."

Walt chuckled at the joke, and then hit him with the question. "So let's have it. What happened? What made you beat up Trent this time when you've managed to swallow down his crap for two years?"

"When we used to tour together, it was fun. You know, five guys traveling around the country in a bus, laughing and joking and drinking together. We'd kill it on stage, then party our asses off until dawn. We were there because we loved the music, loved the life."

"And with Trent?"

"It's fucking brutal. Most you and me ever did was drink whiskey and smoke a little weed. These guys are into snorting coke, popping pills. Trent is the worst."

"That's not exactly new information, Glen. You've been saying that since the beginning. And you've been dealing with it."

"He's the biggest name in town. I'm getting paid a shit ton

of money to 'deal with it'. Somewhere along the line, I became his fucking babysitter. Our manager looks to me to keep him in line and not let him go too wild. Problem is, it gets hard to stomach his attitude after a while."

"I know you; you don't just snap without provocation. What did he do?"

"After the show Saturday night, Trent's bodyguards showed up with several fans who had backstage passes. Me and the rest of the guys were just sitting around, drinking some beer. The usual groupies were there, but I wasn't into the party. Had a wicked headache and I was considering bailing early, but Trent was in rare form, stoned out of his mind. Figured I'd better stick around a while to keep an eye on him. Just in case, you know?"

"Damn. You *are* the babysitter."

Glen grimaced. "Music's blaring, people are dancing and making out—you know how it is. And I'm watching Trent with these fans. Two of the girls couldn't have been more than seventeen years old. They were giggling, excited about meeting the big fucking star. Next thing I know, Trent's offering them booze and pills. One of the girls said no, but the other didn't. Little bit of time goes by and suddenly Trent is leading the drugged-up girl back to his dressing room. Her friend was trying to keep her from going, trying to convince her to leave instead."

Walt sighed. "I guess I know what happened next."

"I walked across the room and stopped Trent, said the girls needed to leave. Pompous little jerkoff was blitzed out of his mind. Told me I could fuck the other girl or fuck off."

"Famous last words of a fool," Walt muttered.

"I swear to God, it felt like slow motion. Like I was in an episode of that old *Batman* show. Started with a right to his eye, followed by a left to his jaw."

"Bam! Whap!" Walt joked.

"Kapow!" Glen had been feeling like hell since he started this trip halfway across the country. Within minutes, Walt had him laughing, and the weight that had been pressing on his chest lifted a little. "It was just about that comical. After the second punch, Trent's head flew back, his eyes rolled so far up all I could see was white. He hit the floor like a bag of potatoes."

Walt eyed him. "I don't see any bruises, so I can only assume no one had Trent's back."

"Nope. Told you. The guy's not very well liked. One of the bodyguards just laughed, which pissed Trent off. He was trying to get up. and I'd actually clenched my fist to put him back down, when the two *girls* hopped in on the action, started kicking Trent, calling him all kinds of nasty names."

"No way! Jesus. I wish I'd been there to see that." Walt's enjoyment of the story continued to help Glen find humor in a situation that—until that moment—had just felt like a damn bad night.

"Trent curled into the fetal position with his arms over his face, because even as stupid as the jackass is, he knows his looks are all that really matter. Of course, I'd already done a fair amount of damage there, so I don't know what he thought he was preserving. One of the girls rammed the toe of her high heel into his ass while the other one kicked his shins. I considered adding my boot to the action, but kicking a guy while he's down isn't exactly honorable. Even if he deserves it."

"Not sure I would have taken the high road."

Glen knew Walt would have, but he appreciated his friend's support. "The bodyguards were still chuckling, letting the girls blow off some steam. I know it sounds like it was a long, drawn-out thing, but in truth, the whole episode only lasted a minute or so. I punched him, the girls kicked him, the rest of the band started cheering the girls on. Whole thing ended when one of the girls got Trent right in the balls and he started crying."

Walt winced. "Shit."

"Yeah. I guess that's when even the bodyguards realized things had gotten out of hand. That, and the fact a few of the groupies had pulled out phones. Place went on freaking lockdown. Phones collected, shit deleted fast and furious. The girls were taken to God knows where. I figure our manager, Toby, must've used that *Men in Black* memory-eraser thing on 'em because there hasn't been a peep on social media about it."

Walt snorted. "Pretty sure he gave them a lot of money to keep their mouths shut."

"Yeah. Worked out good for them in the end. They got paid to kick Trent in the balls." Glen picked up his whiskey and downed it, welcoming the heat of the liquor as it slid down his throat. "I wouldn't have minded some payout for my piece of that action."

His friend grinned and slapped him on the back. "You know, I sort of like this superhero look on you. Glen Rodgers, champion of backstage groupies everywhere. Might see if I can get the local tailor to whip up a costume for you. Something with a long denim cape."

"Let me just go ahead and shut that idea down there."

"I'm being serious." Walt raised his hand at Glen's narrowed eyes. "Not about the cape, you jackass. But the rest. You've always been so easygoing. Live and let live. I like this new leaf you've turned over. Nice to see you caring about something."

Glen wasn't sure how to respond to that. He didn't think of himself as heartless, but when he considered his past, he could see why Walt viewed him as a bit cavalier, maybe even uncaring. He dropped out of high school and ran away from home at sixteen after a falling-out with his dad. He'd never looked back. Just cut all ties with his family so he could do what he wanted. Liked to brag about how he didn't live by anyone's rules but his own. It had been a young man's arrogance.

"So what now?"

Glen shrugged. "Toby suggested that I get away for a little while until the dust settles."

Walt looked surprised. "So you're really *not* fired?"

He shook his head. "No. The label knows that all Trent has in his corner is good looks and showmanship. It's the band that's making the music work."

"It's *you* making it work," Walt said. Glen tried to brush off the compliment, but Walt continued, "You're one of the best musicians in the world, Glen. Yet you're always content to play second fiddle—to me, to Trent."

"I don't like the spotlight, Walt, you know that. I'd rather somebody else shoulder that burden, so I can just play. The music is the only thing that's ever mattered to me. Would have made my life a lot easier if you'd stuck with pure country instead hooking up with that other guy and changing your sound."

"You could have come with me."

Glen sighed. He could have. But he preferred the traditional, old country style. At the time, he hadn't been sure he'd be a good fit with the changes Walt was planning to make. Plus the record label had offered him a small fortune to play with Trent. Walt had encouraged him to move on, even though it was tough as hell for them to split up. Glen figured Walt was about as close to a brother as he'd ever get. "Yeah. I know."

"Toby is a good manager. You're lucky to have him. He'll get all this crap sorted out soon enough."

Walt was right. Toby was a great manager. He was the one who'd landed him the gig with Trent along with a hefty salary.

"So what now?" Walt asked. "You're just going to lay low in Maris until they call you back to Nashville?"

Glen feigned a shudder. "Shit no. I only plan to be here a few days. Didn't get much time to visit you during the last trip. This is just a quick stopover. Figure I'll hang out here until I get bored, which should only take about three minutes, then head over to Vegas and then...who knows."

"I've got a guest room and it's all yours."

"Naw. I appreciate the offer, man, but I've already booked a room in the B&B. Last thing you need is my grumpy ass, moping around on your couch, feeling sorry for myself. Besides, I was kind of hoping—"

"Isn't it a bit early to be tying one on, Walt?"

Glen glanced up at the two men who stood behind him and Walt at the bar.

Walt grinned and gestured to the empty chairs flanking them. "Never too early. Pull up a seat," he said. "Tucker, Evan, you guys remember my friend, Glen? He played at Coach's party a few months back."

Evan claimed the stool next to Walt as Tucker shook Glen's hand. "Y'all were former bandmates, right?"

"Yep," Glen replied. "Toured together for a few years before I joined up with Trent Maxwell and Walt started stretching his wings with a different sound." At the time, Glen couldn't understand his friend's reasons for the change. Country music and the road were Glen's life. He'd never felt the need to walk away from the tried and true. Walt had taken a big risk switching up his sound. And it appeared to have paid off.

Then Walt had left Nashville altogether to move back home after his coach's heart attack. Once again, Glen had expected his friend's music to fall to the wayside, but Walt was making it work. And work well.

Now, Glen was starting to wonder what life looked like on the other side.

"You off duty?" Walt asked Evan.

Evan nodded. "Ran into Tucker at the hardware store. We decided to grab a late lunch and a couple of beers."

"If we're going to do a little day drinking, let's do it right. Two more glasses," Walt said when Sadie walked over to serve them.

"Damn. It's a regular party. Starting to wonder if I should have hired a band," she teased. "Of course, now that I think about it, the band is already here."

"Good to see you again, Glen," Evan said. "What brings you back to Maris?"

Glen took a long sip of the whiskey Sadie had just added to his glass, but he stopped short of chugging the whole thing. Last thing he needed in his current state of mind was to get wasted.

Then he reconsidered and downed the thing. Wasted was *exactly* what he needed.

Now that he'd talked out the whole kicking-Trent's-ass thing with Walt, he was feeling better. He was a professional when it came to partying hard, and it had been a long time since he'd done it with guys who actually got the concept and did it right.

Cruisers appeared to offer just what he needed: bunch of fellas with whom he could play a little pool and drink a lot of whiskey, and maybe, with a little luck, a girl to dance the night away with later. The jukebox in the corner was chock full of his favorites, if the past few selections were anything to go on.

"I'm only in town for a few days. Noticed y'all seem to have more than your fair share of pretty girls down here in Texas. Felt like sampling some of the southern hospitality."

Tucker grinned. "Is that right? Well, I can't fault your observations. We do grow 'em pretty here. And sweet."

"Been a long time since I've danced with a pretty girl." Danced, kissed, or otherwise. Maris felt like a good place to break the dry spell.

Tucker took a sip of whiskey. "I'm sure Walt's glad to have you back in town. You'll have to come out to the lake with us this weekend. We're all planning to do a little fishing Saturday."

Evan lifted his glass in a silent toast. "That's actually code for sitting in a boat all day and drinking beer. Not sure any of us has ever caught an actual fish."

"Might help if one of us remembers to buy bait this time," Tucker joked.

Glen wasn't really the one-with-nature type. He didn't hunt or fish or hike. His idea of spending time in the great outdoors was playing summer festivals, but something about the idea of floating around with a line in the water suddenly seemed damned appealing. "That sounds good to me, but I'll need to borrow a rod."

"I got extras," Walt offered. "I was trying to convince Glen to give up his room at the B&B and stay with me."

"I told you, man, I'm hoping to hook up with a pretty Maris girl. Speaking of pretty, what's the story with Lorelie? She got a boyfriend?"

Just like that, the cheerful welcome he'd been receiving dried up.

Tucker scowled. "She's a little young for you, isn't she?"

Glen shrugged. "I have no idea how old she is."

"Twenty-eight," Evan replied.

"That sounds about right to me," Glen joked.

Then he recalled Lorelie's comments about the overprotectiveness of her dad's former team. Apparently, she hadn't been exaggerating. Even Walt had hopped on the bus that seemed determined to run him out of town on a rail for daring to speak Lorelie's name.

"There're plenty of women in town who would be more than happy to spend a night or two with a famous musician. Lorelie's not one of 'em." Walt tried for nonchalant—but Glen knew better.

"She doesn't like music?" He was purposely pushing their buttons, partly because it was entertaining and partly because he felt like Lorelie would appreciate his efforts on her behalf. She struck him as the type who liked pushing buttons herself.

Evan seemed the least perturbed by his comment, opting to try a different tack. "Lorelie's the kind of woman you date. She's special. Definitely not the type to have a one-night stand."

He couldn't fault the man's reasoning. Lorelie was sweet. But there had been something else there as well. Something hovering just beneath her skin, wild, untamed. She had reminded him of a caged bird, one who longed to be free.

Glen dismissed the thought. Just as he had at least a hundred times since his last visit to Maris. For some reason, he couldn't shake the memory of his little butterfly. And while he'd told Walt he had come here to spend more time with him, in truth, he'd hoped to see Lorelie again too.

If for no other reason than to get the woman out from under his skin. She was consuming far too many of his thoughts lately. And fantasies.

"Tell you what," Walt said, clearly hoping to move them to safer waters. "Evan's wife, Annie, has got a few single girl-friends who would probably get a kick out of hanging with a singing cowboy for a date or two. Why don't you come over tomorrow night for dinner and we'll introduce you?"

Glen shrugged noncommittally, his interest definitely residing firmly in Lorelie Carr's camp. Even so...

He hadn't been with a woman in nearly nine months.

Which was basically the longest he'd gone without sex since he'd lost his virginity to Allie Froehlich in the tenth grade.

Maybe losing himself in the arms of a sexy woman would help him forget what a fucking mess he'd made of his job.

He nodded, reconsidering the offer. "Dinner sounds good. Been a long time since I've had a home-cooked meal."

"Perfect. Tucker, Evan, why don't you guys bring Lela and Annie and we'll make a party of it."

Sadie had wandered back over. "You guys need anything else?"

"You working tomorrow night, Sadie?" Walt asked. "I'm putting together an impromptu dinner party. If you're free, you could come with Oakley and Joel."

"That'd be cool. I'll text my guys and see if they're up for it. Mind if Lorelie tags along too?"

Walt hesitated a second too long, and Glen realized his friend did indeed seem determined to keep Lorelie away from him.

Huh. Since when had Walt begun to view him as the Big Bad Wolf? Hell, back in the day, they were equals when it came to female conquests. Marriage didn't suddenly make a man a saint.

"Sure. If she wants," Walt said at last.

Sadie began texting, calling over her shoulder as she walked into a back room, "I'll let you know if we're in."

"Sadie has two guys?" Glen asked.

Evan grinned. "Yeah. A real life ménage a trois. And they aren't the only one in town. I have two cousins currently living that same lifestyle with their chosen partners. Never seen Tyson and Jeannette happier."

Glen's brows rose. "Seriously? Damn. I may have to reconsider my previous opinion about small-town life being boring."

Tucker chuckled. "I used to feel the same way. Couldn't

wait to get the hell out of this two-horse town right after graduation. And for a dozen years or so, I thought I'd really found the good life, traveling with the football team and spending the off-season at my place in Turks and Caicos."

"What changed your mind?" Glen asked, realizing Tucker, as former quarterback of a professional NFL team, had probably lived a life very similar to his own. And like Walt, he'd given it all up for Maris.

"Came home in June for the first time since I was eighteen. Realized I'd actually missed the town and the people. It's a tight-knit community and we're all friends. It's nice."

Glen couldn't imagine ever wanting to live in a place where everyone knew everything about everybody. "I think I prefer obscurity."

Walt took another sip of whiskey. "You're not sick of that loner lifestyle yet?"

Glen shook his head. "It's too late to teach this old dog a new trick. Spent enough years on the road to know there's no place I'd like to hang my hat for more than a few months or so."

It was clear the men sitting with him didn't agree.

Different strokes for different folks.

"Me and Bertha are destined to keep on rolling."

"Bertha?" Evan asked at the same time Walt laughed. "Please tell me you are *not* still driving that piece-of-shit truck. There's no way that rust bucket made it from Nashville to Maris."

"She's sitting right out there in the parking lot as we speak. My one true love." Glen had owned his truck for fifteen years. Given the fact he was out of town more than in, it wasn't like he drove her all the time. Most of his travel was done on the tour bus.

However, it was clear that this was most likely going to be Bertha's last road trip. She'd overheated four times on the way here and had acquired a pretty loud banging noise right around Dallas that was growing worse.

He wasn't sure why he was so determined to hang on to the ancient thing, but it felt like Bertha was all that was left of the goddamned good old days he was missing more and more lately.

The four of them continued to drink and chat, the conversation warming up once the subject had moved away from Lorelie. Eventually, one by one, they began to peel away, each man returning home, Evan and Tucker to their ladyloves, Walt to his bachelor pad.

Sitting alone at the bar gave Glen too much time to think. About the asshole Trent. About his future. About what would entice men like Walt and Tucker, who had made their escapes from Maris, to return to such a boring existence.

And then, as always, his thoughts returned to Lorelie.

He'd had one conversation with the woman. The two of them probably hadn't spoken more than a couple hundred words to each other. Yet her pretty face, her sweet laugh, and that sparkle in her eyes just kept coming back to him. If he was being completely honest with himself, it was Lorelie who'd brought him back to Maris—and nothing else.

The woman appealed to him in ways he couldn't define. While she was beautiful, all legs and ass, and that wavy blonde hair that flowed over her shoulders like honey, the attraction seemed to stem from something less physical.

On Saturday, Glen had walked the streets of Atlanta in the wee hours of the night, trying to burn off the adrenaline pumping through him right after he'd thrown that hard right to Trent's face. And he was still riding high on anger when he'd returned to the tour bus and found Toby waiting for him. The manager told him he needed a break, a vacation, and explained it would be best if he took a few weeks away while Toby cleaned up the mess.

A man without a home, the first place Glen had thought of was Maris. Actually, it wasn't the place that popped into his head. It was a face.

Lorelie's.

And because he'd been low on steam and not thinking clearly, he'd flown back to Nashville, loaded up Bertha and headed southwest, until he made it here.

With any luck, she'd show up at the dinner party tomorrow night. He would have a chance to talk to her again—and hopefully see that there was nothing special there after all.

Then he could move on, just like he always did.

Chapter Two

TOBY

Where are you again?

GLEN

Maris, Texas. Visiting Walt Bennett

TOBY

Good. Stay there a bit. Trent's on the warpath

GLEN

Don't care

TOBY

Just do me a favor. Lay low. This shit's gonna take time to clean up

GLEN

Fine. I'll let you know my next move when I make it. Thinking Vegas

TOBY

Don't get drunk and marry a stripper

GLEN

Never tell me not to do something, Toby.
Always feels like a dare

TOBY

Fine. Get wasted and marry a pole dancer

GLEN

Will do. Later, chief

Lorelie walked into Walt's kitchen to find four of her best friends sitting around the table, wineglasses in hand, looking at her.

"So..." She studied the tableau and felt a sneaky suspicion she'd missed something. "Start happy hour without me?"

Annie, Sadie, and Paige all looked at Lela, who had apparently been chosen to take the lead in whatever the hell this was.

"Why don't you have a seat?" Lela invited, sounding too much like the spider calling a fly to the web.

"Think I might just stand."

Annie laughed and rose, grabbing a wineglass for her, filling it with her favorite Chardonnay. "Stand down, girls. We're freaking her out and we haven't even started."

"Started?" Lorelie prompted.

"Your intervention," Sadie chimed in.

"Should you be pouring someone a drink at their intervention?"

"It's not that sort of intervention," Lela explained.

"Well, that's good, because that would definitely be the pot calling the kettle black. You girls drink as much as me. Maybe more. So what are y'all interventioning me about?"

"Pretty sure that's not a word," Paige said as Lorelie debated whether she should go with the flow on this or not. Her friends were forces of nature and if they had something to say, it would be said.

Then she decided she wasn't sure she wanted to know what she was apparently doing wrong, so she went for distraction instead.

"Where are the guys?" she asked.

Lela perked up. "Tucker got a new truck. They're all out back admiring it. New F-150 limited. EcoBoost turbo V6 engine, SuperCab. Torque out the ass. That thing is sa-*weet*."

"You should be a dude, Lela. No normal woman gets that worked up over a new truck." Lorelie could never understand why men got such hard-ons for cars either.

Lela laughed. "I don't mean to brag, but there seems to be a direct correlation between that V6 engine and Tucker's sex drive. It has heated backseats too."

"Already christened it, huh?" Lorelie didn't care much for cars, but she didn't really want to see the conversation return to its original destination.

Sadie shot Lela an exasperated glance. "Lela. Focus."

"Sorry." Lela pointed to the empty chair that had been clearly set in a position of honor—if she could call it that—specifically for Lorelie. "Come on. Sit down with us. We need to talk."

Lorelie grabbed the chair at the table and waved a hand, gesturing for one of them to clue her in on what the hell she'd been doing wrong. "Fine. Let's get this over with."

Lela opened her mouth, but before she could speak, Sadie spilled it. "We want our friend back."

Lorelie stared at her for a minute, thinking Sadie would clarify. When she didn't, Lorelie took the bait. "Who went missing?"

"You," Paige said softly. "We lost you just after Coach's

heart attack. The changes were subtle and they took a little time, but now...”

Annie looked at Lorelie, clearly uncomfortable. Of all the women at the table, Annie had the softest heart, felt everything the deepest.

“You think I’m acting different?” Lorelie thought she’d done a better job at hiding her anxiety. So much for that.

Sadie nodded. “You’re a shadow of the wild child we know and love.”

Lorelie laughed at the description. “Wild child, huh?”

Annie leaned forward, putting her wineglass on the table. “We know you’re worried about your dad, but he’s so much better.”

Lorelie swallowed heavily. She couldn’t fault their observation. She was perfectly aware she hadn’t been herself since last June, so her friends weren’t telling her anything she didn’t know. In truth, she’d intended to turn this corner back in October after the party.

The problem was, she didn’t know how to bounce back.

Dad had called her out on the dance floor as Glen sang for her. He’d recognized her fear, and the lovely man had thought that by simply saying, “I’m okay,” *she* would be too.

It didn’t work that way. She still spent far too much time worrying about him, something he’d noticed and pointed out more than once since that night. In fact, she was here tonight because Dad had put his foot down. Insisted she start hanging out with her friends more often as opposed to constantly hovering around him.

Before his heart attack, wild horses couldn’t have kept her at home. She had a reputation as being the life of the party. She never hesitated to do something outrageous or crazy or fun. But now, she couldn’t summon up the energy for anything.

"Are you worried he'll have another heart attack?" Lela asked.

Lorelie shrugged. That fear would always be there, but it was losing its power over her as he continued to grow stronger with each passing day.

It would be very easy to brush this conversation off by simply saying she was worried about him. But it was starting to feel like perhaps that wasn't the only thing at the root of her sudden...quietness.

After his heart attack, her father hadn't been able to carry out a lot of the duties he'd performed for years, so she'd stayed close to take care of him and the house and as much of the ranch as she could. However, he was getting better and acting more like his old self every day, taking back a lot of those chores.

Which left her feeling...what? Restless? Useless?

She let several words play through her mind. She wasn't depressed, discontent, sad, or even lonely. She wasn't suffering from wanderlust because she loved her home and couldn't imagine anywhere on the planet was better than their ranch and Maris.

No. None of that described her feeling. In fact, the only word that felt right was...bored.

Lorelie was completely bored.

All the usual activities, daily happenings, chores, and even those occasional nights at the bar with friends couldn't break through the fact that she was bored out of her mind and in danger of coming out of her skin.

Then she was forced to admit that some of that boredom had been there before her father's heart attack. She'd let his illness fill a void that had started to form well over a year earlier.

"I'll probably always worry about Dad."

"So much so that you'll let it cripple you? Because that's what this feels like." Paige didn't mince words, and Lorelie appreciated that.

"I'm trying. Honest. I'm trying to remember how to be me, but it's not coming back that easily."

They all studied her face just long enough to make Lorelie uneasy.

Then, as always, Sadie announced her prescription. "You need to get laid."

"Oh my God," Lela exclaimed. "How can you make a leap like that? The woman is depressed. Sex isn't going to—"

"Actually," Lorelie interrupted, "I think sex might help."

Paige's grin grew as she exchanged a look with Sadie. "Then I think I know just the cure."

She stood up and gestured for Lorelie to join her at the kitchen window. Glancing toward a barn in the backyard, she spied him.

Glen Rodgers.

"Glen's back in town?"

Paige nodded. "He's on a hiatus from touring. Some sort of issue with the lead singer."

Lorelie could tell from Paige's vague comments that there was a story there, but she was too busy admiring the scenery to care.

At her dad's party last fall, Glen had been wearing tattered jeans, a black T-shirt and a cowboy hat, and it had looked like his face hadn't seen a razor in days. Tonight, he was less bad-boy rocker in dark jeans that looked new, a light blue button-down shirt and a freshly shaven face. Apparently, he'd left the hat at home.

Lorelie was no stranger to cowboy hats *or* the men who wore them. More often than not, the hat hid the fact the wearer was balding. Glen didn't suffer from that problem. His dark brown hair was thick and just long enough to brush the collar of his shirt.

He was—in a word—gorgeous.

Unfortunately, that fact wasn't lost on Stacy Shell, who was giggling at something he'd said.

"Why is Stacy here?" Lorelie asked, silently chastising herself for being disappointed that Glen had brought a date.

Paige sighed. "That was Walt's doing. He thought Glen might enjoy having someone to hang with while he's in town, so he invited her along as a setup."

"If Walt's trying to set Glen up with Stacy, why are we standing here looking at him through the window?"

"That's the part of this intervention you *aren't* going to like." Sadie had joined them at the window.

"Great." Lorelie took another sip of her wine and girded her loins, so to speak.

"I overheard the guys talking at the bar yesterday. Glen asked about you. Tucker, Walt, and Evan shut him down pretty quick. Told him to look elsewhere."

Lorelie's temper spiked. "Are you fucking kidding me?"

Glen asked about her?

And the boys of fall fucked up her chances with him?

That was Lorelie's nickname for the guys who had played on her dad's high school football team. Tucker and Walt and all the others had been a part of the state championship team, a feat the classes who followed had yet to recreate. As such, they were legends in town.

And a pain in the ass for Lorelie.

Back when she was just starting high school, the guys on the team became her self-proclaimed older brothers, taking it upon themselves to run off anyone they deemed unworthy of Coach's only daughter. She was two years younger than them, which instantly cast her into the role of "little sister." She would have preferred to be the damn mascot, donning that sweat-stenched, cartoonish, big-headed Titan costume, over dealing with the army of guys determined to protect her virtue at all costs.

She was fairly certain it was her dad who'd issued that "big brother" directive to begin with, which made it even worse. The boys on her father's team would walk through fire for their coach. So once he'd made the request, the damn thing had been chiseled in stone and was more binding than the freaking Ten Commandments.

She'd bucked them every step of the way, getting away with a hell of a lot more than they realized back in high school. And then for a brief, glorious time, most of them scattered after graduation and dating was easier. Though not exactly successful. All she'd managed to find were a few frogs and more than a handful of regrets.

Just like that, Lorelie felt a spark. And then a blaze.

She'd let the guys get away with their overprotectiveness since returning to Maris because, in truth, they weren't keeping away anyone she was interested in.

Glen didn't fall into that category. She was interested in him. Big time.

"Yeah," Lela said, clearly disappointed in her boyfriend's participation in that conversation. "Twelve years later and it appears those guys are still determined to protect your virtue."

Lorelie snorted. "You mean the virtue they failed to protect back in high school. Jesus, those guys are tools. What the hell did they think I was doing while they were playing football every Friday night?"

Sadie laughed. "Oh, here's a story I haven't heard. Do tell."

"Making out under the bleachers. There was this super-cute trumpet player in the band. His family only lived in Maris a couple of years, but damn if that boy couldn't kiss like a champ. Personally, I credit all that practicing on his instrument. His lip work..." She released an exaggerated sigh.

Annie chortled, choking on her wine. "God, Lorelie. Only you."

"All I'm saying is it seems really stupid for a bunch of grown men to try to protect something I don't want protected— or actually have. My virtue is long gone. I'm twenty-eight, yet they still look at me like I'm some gangly fourteen-year-old virgin standing in the middle of a lion's den."

Lela topped up all their wineglasses. "We agree. Which is why we're going to help you."

Lorelie glanced back toward the yard and it took some effort for her not to roll her eyes at Stacy's flirting.

Sadie followed her gaze, watching Stacy as she propped her arms up on the hood of Tucker's new truck, pretending to be fascinated by the engine. "Stacy looks as happy as a tick on a fat dog."

Lorelie laughed. "Can't blame her, really. Most of the Maris hotties have been claimed lately. Makes it tough on us poor single girls. Especially when some women are greedy...."

Sadie didn't bother to feign guilt or remorse over the fact she'd hooked up with not one, but two of those available men. "What you call greedy, I call inspired. And sexy. And hot. And—"

Lorelie held up her hand. "Please. I'm perfectly aware how great your love life is without the descriptions. Joel and Oakley walk around every day at work with those shit-eating grins on their faces."

Sadie winked, her own smile growing wider.

Lorelie pointed at her face. "Yeah. That's it. That grin right there."

Paige turned the conversation back to Glen. "He's not hard to look at, is he?"

"He's okay," Lorelie said, trying to downplay her interest.

It was a stupid move. Since she'd begun dating Oakley and Joel, Sadie had become a very close friend. A close friend with an annoyingly high aptitude for looking straight through a person's bullshit to find the truth.

"Sell that lie to someone else, sister. I ain't buyin'. You forget I was sober at your dad's party back in October, manning the bar. I saw the way that guy only had eyes for you. And you weren't exactly looking away from the stage yourself."

Lorelie couldn't deny it. She didn't want to. Her friends were offering to help, and considering it was *their* significant others doing the cock blocking, she was going to accept. "Okay. Fine. I'll admit it."

Sadie jerked her head toward Glen. "A nice, hot, sexy cowboy has just been dumped in your front yard. Are you going to let Stacy get the jump on him?"

"Hell no. But I need a little time to work the situation. How long is he here for?" Lorelie asked Paige, who appeared to have more information that the rest of them.

"Just a few days, but I think that time could be extended. With the right enticement. According to Walt, he has a few weeks off. He's planning to drive to Vegas from here at some point."

"I see." It had been too damn long since Lorelie had felt excited about something. And Glen would be a challenge. The man didn't like small towns or staying put. She liked the idea of trying to change his mind, at least for a short while.

"Oooo, I know that look," Sadie said. "You're going for it, aren't you?"

"I've been more than ready to shed this nun-like existence for months. My problem is there hasn't been anyone around who interested me enough to bother."

"He'd be worth getting hot *and* bothered about," Lela said, joining them at the window to look at Glen.

Lorelie agreed. "Which leaves the issue of Stacy."

Stacy leaned closer to Glen and slightly forward, obviously attempting to give him an ample view of what she was packing beneath her shirt. Which Lorelie had to begrudgingly admit was more than she possessed. Her damn B cups couldn't compete with Miss DD.

"Don't worry about that. We've got it well in hand," Paige said. "Walt got in touch with me yesterday to ask if I'd help him with dinner tonight. Sadie called me last night to tell me about the cock block initiative, so when I got here this morning to get the dinner prep rolling, I got all the intel on Glen and his plans, and then...I came up with a countermove. In fact..." She pointed toward the front of the house, where they could hear a car coming down the long driveway. As they all watched, Buck Davis pulled his car next to Tucker's truck and hopped out.

"Buck?" Lorelie asked.

Sadie nodded as if Paige was the smartest person on earth. "Well played, you clever puss. I've been watching him and Stacy make moon eyes at Cruisers for weeks now."

If this was her friends' idea of help, Lorelie suspected she'd be better off on her own. Buck was a math teacher who taught at Maris High School. He was too tall and too skinny, with flaming red hair and freckles. He looked almost clownish standing next to Glen, whom he'd just been introduced to.

"Um..." Lorelie had her doubts this would work. No sane woman would walk away from Glen the God toward Howdy Doody.

However, from the moment Buck emerged from the car, Stacy's entire stature changed. She took a step away from Glen and when Buck spoke to her, she blushed.

Hell, they *both* blushed.

"Well, I'll be damned," Lorelie muttered. "Walt doesn't look too happy to see Buck."

It had been apparent from the second Buck arrived that Paige hadn't clued their host in on the additional dinner guest.

Paige grinned. "I invited Buck this morning...the second I found out Stacy was coming. He's a bachelor and he lives on his own. Even with the late invite, he wasn't going to turn down a free home-cooked meal."

They continued to watch the men in the yard, as well as Buck and Stacy's bizarre mating dance, which seemed to consist of blushing furiously every time one of them spoke to the other.

If losing the girl bothered Glen, he gave absolutely no indication of it. In fact, Lorelie thought he looked just the slightest bit relieved. But that was probably wishful thinking on her part.

They were forced to change the subject from Lorelie's intervention to more mundane things as the men headed toward the house.

Paige pulled a tray of fresh-baked rolls from the oven as the other women began filling the serving bowls.

Lorelie hung back as Glen filed into the kitchen behind Tucker, Evan and Walt, Joel and Oakley on his heels. Buck and Stacy remained in the yard.

She tried to fight down the butterflies in her stomach, as well as the fluttering in regions farther south. Sadie was right. Lorelie *did* need to get laid. Badly. She wondered briefly if Glen would even remember her.

Then she recalled what Sadie had said. He'd asked about her.

She was glad to know she'd at least been memorable. As for her, she had recalled her conversation with Glen countless times since October, and she'd listened to that damn Miley

Cyrus song so many times, Dad finally put his hands over his ears and begged her to find something else to play.

Glen's gaze landed on her the moment he entered. She feared for a second he'd take to heart the guys' warnings to steer clear.

She should have known better. He smiled when he saw her, crossing the room until he stood right in front of her.

"Hey, Lori."

"Lorelie," she corrected, despite loving the way he said her name. She held out her hand for a handshake, but Glen used the grip to raise it to his mouth, where he kissed her knuckles. It was charming, old-fashioned, and had her pussy clenching.

"That's quite a move," she teased.

"Yeah. I've had that in my back pocket for a while now." He winked at her. "I was hoping you'd be here tonight."

Lorelie grinned and fought down her own blush. God, she was as bad as Stacy and Buck. A fact that didn't sit well with her. She was never shy or demurring or any of that silly crap around men. She really *had* lost sight of herself.

Glen still held on to her hand, his grip strong and warm.

"So you came back, huh? Despite how boring our small town is?"

"The town might be boring, but the people aren't. You look pretty tonight. Still flitting around, Butterfly, or have you managed to settle down?"

"I'm doing just fine."

"Still single?"

Oh yeah. She wanted this guy. "Yep. How about you?"

"Yep."

"How's life on the road?"

For the slightest second, she saw something sad flash in his eyes. But Glen was clearly better at hiding his problems than she was. Especially if the fact her dad and all her girlfriends were calling her out for them was anything to go on.

"It's good. Just taking a vacation."

"Paige said you're thinking of heading to Vegas when you leave here."

"Yeah. Thought I'd try my hand at sitting in the audience at a couple of shows, as opposed to standing on stage. And I'm no stranger to the tables. Gambling can be good for the soul every once in a while."

"But bad on the pocketbook."

"Only if you lose. And I don't lose."

There it was. That certain something that set Glen apart from most of the men in Maris. With the exception of the guys in this room, there were too many single men in town who were lacking that bravado, that self-confidence.

It was why Lorelie had been so damn bored. She preferred a guy with a backbone, not one with as much spine as a jellyfish.

"Still cocky, I see."

Glen didn't get a chance to respond as Walt stepped over to them. "Y'all ready to eat?"

Walt gave Glen what the fool obviously thought was a surreptitious warning glance.

Lorelie rolled her eyes.

Stacy and Buck walked into the kitchen, so the entire group grabbed serving bowls, platters, glasses and bottles of wine, carrying it all to the dining room.

It was a loud, fun gathering of old friends, which meant there was nothing formal or serious going on. Instead of mature adults, the group looked more like a gang of rambunctious siblings who'd grown up together. Which was essentially true.

Sadie had made some joke about Tucker buying the big truck to compensate for other things. Tucker's reply was to toss a slice of cucumber from the salad at her, telling her a woman with two men in her bed had no business talking about over-compensating.

Evan teased Joel about the dark purple shirt he'd chosen to wear, calling him Barney—until Oakley revealed it was a gift from Joel's mom. Then the joke turned into one of those "So your mom is still dressing you" gags.

That whole conversation led to a discussion about the relationship between Joel's mom and Sadie's dad. Everyone always had fun giving them shit about the possibility of the lovers becoming stepsiblings as well. Apparently this was all news to Buck, who was slightly horrified by the prospect.

Glen took in all the banter, hopping in more than a few times to add some witty retort. The guy was seriously funny.

He'd claimed the seat next to Lorelie at the table, and every now and then he rested his arm on the back of her chair. Lorelie took great pleasure in leaning toward him whenever he did so, provoking her male friends to shoot them *both* annoying glances.

Then he ran his hand along her hair.

She gave him a quizzical look.

"Wanted to see if it's as soft as it looks."

"And?" she asked, leaning even closer.

"Like silk."

Her heart started to beat a little faster. Lorelie had never felt such an instant and powerful attraction to a man.

Tucker broke them apart when he held the breadbasket out to Glen. "Want another roll?"

Glen grabbed one. "Thanks." He tossed the bread on his plate, and then wrapped his arm around her chair once more, winking at her covertly.

Glen was baiting them on purpose. Lorelie giggled softly, only too pleased to play along.

Too many bottles of wine later, the dinner ended, everyone relaxed and full. Walt suggested they move to the front porch. "You bring your guitar, Glen?"

"Never go anywhere without it."

Glen consented to grab his instrument from the truck and they took their dessert and coffee outside. The evening was crisp, but not too cool. One of the benefits of living in Texas was fairly mild winters, and this year's had been unseasonably warm and dry.

As the men played everyone's favorites, they all sang along. Whenever they couldn't remember the words, Walt and Glen would make up raunchy lines, something they'd clearly had quite a bit of practice with.

"You guys are really great," Stacy said as she and Buck rocked on the porch swing. Sometime during the long meal, they'd overcome their shyness with each other, and Buck had even grown bold enough to hold Stacy's hand the last half hour.

Once they'd sung themselves out, Walt and Glen put their guitars away. Glen walked over to sit next to Lorelie who was perched sideways on the top porch step, her back against a post. Glen claimed the other post, facing her. Lorelie stretched one of her legs toward him. Glen grasped her foot, pulling it into his lap and pointedly ignoring the exasperated scowls from Tucker and Evan.

As so often happened when they all got together, the conversation turned to her dad.

"How's Coach doing?" Tucker asked. "Didn't he have a doctor's appointment today?"

Lorelie nodded. "Yeah. It actually went really well. Or so I heard."

"What do you mean?" Paige asked.

Oakley answered for her, grinning. "Coach was being Coach this morning. Said he was tired of being treated like an invalid. Insisted on going to the doctor on his own, even though Lorelie usually drives him."

"Good," Lela said. "Just proves what we were saying earlier. He's well on his way back to a complete recovery."

Lorelie begrudgingly agreed. "Yeah. Doctor even cleared him to start doing more chores around the ranch. Within reason, of course."

"I'll be damn glad to have the guy back out there with us," Oakley said. "Days go a lot faster with him working beside you."

"What do *you* do on the ranch, Lori?" Glen asked.

"Same as the guys, I guess. We all have our chores. I take care of the house, cook the meals, tend the garden, feed the chickens, and spend a lot of time in the stable with the horses."

"Lorelie was a state-champion roper," Joel added.

"It was high school rodeo, Joel. Team competition." She looked at Glen to explain, "I was the header. My friend, Allison, was the heeler."

Glen nodded slowly.

"You don't have a clue what that means, do you?"

He chuckled. "Not a bit. I'm a Philly boy. City kid through and through."

That fact surprised her, given his love of country music. Of course, it was silly to think just because a person was from the north they wouldn't like a genre of music.

"I roped the calf's head. Allie roped the hind feet," she explained.

"And you do all this while chasing the calf on the back of a galloping horse?"

"Yep."

Glen's expression was sheer amazement. "*That* is something I'd really like to see."

"So much for a singing cowboy," she teased.

Glen didn't take offense. "I sing the songs. I don't live the life."

Lorelie spied an opening to advance her plans to seduce Glen. "Stop by the ranch this weekend. I'll give you a tour and a demonstration."

"We're going fishing on Saturday," Walt interjected.

"Don't see any reason why I can't do both. How about Sunday, Butterfly?"

"That's perfect. Around three? And then you can stay for dinner if you'd like."

Glen smiled. "I would like that a lot."

"Then it's a date."

Before the guys could come up with reasons for Glen not to visit Lorelie on Sunday, Annie starting making plans with the women to get meals to the Phillips family. Georgette Phillips had taken a tumble a few days earlier and broken her leg. The mother of three boys, all under the age of six, Georgette's tumble left her husband struggling to keep the rambunctious kids on his radar, so meals were hit or miss.

"I'll make spaghetti and take it over tomorrow," Annie added.

"Oh God," Sadie said. "I suck at cooking. On my night, I'm picking up the phone, calling in a pizza order, and having it delivered to their house."

Lorelie laughed. "We appreciate your efforts, Martha Stewart. I'll stop by their place on Saturday morning, clean the kitchen, and nag the boys into tidying their bedrooms. I can only imagine what sort of mess they've made. I'm sure Georgette is going nuts surrounded by the chaos, helpless to pick it all up. The woman's house is usually so clean you can eat off the floors."

"That's awful nice of you ladies," Buck remarked.

Even though it was a Thursday night and everyone had

work in the morning, no one seemed anxious to leave. There was a cool breeze blowing and for a moment, Lorelie imagined how nice it would be to just close her eyes and sleep there in the fresh, clean air.

Buck and Stacy were the first to leave, followed by Evan and Annie. Lela and Paige had gone into the kitchen to clear away the dishes.

Sadie, Oakley, and Joel had come in their own car. Lorelie had been confused by why they'd left so early, and without her, but now it was obvious Sadie had been plotting with the other women in regards to her intervention.

As she considered their words, Lorelie was touched by how much her friends cared about her. Having grown up on a ranch, without a mother and surrounded by men and football players her whole life, it was nice to now have so much female companionship. It wasn't something she'd ever missed simply because she didn't know to. Now, she couldn't imagine a life without her girlfriends.

In the days following Dad's heart attack, they'd rallied around her, doing pretty much what they planned to do for Georgette. They kept her and Dad fed, cleaned up, and provided support so she didn't fall apart. She wouldn't have made it through those dark days without them.

Glancing at Glen, she wondered what he thought of their plans to help a neighbor. Even in their short acquaintance, she got the impression he had lived his life pretty much alone. She'd hate that type of existence.

"Wanna ride to the ranch?" Oakley offered to Lorelie. "I can drive you back in the morning to pick up your car."

Lorelie shook her head. "No thanks. I only had two glasses of wine and that was hours ago. I'm okay to drive myself home."

Glen was the next to rise. "Well, guess I'll head back to the B&B. See you on Sunday, Butterfly." He gave her hand a little squeeze. She liked that he was completely unbothered by the constant looks the guys on the porch were casting his way.

She said good night and watched him walk away, his truck farther down the driveway. She'd wondered whose vehicle it was when she'd parked behind it.

Lorelie felt a twinge of disappointment once he was gone. Tonight had been fun. Between Glen's compliments and occasional "accidental" brushes and her attempts at finding her flirting wings again, she was sorry to see it end. It had been too long since she'd felt this...energized.

She did a mental eye roll.

Energized. Yeah right.

She was horny as fuck.

She considered going into the house to help the other women tidy up, but she was too content where she was. She was glad she'd stayed put when the voice she'd just started missing began speaking once again.

"Bertha won't start."

"Bertha?" Lorelie asked.

Walt shook his head. "Not a bit surprised, man. That truck needs to go."

"Yeah. I know." Glen didn't look as bothered by his broken-down vehicle as she thought he should.

"I can give you a ride into town," she offered.

Glen looked like he might have taken her up on the invitation, but Walt spoke first. "You can just crash here tonight, Glen. We'll take a look at the truck tomorrow morning. See if she can be fixed."

Glen nodded his assent, even though Lorelie could tell he was disappointed to refuse her. The idea pleased her more than she could say.

"Thanks, man." Though he was speaking to Walt, his gaze remained on Lorelie's face. That was when she realized he was feeling *energized* too. There was something hot and hungry and almost dangerous in his eyes. And despite her growing need, it provoked something she wasn't used to feeling when approaching sexual encounters.

Nervousness.

God, she'd let herself get too out of practice. And she'd spent way too much time fantasizing about the singing cowboy. It was freaking her out a little.

"I guess I should go," she said at last, when the silence lingered a touch long. She stepped off the porch.

"I'll walk you to your car," Glen offered.

Lorelie didn't bother to turn around to see what the other guys thought about *that*. She could feel their scowls and disapproval without the visual. Glen, lovely man, ignored it all as usual. The way he stood up to the guys was becoming a huge turn-on for her.

They walked down the driveway until they reached her car.

"If looks could kill," he muttered.

"What?"

"How can you stand that?" he asked.

"Stand what?"

"Lori, it's not normal for guys to be that protective of a grown woman, especially one who isn't a sister."

She considered his comment, and then discounted it. "Actually, you're wrong. They're my friends. It *is* normal for them to be protective."

Her response didn't seem to soak in, and again, she was struck by the fact that Glen really didn't seem to get it. Did he even *have* friends? A family? A sister? She was fascinated, and suddenly interested in knowing everything about him. She might have to corner Walt sometime in the next few days and ask some questions.

"Well, then I guess I'll just have to weather the dirty looks. Because I'm not staying away from you."

His deep-voiced assertion had her panties going damp. "Oh, it's not going to be just dirty looks. I think the guys are planning to set you up with some of the local women."

"Like Stacy?"

She nodded.

"That's not going to work either. Only found one butterfly in Maris worth studying."

She leaned closer. "You think you're up to catching her?"

He chuckled. "I feel pretty good about my chances."

"Cocky."

He ran a gentle finger along her cheek. It sent a wave of tingly warmth flowing through her. "You okay to get home?"

"Yeah. Still coming by Sunday?"

He lifted her hand the way he had in the kitchen and placed a soft kiss on the knuckle. "Wild horses couldn't keep me away."

"Good. I'll see you then."

She got in her car and as she pulled away, she could see him standing in the driveway, watching as she left.

And just like that, her life got a lot less boring.

Chapter Three

TOBY

Trent try to contact you?

GLEN

Couple of texts. Guess it's safe to say the dust isn't settling

TOBY

Yeah. He's still pissed. You reply?

GLEN

No. Don't have anything to say to the fucker

TOBY

Keep it that way. Tonight is first show since the incident. Don't want him distracted

GLEN

Let me know how it goes

TOBY

Yeah. Will do. Know you're not religious, but prayers might help

GLEN

Not enough praying in the world to help that asshole

TOBY

Gotta go get my ulcer prescription refilled. Talk to you later

"My night just got a hell of a lot better," Glen said with a grin. He had spotted Lorelie sitting with Paige in a corner booth of Cruisers as soon as he walked into the bar.

Walt had texted earlier to apologize for Stacy not working out. Glen didn't have the heart to tell his friend he'd clearly lost sight of Glen's type, if he thought Stacy was it. Woman had been nice, but giggly in an almost silly way. It had been readily apparent that Buck was a much better match for her.

"Hey, Glen," Lorelie said, scooting over to make room for him next to her in the circular booth. He was more than happy to claim the spot.

Walt appeared at the table with two beers, looking at Lorelie with surprise. "When did you get here?"

"Just a couple minutes ago," Lorelie replied. "Paige invited me to join y'all."

Walt didn't look particularly pleased to see Lorelie at the table, but he put on a good face and placed the bottles in front of Paige and Lorelie. "Guess I'll go grab a couple more beers from the bar."

"Why do I get the feeling I crashed the party?" Lorelie asked.

Paige rolled her eyes. "You'll see in a minute."

Glen got the impression he'd missed the point of that conversation, but he didn't bother to press either woman for an explanation. He'd spent the better part of the day on the lake with Walt, Tucker, and Evan, kicked back with a fishing pole in one hand and a beer in the other.

The soft rocking of the boat, the warmth of the sun, and the peace and quiet had worked its magic. He'd said his goodbyes with every intention of crawling into his bed at the B&B and falling asleep in front of the TV before the sun went down. Those plans changed when Walt texted to invite him to Cruisers.

He'd considered turning his friend down and riding out the wave of complete relaxation until tomorrow. After twenty-two years of perpetual motion, he was trying to get the hang of the slower pace of small-town living. He figured that concept would wear thin in a day or two, but until then, he was pretty happy to try his hand at a life of leisure.

Then he'd decided to rally, hoping Lorelie would be out as well.

Mercifully, he was rewarded for his efforts. Because it had been damn hard climbing off that bed and putting his boots back on.

"You got some sun today," Paige said, gesturing to his face. "Nice tan."

"Gotta admit I'd never understood the appeal of fishing before. I get it now."

Paige gave him a confused look. "Walt said y'all didn't catch a thing."

Glen shrugged. "That's not the point."

Lorelie laughed. "You guys are all the same. Thank God the womenfolk around here aren't relying on those fish to feed their families."

Walt came back to the table with three beers and a woman in tow.

"Look who I ran into."

Glen wasn't fooled by his friend's nonchalant tone for a second. And even if he had been, the exasperated looks exchanged by Lorelie and Paige would have clued him in to the fact he was being set up again. He appreciated his friend's efforts on his behalf—hell, he'd sort of encouraged him to try— but now that he'd seen Lorelie, Glen wasn't interested in meeting anyone else.

And he'd tell Walt that, if the man wasn't such a lunatic when it came to protecting his coach's daughter.

"Hey, Ruby," Paige said.

"Ruby Daniels, this is my good friend, Glen Rodgers. Glen is a musician from Nashville. He used to play in my band, but now he's playing for some upstart named Trent Maxwell."

Glen was amused by Walt's efforts to downplay Trent's fame, but it was wasted on Ruby, whose eyes widened.

"Trent Maxwell? No shit! Damn, that's one man I wouldn't kick out of bed for eating crackers."

Walt sighed quietly, but proceeded with his plan, gesturing for Glen to scoot over to make room for the woman.

Glen didn't kick up a fuss because the action forced him to move closer to Lorelie.

Lorelie seemed to appreciate the tighter quarters as well. She pressed her leg against his and gave him a covert wink.

Walt dove back in. "Ruby is a big fan of country music. She was just telling me about her plans to hit the Brad Paisley concert in Dallas in a few weeks."

Glen looked at Ruby, who didn't appear any more interested in this setup than he was. In fact, she was scowling at some couple across the room.

"Brad does a good show. I think you'll enjoy it," Glen said, failing to come up with anything more exciting to say.

Ruby looked back at him when it became apparent she was expected to respond. "Yeah. I won the tickets from the radio station. I was actually considering selling them on StubHub. I could use the money."

Walt continued undaunted, even in the face of imminent failure. "Glen's headed to Vegas after this. You ever been, Ruby?"

She shook her head. "Nope. Hate slot machines. Talk about a time and money suck."

Lorelie took a sip of her beer, but it was obvious she was using the bottle to hide her grin. Neither she nor Paige made any effort to make this awkward situation less so. In fact, they were clearly enjoying it.

Mercifully, a slow song came on. "Oh," Paige said. "I love this song. Dance with me, Walt, please."

For a second, it looked like Walt would actually turn her down. Then his friend's brain engaged and he recognized his chance to cut his losses and escape. "Okay."

He rose and took Paige's hand, leading her to the dance floor and leaving him alone with Ruby and Lorelie. Lorelie shifted away from him, filling the space Paige had just vacated. That allowed him to move over as well. Ruby remained rooted to her spot.

"So how's life, Ruby?" Lorelie asked. "Haven't seen you much since the divorce."

Ruby sighed, and then jerked her head to the couple sitting at a table on the other side of the room. "My ex is here with the hosebag."

"Hosebag?" Glen asked.

"I left the jackass because he was having an affair with *her*." Ruby pointed at the couple quite openly, not caring who saw the gesture. The hosebag glanced over and gave Ruby a dirty look. Ruby snorted and rolled her eyes.

"Damn. I'm sorry." Once again, Glen was struck by a big

case of "What the fuck, Walt?" In what world would Glen want to tangle with a recently jilted woman?

"I'm not sorry. Been the best four months of my life," Ruby said, taking a big swig of her beer. "Married Earl when I was twenty. Missed kicking up my heels as a single girl when I was younger, so now I'm making up for lost time."

"If you don't mind me asking, how did you find out about the affair?" Lorelie asked.

It appeared they'd touched on a subject Ruby could sink her teeth into. She was suddenly all-in on the conversation, her face brightening.

Once she started telling her tale, Glen realized the woman was a born storyteller. "Earl wasn't the sharpest tool in the shed and he wasn't exactly subtle. Started dying his goatee and wearing tighter T-shirts. As if any woman in her right mind would find that attractive. That man had a beer gut back in high school, so when he decided he was going to start working out, I got suspicious. Then I realized the workout clothes were never hitting the laundry basket. One day, the idiot puts on his exercise stuff and has the nerve to ask me if I switched laundry detergent. Said his shorts were itching him. I told him I hadn't switched laundry detergent, *he'd* switched Laundromats. Suggested he tell her to use Arm & Hammer."

Lorelie laughed loudly. "Oh my God, Ruby. You're a hoot."

Ruby grinned, pleased her story was entertaining them. "Yeah. Last straw came when he started working early. Like I didn't know he wasn't meeting her for a quick screw in the backseat of his car. One morning, he comes in to kiss me goodbye and says he's going to work. I told him if he considered that work, he obviously wasn't doing it right. He left and I got up, packed my bags, and parked myself right outside the lawyer's office, waiting for it to open, so I could file for divorce."

Ruby told the story with such gusto, it was impossible to keep a straight face.

"Your life is a country song waiting to be written," Glen declared.

It was clear she liked the sound of that. "Oh, I got a million more stories like that if you're serious. We could fill an album."

The three of them laughed as they brainstormed possible song titles.

"Hiya, Ruby."

Glen glanced up when a stranger approached the table.

Ruby lit up when she saw the man. "Rodney Babcock. You old scoundrel. What are you doing in town?"

"Changed jobs. I'm a Maris boy again."

"I had no idea. Been in my own little world since leaving Earl."

Rodney didn't look surprised by the news. In fact, Glen thought he looked a bit like a man on a mission. "Yeah, a little birdie behind the bar was telling me about that. Was hoping I could come steal a few dances from you."

Ruby was up and out of the booth in record time. "I'll see y'all later," she threw over her shoulder as she followed the tall cowboy to the floor.

"Ruby's sweet on Rodney?" Glen asked.

Lorelie nodded. "They dated back in high school, but he moved to Phoenix for a job after graduation and she married Earl on the rebound. He moved back a few weeks ago. We think he found out Ruby was single again and decided he wasn't going to miss his chance at scooping her up."

"Who's 'we'?"

"Me and Sadie and Paige and the rest of the girls."

"Y'all are a pretty tight-knit group, aren't you?"

Lorelie smiled. "Hell yeah. They're my best friends. I love them."

"Trying to figure out if I should be grateful or upset that you keep trying to sabotage all these hookups Walt and his friends are putting together for me."

Lorelie feigned innocence, but he wasn't fooled for a minute. "I don't have a clue what you mean."

"Walt wasn't expecting Buck at the dinner party. And he wasn't expecting you to be here tonight."

"He wouldn't have invited you out if he'd known I was coming."

Glen realized that was true. "I'm going to have to give him a word. Tell him to back off on setting me up."

"Thought you wanted to meet a pretty Maris girl and have some fun?"

"Sadie's been telling tales, I see. I already met the prettiest woman in Maris." As he spoke, Glen scooted closer to her. He was pleased when she moved toward him at the same time.

The music changed, a faster tune. Neither Walt nor Rodney were finished dancing with the girls. Then Glen recognized the song and groaned.

Lorelie didn't miss the sound. "Big Trent Maxwell fan, huh?"

He lifted one shoulder, hoping to appear casual. The last thing he wanted to talk about tonight was the asshole. Part of him was afraid Lorelie would start waxing poetic over the idiot's sexy eyes and chiseled jaw and dimples and whatever the fuck else women saw in the jerkoff, and Glen's fantasies of her would be ruined forever.

"He strikes me as too pretty to be a country singer," she said. "More the type to be in one of those cheesy boy bands. And what's up with his voice?" She pointed one finger in the air, cueing him to listen to the song. "Seems like the studio takes a lot of liberties. Always covering up his actual singing with that fancy stuff."

"That's because he can't carry a tune in a bucket."

Her eyes widened and she laughed. "Seriously? That makes sense then. I guess. How does someone who can't sing make it so big?"

Glen had never talked to anyone—with the exception of Walt, who'd been in the business and knew how it worked—about Trent's lack of talent. In fact, it was highly unprofessional for him to continue this conversation.

Of course, punching his lead singer hadn't exactly put him in contention for Employee of the Month.

Glen decided fuck it. Might feel good to get some of this pent-up Trent aggression off his chest. And Lorelie didn't strike him as the type to sell his story to a tabloid. Something told him she'd be a good listener. Maybe even a sympathetic one. He wasn't one to want pity, but he wouldn't mind a little petting if it was Lorelie doing the stroking.

"He's got the right look and he can shake his ass with the best of them onstage. The studio can fake the rest."

"On the recordings, sure. But how can they fake it during concerts?"

Glen blew out a frustrated sigh. "Depends on the venue. Sometimes he lip-syncs, sometimes they turn his mic down low and mine up high. I drown him out."

"No way." She didn't say anything for a few minutes, but he could see the wheels turning. When she finally did speak, she surprised him. Something very few people were capable of nowadays. He'd grown too jaded for shock.

"You must hate that."

She hit the nail on the head. Despite his fascination for her, her words were surprising, considering neither of them knew each other very well.

"What do you mean?" he asked, wondering if she'd interpreted it the way he thought.

"You strike me as a serious musician, Glen. You don't half-ass it and you don't fake it. Why would you work for someone who does?"

Now it was *his* turn to go quiet. Mainly because he didn't have a fucking clue why. Well, actually, he knew all the reasons he'd been telling himself lately. But he was almost embarrassed to say them out loud. They painted him in a shallow, mercenary light.

"He's one of the biggest names out there right now."

Lorelie didn't respond to that, didn't seem to consider that an answer.

"I'm at the height of my career in terms of earnings and name recognition. The studio is paying me a hell of a lot of money for my guitar playing and my singing."

And my babysitting.

He didn't add that part.

"I've heard both. You're obviously the true talent in the band. So why is he the star?"

Walt had asked him the same thing. And his answer was going to be the same. No matter how screwed up he was, the only thing Glen had ever known, had ever accepted about himself, was that he did not crave the limelight. In fact, he hated it.

"There's too much bullshit attached to being the one front and center, Lori. When they put that spotlight on you, it stops being about the music. All the studio cares about is image and dollar signs. Rugged, aging cowboys aren't the rage anymore. No one's racing out to sign the Merle Haggards or the Willie Nelsons these days. Right now, it's all about fitting that sex-symbol, six-pack, make-the-girls-melt mold. That ain't me."

She narrowed her eyes, looking confused. "You're kidding, right? You're about a million times hotter than Trent Maxwell.

And a gazillion times more talented. I've never bought a Trent Maxwell song. I'd buy every one of yours."

Right then and there, Glen decided he wanted to write Lorelie Carr a song.

He wasn't much of a songwriter. It wasn't that he'd never tried. He had. Walt had even recorded one of his songs once and included it on an album. It hadn't gotten a ton of airplay, but they'd pulled it out every now and then at a concert and the true fans had sung along.

Lorelie's support of him, her belief in his talent, went a long way toward soothing some edges that had gotten rougher ever since he'd signed on to play with Trent.

He glanced around the room and caught more than a few pairs of eyes on him. While Walt was concentrating on this feet and following Paige's lead on the line dance, the same didn't hold true for Oakley and Joel, who were helping Sadie man the bar tonight. Or Tucker and Evan, who were drinking with another guy Glen didn't know.

"How many of those former football players are in here?" he asked.

Lorelie scanned the room and he could see her doing a mental count. "I see five. The usual suspects."

"The guy with Tucker and Evan?"

Lorelie nodded. "Jack. He was on the team too. Running back to Tucker's quarterback."

"And what do you think they'd do if I kissed you right now?"

A seductive smile appeared. "I don't have a clue, but the suspense is killing me. Should we give it a try?"

He wrapped his arm around her shoulders as she turned to face him. "Lori."

"Yeah?"

"I don't give a shit about those guys. I'm kissing you because I can't stop myself."

She reached up to touch his cheek. It was rough from a day's worth of growth. He was suddenly sorry he hadn't taken a second to shave again.

They both moved forward and met in the middle. He liked that. Liked that she wanted this as much as he did. His lips touched hers softly at first. She tasted sweet and smelled like sunshine. He didn't have a clue what sunshine actually smelled like, but she was it. Fresh air and heat and a mountain lake—all rolled into one.

Her hand remained on his face, the touch as potent as the kiss. He tilted his head slightly, pressing her mouth open with his. Her tongue was there, stroking his, driving them out of the "sweet" range and straight into "sin city" in seconds. He tightened his grip on her shoulders with one arm while his other hand cupped her cheek. Her skin was as silky soft as her hair. The woman was the epitome of sensual perfection.

After a minute or two, Lorelie broke away.

He scowled.

"Gotta breathe," she said, placing one, then two more quick kisses on his lips.

It took Glen a few minutes to catch his bearings, to recall he was in a crowded bar with loud music and laughter, surrounded by Lorelie's friends. All those things had faded away when he'd kissed her, leaving only the two of them in a silent world where nothing else existed. He wanted to go back there.

"Lori," Glen whispered. His head was spinning, everything except her face was blurry, gray.

"I..." she started, licking her lips. "That...."

He nodded slowly. "Yeah."

She blinked rapidly as if trying to regain her own focus. "I'm a little rusty."

He chuckled. "God help me when you get your sea legs back then, because that kiss rocked my world."

She smiled and flushed slightly at his compliment. "It's been a long time since I've kissed a guy. I don't remember it ever feeling so...overwhelming."

"That's a good word for it. You keep talking about your lack of dates and as always, I find it hard to believe there's not a row of guys from here to the next state waiting to ask you out. No matter how deep the defensive line of football players around you."

He meant his words as a joke, but Lorelie sobered. "Sort of lost track of myself after my dad's heart attack. It's taking me a little time to bounce back."

Glen recalled his first impression of Lorelie back in October. "Caged bird," he murmured.

She frowned. "What?"

"First time we met, I thought you looked like a caged bird."

Lorelie considered his description. "That's not too far from the truth. Let's just say my dancing shoes are dusty from lack of use. I was there the night my dad had his heart attack. To say it scared me shitless is an understatement. For months, I never strayed far from home because I was afraid it would happen again and I wouldn't be there to save him."

"Where's your mom?" It was a personal question, but the more he learned about Lorelie, the more he wanted to know.

"Died when I was born. Dad raised me on his own. He's all I have."

His chest tightened as he thought about the stress Lorelie had been under since last June. Walt had called him shortly after finding out about Coach's heart attack. Told him he was going back home. At the time, Glen thought Walt was a fool for leaving Nashville and he'd banked on his friend coming back. Even though they hadn't toured together for a couple years prior to that, the two of them had found plenty of opportunities to meet for drinks at the bar and talk shop. Then Walt reconnected with his friends in Maris and stayed gone. Glen had missed him.

"He's doing better though, right?" Glen asked, recalling the conversation about Coach's doctor's appointment.

"Oh yeah. He's on the mend. Has been for a while."

"But you're still worried."

She nodded. "That's not going to go away. Ever. I know that. I just need to find a way to deal with it."

"Sounds to me like you need to let go. Have some fun."

Lorelie gave him the sexiest grin he'd ever had the pleasure of being on the receiving end of. "My friends suggested I get laid. But your idea sounds okay too."

He cleared a throat that had suddenly gone tight. "I think you should listen to your friends. They know you better than I do."

Lorelie laughed loudly. "Wanna help me shake off some of this rust?"

As far as invitations went, Glen was pretty sure that was the hottest offer he'd ever received. Lorelie twisted toward him again and he answered with a kiss rather than words.

Any tentativeness or hesitance was gone. There was no denying they both felt the attraction. And they were both diving off the cliff.

He lifted Lorelie's legs, tugging them over his thighs, running one hand over her hip. She was wearing tight jeans that fit her like a second skin. She was long, lean, and the most beautiful woman he'd ever met. As they kissed, he imagined lowering her to the booth and—

A loud knock on the table distracted them and had Lorelie jumping slightly.

As they broke apart, they looked over at the three new bottles of beer Evan had placed on the table. With a very heavy hand.

"Okay, darlin'," Evan said, looking directly at Lorelie. "I might be off duty, but that doesn't mean I won't arrest you two for public indecency if you don't knock it off."

Lorelie narrowed her eyes, undaunted. "Listen, Evan—"

"No," Evan interrupted. "You listen. You're lucky you got *me* instead of one of the other guys." He turned his attention to Glen. "I'm the peaceful one."

Glen chuckled. He'd spent the better part of the day in a boat with Evan, and he really liked the guy. He actually liked all of Lorelie's protectors. "I appreciate you taking the lead then. Don't suppose we could call a truce, could we?"

Evan dropped down next to Lorelie in the booth and took a swig of one of the beers. Glen picked up another, lifting it in a quick toast of thanks. Lorelie remained quiet, her scowl growing darker by the minute.

"What do you have in mind?" Evan asked.

"While I appreciate the introductions to all the single ladies around here, I'm afraid I'm not interested in Ruby or Stacy—or whoever else y'all might have waiting in the wings."

Evan glanced from Glen to Lorelie. "Yeah. I can see that."

"Evan—" Lorelie started again, her tone still fairly hostile.

Glen placed his hand on her knee under the table to stop her. If Evan saw the action, he didn't let on.

"I'm hoping to spend more of my time in Maris with Lorelie. I appreciate that you guys feel protective of her. And I understand why." Glen gave Lorelie a smile. "She's something special."

Lorelie rolled her eyes, but her face reflected pure delight. "You trying to sweeten *Evan* up or me?"

"You wanna go out with me one night next week, Lori?"

She nodded. "Yeah. I'd like that."

Evan frowned. "Thought you were heading to Vegas."

"Haven't fixed my truck yet."

Evan remained undaunted. "I'm struggling to find a truce in any of this."

"I'm here for a few days more. Probably a week. I'd like to spend that time with Lorelie instead of trying to play nice with all these women you and Walt keep lobbing my way. She's an intelligent woman who has agreed to go out with me. If you're really her friend, you'll trust her to make her own decisions."

"Yeah," Lorelie threw out hotly. "You will."

Evan sighed. "Old habits die hard, Lorelie. Coach asked us—"

"To keep an eye on me in *high school*. Dear God, Evan! You guys gotta let this go."

Evan smiled. "It's easier for me. I never left Maris. So I've watched you date more than your fair share of yahoos. Walt, Tucker, and Jack are still trying to figure out what's changed and what's the same around here. And let's face it—Joel and Oakley consider you their kid sister. That will *never* change. You're gonna have to sort them out on your own time."

She glanced toward the bar, where Oakley and Joel both stood. When they saw her looking, they quickly pretended to be busy pouring drinks. "Oh, I will."

Glen was glad he wasn't Joel and Oakley. Given the current level of Lorelie's annoyance, both men were in for it later.

"Do I fall into that 'yahoo' category?" Glen asked.

Evan considered the question for just a moment, and then shook his head. "No. I don't think you do."

"So it's settled. I'm taking this pretty woman out for dinner," Glen said. "And all the intimidating looks in the world aren't going to change that."

Evan sighed. "Not much of a truce. Sounds more like an ultimatum."

Lorelie leaned closer to Glen, her shoulder brushing his. "We're just having fun, Evan. Is that such a bad thing?"

"Fun, huh? Is that what y'all are calling that show?"

Lorelie giggled. "*I* thought it was fun."

Evan reached over and tugged on Lorelie's hair. "Do me a favor, darlin'. Try to have that fun somewhere a lot more private. You're getting all the rednecks in here worked up."

"Deal." Now that peace appeared to have been made, Lorelie reached for the beer Evan had brought to the table. Tipping it back, she chugged nearly half of it in one long gulp. "Feel like making out in the backseat of my car?" she asked Glen.

Evan groaned, but Glen laughed. "I could probably be persuaded."

"Great," Evan muttered. "Second y'all leave here, it'll be *my* ass that's grass for not stopping you. Don't suppose I could convince you to leave separately? Or maybe sneak out the back?"

Lorelie shook her head as Glen stood and reached for her hand, helping her out of the booth. "Nope. I'm not about to pussyfoot around, pretending for a bunch of busybody boys who should all be more worried about keeping their *own* women satisfied and less worried about who I'm sleeping with. Or not sleeping with."

"Which side of that line am I falling on?" Glen teased.

"That remains to be seen."

"Damn. About time." Evan chuckled, the sound prompting Lorelie to turn around and look at her friend. Evan answered the unspoken question in her quizzical expression. "It's nice to have you back, Lorelie."

She smiled, then bent over and placed a quick kiss on Evan's cheek.

Glen wasn't sure what the exchange meant, but clearly it pleased both of them.

Lorelie took Glen's hand, the two of them heading for the exit. Glen was sort of surprised no one else approached. Once they were outside, they paused.

Glen kept hold of her hand as he turned to face her. "If you were just trying to teach your friends a lesson, I'm okay with playing along. We can say good night here, or..."

He let her fill in the blanks. Right now, he'd give just about anything to spend more time with her—whether it was kissing her or simply talking. But it had to be her call.

"I don't want to say good night." Lorelie looked around the parking lot. "How did you get here?"

"Walked. My truck is still DOA and the B&B is only a few blocks away."

"Feel like taking a drive? I can drop you off later."

He wrapped his arm around her shoulders, placing a quick kiss on top of her head. "There's nothing I'd like to do more."

She graced him with the sweetest smile that had ever been sent his direction, and then led him to her car. They hopped in and pulled out of the parking lot.

"Where we headed to?" he asked.

"It's a surprise."

He liked the sound of that.

Lorelie pointed to the dashboard. "Radio?"

He fiddled with the dial until he found an old Keith Whitley song. He quietly sang along as Lorelie drove. Neither one of them felt it necessary to fill the ride with chatter, letting the soft country melody add to the peacefulness of the night.

Glen recognized her driveway and he was slightly surprised that she would bring him to the ranch. Then she bypassed the house and the barn, taking a dirt road he hadn't seen before. Within moments, she was pulling next to the same creek where they'd chatted last October.

It was chillier now than it had been in the fall, so neither of them left the car. Instead, Lorelie turned off the engine, but kept the battery engaged so the radio continued to play.

Then she unhooked her seat belt and twisted in her seat to look at him.

He followed suit. "I like it here."

She nodded. "It's my favorite place on the ranch. Do some of my best thinking by this creek."

"What do you think about?"

Lorelie sighed. "Everything. And sometimes nothing."

Glen glanced out the windshield. The night was clear and bright, the sky filled with a million stars. "Sometimes I forget how many stars there are. Rarely see them in the cities where we play."

"So you really like life on the road?"

He started to nod, and then stopped, unwilling to lie to her. "I used to."

"But not anymore?"

He shrugged. "It's getting harder."

"Because of Trent?"

"Yeah."

"Why are you in Maris?"

Damn woman was too astute, too clever. "I punched Trent after the last concert."

Her eyes widened, first with shock, then he thought with amusement. "Wish I'd been there to see that."

He chuckled, but said, "Not my finest moment, I can assure you."

"Why did you hit him?"

"He was trying to take advantage of a young fan. Gave her drugs, shit like that."

Lorelie gave him a confused look. "Sounds like that *was* your finest moment."

Glen sighed. "I think I'm getting too old for a lot of crap that's going on around me lately."

"How old are you?"

"Thirty-eight."

She snorted. "That's hardly old."

"I got a decade on you. And believe me, I'm feeling every minute of it these days."

"I'm going to circle back to my original question. Why are you here? Did you get fired?"

He shook his head. "According to my manager, I'm laying low until the dust settles."

Lorelie frowned. "You would actually go back to working for that asshole?"

Glen didn't respond. Mainly because the answer was yes, and he was ashamed of that. Ashamed to tell her that he would. But what choice did he have? His life was spent on the road.

When he considered what that entailed—basically just playing his guitar and his crummy, sparsely furnished apartment in Nashville that he rarely saw—he realized it wasn't much of a life.

When the silence lingered too long, she figured out the answer without him speaking. "There must be other bands you could join. I can't believe you have to keep playing for someone you clearly don't respect."

"There are other bands."

She lifted her hand as if the answer was simple. And maybe to her it did seem that way. To him, it meant starting over again—and for the first time since he stepped foot in

Nashville at sixteen, Glen wasn't sure his heart was in it anymore.

Problem with that feeling was...music was all he knew. He'd never had a job that didn't include a guitar. Which left him three paths—returning to Trent, finding a new gig, or leaving the music behind to do God only knew what.

The idea of leaving Nashville terrified him. He took no pleasure in admitting that to himself. He had too much damn pride and the fact that he was scared tweaked the fuck out of it. Left him feeling weak.

She reached out and took his hand. "I can see I've hit a nerve. That really wasn't my intention in bringing you out here."

Lorelie was offering him an out and he grabbed it with both hands. "What *was* your intention?"

"To seduce you."

Just like that, Glen's concerns about the future vanished as all the blood in his body rushed to his cock.

"Lori, darlin'."

"Yeah?"

"Seduce me."

She laughed softly, and then glanced over her shoulder at the backseat.

He answered her suggestive look. "Yeah. I like where you're going with that." Glen opened the passenger door and quickly walked around the front of the car to open hers. "Hop out."

She did as he said, smiling widely when he opened the back door. She owned a nice-sized Yukon. Lots of room for what he had in mind.

Lorelie climbed in and turned around, crooking her finger in invitation.

He followed her onto the backseat and shut the door.

Neither of them said a word. They knew what came next, knew what they wanted. So they took it.

Glen tugged her close, kissing her as if they'd been apart for years. Lorelie wrapped her hands around his neck, her fingers playing with his hair. He opened his mouth, their tongues touching, tasting.

He slid his hands along her arms, loving the way she shivered in response. Tugging at her shirt, he reached beneath the cotton until he found the soft skin of her waist. She sighed against his mouth.

Glen had kissed more than his fair share of women in his lifetime, but none of them held a candle to Lorelie. She didn't hold back, didn't hesitate or demur. There wasn't a drop of shyness in her. She wanted. She took.

She found the top button of his shirt and slipped it loose, then the next. And the next. Within seconds, his shirt was hanging open. Lorelie took advantage of the skin she'd bared, running her fingers along his chest, his pecs.

Her lips slid along his neck, sucking lightly.

Glen ran his fingers through her hair, tightening his grip on the soft, thick mass. "You're so fucking beautiful."

She lifted her head, her blue eyes finding his. "So are you."

He grinned, and then leaned closer. "You need glasses, Butterfly."

Lorelie moved quickly, catching him off guard as she pushed him back and straddled his hips. "My eyesight is just fine." She bent forward and initiated the next round of kisses.

Glen did his own exploring, beneath her shirt, stroking her back and toying with the clasp to her bra. He didn't typically hesitate, but he couldn't quite let go of what Lorelie had said in the bar. It had been a while for her. She was still trying to find her way back after a rough patch with her dad.

In the past, he hadn't been one to pull away, to refuse an

offer as tempting as what Lorelie was dangling in front of him. But something held him back, had him thinking that making out with Lorelie—and not taking it any further than that—would be perfect enough.

He left her bra in place. God willing, he'd find himself alone with her again, and then again. He'd get where he was aiming to go, but he wasn't going to rush her.

It was those damn gridiron guardians of hers. They were fucking with his head.

Lorelie *was* the type of woman a guy dated. Too special for a one-night stand. Glen had spent a lifetime of wham-bam. His lifestyle didn't afford him the opportunity for long-term relationships or even part-time affairs. And in truth, he didn't have the time here either. But he still wanted to do things differently with Lorelie.

Her lips found his earlobe and then his neck once more. His cock was hard enough to pound through concrete. Lorelie had discovered that fact for herself, given the way she was rocking her denim-clad pussy against his crotch. Too much more of that and he'd explode.

"God, Lori," he murmured, pulling his lips away from hers. "We need to stop, darlin', before we can't."

She looked like she wanted to fight him, so he placed another quick kiss on her lips.

"I mean it." He'd hoped his stern, no-nonsense tone would make an impact, but Lorelie wasn't that easy to maneuver.

"I don't want to stop."

"I'm going to be honest with you. I don't want to either. But we're going to. Let me take you out to dinner. We'll talk a bit, get to know each other better."

"Is this your standard operating procedure?"

He laughed. "Nah. I just want to spend more time with you."

"Why?"

Glen didn't hesitate. "Because I like you."

He thought his answer would prompt a smile, but Lorelie only looked more confused.

"You're not staying long."

He could hang out in Maris if he wanted to.

That realization came unbidden and took him by surprise. He wasn't living on anyone's timeline but his own.

"I can stay longer."

She smiled as if he'd given her the moon on a silver platter. "You can?"

"Yeah. I've got nothing but time on my hands right now. And I can't think of anywhere else I'd rather be."

"I'm glad. You still coming by the ranch tomorrow?"

"Wouldn't miss it. Looking forward to my personal rodeo."

Lorelie laughed. "Don't get too excited. I'm out of practice. I'll probably toss my rope and catch a bunch of air."

"Wouldn't mind taking a real tour of this ranch of yours too. Seeing what life is like here. Who knows? Might inspire a country song or two."

"Not sure you'll have time to write any more songs once you've covered all of Ruby's albums."

He kissed her again. He meant to keep the touch brief, soft, but that went to hell the second Lorelie opened her mouth and stole another taste. Her fingers still rested on his bare chest. What would he give to guide them farther south so she could touch the part of him that was really aching?

Glen pulled away and tried to shake some sense into himself. "You're making it really hard for me to be a gentleman here, Lori."

"What gave you the impression I wanted a gentleman?"

He decided it was time to give the woman a taste of her own medicine. So far he'd let her hold the reins, make the moves. That wasn't something that came natural to him. And it wasn't something he'd do for long.

Twisting, he tossed Lorelie to her back on the wide seat, caging her beneath him. He gave her a quick, hard kiss, and then held himself over her, forcing her to look him straight in the eye.

"I know exactly what you want. I pay attention. And I'm pretty sure I know some things you might like, but don't even know you want yet."

Lorelie's legs were parted. He had to force himself to hold his stern expression and not laugh when she wrapped her ankles around his waist, rubbing against him like a purring kitten.

"Not here, Butterfly. When I take you, it's going to be in a bed and we're going to have hours to do it right."

"Glen. It's been too long. I don't need fancy, trust me."

"Maybe you don't. But I do." He gave her a longer kiss, and then, much as it pained him, he sat up and opened the back door. For a second, he wasn't sure Lorelie was going to follow him. She lay there quietly looking at the roof of the car until her rapid breathing slowed.

Then, she sat up as well. "Figures," she muttered as she got out of the car.

"What does?"

"I'd manage to find a sexy singing cowboy with morals, principles. Patience."

He chuckled. "My patience is being seriously tested, believe me. And I'm going to have the mother of all blue balls tonight."

"Simple solution," she said in a sexy singsong voice.

"Soon." He glanced around at the dark, quiet night. "Hate the idea of you having to run me all the way back to the B&B, only to have to drive here again."

"You can drop me off at my house and take my car tonight. Then you can just bring it back when you come to visit tomorrow afternoon."

"You sure?"

She nodded.

"Okay. I like that better than thinking of you on the road alone this late."

Lorelie kissed him on the cheek. "I'd say you're doing a bang-up job being a gentleman."

"It's a whole new me."

"I like it, even if it does sort of piss me off."

They got back in the car, but this time, he climbed behind the driver's seat. When he pulled up in front of her house, Lorelie leaned over and kissed him. As their lips parted, he leaned his forehead against hers.

"Going to be hard driving away from you."

She cupped his cheek. "Going to be hard falling asleep tonight. You've sort of left me in a..." She paused, seeking a word, then she landed on, "State."

"Tell you what. I'll think about you while I'm dealing with *my* state, and you can think about me. Builds up the anticipation for next time."

"So long as that next time is tomorrow," she added.

"That was never in question."

He gave her another quick kiss before she climbed out of the car. He waited until she got into the house and then he put the car in drive and headed back to town.

Small town life had suddenly gotten a lot more interesting.

Chapter Four

TOBY

How long you planning to stay in Maris?

GLEN

Thought that was up to you

TOBY

You can come back now

GLEN

Hell no. Last night bad?

TOBY

Disaster

GLEN

Trent want me back?

TOBY (AFTER LONG SILENCE)

No

GLEN

Then I'm staying put

TOBY

Don't stay gone too long

GLEN

You're the one who told me to go away

TOBY

Regretting that

GLEN

He's your problem now

TOBY

I don't get paid enough for this shit

GLEN

Gotta go. Date with a beautiful cowgirl

TOBY

You're a heartless fucking bastard

GLEN

I love you too

L orelie glanced out the front kitchen window and sighed.

"Okay. What are we waiting for?" Dad asked from his seat at the table. They'd been snapping the green beans she was going to cook for dinner.

She turned around and gave him a confused look. "What?"

"You've looked out that window no less than fifteen times in the last five minutes. What's about to happen?"

"Oh." She hadn't meant to give herself away. She wasn't sure why she hadn't told her dad about Glen coming to visit. For some reason, she felt sort of nervous about the two of them meeting.

Well, they'd actually already met at the party in October,

but that had been little more than an introduction and hand-shake between strangers.

She wanted her dad to like Glen. And she wanted Glen to like Dad. Completely silly desires when she considered how short Glen's time in Maris was going to be. She had to keep reminding herself that this attraction between them was destined to be a short-term affair and nothing more. She was okay with that. Glen was helping her break free of the doldrums that had plagued her for too long.

"Do you remember Glen, Walt's friend from Nashville? He played the guitar at your party."

"That tall, nice-looking fella who couldn't keep his eyes off you?"

Sadie had alluded to the same thing. How had Lorelie missed all those stares?

She knew how. She'd been obsessed with watching over her father, making sure he didn't overdo it at the party.

"I don't know about that. Anyway, he's back in town for a longer visit. He was at Wade's dinner party the other night. I invited him for a tour of the ranch and Sunday dinner."

Dad studied her face with way too much interest. "Is that right?"

He'd masked his tone, making it difficult for her to figure out what the heck he meant with his casual question.

"He's never spent any time on a ranch, so he's curious to see how it works."

"Mmmhmm."

Lorelie narrowed her eyes. "What's that mean?"

"In twenty-eight years, you've never invited a man here for Sunday dinner."

"So?"

Dad grinned. "So I'm just wondering what that might mean."

"He's a musician, Dad. He tours with Trent Maxwell. The man is on the road most of the year. Which means he's only in Maris for a little while."

"Mmmhmm," her father repeated.

Lorelie rolled her eyes. "You're driving me mad."

Before they could continue the conversation, the crunch of tires on gravel sounded out front.

"He's here."

Lorelie started to walk outside to meet Glen, intent on leading him straight to the stable, putting off the dad/future lover—God please—meeting until later. Maybe the introduction would be easier with Joel, Oakley, and Sadie around.

She was almost to the kitchen door when her father caught her by the upper arm, gently halting her escape.

"Not so fast. I want to meet him." Dad glanced out the window. "Why is he driving your car?"

Lorelie had sort of hoped her dad wouldn't notice that detail. "His truck broke down. We drove back here from Cruisers together and then I let him borrow my Yukon, so he could get back to his room at the B&B. He didn't want me driving alone so late at night."

"I see." More of the elusive tone.

Lorelie huffed. "Dad," she started.

"Go open the door, Lori."

Glen's footsteps sounded on the porch. Lorelie took a deep breath as her father released her and she headed for the front door. Dad followed closely behind.

She opened the door at Glen's knock, and then he stepped inside at the invitation her father issued from behind her.

"Dad," Lorelie said, "you remember Glen Rodgers."

The men shook hands.

"Nice to see you again, Mr. Carr."

Dad shook his head. "No need to be so formal. Everyone around here just calls me Coach."

"Have to admit I feel like I know you. Walt thinks the world of you. Quoted you quite a bit when we used to tour together."

Dad was clearly pleased to hear that. "Nice to know my boys were listening."

Glen turned his attention to her. "You look pretty today, Lori."

She snuck a quick glance at her dad, wondering how he would react to Glen's nickname. No one had ever used that name for her except her father. As she expected, his gaze was on her face, probably waiting for her to correct Glen.

She didn't bother. It was too late now, and Glen would think she was nuts if she suddenly pretended to take offense again. Besides...she liked when he called her Lori. And Butter-fly. She was *really* fond of Butterfly.

Then Lorelie glanced down in the face of his compliment to study her attire. She was in faded blue jeans, a Maris Titans T-shirt, and dusty boots. Her hair was pulled back in a ponytail and she'd tossed a cowboy hat on as well. "Oh yeah," she teased. "I'm a regular rodeo queen."

"Lori says you're visiting for a few days before heading back out on tour."

Glen nodded slowly. "Yeah. That was the original plan." He looked at Lorelie. "Bertha is officially out of commission."

"Bertha?" her dad asked, as Lorelie smiled widely, not bothering to hide her delight.

"Oh yeah?" she asked.

"Walt called a local mechanic to come out to his place to take a look at it. Bertha is down for the count, so it looks like I'm going to be stuck in Maris for a couple weeks rather than days.

The mechanic has to order a part before he can get the truck up and running again."

"Wow. How will you survive without the bright lights of the big city?"

"I think you're glad I'm trapped. You've raised a cruel daughter, Coach."

Dad lifted one shoulder, enjoying their banter. "Well, I did my best, Glen. So you're a city boy?"

"Philly, born and raised."

"Your folks still live there?" Dad asked.

Glen hesitated. "I assume so. I haven't seen them in twenty-two years."

"Seriously?" Lorelie asked, doing the math. He hadn't seen his parents since he was sixteen?

Glen shrugged good-naturedly. "We weren't all blessed with great fathers, Butterfly."

Once again, she felt her father's gaze on her face and was left to wonder what he'd noticed this time. The lack of parents or the term of endearment. Glen wasn't trying to hide his interest in her at all. Not that she minded. It was just...foreign territory for her.

Dad was right. She'd never brought a guy home for Sunday dinner. Never dated anyone for longer than a few weeks after high school. And none of those relationships had involved much more than hanging out at Cruisers and occasionally hooking up.

Lorelie had always blamed the boys of fall for her lack of serious boyfriends, but she realized Glen had actually latched onto the real reason for her life of solitude. No man had ever measured up to her dad.

Oakley and Joel appeared at the door. Neither of them looked particularly overjoyed to see Glen.

"Hi, Glen," Oakley said, while Joel merely nodded his greeting.

Glen, as always, was more amused by their cold shoulder than offended. "Oakley, Joel, good to see you again."

Joel glanced at Coach. "We were just about to load the truck with the new fence posts. You want to ride out to the south pasture with us in about an hour to show us where we should start?"

Dad nodded then he glanced at Glen. "Lori tells me you're interested in learning about the ranch."

"Yeah. Curious to see what goes on around here."

"Sounds to me like you're about to have a little time on your hands. If you want a real up-close look at the lifestyle, maybe you'd like to try to live it."

"What did you have in mind?" Glen asked, his tone laced with what sounded like genuine interest.

"Me and the boys are starting a new project, building a new fencerow. Going to take us some time, as we have our regular chores to do as well. Strong backs are always welcome. Fancy playing ranch hand this week?"

"Me and Oak can handle the fence," Joel interjected. It appeared he hadn't given up hope that he could keep Glen away from Lorelie.

She was ready to rip Joel a new one when Glen piped up. "I'd like that a lot, Coach."

The idea of having Glen around all day, every day, sounded like heaven on earth, and if her dad wouldn't think she'd lost her mind, she'd hug him for suggesting it.

"Great," Dad said. "Then it's all settled. You can start first thing in the morning. By the way, we get rolling at five thirty."

Glen's eyes widened and Lorelie fought to hide her grin.

"A.M.?" he clarified.

Oakley chuckled, while Joel just shook his head.

"I think you're going to like working here, Glen." Dad started upstairs, looking back at Joel and Oakley. "Let me finish a couple things around here and then change into my work boots. I'll meet you boys by the barn in an hour. And, Lorelie, why don't you give Glen that tour so he's not lost tomorrow?"

Joel and Oakley left the house, clearly not excited about the new turn of events. She imagined Joel wouldn't make it twenty paces from the house before he'd texted all the guys to tell them about Glen's extended stay and new part-time job.

"You didn't have to say yes," she said, when they were alone again.

"I like the idea of playing ranch hand. Besides, your dad just handed me the perfect way to spend every single day with you."

He was right. Her father *had* done that.

Why had Dad done that?

She added that to the list of "what the hell's going on" items rattling around in her brain that she'd have to try to decipher at some point. "Thought we'd do the rodeo demo first. Though I warn you, it's going to be a far cry from what really happens. I'm ten years away from competing and I haven't tried this in ages."

He took her hand, the two of them walking to the stable together. "Sweetheart, I wasn't kidding about the city boy childhood. The fact that you can ride a horse at something faster than a ramble will impress the hell out of me."

"Oh, well, in that case, I hope you're ready to be amazed."

As they entered the stable, Lorelie led him to a stall near the back. Reaching into her back pocket, she handed Glen a carrot. "This is Penny."

"Penny?"

"Probably not a very original name. She has a shiny copper-colored coat. Reminded me of a new penny, so..."

"Suits her. She's yours?"

Lorelie nodded. "Yeah. She's my spoiled baby. She's a sucker for treats. Give her this and she'll love you for life."

Glen stroked the horse's head as she claimed the carrot, munching slowly and then butting her head playfully against his shoulder.

"You familiar with horses at all?"

Glen shook his head. "I've been on one a couple of times, but I'm not going to tell you why."

"Too late. You can't say something like that and not divulge all."

"We were shooting a music video."

"With Walt or Trent?"

"Trent," Glen said, never managing to conceal his disdain for the guy. "It was a ridiculous video. I'm sitting on top of this ancient horse with my guitar. Bass player is on one as well. The drummer was sitting on top of some mound of dirt, just behind us, while Trent is strutting and dancing around with three supermodels. I felt like a complete jackass."

"I'm pulling that up on YouTube the second we get back to the house."

Glen laughed and tugged on the end of her ponytail. "If you have any compassion in you, you'll forget that video exists and never go looking for it."

"Like you said to my dad, I'm a cruel woman."

"Damn. Now I'm really sorry I mentioned it."

Penny nudged Glen once more, obviously hoping for another carrot. Lorelie slipped another out of her pocket and handed it to him to feed her horse. Penny rubbed her nose against his chest when he teased her with it, holding it just out of reach for a second before giving it to her.

"She's a total flirt," Lorelie said.

"Just my luck," he said with a sigh.

"What do you mean?"

"Wrong girl is flirting with me."

Lorelie moved closer. "Feeling neglected?" She ran her hand along his chest, tempted to unbutton his shirt like she had the night before. The man was built, a wall of muscles. She'd always been a sucker for a six-pack. Lorelie attributed that appreciation to the abundance of eye candy in her neck of the woods. Between football players and cowboys and the hot Texas sun, she'd spent a lifetime spoiled by sexy, shirtless man-flesh shows.

She would put Glen's chest up there with the best of them, which was surprising considering he was neither an athlete nor a cowboy. She played with the top button of his shirt, ready to say to hell to the rodeo show, but Glen caught her hand and stopped her.

"You start that and I'm in trouble. I think your dad likes me. Hate to ruin that this early in the game by dragging you into one of these stalls and doing dirty, dirty things to you."

Lorelie's pussy clenched. "That's a chance I'm willing to take."

Glen laughed. "Yeah. I'm sure you would."

She frowned. "How many women have you had sex with?"

It was Glen's turn to sober up. "Where did that question come from?"

"I told you my number by the creek last fall. Four lovers."

"I'm not answering that question, Lori."

"Why not?"

He sighed. "For one, I didn't keep count, and for another, I'm not exactly proud of how many women there have been."

"Which proves the point I was hoping to make. It's just sex for you, right?"

Glen didn't answer.

"I'm not going to think less of you," she added, hoping he

wasn't misinterpreting her meaning. "It was always just sex for me too. I've never had a real boyfriend. I wasn't in love with the guys I took to bed."

"Okay," he answered slowly. He was obviously confused by where she was heading with this conversation. She was sort of sorry she had started it, but now that she'd gone this far, she figured she'd just take it to the end.

"Isn't this just about sex between us? I don't mean to sound callous or insensitive, but I'm a Maris girl, Glen, and you're only here for a week or two. Seems to me like you're wasting a lot of time wooing me. In case you couldn't tell, I'm sort of a sure thing here. I want you. You want *me*. I'm not expecting flowers or chocolates or love songs."

She thought perhaps her comments would set his mind at ease. Maybe it was the overprotectiveness of the guys working on him, making him feel guilty or something. However, rather than smile and take her up on her offer to get down to business, his expression darkened.

"It's not just sex."

His response caught her off guard. "What?"

"You're right, Lori. I *am* leaving in a couple weeks." He released a long, frustrated breath. "I can't tell you why you're different, but you are. Two weeks is the longest I've ever stayed anywhere at one time with the exception of Nashville. And even when I'm there, I'm always working nonstop. I've had way too many one-night stands because that's all there have ever been time for. I don't want to do that with you. I want to get to know you. I want to watch you ride your horse, go out on a date with you, eat Sunday dinner with your family and then, well...fuck it. I want the damn romance. I've never had that. And from the sounds of it, you haven't either."

Lorelie didn't have a clue how to respond. For the first time ever, the woman who was never at a loss for something to say couldn't form a single word if her life depended on it.

She stared at him, wondering if she'd ever heard anything more wonderful in her life. More romantic. More...just...God. If he put that to music, it would be the most beautiful love song in the world.

She'd started the conversation as much to convince herself as him that she could do this. Do casual. Start the affair with no expectations and end it the same way. He just made damn sure that would never happen.

"Freak you out?" he asked when the silence drifted on too long.

"No," she whispered.

He grinned, the look so affable and sweet, she had no choice but to return it.

"Because you look completely freaked out."

"I'm not freaked out." She wasn't. She was...what? "I'm sort of touched and amazed and..." He'd laid it all on the line for her, so didn't she owe him the same?

"And?" he prompted.

"Really happy. Everything you just said made me feel happier than I think I've ever been in my life. You should put all that in a song."

He grinned. "Might just do that. John Denver had 'Annie's Song'. I'll call mine 'Lori's Song'."

"I find it hard to believe you've never done romance before. Because you're really good at it."

"Pent up for thirty-eight years. Guess I finally found the right outlet."

She reached up on tiptoe to give him a kiss on the cheek. Then, because she was *that* girl and she could never resist a joke, she took them right out of romance and straight back to raunchy. "Yeah, well, speaking of pent up, I haven't had sex in well over a year, so while the sweet words are nice and all, I'm going to need you to dig deep to give me a little bit of that bad boy rock star action too."

"So noted. And not a problem. I'm fairly certain we can reach a compromise where we both get what we want...and need." He reached around her, cupping her ass to pull her against him. She felt his erection pressing against the denim of his jeans.

He released her too quickly for her tastes and turned back to Penny. Stroking the horse's nose once more, he said, "When do I get my rodeo?"

Lorelie sucked in a deep breath, hoping to clear some of the horniness away. It didn't help much.

As she issued instructions, Glen helped her saddle her horse. The man really didn't have a clue when it came to working on a ranch. Twice, she'd laughingly showed him what she meant when she'd used lingo he didn't understand.

Once the horse was ready, she held on to the reins as she explained what she was planning to do. "This is going to be the lamest demonstration of team roping ever. I asked Oakley to move one of our steers into the corral this morning. Typically, the steer is released from a chute and given a little bit of a head start. I'm lacking my heeler, so basically all I'm going to do is chase a steer who probably won't run all that fast and rope him. You're missing the second part, where the heeler ropes the legs. Unless *you* want to try that part, of course."

"I'll be fine...on the other side of the fence."

Lorelie tsked. "If you're going to be a ranch hand, you're going to have to give up this aversion to horses."

"Pretty sure I can do my duties in that truck we passed on the way over here just as easily."

Lorelie laughed and didn't tell him that—for the most part —he was right. "Go on out there and find yourself a spot."

Lorelie found her rope and made sure everything was adjusted correctly. So much of what she was doing was second nature to her, she couldn't imagine not knowing anything about horses. Despite his hesitance, she hoped Glen would give her the chance to teach him how to ride while he was here.

When she was ready to go, she led Penny out of the large stall and climbed onto her back. They entered the corral at a slow pace so that Lorelie could figure out her best approach. The steer wouldn't have too much time to build up speed once she and Penny started.

Checking her grip on her rope, she spurred Penny to run. The steer—startled by the approaching rider and horse—took off. Giving chase, Lorelie lifted her arm, swung the rope and released, delighted when it fell into place, perfectly wrapping the steer's horns.

Once secure, she leapt off the horse to release the rope and the steer ran to the far end of the corral. That was when she realized Glen was clapping and cheering for her. She climbed back onto Penny and rode over to where he stood by the fence.

"That was great."

She crooked her finger. "Come here."

His brows furrowed in confusion, but he climbed the fence anyway, jumping down into the corral.

"Hop on. I'll give you a ride back to the stable."

Glen laughed, but took the hand she proffered, straddling the horse behind her. His cock felt even harder and bigger than it had earlier.

A fact she didn't bother to ignore. "Liked that, did you?"

He wrapped his arms around her waist, a little on the high side, so his hands were just touching the underside of her breasts. If she had been sure her dad, Oakley, and Joel were out of sight, she would have encouraged him to cup her breasts.

That way they'd both benefit—he'd have a way to hold on and she'd have a way to get off.

But she had no idea where anyone else was at the moment. For all she knew, everyone was watching them. In fact, she'd bet twenty bucks that's exactly why her dad had gone upstairs. To stand at his bedroom window so he had a better view of the corral.

"You are one hell of a sexy cowgirl," he murmured in her ear as they rode back to the stable. "The way you ride and rope. Jesus. I'm not sure I've ever been this turned on."

She glanced over her shoulder at him. "You think those skills translate to the bedroom?" she teased.

"I fucking hope so."

They were still laughing when they entered the stable. Lorelie took the saddle off Penny. "I've got a surprise for you," she said when she was finished.

"I like surprises."

She led him to a ladder that led to the hayloft. Lorelie had had a one-track mind all morning as she waited for Glen to arrive. Given the fact that his current state matched hers perfectly, she was hoping to entice him to expand on the make-out session they'd started last night by the creek.

He climbed the ladder closely behind her. When they arrived at the top, he chuckled. "Hmmm, I wonder what you could possibly have in mind?"

There was a huge pile of hay against the back wall. She'd thrown a couple of thick, soft blankets on top of it. Next to the makeshift bed were two bottles of Bud Light icing down in a wine bucket.

"I noticed you weren't much of a wine drinker the other night at Walt's. Figured you might like beer more."

"You know, you're not too shabby when it comes to romance yourself, Ms. Carr."

She led him to the blankets and they sank down together. Glen twisted the top off one of the bottles and handed it to her before opening the other for himself.

Tapping the bottle against hers, he said, "To trying new things."

"To new things," she repeated as they both took a drink.

Glen glanced around the hayloft. "Surprisingly private up here."

It was why Lorelie had chosen the place for their quiet drink and hopefully more.

There was a railing at the edge made of wide planks. Given their distance from it and the fact they were sitting down, they were completely hidden from anyone below who might venture into the stable. Not that Lorelie was expecting visitors. Her dad, Oakley, and Joel should be heading out to the south pasture any minute and Sadie was working at Cruisers for a couple more hours. It was rare to be alone on the ranch, so Lorelie had learned to find quiet hiding places for the times she needed solitude.

The creek was one of those places. This hayloft, another.

They sipped their beers quietly for a few minutes before Glen put his back in the wine bucket. Lorelie followed suit.

And then he was there, kissing her. She'd never had anyone kiss her so passionately, so hungrily. Lorelie wondered if he could feel the same intense need in her kisses.

For a split second, she recalled that he was leaving in a couple weeks. And then, like always, she forced the thought away. She wasn't about to waste a single second of their time together worrying about that.

Ever since her dad's heart attack, she'd wallowed waist-deep in anxiety, constantly playing out every horrible ending to that story. She had lost months of her life consumed by the fear of what her future might hold. As such, she hadn't enjoyed or paid attention to the here and now. So much lost time.

Glen pressed her to her back on the blanket, leaning over her. She wasn't a short woman by any means, but Glen still made her feel almost delicate. His lips traveled from hers, along her neck, and he drew lines with his tongue on the sensitive skin there.

She'd been a bit chilly before, but between the blanket, the hay and Glen, she suddenly felt warm, feverish even.

Reaching down, Lorelie grasped the hem of her T-shirt and pulled it over her head. Glen had risen slightly, giving her room to move. Once she was in just her bra, he didn't seek to resume his kisses. Instead, he looked his fill. He ran just one finger along the top of her bra, tracing the line against her breasts. It kept moving until he reached her shoulder. When he was there, he slid the strap over, then repeated the action on the other side. He used both hands to draw down the cups of her cotton bra, baring her breast while leaving the thing hooked around her upper torso.

She didn't speak. Hell, she wasn't sure she was breathing, when he bent his head lower and sucked one turgid nipple into his mouth. Given the gentleness of his previous touches, she was surprised by the amount of pressure he applied. Sparks flashed along her spine and her pussy constricted, painfully empty.

While she'd adored Glen's comments about wanting this to be about something more than sex, her body was having a hard time agreeing with that.

Glen turned his head and applied the same pressure to the other nipple as she gripped his hair, tugging it to hold him close. She'd never had so much beautiful attention paid to her breasts. Glen sucked, kissed, licked, nipped, pinched and played with them like he had all the time in the world. She loved every minute of it, even though her body was demanding more. Way more.

After a hundred years, he lifted his head to look at her.

"Please take your shirt off," she said.

Glen didn't hesitate. He unbuttoned it, tossing his next to hers.

"Take your pants off," she added after the first request was granted so easily.

He chuckled. "Nope."

"You aren't a very nice man."

Glen gave her a quick kiss on the cheek. "I think you're going to regret those words when you see what comes next."

She didn't have time to question him—or even feel the need to—when he reached for the button on her jeans, slipping it free. She held her breath as he slid the zipper south and then she lifted her hips, so he could tug the jeans down.

Glen clearly wasn't the type to mess around, because the panties went with the denim. She was wearing her damn cowboy boots, but he wasn't deterred. He pulled one boot off, and then worked that leg of the jeans and panties off as well. She expected him to do the same to the other leg, so she was surprised when he moved back up, covering her with his body. He was shirtless, which gave her hands plenty to enjoy, but still wearing too many clothes below the waist to do her any good. Even though she was way more naked than dressed.

"Your turn?" she asked.

He shook his head. "Just you this time. I'm already going further than I'd intended, but it's too damn hard to keep my hands off you."

Glen began kissing her again, not bothering to acknowledge the parts of her he'd just undressed. Lorelie wrapped her ankles around his hips, dragging the half-on/half-off jeans along for the ride, and began to gyrate against his crotch. She hoped the action would stir Glen to, well, action.

It didn't work.

Then she ran her fingernails along the muscles of his bare back, digging in deeper than she normally would have, hoping that would get his attention. If anything, Glen's kisses became softer, calmer.

Lorelie was an impatient person on good days. This wasn't a good day, and the man was driving her out of her mind.

When her unsatisfied arousal reached fever pitch, she twisted her face away from him. "Glen, I—"

"You finished?" he asked, interrupting her before she could read him the riot act.

"Finished what? We haven't even started!"

Glen leaned up on his elbows, cupping her cheeks. His face was only inches above hers and she was confused by what she saw there. Amusement and...maybe frustration.

"Four lovers, you said."

Lorelie nodded, wondering where the hell that comment had come from.

"I understand now why you think those four were plenty. Did any of them ever make you come?"

"I had orgasms with them."

"That's not what I asked."

She knew that. And she knew exactly what he was alluding to. She'd had orgasms with her other lovers. Orgasms that wouldn't have happened without her doing everything in her power to help the situation along.

"I'm perfectly capable of taking care of my own needs," she said at last.

"Jesus. Add another thing to our agenda for the next two weeks. In addition to romance, I'm going to show you what it's like to go to bed with a man who knows what the fuck he's doing."

"You're being cocky again."

"Call me that after."

"After what?"

Glen didn't answer. Instead, he reached for his shirt. "First thing I need to do is get *you* out of the way."

She snorted. "Won't that defeat the purp—"

Her words died abruptly when Glen grasped both her hands and pulled them above her head. He used his shirt to bind them together. "I don't have anything to tie the shirt to, so you're on the honor system. Keep your hands up there. Don't lower them. At all. Understand?"

She nodded, while trying to discreetly test the cotton binding her. He may be a city boy, but damn if he didn't know how to tie a knot.

"It's gonna hold, darlin'. You can quit trying to break free."

"But I can't touch you this way."

"That's the point."

Lorelie had never considered herself sexually inexperienced until that moment. Everything with Glen felt foreign and exciting as fuck. She'd never considered bondage something she would find sexually stimulating, but the idea of being held captive by him was provoking tingles she had never felt before.

Glen slid lower, returning to her breasts. While he sucked on one nipple, he pinched the other. His touches were even rougher, stronger.

Lorelie's hips started the same rise and fall, almost of their own volition. She'd never experienced such painful need. Her pussy was throbbing, clenching tighter with each hard suck, each pinch.

"God, Glen," she gasped. "Please."

Several minutes passed before he gave in to her pleas. By then, her breathing was ragged, her chest rising and falling, her heart thumping louder than a bass drum.

When he touched her clit, her body jerked as if she'd been struck by lightning.

Jesus. One touch and she was poised to go off like a bottle rocket.

Glen's finger slid lower, swirling around the opening to her body. It probably felt like a Slip 'N Slide down there. She'd never been so wet in her life.

When he pressed that lone digit inside her, Lorelie felt the uncontrollable desire to cry. Not from pain or sadness, but with overpowering relief. He thrust the finger in and out several times before adding a second.

It had been too long. She hadn't even masturbated since her dad's heart attack. That fact was driven home as she marveled over how full she felt. He was only using two fingers.

Glen continued to work them inside her, setting an easy, gentle pace, giving her time to get accustomed to him. Or maybe he was trying to slow down the inevitable orgasm. She was so freaking close.

Lorelie had just opened her mouth to ask him to move faster, take her harder, when they heard voices in the stable below.

Both of them froze when they heard her dad talking to Oakley. "You got the truck loaded?"

"Yeah," Oakley responded.

Lorelie didn't move a muscle as she considered what would happen if Dad or Oakley climbed the ladder. She was lying almost completely naked in the hayloft, her hands tied above her head, and Glen had two fingers buried deep inside her.

If she weren't on the verge of panic, she'd laugh her ass off.

She'd been looking toward the railing—but her gaze flew to

Glen's face when he began thrusting his fingers inside her again.

Her eyes widened and she shook her head no. This time he was giving her *exactly* what she'd just been about to ask for. Instead of two fingers, he used three, and while his movements were quiet, they were deadly to her self-control. Her mouth flew open as she tried to suck in some much-needed air. Then she mouthed, "What are you doing?"

Glen, the gorgeous bastard, just winked at her. Then he stroked her clit with his thumb.

She closed her eyes tightly and bit her bottom lip so hard she thought she tasted blood. Her dad and Oakley were having some discussion about what tools they needed.

Jesus. She was going to come. Right here. Right now. With her dad no less that twenty-five feet below her.

She was going to kill Glen when this was over.

Maybe.

Glen continued to thrust his fingers inside her as he leaned closer, his face only an inch or so from her ear. "Do you have any idea how beautiful you are right now?" he whispered.

Shit. She'd been able to battle the orgasm on a physical level, but now he was adding emotional warfare to the game. She couldn't win.

She was going to come. And it wasn't going to be quiet.

Glen's thumb grazed her clit again and she jerked, everything inside her turned to static. Static and this screaming white noise that deafened her. Her body trembled and shook as the orgasm rumbled through her like a freight train.

It was so powerful it almost hurt. The world turned to black as she closed her eyes and gave in. It was lightning, thunder, crashing waves, and every other crazy description she'd ever heard used to describe a sensation that simply couldn't *be* put into words.

When she finally opened her eyes, she realized she'd lost time. Glen was sitting next to her on the blanket and the voices below were gone. In fact, she could just make out the sound of the old ranch truck in the distance.

Glen reached out and ran his fingers along her cheek, clueing her in to the wetness there. Was she crying? Why would she be crying?

She touched her own face and found his shirt gone. "You untied me."

He nodded, his expression one of almost wonder.

"What?" she said.

"We're in trouble, Lori."

She sat up quickly, pulling the blanket over her as she glanced behind him for her father. Had they been caught?

"What do you mean? Dad?"

Glen shook his head. "No. Nothing like that. They were gone before you came. They didn't hear a thing."

That surprised her. She really *had* lost track of time. Because she could've sworn Dad and Oakley had just been here a minute ago.

"Then what's the trouble?"

"Two weeks isn't going to be enough."

She smiled, even as his reminder of the time limit looming over their heads sent a sharp stab straight through her heart. She agreed with him, but old habits died hard. When Lorelie was stressed out, she turned to humor. "Most people decide that two hours with me is enough. Give it time."

He grinned, and she was relieved. When he reached out to brush a strand of hair away from her face, she pretended the tightness in her chest had nothing to do with this unfamiliar feeling. She'd seen this man a total of four times in her life. Four times.

It was too soon to attach any sort of name to what was

happening here. In truth, it was better if they didn't try to name it. So she sought for a way to change the subject.

"Glen. I take back what I said. You're not cocky. Or well, actually, you kind of are. But you have every right to be. That was amazing. I didn't... I never—"

"You're going to do it again for me. Because that was the most incredible thing I've ever seen. And next time, I'm going to be right there with you."

She pressed her legs together, shocked that he could make her feel so needy again after an almost brutal orgasm. "I swear to God, I think I heard my bones rattle when I came. I didn't realize orgasms could feel like that. Maybe we could set up some sort of same-time-next-year deal, because I'm going to need a hit of that at least every twelve months, and God knows the yahoos around here aren't capable enough."

"You think once a year is enough?" he asked.

It was on the tip of her tongue to say hell no. To tell him once a day wouldn't be enough, but they were already tiptoeing around an issue that was going to bite them in the ass.

She strengthened her resolve once more, merely shrugging rather than lying.

Live in the moment, Lorelie.

"So what next?" she asked, her gaze drifting lower. There was no denying Glen was still hard. He had to be hurting.

"I thought maybe we could finish the tour."

His answer surprised her.

"What about..." She pointed at his crotch.

Glen chuckled. "Quick trip to the bathroom and I'll fix that right up."

"Or I—"

"Don't finish that sentence, Butterfly."

"It's just—"

"I told you my reasons before. They still stand."

She sighed. "I'm sorry. I keep pushing."

He laughed. "Don't apologize. I assure you. This is uncharted territory for me too. Never wanted a woman as much as I want you. But I'm not willing to rush it."

Lorelie tugged her bra back in place, and then put her T-shirt on. Glen did the same and then he helped her pull her jeans back up so she could put her boot on.

"Do you want to see my garden?"

He nodded. "Yeah. I'd like that."

They climbed down the ladder and spent the next two hours holding hands as she showed him the ranch, pointing out all her best hide-and-seek spots as a child and the place where her beloved dog, Scooter, was buried underneath the cherry tree next to the house. She told him that her garden had actually been her mother's before she'd died, and that she was still planting the same vegetables and herbs. She showed him the kitchen and the small ranch manager's house, where Oakley, Joel, and now Sadie lived.

She gave him a quick tour of the building they called the barracks, as well as the history. The barracks had been built nearly fifty years earlier by Lorelie's great-grandfather. At that time, the ranch had been a larger operation, and as such, it had employed nearly a dozen ranch hands.

Her grandfather had sold a large tract of land to the state, so that they could build a road, and the need for extra hands dwindled.

Back when her dad was football coach, a lot of the boys on the team worked on the ranch, sort of an old-school version of off-season conditioning. Occasionally, they'd spend weekends in the barracks, something her dad called a team-building exercise, and they roasted hot dogs over the fire pit and talked about girls, family issues and occasionally game strategy. The Maris boys' version of Boy Scouts.

However, the place hadn't housed anyone in over a decade, so it was dusty and badly in need of a coat of paint. Regardless, Lorelie had always loved the place.

"One of these days, I'll come out here and fix it up."

"For you?"

There had been a time Lorelie had considered taking over the barracks and making it her own little house. That idea had been squelched after her dad's heart attack. The thought of leaving him in the big house alone now wasn't something she'd consider.

"No," she said. "I can't leave Dad alone."

Glen nodded, but she could see he didn't necessarily agree with that assessment. However, he didn't question her on it.

"I need to get dinner started. Still staying?"

"Hell yeah. Home-cooked meals are few and far between in my life."

"Did you bring your guitar?"

He tilted his head. "Are you going to think I'm crazy if I say yes?"

She shook her head. "No. I heard you tell Walt you never go anywhere without it."

"I swear the thing feels like an extra limb."

"I'm glad you've got it. Grab it from the Yukon and I'll let you serenade me while I cook."

Glen wrapped his arm around her shoulders as they walked back toward the main house. "You'll let me, huh?"

"Yep. And I'm warning you now, I have a long request list. Might take you a few hours, or days, to get through it."

"I like singing to you, Lori." He placed a quick kiss on the top of her head.

Two hours later, they were still in the kitchen. Lorelie had just pulled the roasted chicken out of the oven as Glen played her favorite Zac Brown song for her. For some reason, "Colder

Weather" had always seemed romantic to her...until Glen sang it. Now it just reminded her that he would never stay in Maris forever. No matter what happened between them, he would leave. She pushed that idea down into concrete in her brain and tried to force the stuff around it to dry.

He *would* leave.

"That's a nice song."

They both glanced over, surprised to find her dad standing in the doorway. "And dinner smells delicious, Lori."

She walked over, kissing Dad on the cheek. She didn't even consider her actions until her father gave her a pleased look. "That's a nice welcome, too."

God. What the hell was she doing? She loved her dad more than anything, but they weren't overly affectionate.

She tried to brush off her uncharacteristic behavior. "Oakley and Joel behind you?"

"Yeah. They stopped by the house to grab Sadie. I'll go wash up."

"Okay."

She started to turn around, but her dad grabbed her hand, tugging her a step closer so that he could place a quick kiss on her forehead. "Owed you one."

Lorelie laughed and rolled her eyes. "Dinner will be on the table in fifteen minutes."

Dad left the room with a chuckle, and Lorelie turned to find Glen watching them with an expression she couldn't even begin to read.

Before she could question him, Glen leaned back in his chair. "He's a great guy." She nodded, pleased by his words, until he added, "And I was right. It's not the football guys getting in your way."

Lorelie shrugged. She'd had a few months to consider Glen's comment about her dad being a tough act for another man to follow. And she'd found a way to come to peace with it. "There are a lot of good men in the world, Glen. My dad is one of them. But he's not the only one. So my bar is set higher. I'm not going to lower it and not going to apologize for what I want."

Glen stood and placed his guitar on the table. "I'm not asking you to do either one of those things. You deserve nothing but a man's very best."

He reached out to her and Lorelie stepped into his arms without a moment's hesitation. Her entire family would be here any minute, but she didn't care. After the intensity of their interlude in the hayloft, she was surprised by how this simple hug seemed to affect her just as strongly.

They broke apart at the sound of the front door opening, and Oakley, Sadie, and Joel's voices coming from the foyer. Dad followed them all into the kitchen.

As they gathered around the dining room table, talking and eating, Lorelie was aware of two things. One was how closely her dad was watching her and Glen. And the second was how much she liked having Glen with them. Even Joel and Oakley seemed hard-pressed to keep up their chilly treatment in the face of his sense of humor and tales of life on the road.

He was a really nice guy. A romantic.

And she was going to fall completely in love with him.

Shit.

Chapter Five

TOBY

Last night's concert was worse than
Saturday's.

Silence

TOBY

Glen? You there?

Silence

TOBY

Come on, man. Throw a dog a bone. Would
you consider apologizing to Trent?

Silence

TOBY

Glen?

Silence

TOBY

Fuck. Text me when you get this

Glen leaned against the truck and stared at the main house like a zombie. He'd arrived at the ranch when it was still dark this morning. Dark, in *his* mind, indicated night and sleeping, and his body had rejected being up at that ungodly hour until the third cup of strong, black coffee kicked in.

Now, as the sun was just beginning to set, he was fairly certain he'd never been in this much pain in his life. Merely getting up early had been a cakewalk to the physical anguish he was experiencing now. What kind of person chose to live in a place like this?

Mentally, Glen tried to figure out how many steps he would have to make to get from here to the house. Too many, he decided, as he continued to lean. He was fighting like the devil to make his stance appear casual. In truth, the truck was the only thing keeping him upright.

Coach walked back from the stable, where he'd gone to check on a few things, and slapped Glen on the shoulder. Glen fought not to wince. The older man had been right beside him all damn day. And while he hadn't done as much of the back-breaking work as Glen, he'd still done his fair share. Something Glen was certain Lorelie would not have approved of if she'd seen it.

"You did good work today, Glen. There might be city blood in your veins, but you've got the spirit of a rancher."

Glen could not disagree more. If this was what it meant to be a ranch hand, he'd stay on the road with Trent Asshole Maxwell until the day he died.

"Thanks," he said, "but I'm not so sure about that. I've played my guitar until my fingers bled and cramped and not felt as bad as this."

Coach laughed. "Hard work never killed anybody. It'll get easier."

Glen couldn't imagine that, but before he could contradict him, Lorelie appeared on the porch. Glen forced himself to stand up straighter.

Mercifully, she crossed the yard to them, granting him a few more minutes to figure out if he could get his legs moving again.

"You're back." She gave her dad a quick kiss on the cheek. "How did the post digging go?"

"A lot faster with this man's help." Coach was smiling at Glen. "Covered double the distance I'd hoped today."

Digging holes for fence posts was excruciating work. As much as Glen was worried about getting his legs to function again, he didn't even hope for the ability to lift his arms. That wasn't going to happen for days.

He'd been too busy this afternoon to reply to Toby's texts and now he couldn't even if he wanted to. Which he didn't. Apologize to Trent? The idea had pissed him off so much, he'd started digging holes faster. So fast that Oakley had teased him about making them look bad in front of Coach.

Even if Toby called and told him all was forgiven, playing the guitar was definitely out for a day or eight...or maybe forever.

Lorelie's attention turned to Glen, and she laughed. "Did you leave any dirt in the field?" She reached out to swipe her fingers along his cheek.

Glen shrugged, but the motion was cut short when it sent a sharp shooting pain straight down his arms. "I'm afraid some of this might still be manure from mucking out the stalls this morning and composting the crap."

Lorelie gave her dad a quizzical look. From the way Coach raised *his* shoulders, it was clear he was confused too.

"You mucked the stalls?" she asked.

He nodded. Joel and Oakley had been waiting for him as soon as he pulled into the driveway this morning, pitchfork in hand.

"I wondered who had done that. Joel, Oakley, and I take turns because composting is such a smelly job. I said I'd take care of it this week, since digging postholes is grueling work. I actually thought maybe Joel or Oak had forgotten…and I figured they were paying for it right about now."

Oh, someone was paying for it, Glen thought, but it wasn't Joel or Oakley. Yet. They'd been hazing the new guy, and, like a jackass, he'd fallen for it, not realizing what the day had in store.

And then, speak of the devils, they appeared.

"Hey, Lorelie," Joel said, confused at her hostile look, until she spoke.

"You had Glen muck out the stalls?"

Joel was a decent enough guy to look a little bit guilty. Oakley just grinned, clearly pleased with the gag.

"Glen said he wanted to learn how to be a ranch hand," Oakley explained. "We were just giving him an overview."

"All in one day?" Lorelie wasn't backing down. She was pissed. "Listen—"

Glen cut in before things got too bad. "It's okay, Lori."

She paused, mid-tirade, to look at him. "No. It's not."

Though it cost him a bit in terms of effort, Glen managed to reach out and grasp her hand. "It's a guy thing. We do the same thing to new bandmates when they first join. Make them carry the heaviest amps, do all the grunt work nobody else wants to. Takes them a few days, but eventually they figure it out and the initiation is over."

Coach chuckled. "Nice of you to be so forgiving. If I'd known you'd put in all that work before the fence building, I would have called a halt earlier. As it is," Coach looked at Joel and Oakley, "we're going to call this initiation over right now."

Oakley and Joel didn't look happy with that edict. No doubt they'd had more torture planned for tomorrow.

But Coach wasn't finished. "Tomorrow, Glen and I will start setting the posts, while you two finish digging."

"You're coming back tomorrow?" Lorelie asked him, sounding somewhat surprised.

Prior to her appearance, he'd been trying to figure out how to get out of working the rest of the week. Now his pride was involved. It was clear none of them expected him to return.

"Of course I am. I promised to help your dad build the fence."

It was worth every ounce of agony he was now suffering to see Lorelie's face light up.

"Besides," he added, not able to resist getting back a little of his own with the ranch hands, "I'm not about to throw away my chance at seeing you every day."

Her grin grew.

"I see," Coach muttered.

Damn. Glen had forgotten her dad was there, listening to him flirt. While he hadn't given Glen any indication that his interest in Lorelie bothered him, he couldn't help but wonder if maybe Coach felt the same way as the football players.

He dismissed the concern. If he did, why would he invite him to work on the ranch? Unless he was testing Glen the same way Joel and Oakley were.

"Well, I just took a big-ass chicken potpie out of the oven, so why don't you guys go get cleaned up?" Lorelie suggested.

As tempting as food sounded, Glen had officially reached the end of the line on strength. He wasn't even sure how he was going to manage to drive back to the B&B. He looked down at his dust-covered clothing. "Butterfly, I'm not sure anything short of a three-hour hot shower and burning these clothes is going to get me clean again. I'm afraid I'll have to pass on the food. I'll just drive back to town now."

It did funny things to Glen's stomach—things that had nothing to do with hunger—when Lorelie looked disappointed to hear he was leaving. It wasn't an expression he'd ever seen thrown his way. People didn't expect him to stay, so they weren't sorry to see him go. The idea that Lorelie didn't want him to leave stirred something inside him he'd never really felt before.

Regret.

Regret at the idea of walking away from her. Even for just a night.

"You know what," Coach said. "It seems silly for you to keep that room at the B&B when you're going to be working here all week. We put in long hours and the last thing you need is to tack a drive to town at the beginning and end of that. Why don't you go into town with Glen, Lori, and help him pack his stuff? You can stay in our guest room while you're in Maris."

Lorelie's face flashed pure delight, while Joel and Oakley exchanged a somewhat horrified glance. As for Glen, he didn't know what to think. He was sure sleeping under the same roof as Lorelie and her dad would be pure torture. At the same time, he wasn't gentleman enough to say no.

"That's real nice of you, Coach."

"What about the barracks?" Joel interjected. "I mean, we've got a building right on the property all set up for ranch hands. He can have the whole place to himself."

Coach shook his head. "The man's lookin' to get that inch of dust *off* him, Joel. Not sleep in more of it. That place is filthy, and you know it."

"We can clean it up," Oakley offered. "We'll start right now."

"No." Coach wasn't going to be swayed. "He's only here for a week. Doesn't make sense to do all that work for a few days when there's a perfectly nice room ready for company in the house."

Lorelie reacted before the ranch hands could offer any more reasons why Glen couldn't stay. "Let me go grab the keys to my Yukon. You guys go ahead and eat the potpie now while it's hot. I'll reheat a couple slices for Glen and me when we get back from town."

She darted back to the house and Glen envied her ability to move so quickly. As it was, he anticipated it would take him an hour or so to travel the twelve feet to her car.

"I'll see you in a little while," Coach said, heading in the direction Lorelie had just gone. "You guys coming?"

Joel and Oakley followed after a brief wave. Glen didn't doubt for a moment that they weren't finished fighting the good fight. That idea was sort of solidified when he watched Joel tug his cell phone out of his back pocket and start texting. Rallying the troops, he figured.

Glen grinned at the thought.

While the overprotectiveness of the men in her life annoyed the crap out of him, Glen couldn't help but be grateful that she had people who cared about her. He wasn't going to be here forever, and it set his mind at ease to know Joel and Oakley and Evan and Walt and all the rest would keep her safe.

When Lorelie reappeared, Glen pushed himself away from the truck with some effort and took that first excruciating step toward her car. Every muscle in his body rejected the movement. He'd stood still too long. Regardless, he ploddingly put one foot in front of the other, not wanting to lose face in front of her. He wasn't about to look like an invalid after her dad, Joel and Oakley bee-bopped into the house without so much as a limp.

Lorelie met him at the Yukon. She was standing by the driver's side door—thank God—and looking at him with concern. So much for hiding his pain.

"Ready?" she asked.

He nodded and gingerly settled into the passenger side. They made the ride into town in silence and Glen almost fell asleep.

He jerked when the car came to a stop, surprised to realize they were already at the B&B.

"I can grab my stuff if you want to wait in the car." There was no way he'd manage to climb the stairs to his room without groaning every step of the way.

Lorelie opened her door and hopped out. "That's okay. I'll help you pack."

"There's not that much to pack," he said when she stepped next to him on the sidewalk.

"Let me reword that. I'll pack while you get cleaned up."

They entered the B&B together and while she didn't say anything, he noticed Lorelie had slowed her pace considerably.

Once they were in his room, she walked straight to the bathroom, and he listened as she started the water. When she returned to the room, he was still standing just inside the doorway. Glen eyeballed the bed. What would he give to fall face down on the mattress and lay there for the next six years or so, dirt, manure and all?

Lorelie read his mind. "No. If you lay down now, you'll regret it in the morning. Best to work some of the kinks out. Plus there's the stink factor."

He chuckled wearily. He smelled like shit. Literally.

"I have to admit that's the first time a woman has said the

word *kinks* to me, and my mind didn't go straight to the gutter," he joked.

"Well, I'll have to work it into conversation later and see if I get a better response. Come on." She took his hand and led him to the bathroom. She'd run him a steaming hot bath and he realized she had the right idea. A bath and then a Rip Van Winkle sleep.

At least, that was what he thought until she reached for his shirt and began unbuttoning it. He was grateful for her help, because God knew he couldn't have gotten out of it himself. It stank of sweat and manure. He hadn't been kidding back at the ranch. He was burning the thing.

The problem was Lorelie wasn't intent on just stripping him out of his shirt. Her fingers started working on the button and zipper to his jeans.

He gripped her wrist. So far, he'd managed to keep his dick in his pants around her. Barely.

And tired as he was, his cock apparently hadn't gotten the message that his body was out of commission. While the contrary appendage appeared willing to give it the old college try, the rest of him had checked out.

"Lori, I—"

"I'm not going to jump on you, Glen. I know you're worn out. I just want to help ease some of the hurts."

His brow creased and she laughed.

"Not that hurt," she added. Then she shook off his grip—not that it was hard to do, he had zero strength left—and finished unfastening his jeans.

She worked the stiff denim and his boxers over his hips and down his legs. Then she put the lid down on the toilet and told him to sit while she tugged off his boots and finished divesting him of his clothing.

It was the first time in his life he'd been naked with a

woman without hope of having sex. Lorelie guided him to the bathtub, and he groaned in absolute pleasure as the hot water hit his fatigued muscles.

"Jesus Christ, that feels good," he muttered.

Lorelie tossed a folded towel on the floor next to the tub and sank to her knees. She reached for a bar of soap as he watched, fascinated.

"What are you doing?" he asked as she worked suds up on a washcloth.

"Washing you off."

Glen was thirty-eight years old and couldn't remember the last time anyone had ever taken care of him. Probably his mother when he was a little kid. He'd suffered through injuries, flu bugs and food poisoning on his own, laying alone in bed and dealing with whatever was wrong the best way he could until it passed.

He didn't resist when Lorelie ran the washcloth over his chest and along his arms. His whole body hurt, but that pain disappeared in the face of the amazement he was feeling.

"Lean forward," she instructed, and he moved without question as she ran the soapy cloth over his stiff back. She applied pressure to her scrubbing, so in addition to getting him clean, she was massaging the soreness out. It felt like heaven.

Moving toward the other end of the tub, she offered the same cleansing kneading to his feet, calves, and thighs. She hadn't ventured toward his waist/hip region, and it occurred to Glen, he hadn't even been thinking about that, about sex.

Here was the most beautiful woman he'd ever met, rubbing her hands all over his naked body, and sex hadn't even entered his mind. Instead, he was blown away by the idea that she was taking care of him.

Rising, Lorelie grabbed a cup from the sink, dipped it into the water and poured it over his head. She repeated the action several times before squeezing a dollop of shampoo into her palm and washing his hair.

Part of him wondered why he wasn't resisting. He wasn't helpless. In fact, the longer he sat in the tub, the stronger he felt. The stiffness was fading, along with the twinges, aches and pains.

"You don't have to do this, Lori," he said when she started to rinse the shampoo out of his hair. He slid down in the tub, submerging his head in the water to sluice out the rest. When he came up for air, she was still kneeling there.

"I like taking care of you."

"Just me?" Glen didn't have a clue where that question came from or why it mattered. It shouldn't make a damn bit of difference to him. But it did. If she was one of those natural-born caregivers, that was one thing. However, he wanted to be special to her. Liked thinking her gentle ministrations were just for him.

He was a jackass. And he was letting himself wander down a road he had no business taking.

"Never mind," he muttered.

"Yeah," she answered anyway. "Just you. This feels weird to me too, you know?"

Lorelie never minced words, but more than that, she was really good at reading his mind and finding the words to make him feel like less of a fool.

"Never given anyone a bath?"

She shook her head. "Not like this. Shortly after my dad's heart attack, he was bedridden. I gave him sponge baths, but that was just me running a warm rag over his arms and legs and face. This…"

She didn't finish her sentence. Maybe she couldn't find a word for it any more than he could.

"I like *this*," he admitted.

"So do I."

"You worked a miracle. I feel alive again. Don't tell your dad, but today nearly killed me."

She laughed. "I'm pretty sure he knows that. Actually, we all knew it. You really don't have to go back tomorrow if you don't want to."

He knew that. But he was going anyway. Initially, he'd been trying to impress Lorelie and her dad, to prove to the ranch hands and the football players that they were wrong about him. But now, it felt like he needed to prove something to himself.

"I'm going back."

His answer pleased her, which pleased *him*. More than he cared to admit.

Lorelie stood and grabbed a clean towel. Glen rose as well and took it from her. He was ready to take the reins back. Drying off, he worked quickly and efficiently, so that he could use the towel as a shield. His cock was rock hard and pretty much impossible to miss.

Not that Lorelie was trying at all. Her gaze left his face and traveled south, hanging out for a nice long time.

She licked her lips and he groaned, prompting her to glance at his face once more.

"Can you answer something for me, Butterfly?"

She nodded.

"How far is the guest room from your bedroom?"

Lorelie tried to look innocent but failed miserably. "They're right next door to each other."

"Fuck," he whispered as she giggled.

While he felt better than he had when they'd walked into this room, he was still physically wiped out. He wanted Lorelie with a need that was becoming painful, but there was no way he could do that passion justice in his present state.

With the towel wrapped securely around his waist, he only felt minimally better. It didn't do much to hide his erection.

"Let me throw some clothes on and then we can head back to the ranch."

Glen tried to step around Lorelie in the small room, but she didn't give way, remaining resolutely in his path. "There's no rush. There's something else I'd like to take care of first."

He knew what she meant. Lorelie had made no secret of her desire to have sex with him.

"Lori. I know it looks like I'm good to go, but—"

"Glen?"

"Yeah?"

"Just stand still."

Before he could respond, she jerked the towel loose and dropped it to the floor. And then she wrapped her hand around his cock.

He sucked in a deep gasp. "Lori, baby."

She stroked him from root to tip...and Glen reconsidered his previous assessment. Maybe he could find the strength after all. Lorelie stretched up on tiptoe, giving him a soft kiss on the cheek. He reached to catch her lips, to give her a longer, deeper kiss, but she moved too quickly.

One minute she stood in front of him, the next she was on her knees. Glen grasped her cheeks, forcing her gaze upwards.

"Lori, honey, you don't have to—"

"Not a question of having to. I want to. Now hush."

One of these days, Glen was going to find a way to hold on to the reins this cowgirl kept yanking out of his hands. He stroked his fingers through her hair, his eyes closing briefly when she sucked the tip of his cock into her mouth.

Jesus. She'd barely touched him, and he was already perilously close to blowing. He blamed it not just on tonight, but the last few times they'd been together, and every night he'd spent alone since the first time he'd met her. Her face was the last thing he saw every night when he closed his eyes, and he'd woken up too many times in the wee hours after midnight, hard and hurting and wanting her.

She took him deeper as she wrapped her hand tighter around the base of his dick. His fingers gripped her hair as he struggled to hang on.

Lorelie either didn't notice or care about the way he was pulling her hair or the instant, overwhelming effect she was having on him. She wasn't giving him an opportunity to steady himself, to catch his breath. Instead, she started sucking him harder, moving faster, gripping him tighter.

"Dammit," he muttered. "I'm not going to last long if you keep..." His words faded away when Lorelie used her free hand to grip his balls.

He sucked in some much-needed air, but it didn't help. She was too fucking good at this. When she giggled, the action vibrating along his hard cock, he realized he'd said those words aloud.

Glen decided it was pointless to wage a battle he wasn't going to win. Tightening his grip in her hair even more, he started thrusting toward her. Lorelie hummed her approval, so he gave in. Taking her the way he'd dreamed of every night since October.

Lorelie met him thrust for thrust and then put the final nail in the coffin when she dragged one fingertip between his ass cheeks and circled his anus.

"God. Dammit!" Glen tried to pull out of her mouth, but Lorelie followed him as his come erupted. And then, holy mother, she swallowed. Neither of them sought to separate as his dick softened. Lorelie simply held him there until the gray spots that blinded him began to fade.

Then he realized his fingers were still in her hair. He loosened his grip and pulled his hips away from her.

"I'm sorry, Lori. Did I hurt you?" he asked, rubbing her scalp.

She shook her head. "Not at all. That was hot."

He reached under her arms and helped her stand, tugging her into his embrace and holding her. Stroking her back, Glen tried to find the words to thank her for...well...every single thing she had done since they'd walked into this room.

Lorelie's arms were wrapped around his waist, and he realized he could spend the rest of his life standing here just like this, and never want for another thing.

He wasn't sure what the hell that meant, but he understood that he'd just taken a hard left...and his life was never going to be the same again.

Chapter Six

Lorelie stood on the front porch as afternoon gave way to evening and hugged her dad. He chuckled when she finally released him.

"I'm only going to be gone overnight, Lori," Dad said.

"I know that."

It would be the first time she'd spent a night away from her father since his heart attack. He and Joel were driving to Austin for a stock sale. They planned to put most of the driving behind them tonight, pull over at a hotel off the interstate when they got tired, and then drive the rest of the way early in the morning. Stock sale started at nine and her dad liked to get there early to check out the cattle.

"Besides, Joel will be doing most of the driving."

The only reason she was feeling partly okay with the trip was the fact Joel was going.

But currently Joel was glancing at Glen, who was standing next to her on the porch.

It had been one week—seven days exactly—since Glen had moved into the guest room. Oakley and Joel were warming up to him, but every now and then—like now—they'd revert to protector mode. Joel clearly wasn't happy about Lorelie and Glen spending the night alone together in the house. He'd even made a pretty strong case for why Glen should go with Coach instead of him, but her dad didn't bite.

The only person she didn't have to worry about accepting Glen was Dad, which surprised her. Dad had welcomed Glen with open arms from the beginning, and, while he'd done nothing overt, there was a tiny part of her that felt like Dad was even trying to push her and Glen together romantically. She usually dismissed that idea whenever it reared its head. Her dad had never taken an interest in her love life. Of course, she'd never had one worth paying much attention to before now.

"Okay—text when you stop at the hotel and let me know where you're staying," she said to Joel, who nodded even as he sighed.

"We've made this trip at least twenty times before, Lorelie. We know what we're doing."

"Fine. You guys better hit it, or it'll be midnight before you get to lay your heads down." She waved as they walked to the truck.

Her dad turned before climbing in. "Take care of my girl, Glen."

Glen smiled and gave Dad the thumbs-up. "Will do, Coach."

Joel frowned. "Oakley will be back soon."

If he meant his words as a threat, they missed the mark by a mile. Lorelie laughed, which clearly annoyed Joel even more. Regardless, the two men got in the truck, fired it up, and were on their way.

"What's so funny about Oakley?" Glen asked.

"He's closing Cruisers with Sadie tonight. He won't be back *soon*, and there's no way he'll be checking on us afterwards anyway. I have Sadie in my camp. She'll have him seduced out of his pants five minutes after they get back—and Joel knows it."

Glen gave her a look so sexy, she realized Oakley wasn't the only one in danger of being seduced. "If I'm not inside you in the next fifteen minutes, I'll explode."

Though she and Glen had found countless opportunities to mess around during the past week, they hadn't managed to seal the deal, so to speak.

For one thing, the stubborn asshole was insisting on a bed and romance. No matter how many times she dragged him to the hayloft, he wouldn't do more than some seriously heavy petting.

And then there was the issue of her dad. Glen said it would be extremely disrespectful to sleep with his boss's daughter while he was in the house. When she pointed out that Dad wasn't technically his boss, Glen made some very sweet speech about being grateful for the opportunity to work on the ranch and spend time with her and how there was no way he'd take advantage of her father's kindness.

It was a nice sentiment—that left her alone in her bed every night, and so freaking horny she'd wanted to scream. She'd considered throwing caution to the wind and sneaking over to his room just last night, but then she recalled the squeaky floorboards, and realized the mattress springs were bound to be just as squeaky. Despite how badly she was hurting, the idea of her father hearing any of that was too mortifying to consider.

But now...Dad was gone. The house was empty. They were alone. At last.

"Come on." She took Glen's hand and led him into the house and straight up the stairs. Lorelie hesitated briefly just inside the doorway to her room.

Glen placed his hand at the base of her spine. "Now you're having second thoughts?" There was no anger in his tone. In fact, she didn't doubt for a second if she said she was, he'd call a halt to the whole thing.

Lorelie shook her head. "No. No second thoughts."

"Maybe you should think harder." His words were said lightly, almost as a joke, but she could read the seriousness in his eyes.

Ever since he'd arrived, she had been the aggressor in their sexual exploits. She'd been the one constantly pushing for more, while he'd tried to put on the brakes, to give her space and romance and time and...

She bit her lower lip, trying to figure out why she was hesitating. "I want you. So badly."

"I don't want to hurt you, Lori."

And then she knew why. It was a little late to hope that Glen wouldn't hurt her. If he'd gone the one-night-stand route, maybe she would have had some hope of holding on to her heart.

Now...yeah. It was definitely too late.

Then she saw something in his expression that told her this wasn't a one-way street. "I don't want to hurt you either."

Lines formed in his forehead, as if he hadn't considered that. Hadn't realized that she wasn't the only one who was vulnerable.

"We're playing a game we can't win here."

She nodded. "I know that."

"I can't get up from the table and walk away."

Lorelie reached for the hem of her T-shirt and tugged it over her head. "Good."

Glen's gaze drifted to her breasts as he reached out to cup one. "Lori?"

"Yeah?"

"I'm going all-in. And I'm playing my wild card."

They'd turn the corner together. Whatever happened in the future was going to happen. None of that mattered right now. It couldn't.

Glen's hands slid to her back, and he unhooked her bra, pulling the lace off and dropping it to the floor with her shirt.

Lorelie went to work on his clothing while he freed her of her jeans. As far as finesse was concerned, neither of them bothered. They needed naked and they needed it now.

They'd both seen each other before, but once the clothes were gone, Glen took a step away, eating her up with his eyes. She followed suit. It was amazing what just one week of working on the ranch had done to Glen's body. Lorelie had thought he was built before, but now...

"Holy Moses."

He chuckled. "Ditto. You're fucking gorgeous, Butterfly."

She glanced across the room. "Bed?"

"In a minute."

Lorelie put her hands on her hips. "Glen..." she started.

He'd put her off for days. They were alone and the requisite bed he kept insisting on was right there. She wasn't about to wait much longer.

Before she could tell him that, he gripped her waist, pulling her against him. His erection brushed her stomach. "You gotta stop trying to run the show, Lori."

He'd said as much before. And he'd shown her what benefits came from trusting a lover to give her what she needed.

"I know. It's just—"

"We've got all night. We're both going to get exactly what we want. There's no need to rush things or force them."

"Okay," she whispered, resting her cheek against his chest. She could hear and feel his heart pounding, racing. It matched hers.

Glen's hands drifted lower, leaving her waist to stroke her ass. "I can't begin to list all the ways I want to take you."

She lifted her head to look at him. Her past experiences with sex were fairly tame and certainly nothing to write home about. "Tell me."

He shook his head. "No. I'm going to show you." He led her to the bed. She sank down on the edge of the mattress, slightly shocked when Glen knelt in front of her. He pressed her legs open. "Put your knees over my shoulders."

She moved into position, squeaking when Glen lost no time running his tongue along her slit.

"Oh my God."

Glen applied pressure to her clit until she squirmed, then he pushed two fingers into her.

Lorelie fell to her back, her fingers gripping the bedspread as he evoked the most incredible sensations. The best part was that he wasn't in a hurry. For several minutes, he focused solely on her, on provoking a nonstop litany of moans, groans and squeals.

"Glen, I..." She was going to come.

"Wait one second."

Wait? What? Um...hell no. He'd worked her up into a frenzy. There was no way she could hold on.

Then his fingers left her, and she cried out, calling him an asshole.

He grinned. "Speaking of..." He pressed the tip of one wet finger into her anus and her hips jerked roughly.

Now it was *her* turn to make the "wait" demand.

"Don't worry. Just a little bit more, and then..." His words faded as he pushed his finger in to the second knuckle. His tongue found her clit again before dropping lower to thrust inside her. He fucked her with it, the finger in her ass moving in and out slowly.

The sensations were foreign, overwhelming. Amazing.

She tightened her knees on his head, her ankles digging into his back to spur him on. God, she'd never been so demanding, so needy.

"I have to...I...God..."

Glen didn't stop, didn't ask or give permission. Instead, he pushed her onward, toward the point of no return until...

Lorelie cried out, her body trembling as she came. Glen slowed his motions but didn't stop until the storm had passed completely.

Her legs fell off his shoulders as if they weighed two tons. He rose, standing next to the bed. Lorelie let her gaze travel along his body leisurely, starting at his hungry eyes, working their way over his muscular chest and not stopping until she found what she really wanted.

She crooked her fingers, her legs sliding open. She was empty when she needed to be full.

Glen grasped his cock, stroking the hard flesh slowly.

"Glen," she whispered, her voice hoarse from her previous cries.

"Crawl up in the middle of the bed."

She moved into position as he watched.

"Don't move," he instructed as he turned to walk toward the door.

"Where are you—"

"Shh. Don't worry, darlin'. Just forgot to grab a condom." He bent over to pull his wallet from his pants before returning to the bed. "You're an impatient little thing."

"If you expect an apology, you're destined for disappointment. My current state is your fault. You and those romantic notions of yours."

His smile faded. "Damn. Thanks for the reminder."

She narrowed her eyes. "I swear to God, if you say we're stopping—"

"We're not. But we're missing some stuff." She pushed herself to a sitting position, watching as Glen closed the blinds, making the dim room even darker. It was dusk and the sun was already low in the sky. He lit the candle that sat on her dresser and then the one on her nightstand. Then he pressed his iPhone into the speakers on her bookshelf, tapping the screen until he found what he was looking for.

Glen was a musician. He lived for the song. So it didn't surprise her that he had the perfect music for the occasion. She was pretty sure there wasn't a girl in the world who didn't melt whenever a George Strait love song played.

"What do you think?" he asked as he returned to the bed.

"It's perfect." It really was. No one had ever taken such care to make her happy.

Glen climbed on the bed, not stopping until she was caged beneath him. Then he bent lower and kissed her. Whatever control he'd managed to maintain until that moment appeared to have vanished. He took her lips in a bruising kiss she felt all the way to her toes.

He ran his fingers through her hair, tugging it until she gasped, the sound swallowed by his mouth.

"Tell me if I hurt you," he murmured.

"You won't." She wanted the roughness. After a lifetime of lukewarm sex, she wanted the craving, the ravenousness. She wanted to indulge in her own need to leave a few marks on Glen. As such, she dug her nails into his shoulders. This time it was *his* turn to gasp.

"Wildcat, huh? I like that."

He kissed her again, his tongue stroking hers. She lost all concept of time as they touched and tasted, pinched and pulled.

By the time he rolled the condom on, she was on fire.

Glen paused when he placed the head of his cock at her opening, his gaze seeking hers.

Neither of them spoke as he pressed inside, but to Lorelie, it felt as if he'd sung her an entire song with just his eyes. Once he was seated to the hilt, he smiled, and she returned it.

"Finally," she whispered.

He released a quiet snort. "It's only been a week, Lori."

"Felt like forever."

"Forever," he whispered as he began to move inside her. His motions were slow and easy at first, but neither of them was satisfied with that for long.

Lorelie wrapped her ankles around his waist, lifting her hips to meet him thrust for thrust.

Glen kissed her again as they moved in unison. When Lorelie was close, he helped her along, rubbing her clit until she saw stars and came, screaming his name.

As her orgasm began to wane, she realized Glen was still inside, hard, moving slower.

"Ready for more?"

There was more? Damn. A girl could get used to this.

She nodded, and then scowled when Glen pulled out of her completely. "I think you need to look up the word *more* in the dictionary, then flip back to the word *less*."

Glen laughed. "Roll over, smartass."

"Oh," she said in delight, twisting until she was face down on the bed. Glen knelt behind her and lifted her hips until she was on all fours.

"Hey," she said loudly when he placed a slap on her bare ass.

"For your information, I know exactly what the word *more* means."

He proved it when he touched her. She was wet, hot and ready. She sighed with relief when he pushed his cock back inside her, shoving in hard and fast.

Within minutes, he had her right back at the brink of coming, but this time she wasn't alone. Glen's fingers tightened, gripping her hips roughly as he pulled her against him so fast, it took her breath away.

Lorelie went over a split second before him, her orgasm washing over her like a powerful waterfall. It pounded and pulsed so strongly, she thought she'd be swept away forever. Glen called out her name, making it sound like a prayer as he came as well.

Glen pulled away first, rising to dispose of the condom. When he returned to the bed, he wrapped her in his arms, her head resting against his chest once more.

"Think I could convince Oakley to let me skip work tomorrow?" he asked.

She lifted her head and grinned. "Technically, with my dad away, I'm the boss."

"In that case, can I have the day off?"

"Are you sick?" she joked.

He shook his head. "Nope. But I do intend to spend the entire day in bed."

She placed her head back on his chest. "A whole day in bed sounds like heaven."

"Yeah. We haven't even started to put a dent in that list of mine. We're going to need the time."

Lorelie giggled. "I like the sound of that too. Hungry?"

"Starving," Glen said as he kissed her.

"I meant for food," she said. "We missed dinner."

He lifted one shoulder. "Maybe later. Don't like the idea of you putting clothes on again. Besides, I haven't gotten my fill of you yet."

"Well," she said, wrapping her arms around his neck and tugging him closer. "I wouldn't want you to go hungry."

She meant her words as a joke, but when Glen rolled her to her back, she realized he wasn't kidding. "Seriously? That was like zero recovery time."

"What can I say? You inspire me."

"How many condoms are in that wallet?"

"Not enough. We might have to break into Joel and Oakley's cabin and steal from their stash."

Lorelie laughed. "Oh man. I love that idea."

"Something tells me you plan to confess to the crime."

"Of course I do. As far as I'm concerned, they still owe you for that hazing."

"Agreed. But we're covered for this round. And the next one."

Lorelie kissed his chin, then let her lips travel down to his neck.

"I love your mouth on me," he whispered. "And your hands."

His words encouraged her to add to her explorations. She

grasped his cock, stroking it slowly, enjoying his quiet groan. When it became too much for him, he pulled her hand away and slid lower, sucking one of her nipples into his mouth.

Lorelie ran her fingers through his hair and sighed. "One day in bed isn't going to be enough. God, a year wouldn't be enough for this."

She hadn't meant to speak those words aloud. One thing they appeared to have reached a tacit agreement on in this past week was that they didn't talk about the future, about Glen's imminent return to Nashville.

He lifted his head and looked at her, his expression too serious.

Great job, Lorelie. Way to kill the moment.

"You're right," he said. "It *won't* be enough."

Glen looked like he wanted to say more, but Lorelie was too afraid to hear it. So she shoved on his shoulder, pushing him to his back as she straddled his hips. His cock was nestled between her legs, and she began to rub against it.

"We better get that condom, Butterfly."

She twisted to find the wallet he'd tossed at the foot of the bed. Pulling one out, she slid the condom on him, and then lifted her hips. She sank down, her slow pace driving both of them crazy.

Once he was fully seated, she placed her hands on his chest and savored the moment. It was as if Glen was made just for her, their bodies fitting together perfectly.

"Ride me, cowgirl," he urged in a deep, sexy voice that had her pussy clenching. Lifting her hips, she didn't have the patience to keep the pace gentle. When she pushed downward again, she took him exactly the way she wanted. She wasn't satisfied with a canter. She wanted a gallop.

Glen gripped her waist tightly, helping to drive her thrusts, until both of them were sweating, gasping, so fucking close.

"Glen," she said, letting him know she was there.

"Give in, Butterfly. I'm there too."

The beloved nickname did the trick. Lorelie cried out as she came, then she cried out in surprise when Glen flipped her to her back and thrust inside her three, four, five more times, before succumbing to his own climax.

"Jesus," he muttered, dropping to his elbows above her. Though they were both out of breath, he kissed her thoroughly before withdrawing. He fell to his back, his chest rising and falling rapidly. Tugging off the condom, he tossed it into the trash can near her bed.

"Doing okay over there?" she asked after several quiet minutes.

"I'm not sure."

She rolled over to face him, concerned. "Is something wrong?"

He looked at her. "Physically, no. But I'm starting to understand why I stayed away from romance."

"Yeah," she said quietly. "Me too."

"We're fucked, aren't we?"

She nodded. "Afraid so."

"Not stopping, are we?"

"Hell no."

He ran his knuckles along her cheek as if she was the most beautiful thing he'd ever seen. "All-in," he murmured as his eyes drifted shut.

She kissed him on the cheek, and then closed her own eyes, exhaustion coming to take her despite all the shit whirling around in her head. As long as he was here, it was easy to pretend they weren't both headed for heartache.

Mercifully, sleep took her quickly.

* * *

Lorelie cleared the table as Glen leaned back in his chair and sighed.

"Pretty sure I've put on ten pounds in the last week. Damn, I love your cooking."

She rolled her eyes. "There's no way you've gained an ounce, considering all the work you've been doing around here. If anything, you've probably lost weight."

"I don't know. They say muscle is heavier than fat. I've been getting one hell of a workout. Actually..." He lifted his shirt. "What do you think?"

She thought he was ripped, a six-pack sex god. "Are you trying to tempt me?"

"Is it working?"

It was *so* working, but one of them had to be the voice of reason. And for the first time in her life, it looked like it was going to be her. Which sucked. "My dad is going to be home any minute."

Glen lowered his shirt reluctantly. "Yeah. Good point. Dammit."

They'd spent last night and all day in bed, only rolling out a couple of times in search of food, more condoms—which they did indeed steal from the ranch hands' stash—and then once more for a long, hot, sexy shower.

Oakley hadn't been too pleased when she'd called to see if he'd take care of mucking out the stalls this morning. And he'd been even less happy when she'd informed him she was taking the whole day off and he'd have to fend for himself for meals. It wasn't unheard of for Joel, Oakley, and Sadie to make their own food in their cabin occasionally, but given Sadie's disdain for cooking, more often than not, Lorelie was the one who kept everyone fed on the ranch.

Glen stood up and fiddled with the radio as she rinsed off the plates. "Hey. Here's a good one. Dance with me, Lori."

She dried her hands on a towel. "Alan Jackson?"

Glen nodded and started singing along to "Livin' on Love". She loved his voice. When he grasped her hand and spun her toward him, she laughed.

"You know, you're a pretty good dancer," she said as he twirled her around the kitchen. "Seems like you wouldn't get much practice since you're always in the band."

"I can't listen to music without wanting to move."

Neither of them said anything else as they danced to the quick beat. When that song ended and a slower one started, Glen tugged her closer. Rather than spinning, they swayed. He pressed his cheek against the top of her head as she tightened her arms around his waist.

It was a sad song, something about Trisha Yearwood lying to the moon, but Lorelie refused to hear the words. She would have plenty of time to be sad after Glen was gone.

Apparently his thoughts were running along the same lines, the lyrics striking a chord with him, about how he was going to leave her eventually. He leaned away and cupped her cheek. Her gaze met his. "Lori—"

She shook her head. "No regrets. Ever."

Glen pressed his forehead to hers and closed his eyes. "Ever."

She tipped her face up until her lips touched his. He kissed her softly, but with the same passion she always felt from him.

She was in love with him. And she was pretty sure he felt the same, but neither one of them would speak the words. How could they?

It was too soon. And it was going to be over any day.

"That's a pretty song."

They broke away at the sound of her dad's voice in the doorway. Lorelie wasn't sure how long he'd been there, but from the look on his face, she'd say long enough.

Lorelie cleared her throat, struggling to find something to say.

Glen was quicker on his feet than she was. "How was the trip?"

"Uneventful," Dad said. "Looks like it was more interesting here."

"Coach—" Glen started.

"No, no." Dad lifted his hand to wave off whatever Glen might say. "I don't mean that in a bad way." He looked at Lorelie and smiled. "Glad to see you've learned how to dance without standing on a man's feet."

Lorelie laughed. As always, Dad knew just what to say to break the tension. "I was seven years old the last time I did that."

"You can thank me and my broken toes for those dancing skills of hers," her dad told Glen. "You'll have to come to the Valentine's Dance with us at the community center this weekend, Glen."

"I'd like that." Glen looked at her. "I didn't know there was a dance."

"Slipped my mind," she lied. Lorelie hadn't mentioned the dance on purpose, hadn't let herself hope that he'd still be here by then. His truck was fixed. And while Toby hadn't contacted him about returning to Nashville, that didn't mean Glen couldn't decide to move on. He wasn't stuck in Maris. She desperately wanted him to stay, but she wasn't sure she had the right to ask him.

"Save all your dances for me," Glen said.

She smiled. "I'll do my best, but I'm a pretty good dancer, and—at the risk of tooting my own horn—very popular."

He tugged her hair playfully. "Is that right? Did I mention I'm a famous musician?"

"Famous?"

Glen laughed. "Don't have to worry about my ego around you, do I? Fine. I'm not famous. But I *am* able to pay my own bills, with enough leftover at the end of every month to buy a pretty girl flowers if the spirit moves me."

"Just flowers?"

"Your daughter is a mercenary, Coach."

Her dad laughed. "Naw. Truth is, she's not the type you can sway with presents. Never was. She gets that from her mother."

"I see." Glen looked at her father. "Got any advice for the poor sap trying to win her affections?"

Dad tilted his head. "Looks to me like you're doing just fine." Then he ran his hand along his jaw. "If y'all will excuse me, I'm going to turn in early. Want a hot shower, a shave, and my bed."

Lorelie crossed the room to give him a quick kiss on the cheek. "Night. I'm glad you're home. I missed you."

Her dad winked at her. "I missed you too, Lori. Night, Glen. See you bright and early tomorrow. That fence isn't going to build itself, and according to Oakley, not much work got done today."

Lorelie fought hard not to flush and decided she was going to kill Oakley very slowly and painfully. "Dad—"

"Nothing wrong with taking a day off, but tomorrow we're back at it. Agreed?"

"Agreed," Glen answered quickly. "We'll make up for the lost time."

Dad smiled, which sort of set Lorelie's mind at ease. Although she still planned to read Oakley the riot act for ratting them out.

Her father left the room, his footsteps heavy on the staircase.

Lorelie turned to face Glen and was surprised to find he'd

moved closer. Reaching out, he took her hands in his and tugged her close, placing a soft kiss on her head.

"Going to miss sleeping next to you tonight," he murmured.

She nodded. "Yeah. Me too. But my dad spent too many years working with teenaged boys. I don't doubt for a minute he's upstairs setting his alarm for a middle-of-the-night bed check. He used to do the same when the players stayed here during the summer, out in the barracks. He must've walked across that yard a thousand times, making sure everyone was where they were supposed to be and not doing anything they shouldn't."

Glen chuckled. "Gotta admit the concept is a new one for me. I might be thirty-eight years old, but I'm feeling a little bit like a teenager myself right now."

He had a point. They were adults. But her decision not to share his bed tonight had nothing to do with age and more to do with respect. "Glen—" she started.

"No, Lori. That wasn't a complaint. Your father is a good man, and this is his home. We're just going to have to be creative."

She laughed. "Creative sounds fun. How about right now?"

"What did you have in mind?"

"I really need to check on Penny."

Glen grasped her hand. "So you're suggesting a roll in the hay? Literally?"

"Literally."

Chapter Seven

TOBY

It's time

GLEN

What?

TOBY

Band is playing in Houston tomorrow night.
Meet us there. Hop back on the tour

GLEN

Trent okay with that? I'm not coming back if
he plans to start a fight

TOBY

He's cool. It was even his idea

Silence

TOBY

Glen? You there?

GLEN

Yeah. I'll text tomorrow morning. Let you
know my plans

"Just a few more steps."

Glen felt like an idiot with Lorelie's scarf covering his eyes as he walked across the yard. He hoped Oakley and Joel weren't watching or they'd give him shit for it. He'd spent the better part of the morning working in the stable with the other guys. They were all quitting early today in order to get ready for the Valentine's Dance tonight. Lorelie must've been watching the clock, because she showed up just as they were calling it a day.

It didn't help that she'd found him seconds after that text from Toby.

Sunday. Tomorrow.

Glen didn't have a clue how to tell Lorelie. And he hadn't had a chance before she covered his eyes, grabbed his hand and started leading him from the stable to God only knew where.

"Three steps up here," she warned him.

He took them with care, trusting that she wouldn't let him walk into anything or fall. "What's going on, Lori?"

"You'll see. We're almost there."

He heard a door open and then he could tell they'd walked inside something. They hadn't traveled far enough for him to be in the main house, plus she'd gone the wrong direction.

Glen didn't have to wonder for long as she tugged the blindfold free. He blinked a few times to clear his vision and tried to figure out what he was looking at.

"The barracks?"

She'd brought him here before as part of his initial tour. The place looked a hell of a lot different *now* than it had then.

She nodded. "Yeah. What do you think?"

He wasn't sure what answer she was looking for. So he tried to buy himself some time as he glanced around. When he'd first seen the place, it had been covered in a thick layer of dust and there was furniture and boxes and all kinds of stuff stored willy-nilly in every room. It had looked more like an attic than a cabin. Now, the kitchen and living area were spotless and decorated in a style that was downright homey. "It looks great."

"Come look at this." She led him to the first door on the right. When she opened it, he saw that the bedroom was as inviting as the other two rooms.

"You did all this?"

"Me and Sadie. While you guys were out working on the fence this week. I was thinking that if you ever wanted to come back to Maris, you might like knowing there was a place for you to stay here on the ranch."

She'd fixed up the cabin for him?

Glen wasn't sure what to say. He'd never really had a place he considered home. He had an apartment in Nashville that provided a functional living space and nothing more. The walls were bare, and the cupboards didn't hold much either—couple plates, cups and bowls. He ordered in or ate out ninety-nine percent of the time, so he didn't even own a pan.

"You did this for *me*?"

"Yeah."

Glen swallowed heavily, trying to work down the lump that had formed in his throat. Rather than let her see how much her kindness affected him, he meandered around the room, looking at everything she'd done. All the extra touches she had added to make the place special.

Lorelie had hung framed photographs of the ranch and there were knickknacks on the dresser, the kind of stuff women always scattered around that made a place look lived in: candles, a small painted wooden box, a few books.

"Is that quilt on the bed handmade?" he asked once he found his voice again.

"Yes. My grandmother was a big quilter. Quite a few of the beds on the ranch are wearing her work." Her voice was laced with pride as she talked about what the pattern on Glen's quilt represented. He hadn't realized there was a meaning to quilts, until she explained the one she'd put on his bed was a Jacob's Ladder pattern, and that it had been used as a signal by the Underground Railroad.

"It's really beautiful. The whole place is," he said, trying to remember if anyone had ever given him such a thoughtful gift.

She grinned. "Well, I wouldn't go that far. Apart from this room, the bathroom and the front rooms, the rest of the place is a disaster. Don't open any doors that are still closed."

He stepped closer, tugging her toward him for a hug. "I'm serious, Lori. This was..." He struggled for a word powerful enough, but nothing fit. Finally, he just added, "Really sweet of you," which didn't begin to touch what he felt.

She returned his embrace, her cheek resting on his chest. "I'd like to pretend I did it all for you, but this is really me being selfish. I've been trying to figure out some way I could entice you to come back and see me sometimes."

"I was going to do that anyway—without all this. I mean, if you want me to."

Lorelie released her grip to look at him. "If I want you to? Of *course* I want you to come back. Hell, I don't want—"

She closed her mouth quickly. He didn't have to hear the words to know where she was heading. Both of them had been very careful about not showing too much of their hand since the night they'd danced in the kitchen. They had started playing their cards close to their chests. Self-preservation, he figured.

If he hadn't gotten that fucking text earlier, he probably

would have tossed his hand face up on the table and told her everything he felt, future be damned. But now, he didn't know what to do. Was it fair to tell her when the clock was ticking? Less than twenty-four hours left before he'd have to pack up and get on the road.

Then he realized he wanted to give her something back after what she'd just given him.

"I don't want to leave either, Butterfly."

"Well," she said, "we don't need to worry about that right now. Tonight, we're going to dance our asses off and drink shots until we sing too loud, talk too much and laugh too hard. Then we're going to come back here and do scandalous things to each other on my grandma's quilt."

He chuckled. "Is that your plan for Valentine's Day?"

"Did you have something more romantic in mind?"

He shook his head. "Nothing that would top that."

Lorelie laughed. "Nothing *could* top that. Sort of wish we had time for a little pregaming," she said as she glanced at the bed, "but my dad loves this dance, and he'll be chomping at the bit if we're not ready to go on time."

They left the barracks together, heading back toward the main house. Glen didn't tell her about the text. There would be time for that conversation in the morning. Tonight, he wanted exactly what she'd just described.

One last night in heaven.

And then...he was back to hell.

* * *

Glen grabbed a chair at the table where Coach sat alone, grateful for the chance to escape the dance floor. He'd been teasing when he asked Lorelie to save all her dances for him, but apparently, she'd taken the request seriously. They'd arrived at the community center with her dad nearly two hours earlier, and since then, Lorelie and her friends had surrounded him, laughing and dancing in a huge pack in the center of the floor.

"Taking a break?" Coach asked.

He nodded. "I'm not a fan of line dances. Figure the point of dancing is to have a pretty girl to hold on to. Stuff like this defeats that purpose."

Coach chuckled. "Can't fault your reasoning there." The two of them watched Lorelie with a bunch of her girlfriends doing the Cupid Shuffle. Her cheeks were flushed, and she'd pulled her long hair up in a ponytail about half an hour earlier, when the room got too hot. She was grinning widely and leading the ones who struggled to hit the right steps.

She had taken his breath away when she'd come downstairs earlier after getting ready for the dance. For the first time since he'd met her, she had put the jeans away and donned a dress. It was a red sheath thing with a scoop neck that was sexy without pushing the limits.

The skirt part hit her mid-thigh. On a shorter woman, it would have reached lower, but with Lorelie's height, it gave him a better view of her trim legs. Legs he hadn't been able to stop thinking about wrapping around his waist later tonight as he slid inside her.

Best part was, she'd traded her cowboy boots for heels. The added inches put her lips closer to his, a bonus he'd been taking advantage of all night, sneaking kisses as often as he could.

"So what's the plan, Glen?"

Glen glanced back at Coach, confused. "Plan?"

Coach nodded, his smile fading, his eyes concerned. "This is the part where I ask you what your intentions are toward my daughter."

"Oh."

Shit.

Glen had been trying to figure that out himself. Toby's "come back now" edict this morning had thrown him for a loop.

"Yeah," Coach said, when Glen failed to reply. Glen figured he was gaping like a fish out of water. "That's what I thought. Don't have a clue, do you?"

Glen shook his head. "I didn't expect this."

"'This'?"

To fall in love.

That was the true response, but Glen hadn't even told Lorelie yet, so how could he confess to her dad?

"I'm a musician, Coach. It's all I've ever known. All that I'm good at. It's my life."

Coach sighed. "That's an excuse, Glen. Not an answer. People aren't so one-sided. You're actually a pretty fair ranch hand. I know it was tough for you at first, but you stuck it out and now...you're good at it. You're a hard worker, and I suspect there's not much you *can't* do if you put your mind to it."

"Thanks, Coach. That really means a lot." The compliment coming from Coach meant way more to Glen than hundreds of screaming fans cheering for him during his guitar solos. Which took him aback for a second. He wasn't used to wanting someone's approval. But he respected Coach, wanted to make him proud.

What the fuck was he supposed to do with that?

Glen had hated working on the ranch at first, but as he spent more time out in the field with the guys, building things, tending to the animals, the more he'd come to love it. The pace of life in Maris was the exact opposite of life on the road.

When he was touring, he was in constant motion, always rushing from one place to the next without ever stopping to take a look around. They'd roll into town, play, party backstage, then hop on the bus and head off to the next city. He was never still. Never quiet.

And while working on the ranch kept him busy, it was slower somehow. For two weeks, he'd worked out in the south pasture, building a fence, his hands in constant motion. But along the way, he had time to take in his surroundings, to appreciate everything around him. He had watched the sun rise and set on the horizon. He had noticed how many different vivid colors Mother Nature produced. He began to recognize distinct birdcalls, for God's sake.

He'd even spent one night with Coach, Oakley, and Joel, sitting in lawn chairs in the middle of a field, drinking PBR and waiting for the groundhog that was digging holes to emerge. Coach had been waiting for the little bastard with a shotgun across his lap, ready to take care of the vermin who'd dug the hole that caused a cow to break its leg. They hadn't managed to kill the thing, and Glen was pretty sure the shotgun blasts had created as many craters as the groundhog, but they'd laughed their asses off, telling tales and just...being.

"So you're going back?" Coach asked, calling him out and asking him point-blank the question Glen was struggling with.

"I don't have any choice. It's my job."

"Son, you always have choices in life. Always."

Glen heard the sentiment and he appreciated it.

Unfortunately, he got hung up on the word *son*—and how much he liked hearing it.

"I've only been here two weeks. That's hardly enough time to make any life-altering decisions."

"Lori says you don't like working with this Trent guy."

"I don't."

"You like it here, Glen? You like Maris?"

Glen didn't hesitate. He nodded. "I didn't expect to. There

are still some parts of small-town life that feel kind of foreign to me. But yeah. This is a good place with nice people."

"If you take a break from touring, would you forget how to play the guitar?"

He chuckled and shook his head at Coach's teasing question. "No. I'm pretty sure I'll keep hold of those skills 'til the day I die."

"Playing in that band pay pretty good?"

Glen nodded. "Yeah." He'd been around Coach long enough to know that these questions weren't the man's way of prying. He was building up to something, making a case. And Glen was starting to figure out what it was.

"You save some of that money, or spend it all?"

"I've got plenty of money in the bank, Coach."

"Enough that you could afford to extend this vacation."

"Yes, sir."

"You love my daughter?"

Glen couldn't deny it. Hell, he didn't want to. "So much it hurts."

"Sounds to me like you *already* made a life-altering decision. In just two weeks."

Coach's words hit him like a two-by-four between the eyes.

He was right. Glen's life had already been tossed on its ear. And no matter *what* he did next, his life was going to change.

Glen tried to wrap his mind around that fact. He'd been living on borrowed time. Time that had run out this morning. Lorelie had given him a way to return. She'd fixed up the barracks and issued the invitation. He could potentially have his cake and eat it too. Return to the tour and come back here in between concerts and recording sessions. Walt was doing that. Was making it work.

He dismissed the idea instantly. For one thing, Wade set

his own schedule, and he'd scaled back a lot so he could be home more often.

As a member of Trent's band, Glen didn't have that luxury. Which meant he would be away from Maris ninety percent of the year. That wasn't fair to Lorelie. She deserved all of a man's attention, not some walkaway Joe who popped into town whenever he could squeeze in a trip.

And then there was Coach to consider. Glen had felt the man's approval, but he'd never come right out and asked the guy what he thought about him and Lorelie together. "You really wouldn't mind it if I stuck around?"

Coach didn't hesitate, just shook his head. "No. I wouldn't mind."

"You're a lot different from my dad." Glen didn't have a clue where that had come from, but as more time passed, he couldn't help making the comparison.

"Yeah. I got that impression. Your dad a drinker?"

"No. Just a cold son of a bitch. Got my mom pregnant with my older brother when they were younger. Their parents made them get married. Rather than make the best of it, he made us all suffer. Let us know every minute of every day how miserable he was and how it was our fault. My brother is a few years older. He took off right after high school and never looked back."

"Your mom could have left your dad. Found a better place for y'all."

Glen snorted. "She liked being miserable too. Good Catholic girl, raised to believe we were meant to suffer so we could live the good life in the ever-after. She took her suffering very seriously, made it an art form."

Glen was surprised to realize the usual bitter tone that accompanied any conversation about his family was missing. It was as if he'd finally managed to let go of all that. His time with

Coach and Lorelie had shown him he hadn't left behind anything that was worth missing. What they had, their family of two—or five, really, considering they'd extended it to make room for Oakley, Joel, and Sadie—had taught him what a good family looked like.

He had never missed his family. Not once. But if he left Maris, he would miss *this* family intensely.

"Couldn't have been an easy way to grow up," Coach said.

"I got out at sixteen. Enough years have passed that I can't remember much of it anyway."

"You've grown up to be a good man. That's pretty exceptional, when you consider it doesn't sound like you had anyone showing you how."

And there it was again. That unconditional acceptance he'd felt from Coach, right from the start.

"Haven't been here that long, Coach. How can you know that?"

"I've been around long enough, son, to know the lay of the land. I can usually get a feel for a man's character pretty quick. Got good intuition."

"What does it tell you about me?"

Why does it matter so much? Glen didn't know. All he knew was...it did.

"I didn't even have to try to figure you out. Lori did that for me. Knew that day she brought you home for Sunday supper and I saw the way she looked at you. You make my daughter happy, Glen. There's no man on earth who doesn't want that for his baby girl."

"She's something special."

Coach's face sobered, which surprised him. He would have expected the man to be pleased to hear Glen admit that. "She's had a rough time since my heart attack."

"I know."

"I'm going to tell you something I haven't said to anyone else."

Glen swallowed heavily, suddenly afraid by the seriousness of Coach's tone. If he confessed to still being ill...

Glen thrust the thought aside. "Okay," he said at last.

"When I was laying in that hospital bed back after the heart attack, all I could think about was Lori. If I died, she would be alone. I know she thinks I told the football players to look after her in high school, but in truth...I restated it back in June. Made them all promise to look after her, to keep her safe for me, and to make sure she found a man who was worthy of her love and her trust. I also made them swear they'd never tell her why they were doing it."

That explained the defensive line surrounding her. "She's pretty annoyed at those guys."

"Yeah. I know. Thing is...you got by them."

Did Coach think that was a bad thing?

"They didn't exactly make it easy."

"They weren't supposed to. There haven't been any other men with either the backbone to take on her guardians or the vision to see why she was worth making the effort. You had both."

He had Coach's approval. He'd felt like he had all along, but hearing it spoken aloud...it went deep, made him feel happier than he'd been in a damn long time.

Fuck. What the hell was he supposed to do? If Toby hadn't texted, hadn't told him to come back, he would have had time to consider his next move. But he had to go now. Return to the tour tomorrow or lose his job.

"My manager texted me this morning. They want me back on the tour," Glen confessed, relieved to be able to get the truth out there. "Tomorrow."

"You're leaving?" Lorelie had approached the table without him seeing her.

Glen's heart shattered at the sound of her voice. He hadn't wanted to ruin her night, intent on waiting until morning. It had been his cowardly way of prolonging the inevitable confrontation, while holding on to the hope that maybe some easy answer would appear overnight.

"Lori," Glen said, rising. "I was going to tell you."

A million different emotions crossed her face in the course of only a minute. Glen managed to catch every single one. Mainly because he felt them as well. She'd started with upset, which morphed into the briefest flash of anger before she sucked in a deep breath and strengthened her resolve and gave him exactly what they'd promised each other from the beginning.

An easy out.

"Guess we'll need to make tonight count then," she said softly.

He frowned. Not because he believed for one second she was taking this news lightly. But because she genuinely thought he'd want that from her.

Glen stepped closer to her, taking her hands in his. "No."

Her forehead crinkled. "No?" Then her eyes went wide, and she didn't bother to hide her disappointment. "You're leaving tonight?"

"What? Wait. No. God no! I just...we need to talk, Lori. I've been trying to wrap my head around this all damn day. We both knew this was coming. And we were both dreading it. I don't want you to pretend it's okay. Because it's not. This sucks. All of it."

He hadn't noticed the stiffness in her shoulders until they fell. It occurred to him she'd been holding herself stiffly, but his words appeared to release her from that. He was glad. He needed the truth from her, needed to know how she genuinely felt.

"Been thinking all day, huh?"

He nodded.

"No answers?"

He shook his head. No answer.

Just one big fucking realization.

He was in love with her.

"Then come on."

"Where are we going?"

"The gang has decided to move the party to Cruisers. Sadie's created a special shot for Valentine's Day. We're moving ahead with Plan A."

Plan A. Glen recalled her itinerary for the evening. Dancing, shots, laughing, and sex. Lots of sex.

"Lori, I'm not sure—"

"Glen, you don't know what to do. And I don't know what to do. That fact will be the same come sunrise, so let's just give ourselves one more night to pretend like the world doesn't exist. Tomorrow, we'll be grown-ups. We'll talk and figure out what comes next together. Okay?"

He had never, for one second, considered that they would make this decision together.

Together.

The word repeated itself over and over in his head.

He wasn't alone anymore. He had someone standing in front of him who gave a genuine shit about him and his life. Someone who would help him.

"Together?" It slipped out unbidden before Glen could stop himself.

Lorelie smiled, even as she rolled her eyes at him. "Yes, you idiot. Together. What you do next impacts both of us. Don't you think for a second I'm not getting my say-so."

He chuckled, amazed to feel the pressure on his chest disappear. The problem remained, but the idea of not having to face it alone made it seem less dire somehow. "I wouldn't dream of it. I'm actually looking forward to hearing what you have to say."

"Yeah. Well. Don't get too excited. You might not like it."

"You going to tell me to leave and never come back?"

"Nothing even close to that," she replied, clearly horrified that he would suggest such a thing.

"Then I'm gonna like what you have to say. Come on. You promised me Plan A."

They both glanced back at Coach, who shooed them away. "Go on. Have fun. I've had my eye on that pretty woman sitting across the room all night. I'm going to go dance with her."

Lorelie looked in the direction her father pointed and then narrowed her eyes. "Dad, that's Ms. Kinnaman, my fourth-grade teacher."

"I know who she is."

"Seriously?" Lorelie put her hands on her hips, clearly ready to express her opinion on the matter.

Glen decided to run interference. "Let the man work, Lori," Glen teased as he took Lorelie's hand, intent on leading her to the exit. "Where are the others?"

"They already headed over to Cruisers. I told them we'd catch up."

"Good. Then we have time for one more slow dance. I like this song."

Glen changed directions, guiding her to the floor, wrapping her in his arms. Martina McBride sang about her own Valentine as Glen pressed his face to hers. Lorelie laced her fingers behind his neck as she turned until her lips touched his. Glen kissed her softly.

And just like that, the easy answer did appear.

He wasn't leaving her.

Not tomorrow.

Not ever.

* * *

Two hours later, Glen was sitting at a table at Cruisers with Tucker, drinking a beer as Lorelie and her girlfriends stood at the bar, doing some special shot Sadie had created for the holiday called Cupid's Cock. It was pink and fruity, and the women were crazy about them.

It had been a hell of a night. He and Lorelie had done just about everything on her list for a romantic Valentine's Day. There was only one thing left—and Glen planned to give her about twenty more minutes with her friends before he dragged her out of here and back to the barracks. That damn handmade quilt was beckoning him.

Tucker was watching Lela the same way he was looking at Lorelie. Hungrily.

"One more shot, and I'm getting my girl out of here before she gets too drunk for what I have in mind for later," Tucker said. Part of Glen was still amazed every time he hung out with Tucker. The man was a football legend, the quarterback who had almost taken his team to the Super Bowl last year. "And my intentions for the rest of the night do *not* include holding her hair while she gets sick."

Glen chuckled. "I hear that."

Tucker's attention turned away from Lela and over to him. "Hey, listen. I know you've been staying at Coach's while you're working on the ranch." Tucker reached into his pocket and pulled out a ring of keys. "Lela and I are going back to our farmhouse tonight. Won't be using our weekend lake house. If you and Lorelie want to stay there..."

Glen wasn't sure what to say in the face of Tucker's complete one-eighty. The former quarterback had been hell-bent in keeping him away from Lorelie. He was surprised—and touched—by this sudden show of support. He shook his head when Tucker started to hand him the key. "I appreciate the offer, but Lorelie has already fixed us up a nice place to stay tonight."

Tucker smiled. "Good. Figure it can't be easy for you, staying in the same house with Lorelie and her dad."

Truer words were never spoken. But at the same time, Glen had enjoyed his time at the ranch, living in the main house. He'd been struck by all the activity and noise. His apartment was damn quiet in comparison. Joel, Oakley, and Sadie were almost always there for dinner, the six of them sitting around the table, discussing the day, telling jokes, laughing.

"It's actually not that bad. I like being at the ranch."

"Coach is a good guy."

"The best," Glen added.

If he hadn't completely won Tucker over before, his quick response had just sealed the deal.

"Yeah." Then Tucker was distracted by Lela's loud laughter and request for another shot. "That's it. We're out of here."

Glen laughed and said goodbye as Tucker walked to the bar, intent on persuading his fiancée to leave with him. Obviously, the larger-than-life quarterback was outmanned when Lela convinced him to join them instead.

Glen sat at the table for a few minutes more, simply enjoying the chance to watch Lorelie with her friends. Then he realized he wasn't the only one observing the party.

He stood up and walked over to Walt.

"You're standing back tonight," Glen pointed out.

"Feel like being more of an observer," he said. "Besides, I'm not in the same boat as you guys. Got no girl to moon over for the holiday."

"You sure about that?" Glen asked, aware that Walt's hanging back seemed to have less to do with feeling sorry for himself because he had no girl, and more to do with observing the pretty Paige Sparks from afar.

Walt narrowed his eyes. "Leave it alone. Paige and I have been friends forever, since we were kids. I don't have feelings for her. I'm just...worried she's drinking too much. Don't want her to get sick."

Glen laughed. "Yeah, you can sell that shit to someone else."

Walt gave him a half-hearted shrug that proved his friend knew his argument was weak at best. Then he did what Walt was best at. Distraction. "You seem to be holding your own pretty well these days."

"I guess I am."

"Still hate small towns?"

Glen shook his head. "Nope."

"Thinking of giving it all up, your job, your life on the road?"

Glen nodded. "Yeah, I'm thinking about it."

He saw the quick flash of surprise in his friend's eyes. It faded quickly. "You'd really give it all up for Lorelie?"

"She's worth it, don't you think?"

Walt took a drink. "Just so you know, the fact that you think so makes us guys pretty happy."

Glen looked over at Joel and Oakley and the rest of the men. He had been pleased by Tucker's offer to use his lake house tonight. At the beginning, he'd been annoyed by the fact that Walt and his friends didn't seem to think he was good enough for her. Now he knew they were protecting her for

Coach, to ease the man's mind after his heart attack. They were good guys, the whole lot of them.

Regardless, it wasn't their happiness he was worried about. It was Lorelie's. And maybe Coach's, by extension, because he knew how much he meant to Lorelie. And vice versa. "Truth is, I don't care much about making you guys happy."

"Us guys being happy makes *Lorelie* happy."

"Yeah, well, maybe that's why I didn't knock any heads together when you all first started giving me shit," Glen said. "Didn't want to lose points with Lori."

Walt lifted an eyebrow at his use of Lorelie's nickname. Glen was aware of the fact there were only two men she let call her Lori. Him and Coach.

"So tell me again how come you're not over there with your girl?" Glen asked.

"My girl," Walt repeated a little too casually, as if he was trying it on for size.

"What's really holding you back, Walt?" Glen asked.

"She wasn't part of my plan. I'm still not sure she should be."

Glen took a long draw of beer, watching the group, considering what Walt said. Then he nodded. "I've noticed that falling for a Maris girl has a way of fucking up a lot of plans."

"Your plans did get fucked up?" Walt asked.

Glen didn't even bother to pretend to be disappointed or concerned. He just grinned. "Big time."

Walt chuckled. "I tried to get Maris out of my system for twelve years. I can tell you, it ain't easy. Add in a girl you're crazy about, and yeah...good luck."

"Think I have a little Maris in my system too." Glen's gaze was fixed on Lorelie. "But I'm not so sure I mind."

Walt looked at Paige. "Yeah, I hear you."

"So what are you gonna do about it?" Glen asked.

"I'm going to go ask my girl to dance."

Glen nodded. "Good plan."

"How about you?"

"I'm going to take my girl home."

"You're just going to walk over there, in the midst of all of those people who've been looking out for Lorelie all her life, and pull her away?"

Glen finished off his beer, set the bottle on the table right behind him, and nodded. "Yep, pretty much."

Glen pushed away from the wall, but Walt stopped him with a hand on his arm.

"Call me tomorrow before you make any final decisions. I want to talk to you about something. A business proposition."

Glen gave his friend a quizzical look, but it was clear Walt wouldn't go into it tonight. It was also pretty plain the word was out on his possible departure tomorrow. "I'll do that. Night, Walt."

Glen approached Lorelie, who must have sensed his presence because she spun around on the barstool to face him. "Hey, hot stuff."

"I want the rest of Plan A. Right now."

Lorelie laughed. "Ooo. Very demanding and alpha. Me likey."

Glen narrowed his eyes. "How many of those shots have you had?"

She winked as she leaned closer, whispering her answer so her friends couldn't hear. "Not as many as the girls think. Sadie's been sneaking me virgin shots since the first one. Told her I need my wits about me tonight."

Her close proximity and adorable confession was too much for him. He kissed her on the cheek, then the lips. He didn't give a shit about their audience or the scene they were making.

"Goddammit," Evan said, slapping Glen on the back. "What did I say about that public indecency thing?"

Lorelie hopped off the barstool. "You heard the cop, Glen. We have to be indecent in private."

"Guess that's our cue to leave." Glen turned to Evan and feigned guilt. "I apologize, officer."

Evan rolled his eyes. "Get out of here, you lunatics."

The two of them walked out of Cruisers hand in hand. Lorelie might not realize the importance of the evening, but Glen knew exactly what they were doing.

They were about to spend their first night together in their future home.

Chapter Eight

GLEN

I'm not coming back

TOBY

What? Hell no. You have to

GLEN

I'm staying in Maris

TOBY

For how long?

GLEN

With any luck, forever

TOBY

Goddammit, Glen. You can't do this.

GLEN

Guitar players are a dime a dozen in Nashville

TOBY

We've had three subs since you left. Trent's crashing. Need you

GLEN

Not happening

TOBY

You're fucking killing me, man. Please

GLEN

I'm sorry. I just can't do it anymore

TOBY

Does this have anything to do with that cowgirl?

GLEN

Has everything to do with her

Lorelie stepped into the bedroom of the barracks and tried to beat down her anxieties. She had promised Glen they'd spend one more night together without letting the future interfere. She wanted to follow through on that, but her insides were a jumbled mess of hormones, sadness, nervousness, and hope.

She was seriously fucked up.

"Lori," Glen said when she hovered in the doorway. "Let's say what needs to be said now. I don't want to wait until tomorrow."

If he told her he was leaving, she would fall apart. Completely.

She had pretended to be okay with him leaving and maybe she'd convinced him those feelings were legitimate. If so, he was going to be in for a rude awakening. And then their last night together would be ruined for sure when she dropped to her knees, crying, clinging to his legs, begging him to stay.

Yeah. That would be a pretty picture.

She should have had more of those shots. She wasn't ready for this.

"Glen, I don't think we should—"

"I'm not leaving."

The second he spoke the words, the tears she'd been holding at bay all night—hell, for the last two weeks—escaped, streaming down her face.

Glen, startled by her reaction, cupped her cheeks in his palms. "Jesus! Lori. Are you okay?"

She nodded, trying to stop crying. God, he'd just given her exactly what she wanted and she was still falling apart. "I was so afraid... I thought you were... Oh my God, what the hell is wrong with me? I *want* you to stay. I'm really f-fucking happy r-right now!"

Glen grinned and kissed her, not bothered by her very unattractive flood of tears or runny nose. "I know that."

"So why am I crying?"

"Because you just found out you're stuck with me?"

She laughed, the sound combined with a very choked sob. Holy crap. "Yeah. That's probably it."

He wrapped his arms around her, letting her hide her face against his chest until she got her shit together. It took her a few minutes. Then she tried to covertly wipe away the evidence of her insanity on his shirt.

Glen chuckled. "Don't worry. I was going to wash it anyway." To help matters along, he unbuttoned it, and then used it to clean up the rest of her tears, and she could only assume some pretty horrendous makeup tracks left from her mascara when she spotted the black streaks on the cotton. "Better?"

She nodded. "I have no idea where that came from."

"I feel like crying too."

He was completely dry-eyed, but she appreciated the sentiment.

"Because you just committed to staying with me?" she asked.

"Yeah," he teased. "That's probably it."

"We're not finished talking about this, Glen. I have so much more to say. But you took your shirt off and now I'm totally distracted. Maybe we can circle back around to the heavy stuff after..."

She let her words fade away, so he could fill in the blanks.

"After we defile your grandma's quilt?"

Lorelie didn't have a chance to reply before Glen used his grip on her shoulders to turn her away from him. He slid down the zipper on her dress and let the thing drop to her ankles. She kicked it off and spun back to face him.

His eyes widened appreciatively. "Oh, hell yeah. I like." He ran his hands over her matching silk bra and panties set. The pink push-up bra and thong were covered in hearts. She'd bought them special when she found out he was staying for Valentine's Day.

"Thought you would."

"Take them off."

She didn't hesitate. She flicked the front clasp of the bra and let it fall. Then she untied the strings on both sides of the thong. It fell away as well.

Glen blew out a long sigh. "Damn, Butterfly. That might be the sexiest thing I've ever seen in my life."

She stepped nearer, her heels still on. The shoes added a few more inches, which put her much closer to his height.

"Leave those shoes on."

Lorelie hadn't intended to take them off. She liked this new perspective. Especially when he gripped her waist and pulled her against him. He kissed her roughly, one hand rising to take a handful of her hair in his fist. If Lorelie thought she'd felt passion from him before, she'd been a fool. Glen wasn't holding anything back tonight.

Which worked for her. While they still had miles to go in terms of sorting out their future, the idea that he was willing to stay until they figured it out, the realization that he would give up his job to remain with her, was so freaking amazing...

Lorelie had to push the thought away or she'd start crying again. Happy tears were a new emotion for her. And one that Glen seemed an expert at provoking.

They kissed for ages, neither of them in a hurry to rush this along. Now that they weren't racing against that clock that had been ticking in the background for the last two weeks, it looked as if Glen was ready for a more leisurely pace.

She was the first to break the kiss. "While I'm glad to see you've gotten the hang of the slower pace of small-town living, I need you inside me. Like now."

Glen shook his head as if disappointed. "You need to stop and smell the roses, Lori. Can't keep rushing through life."

Lorelie giggled, even as she grabbed his hand and dragged him to the bed. Mercifully, his actions didn't match his words when he pressed her to her back on the mattress, coming over her.

"Pants," she said when he pressed his still-covered erection against her.

"In a minute."

She opened her mouth to blast him, but he kissed her into silence. Then his lips took a trip lower, and she decided the pants could wait a little while longer.

"Gotta say it," he murmured, lifting his head after his tongue had made a trail between her breasts and along her stomach. "I'm a huge fan of the south these days."

She got his meaning the second he dropped to his knees by

the bed and used his tongue to do wicked, wonderful things to her clit.

Lorelie gripped the quilt tightly as Glen drove her higher and higher with his fingers, his tongue, even just his hot breath on her pussy.

She was just about to come when he disappeared.

Her gaze flew to his face as he stood, looking down at her.

"What are you doing?"

"Letting you take a breather before the next round."

She scowled. "We didn't finish *that* round."

He lifted one shoulder, clearly not intimidated by her hostile tone. "You're pretty good at coming at will. Thought tonight we'd practice letting the pressure build. One big blowout. I think you'll like it."

"I won't," she said, not caring that she sounded like a two-year-old about to throw the mother of all tantrums if she didn't get her lollipop immediately. "I'll hate it."

"Tough."

She would have continued the argument, but Glen lay down next to her on the mattress. Sadly, his pants were still on, but she didn't have time to complain about that when he took one of her breasts in his hand, his lips latching onto the nipple.

"Oh," she sighed. She was exceptionally fond of the way he loved her breasts. She'd never had a lover in the past pay so much attention to them. As such, she'd had no idea they were such a hot button for her. When he sucked harder, the pressure growing to the point where she couldn't decide if it was pleasure or pain she was feeling, it felt as if she would—

Glen released her again. Just when she reached the place she most wanted to be.

Her anger was starting to give way to desperation.

"Glen, please." Pride be damned. She'd beg for what she wanted if that was the only way.

He stood again and she sighed with relief, thinking he was ready to take his pants off.

She was wrong.

Glen grasped her hand and pulled her from the bed. "Bend over the edge."

She turned and leaned over the mattress, digging her hands in the quilt. She jerked when Glen smacked her ass twice.

Looking over her shoulder, she narrowed her eyes. "You realize I'm going to keep count. That's two I owe you."

"Not everything in life is tit for tat."

"That will be," she assured him as he chuckled.

"Then I guess I better make it worth my while." He added five more slaps to the tally.

She didn't bother to complain because she was actually starting to enjoy the spanking. When she tilted her ass up farther and wiggled it, Glen ran his fingers over the sensitive skin.

"You like it." His words weren't a question, so she didn't bother to reply or deny.

Bending lower, he kissed away some of the sting. Then bit her ass cheek lightly. And then—holy hell—he dropped between her legs once more, adding even more heat to the powder keg. She wasn't just going to blow, she was going to detonate, blast, shatter.

He ran his thumb along her slit and used her own wetness to allow him to push it into her ass. This time it was *her* turn to try to move away, but he kept a firm grip on her waist. He pressed his thumb in and out of the tight opening a few times, moving deeper with each pass.

Lorelie bit her lip, trying to figure out if she liked what he was doing. Glen *had* promised to introduce her to new things. She just hadn't realized his repertoire was so vast. Or that she had so much left to learn.

She glanced down, her vision focusing on two of the quilt squares. Damn. They really were besmirching the quilt. She giggled before she could stop herself.

Glen paused. His thumb was still playing in her ass. "Lori?"

"My poor grandma is rolling over in her grave."

He chuckled as well, and then, because he was more of a gentleman than he gave himself credit for, he asked, "Are you okay with all of this?"

"So okay," she replied, the sound more air than tone.

"Good." He added his fingers to the game, dipping two inside her pussy while this thumb was still buried in her backside. His strokes were easy at first, but they soon built up speed.

The asshole knew exactly when to pull away. When he did so again, she closed her eyes, fighting the dizziness, the almost painful clenching of her inner muscles.

"Glen," she gasped.

"Get on your back. I want to look at you when I take you. Want to see your pretty face when you come."

Finally, he took off his pants. She was vaguely aware of the crinkling of the condom wrapper and then his hands were on her ankles, tugging them over his shoulders.

She was wide open and so fucking ready.

Their gazes connected as he placed the head of his cock at her opening. "Fast or slow?"

"You really have to ask?"

He laughed, but she was too far gone for humor, hadn't actually meant her words to be funny. She was desperate.

Glen slammed to the hilt in one rough thrust, and she screamed in relief. He didn't give her time to adjust or to even find something to hold on to. He simply took what he wanted and gave her what she needed. He pounded faster, harder as she lifted her hips, trying to add more power, more force, more...

"Oh God. Fuck. Glen!" If he pulled out now, she'd strangle him, kill him with her bare hands.

Mercifully, he didn't even slow down.

"Jesus, Lori. So fucking good. I'm going to..."

He was there too. Hallelujah. Because there was no way she could—

Lorelie came a split second before Glen, her back arching off the mattress as he pumped deeper, his motions erratic as his own climax thundered through him.

It was several minutes before Lorelie became aware of her surroundings again. Glen was lying next to her on the bed, his chest rising and falling rapidly as he tried to catch his breath. She was gasping for air herself. Her heart pounded loudly, the blood rushing in her ears making it hard for her to hear anything.

Glen's lips were moving, but she had no idea what he was saying, so she just nodded and closed her eyes.

The next time she opened them, she could tell it was much later than before. Or much earlier. The room wasn't quite as dark now. She was under the covers and Glen was spooning her from behind, one of his palms cupping her breast. She could tell from his deep breathing he was asleep.

Despite that, she could feel something else. His cock. Erect and resting against her ass.

She moved slowly, careful not to wake him. She wanted him inside her. She didn't need motion or actual sex, but she wanted to be filled by him.

Sliding down slowly on the hard flesh, she sighed when she managed to get most of him where she wanted. Glen hadn't moved. Of course, once his cock was inside her, she changed her mind about not needing the motion. Or the sex.

So she wiggled a little more, then found a slow, easy pace that let her feel the slide, the ebb and flow.

She wasn't sure how long she'd been rocking against him before she got the sense that Glen was awake, cognizant of what she was doing.

Lorelie looked over her shoulder and found his gaze on her.

He gave her a sleepy smile. "Butterfly, I don't want you to think this is a complaint, because I'm pretty sure this is the best way in the world to wake up, but before we let this go too far, you need to let me grab a condom."

She hadn't even considered that when she'd started her drowsy game. She shook her head. "Pill."

His grip on her breast tightened at her response. "You sure?"

She nodded. "Oh yeah. Are you?"

"I've never been inside a woman without a condom. Before this second. Pretty sure I'm going to embarrass myself and come way too fast. You can't believe how different this feels."

Actually, she could. Lorelie started pressing her hips forward and back again. She'd never had sex with a guy who wasn't covered up. It was softer this way. Easier. He was gliding so smoothly.

"Glen?"

"Yeah?" he murmured from behind her.

"I love you."

Glen's hand slid to her hip, halting her movements. Then he pulled out, pressing her to her back beside him. He cupped her cheek.

She was certain she was blushing. It was the reason she'd decided to tell him how she felt when her back was turned. She'd never said those words, and regardless of what they'd said last night, part of her had been nervous she had dreamed the whole thing.

"You and your damned impatience."

Her brows furrowed in confusion. "What?"

"I wanted to say it first. With flowers. And a candlelit dinner."

"More romance?"

"Yeah. Something like that. Of course, now that I think about it, I'm pretty sure you picked the perfect moment."

She smiled. "Don't like to brag, but I'm pretty good at rom—"

"I love you too, Butterfly."

He kissed her gently, sealing those words so tightly in her heart, she'd never get them out. Never want to.

Then he rose over her, and she opened her legs. He pushed back inside, and for the first time in her life, Lorelie understood the difference between fucking and making love.

They rocked together slowly, savoring every stroke, every caress, every kiss. The first ray of sunlight streamed through the window as they came together, Glen filling her, body and soul. And then, once more they dozed.

When they woke again, the room was bright. Lorelie was the first to rouse. Sitting up and glancing outside, she realized it was easily noon.

"Shit," she muttered.

"What's wrong?" Glen asked, lying next to her, naked and gorgeous.

"It's late. My dad is probably wondering where we are."

Glen chuckled. "I'm sure he knows exactly where we are. And what we've been doing."

"Yeah. That's kind of embarrassing."

He sat up and ran his hand along her bare back. "We should get dressed and find him. I need to see if he'd be willing to hire me on for a little longer. And I need to call Walt."

"Walt?"

"He stopped me on the way out of Cruisers last night. Told me to call him this morning before I made any decisions. Said he had a business proposition for me."

Lorelie felt a slight rush of relief. "Really? Call him now."

"Lori—"

"Please? I told you last night. We're not finished talking this out. I want you to stay, Glen. More than anything. But I feel like I'm forcing you to give up your dreams, your music."

He shook his head. "It's not like that. Not even close. I've been on the road most of my life. In two weeks, you opened my eyes to everything I've been missing. The dream is different now. I'm not giving up anything I want. Instead, I'm gaining so much more."

"You don't want to play the guitar?" She would never believe that. He'd said it himself. The thing was an extension of him, an extra appendage.

"I do. But not for Trent. And...maybe not for a living anymore."

She studied his face, trying to decide if he was sincere or if he was saying what he thought she wanted to hear.

He tilted his head and gave her an exasperated look. "I'm not lying, Lori."

She believed him. But that still wasn't enough. "Call Walt?"

He kissed her on the cheek, clearly ready to appease her. "Fine." He rose from the bed, treating her to a bird's-eye view of his sexy ass as he bent over to retrieve his cell from the pocket of his pants.

She tried to follow his conversation with Walt, but it was very one-sided and she was on the wrong side. All Glen said was a lot of "okay", "sounds good" and "mmmhmm." Then, finally, he hung up.

"Well?" she prodded, when the devil teased her by tugging on his pants and socks without speaking.

"He wants me to work with him on a few new tracks he's laying down on his next album."

Lorelie had silently been praying that was the offer. "And you want to do that?"

He nodded. "Yeah. I do. Last time he made that offer, we were both at different places in our lives. I was all about the traditional sound and he wanted to try something new. This time, I'm ready for the change. Hell, I need it. Need to be around serious musicians again, guys who give a shit about their songs, their work. For the first time in months, I'm actually excited about playing."

She smiled. "I'm glad."

"And Walt's schedule isn't as grueling as Trent's. It'll also help that we have the same home base. I'll still be traveling back and forth to Nashville, but I'll be *here* more than I'll be away."

"You can work on the ranch part-time then."

He lifted one shoulder. "If that's okay with your dad, I'd like that."

Lorelie hopped from the bed to grab her dress. While his words last night had made her happy, this morning's talk had given her genuine hope. Everything was going to be fine. Better than fine.

Perfect.

Chapter Nine

TOBY

Still time to change your mind. Bus is driving near Maris this morning. They could take a quick detour to pick you up

Silence

TOBY

Or not. Wanna give me a hint here?

Silence

TOBY

So I looked up Maris on Google maps. You could be in Houston in just a few hours

Silence

TOBY

Goddammit. Glen?

GLEN

I'm staying in Maris. Need to talk to you about the possibility of playing with Walt Bennett again

TOBY

Walt?

GLEN

Yeah

TOBY

Two of you were great together. Trent won't
be happy

GLEN

His happiness means nothing to me. Working
on finding my own instead

TOBY

I'll make a few calls

GLEN

Thanks

C oach was in the kitchen when he and Lorelie returned to the house. Glen couldn't beat down the sudden nervousness as they planned to sit down and talk to her father about what came next.

They had intended to head up to their rooms to change their clothes. After all, she was still in last night's dress and his shirt was wrinkled and stained from using it to dry her tears last night.

Unfortunately, Coach had clearly been waiting for them. "Lori? Glen? You two got a minute?"

Lorelie gave him a so-much-for-that shrug and changed direction, heading toward the kitchen. Glen followed.

"Hi, Daddy," she said as they entered, bending over to kiss her father on the cheek.

"Daddy, is it?" Coach asked.

Lorelie dropped down into the chair next to her father's, while Glen remained in the doorway. Probably a coward's place, but he wanted to get a weather report before he stepped into the room. Coach was wise enough to read the writing on the wall. Glen had been having sex with his only daughter all night...and morning.

Lorelie didn't feel the same need for self-preservation. "I'm sorry I didn't text you, but your light was on last night when we got home. I figured you saw the headlights. And you knew I'd been fixing up the barracks for Glen, so..."

Coach chuckled. "You're twenty-eight years old, Lori. I hardly need an explanation."

"Yeah, but, well, it's just common courtesy, isn't it? And I feel bad."

"Don't feel bad." Coach looked over his shoulder at Glen. "Still here, huh?"

Glen nodded. Then took a deep breath and walked into the room, claiming a third seat at the table. "I'm not going back out on the road with Trent."

Coach smiled. A genuine smile that warmed Glen right to the core. "I'm glad."

It was only two words, a simple statement, but it packed a powerful punch. Lorelie and her dad both wanted him to stay. And given Walt's reaction when Glen said yes to his proposition on the phone, he'd say at least three people were happy with his decision. It would take him some time to get used to the idea that there were people in his life who actually wanted him around.

Lorelie went on to tell Coach about Walt's offer and Glen's desire to continue working on the ranch. Coach didn't blink twice at that and said he was welcome to work there as long as he wanted. She asked if it was okay for Glen to move into the barracks, and again, Coach never hesitated, simply said the cabin was his.

Then Coach asked a question that managed to slow Lorelie's roll. "You going to move out there with him?"

She flushed. "Dad."

Coach chuckled. "I think we both know that's where you're going to be sleeping. And you're getting a little old to be living at home with your old man. I'm fine here, Lori. You won't be that far away, and I think it's time you spread your wings a bit."

"I've only been here a couple weeks, Coach. If Lori needs more time to—"

Coach looked him straight in the eye. "I proposed to Lori's mom on the third date. My folks and my friends thought I was crazy. But I knew I loved her, knew that feeling wasn't a flash in the pan or just lust. I've seen the way you two look at each other. Noticed it that night way back in October. What you've got is the real deal, something special. You can either roll with it or try to play by some set of relationship rules put in place by society. Fact remains, you're going to end up in the exact same place—just farther down the road."

"And where's that?" Glen asked.

"Living together out there in those barracks, planning your wedding and talking about making me some grandkids."

Glen laughed, while Lorelie looked horrified. "Seriously, Dad? I just convinced him to stay last night. You're going to scare him away with all that."

Glen reached for her hand. "Lori..."

"Yeah?"

"I'm not scared. You want to move in together?"

She stood up from the chair with an exasperated huff. "You're both insane," she said as she walked to the kitchen counter, putting a stray coffee cup and plate in the sink. When she turned around again, she added, "Must be why I love you both so much. Birds of a feather and all that."

"Is that a yes?" Glen asked. The idea that they could spend every night for the rest of their lives waking up in each other's arms took root, deep and fast.

She nodded. "Of course it is."

Lorelie turned back to wash the dishes but stopped and turned off the water after just a few seconds. "Um, Glen?"

"Second thoughts already?"

She didn't turn to face him as she shook her head. "There's a big bus coming down our driveway."

"What?" He rose from the chair, Coach right behind him. The three of them stared out the window as the bus Glen had just purposely missed rolled toward them.

"Fuck," he muttered.

The bus came to a stop just in front of the house and the one person Glen had hoped to never see again stepped off, taking in his surroundings liked he'd just landed on Mars.

"Isn't that Trent?" Lorelie asked.

"Yeah."

"He looks different."

He looked like shit. His hair was shaggy and sticking up, as if he'd just rolled out of bed, a far cry from the cowboy hat he never—*never*—was seen without, mainly because he was going bald.

Trent was in a faded, stained T-shirt and ripped jeans, both of which needed a trip to the Laundromat, or even better, to a trash can. And his face was wearing at least three days' worth of beard. On some men, that looked good, but Trent couldn't grow a full beard, so instead the thing came out in patches, some places covered, others bare.

"I don't suppose I could talk you and your dad into staying here while I have this conversation? The man's not pleasant."

Lorelie looked at him with wide eyes that basically told him he was nuts. "I'm coming with you."

A quick glance at Coach confirmed he was already halfway across the kitchen and headed for the front door. "We got your back, son," Coach said, over his shoulder.

Glen grinned, then considered staying in the kitchen himself. It was obvious Coach and Lorelie could handle Trent just fine without him. It was tempting. But not fair. To Trent. Even if the asshole *did* deserve it.

Glen stepped out onto the porch and walked a few steps beyond Lorelie and her dad, who'd already claimed their spots.

"Trent," he said as the man climbed the stairs. "Thought you were in Houston."

"We're heading there now," Trent said. "As soon as you get your sorry ass on the bus."

Glen balled his hands into fists. Trent had apparently gotten stupider in the weeks since he'd been gone. He never would have had the balls to speak to Glen like that before.

"Not going. I quit."

Trent's expression turned even darker. "What is this? Some game to get more money? Fine. You can have a raise. Now let's go."

Glen shook his head. "No. Not enough money in the world to get me back on that bus."

"What am I supposed to do?" Trent's tone lost some of its edge, desperation creeping in. "Apologize? You're the one who fucking punched me!"

Glen considered explaining to the idiot why he'd hit him, but decided Trent wasn't worth his time. The man believed his own press, had for years. There was no reasoning with someone whose head was buried so deep inside his own ass. "I'm moving on, Trent."

For the first time since he'd approached him, Trent looked

at the other two people on the porch, first taking in Coach, who stood with his arms crossed over his chest in a way that all but dared the man to mess with them.

Then his eyes landed on Lorelie—and a hateful smirk crossed his lips. "Because of her? You're giving up your spot in my band for a bit of *pussy*? She's not even that fucking pretty!"

Trent should have been flat on his ass out in the yard, bleeding. That was sure as hell where Glen had planned to put him. With his fists.

But Lorelie caught his arm as it reared back, holding it tightly.

"Don't, Glen," she said softly. "He's not worth it."

She was wrong. He was worth every punch, every broken bone, every drop of blood. "Let go of me, Lori. Man needs to be taught a lesson. One he obviously didn't learn the last time."

"Glen," Coach said. "Calm down, son."

He let out a slow breath. Glen was no match for the two of them. They were the closest thing to a family he'd had in over two decades. Hell, in his whole life. His family had been dysfunctional and broken from the get-go. They'd never meant to him what these two people did. Which was unnerving, when he considered how short his time here had been. How had they gotten so deep under his skin? How had this whole town gotten there?

He knew how. They'd all given him things he'd never had. Trust, support, a chance to prove himself, laughter, friendship, love. They had challenged him to see beyond his own selfishness, and in doing so, helped him to discover the man he wanted to be.

He dropped his fists, let his arm go limp.

Lorelie held tight for just a moment more.

"So that's how it is," Trent all but snarled. "You're pussy-whipped. Jesus, Glen, I didn't realize you were such a wimp. A loser who'd let his dick—"

And then Glen saw it again. The old *Batman* fight scene in action.

Bam! Whap! Kaboom!

Only this time, he was on the sidelines as Lorelie went after the man, taking him down with one punch.

Glen was impressed. It had taken *him* two.

She followed up her wicked right with a couple of kicks after Trent hit the porch boards hard, punctuating each strike with a string of angry words. Glen suspected the words probably hurt Trent more than the blows, when he saw Trent's reaction to them.

"How *dare* you talk to him that way? You wouldn't be here if you had an ounce of talent! You know you need Glen because you're *nothing* without him. Nothing! So stand up, tell him that, and then get the fuck off my property!"

Trent stumbled as he tried to rise, his movements hesitant as his eyes remained glued on Lorelie. He was clearly afraid she'd attack again.

"The tour is in the toilet, man," Trent said after a minute or so. "People are asking for refunds. They figured out I was lip-synching after you left, so Toby said I had to start singing for real. Without your voice..."

"They thought my voice was yours."

Trent nodded miserably. "None of the other guitarists we've hired know the songs well enough and they don't sound like..."

"Me."

"My career is gonna be ruined if you don't come back!"

It was the most humble words he'd ever heard from Trent.

And they didn't change a thing.

"I can't go back. I've got friends here in Maris." He looked over his shoulder at Lorelie and her dad. "A family. And a home. For the first time. I'm not leaving it. Not for money or fame or you." And then, because he genuinely felt bad for the man, he added, "I'm sorry, Trent."

Trent wiped the dust from his jaw, looking somewhat surprised to find blood mingled in as well. "Your girlfriend hits harder than you. My jaw fucking hurts."

Glen grinned as he turned and reached out for Lorelie, wrapping his arm around her shoulders. "Appreciate you testing that out for me. I'll be sure to tread lightly around her."

Lorelie rolled her eyes at him, her smile as sweet as lemonade on a hot day.

"If you change your mind..." Trent started, still holding out hope.

"I won't."

Trent nodded slowly, then descended the stairs gingerly. Apparently, he'd landed on his ass a little too hard. He climbed back on the bus and then, just like that, Trent Maxwell was out of his life.

The man was forgotten before the bus hit the end of the driveway.

Glen turned to look at her. "So you wouldn't let *me* hit the guy when he insulted you, but he was fair game for you?"

"I didn't like what he said about you."

Glen put his hands on his hips. "And I was over the moon with the way he talked about you? Dammit, Lori. What if he'd swung back? He could have hurt you."

She looked at him as if he'd grown another head. "Oh yeah, right. Like any punch he might've thrown would have landed. With you and my dad here. And Oakley and Joel standing right there."

She pointed toward the side of the house at his back. Sure

enough, there were the ranch hands. He hadn't noticed their arrival.

"Y'all been there the whole time?" Glen asked.

Oakley grinned. "Long enough to see Lorelie defend your honor."

"Fuck," he muttered. He figured it wouldn't take them five minutes to have that story spread throughout Maris. He'd never live it down.

"So you're staying?" Joel asked. Glen wasn't sure, but he thought the man actually looked happy to hear that news.

Glen nodded. "Yeah. Looks like you're gonna have to work a little harder if you're still trying to run me off."

Oakley rubbed his hands together. "Damn. I do love a dare."

Lorelie pointed her finger at both ranch hands. "I swear to God, if either one of you—"

Joel threw his hands up in instant surrender, pretending to be scared. "Stand down, Oak, or she'll come out swinging."

They all laughed.

"Don't you boys have work to do?" Coach asked at last.

Oakley and Joel meandered back to the barn as Coach opened the screen door. "You two start packing, and I'll help you move your stuff over to the barracks. Of course, it seems to me if you're going to call that place home, we might want to come up with a better name for it."

Home. He had a home.

Then he realized it wasn't the place that made him feel that way. Without her, he wouldn't want it.

"Don't care what we call it," Glen said, Lorelie still tucked in his arm. "As long as Lori's there with me."

Lorelie gave him a quick kiss on the cheek. "Keep talking like that and my right hook is going to get rusty from a lack of use."

"Better that than your kisses," he said, stealing a kiss to punctuate his point. "I love you, Butterfly."

"Ditto, Music Man."

Coach chuckled. "You're gonna do just fine here, Glen. You've got the same spirit as my boys of fall. Welcome to the family."

Epilogue

SADIE

Hey, where did you and Glen go?

Silence

SADIE

Lorelie? Did you guys go home? You're
missing a great game

Silence

WALT

Glen? The gang is looking for you and Lorelie

Silence:

WALT

You picked the wrong game to ditch. The
Titans are killing it tonight

"Turn off your cell. That constant buzzing is distracting me." Glen started to reach for her phone, but she got to it first. She pushed the off button and then pulled him back toward her, the two of them resuming some pretty hot-and-heavy kissing.

"So this is how you evaded your protectors back in high school?" Glen murmured when her lips moved from his mouth to his neck.

"Mmmhmm. They were too busy playing to worry about me."

"Trumpet player, you say?"

She giggled. "It would appear I've always had a thing for musicians."

Lorelie began kissing his neck again and for a second, Glen let her distract him from why he'd really dragged her here.

"Lori, hang on a second, darlin'."

She pulled back reluctantly. Very reluctantly. He grinned. He was one lucky man. The past six months had been the best of his life.

The songs he and Walt had recorded were getting some serious airplay and they were starting to talk about a potential tour. Lorelie was excited about the prospect of joining them on the road for a few of the concert dates. It was all she could talk about lately.

Coach had become more of a father to him than his own dad had ever been. And the man was starting to hand over more and more of the ranch duties as well. Coach would occasionally talk about the day he retired, and how the land would belong to Lorelie and her kids one day. Up until yesterday, Coach had always said it that way. Lorelie and her kids.

Yesterday, he said it would belong to them—to Glen and Lorelie and their kids.

It wasn't exactly a subtle hint for Glen to get off his ass and propose, but Glen had taken it to heart.

Glen had purchased the ring two weeks ago after securing Coach's permission to ask for her hand. And since then, he'd been looking for the perfect time.

Earlier, sitting with her dad in the bleachers at the high school football game, surrounded by all their friends, and with plans to hit Cruisers afterwards, he'd decided there was no better time.

Reaching into his pocket, he pulled out the box. Lorelie's eyes widened with surprise.

"Glen," she whispered.

"I've been racking my brain for a romantic way to do this, Lori, but the truth is, every single day I spend with you is the best day of my life. This proposal is greediness on my part, pure and simple. Because I want a lifetime of you. You're everything to me. Every song I've ever played, every word I've ever spoken, every step I've ever taken. Everything has led me to you. I love you. I want to marry you, make babies with you, and get old and gray and grumpy with you."

He used his free hand to wipe away the tears streaming down her face. "Crying?"

The tears she shed at moments like this always embarrassed her. When she was overwhelmed by happiness. He could never convince her this was when she was the most beautiful to him.

"Yes," she said begrudgingly.

"Yes, you're crying, or yes, you'll marry me?"

She laughed. "Both. And damn you, what the hell can I say to top that? You always steal the most perfect words and then I'm left with the same three."

"Say them anyway. They're my favorites."

"You're not bored with them?"

He shook his head. "Never."

"I love you." She kissed him, hard. "I love you. I love you. God. I love you so much..."

He returned her kiss and slid the ring on her finger.

Lorelie admired it for a few seconds, and then she grabbed his hand, tugging him out from under the bleachers. "Come on! I want to tell everybody."

He let her drag him willingly toward the rest of the gang, as anxious as she was to share their good news.

It took a moment for that to soak in. He wanted to share his life with all these people. All of them.

The rambler had found his home.

At last.

Did you know there are more stories set in Maris, Texas? Be sure to read about Tyson, Evan, Macie and the rest of the Sparks family in the Sparks in Texas series!

Waiting for Us (prequel)
Waiting for You
Waiting for Her
Waiting for Him
Waiting for Them
Waiting for Love
Waiting for Snow

Fans of Kindle Unlimited - Be sure to check out these red hot reads by Mari Carr!

Erotic Research (sexy erotic role playing while trapped in snowstorm with her rich publisher)

Tequila Truth (friends to lovers "who loves a good spanking" menage)

Power Play (birthday sex with a stranger turns into the gift that keeps giving - a workplace/power exchange romance)

Rough Cut (Hollywood's hottest bad boy in a BDSM romance)

Assume the Positions (older woman, younger cop with handcuffs! romance)

Mad about Meg (mistaken identity - who knew he was a billionaire? - holiday romance)

Do Over (seasoned "they'd be dead by chapter 2 after all that sex" romance)

Making His Play (a hockey player, fake relationship, drunken Vegas elopement free-for-all)

Up in Flames (an...ahem...*extremely* well-endowed firefighter and single mom romance)

Educating Ms. Wright (happy hour between friends turns into menage-a-palooza)

Resisting Mr. Right - (friends with benefits...A LOT of benefits)

About the Author

Virginia native Mari Carr is a New York Times and USA TODAY bestseller of contemporary romance novels. With over two million copies of her books sold, Mari was the winner of the Romance Writers of America's Passionate Plume award for her novella, Erotic Research. She has over a hundred published works, including her popular Wild Irish and Compass books, along with the Trinity Masters/Masters Admiralty series she writes with Lila Dubois.

Find Mari Carr on the web at
www.maricarr.com
mari@maricarr.com